"I came to walk you down to the bar, Brenda."

Was Colin's voice sultry, or was that her imagination? Oh, Lord, however was she going to hold on to her purity with Colin acting like this? She cleared her throat. "Um, thanks, Colin. I'm not dressed yet."

A very faint, very seductive smile visited his lips. "I don't mind."

His words and his manner jolted her. What did he think she was, anyway? Some kind of floozy? A doxie? A scarlet woman? She was no mere plaything, and the sooner he realized that, the better for them both. With a frown, she said tartly, "Well, I do."

His expression didn't alter. Brenda swallowed. Oh, dear. Maybe the opinion of her she deduced from his attitude was the correct one after all. She sure didn't feel like turning him away with harsh words stinging his ears. Rather, she felt like pulling him into her room and ravishing him.

This was really terrible.

"It's going to take me a little while," she said. "I'm going to take a quick bath."

"I'll be happy to wait."

Good heavens, what should she do now? This decision wasn't nearly as easy to make as whether or not she should slide on the baseball diamond. After what seemed like a century, she said, "Wait a minute. I have to get a dressing gown on."

That damned eyebrow of his just lifted.

Dear Romance Reader,

In July, we launched the Ballad line with four new series, and each month we'll present both new and continuing stories set everywhere from medieval England to the American West—the kind of passionate, romantic stories you love best, written by the most gifted authors. At the back of each book, we'll tell you when you can find subsequent books in the series that have captured your heart.

Debuting this month with a fabulous new series called *The Sword and the Ring,* Suzanne McMinn offers **My Lady Imposter.** The pageantry and adventure of medieval England come vividly to life in the rousing story of one incredible family in an age when men lived and died by the sword and a woman's life might be forever changed by a betrothal ring. Next, Alice Duncan continues *The Dream Maker* series with **Beauty and the Brain,** as an actress hiding her intelligence meets her match in a research assistant who knows everything . . . except about love.

Travel back to Regency England with Joy Reed's romantic *Wishing Well* trilogy. In **Anne's Wish,** a marriage of convenience promises unexpected love—unless a jealous rival comes between the newlyweds. Finally, the third book in Elizabeth Key's charming *Irish Blessing* series reunites childhood companions, but will **Reilly's Pride** stand in the way of a love destined to unite two souls in matrimony?

Kate Duffy
Editorial Director

The Dream Maker

BEAUTY AND THE BRAIN

Alice Duncan

ZEBRA BOOKS
Kensington Publishing Corp.
http://www.zebrabooks.com

ZEBRA BOOKS are published by

Kensington Publishing Corp.
850 Third Avenue
New York, NY 10022

First Printing: May, 2001
10 9 8 7 6 5 4 3 2 1

Printed in the United States of America

One

San Bernardino Mountains,
California, 1907

Martin Tafft sucked in a deep breath of fresh mountain air and thanked his lucky stars that this picture wasn't being filmed in the desert. He was sick to death of deserts.

Indeed, Martin felt exceptionally cheerful these days. His good mood had carried him into these gorgeous mountains, and he was eager to begin production of the latest Peerless Studio offering to the world of culture: *Indian Love Song.*

Life was grand—even if he was too busy to cultivate close friends other than those he'd had for years and those with whom he worked. He occasionally wished he had a romance in his life, except that he didn't have time for one. He didn't dwell on the absence of love and intimacy; it seemed silly to do so when he reflected upon the gratifying aspects of his life.

Peerless Studio had produced a string of smash-hit feature motion pictures. Peerless's stature in the infant industry had grown by leaps and bounds, until it was now right up there with Biograph and Vitagraph when it came to producing quality products. And he, Martin Tafft, who for several years had been required to do pretty much everything that needed to be done in his studio's production efforts, from finding locations to acting as wet nurse to temperamental actors, now had himself a research assistant.

He smiled at said assistant, Colin Peters. "Isn't this fresh air invigorating? I really enjoy the mountains." Feeling expansive, he thumped himself on the chest. "Springtime in the Sierras, Colin. You can't beat it."

Colin pushed his thick spectacles up his nose. They had a tendency to slip, as Martin had noticed before. "Actually, these aren't the Sierras, Mr. Tafft. We're presently in a range called the San Bernardinos." He pointed into a clump of trees in a direction Martin presumed was vaguely downhill. "That's San Bernardino down there. The town."

Undaunted, Martin went on. "Ah, but you can't beat the natural beauty of these mountains." Martin, who had grown up in Pittsburgh, where there was precious little of nature left, appreciated natural beauty when he saw it. "Look there!" He pointed at a couple of birds that had just flown, chirping madly, out of a tall cedar tree. "Why, even the birds are playful!"

Colin cleared his throat self-deprecatingly. "Er, actually, I believe that blue jay—the larger bird, you see—just tried to steal an egg from that scarlet tanager's nest. Birds don't generally play with each other. Life's too precarious for them out here in the wild."

Martin's smile twisted slightly askew. As much as he appreciated Colin, who was a bright and enthusiastic fellow and a joy with whom to work, Martin found him a trace too literal sometimes. His scholarly nature had come as something of a surprise to Martin, since Colin looked like a well-built, muscular young man. Martin hadn't anticipated so unemotional a personality as Colin's to be housed in such a hearty, masculine shell.

"These are the moving pictures, Colin," he said gently.

"The San Bernardinos can belong to any old mountain range we want them to, and the birds can play if we say so."

"I see." Colin frowned a little and scanned the scenery.

Martin didn't know how a person could remain unmoved by the pristine beauty sprawled all about them, but Colin seemed to be managing nicely. Martin sighed. He was still happy. He saw a short-tailed chipmunk sitting on a rock, clutching an acorn in its paws and darting glances all around. The thing looked darling to Martin, but he chose not to point the animal out to Colin, fearing he would predict the beast's doom from its charming behavior.

"In that case," Colin went on after a short period of thought, and startling Martin, who'd forgotten what they'd been talking about, "I suppose these would be the Black Hills, since this picture is supposed to be set in the Dakotas."

"Right."

"I see." Colin pushed up his glasses again. He didn't smile.

Martin gave up trying to lure his assistant into thinking about anything but work. Far from gloomy, Colin had yet to exhibit anything resembling lightness of spirit, and Martin considered that something of a shame. His own cheer remained unabated, and he clapped Colin on the back.

Colin, not anticipating the blow, took a startled step forward.

After expelling another, rather more heartfelt sigh, and feeling a good deal of sympathy for Colin, Martin said, "I believe the rest of the crew and the cast have assembled. Let me introduce you to everyone. I'm sure you'll find them all very agreeable to work with."

"Yes. I see." Colin sounded unconvinced.

Martin's natural enthusiasm overcame his sympathy for

his dull assistant, and he took Colin's arm. "This will be a super picture for Peerless. It has all the elements in it that the public craves."

Colin nodded gravely. His glasses slipped a little.

Continuing with zest, Martin went on, "Indeed. The public is wild about cowboys and Indians these days. We're going to give them cowboys, Indians, a beautiful woman, danger, romance—why, we've got everything in this picture. We're even throwing in an absentminded professor, so there will be an element of comedy." Martin hoped Colin wouldn't take the last part amiss.

He didn't seem to. "So I understood from Mr. Lovejoy."

"Yes. The title of the picture is wonderful, too." Martin chuckled. He liked this whole picture a lot. "*Indian Love Song.* It has a good deal of zing to it, doesn't it?"

"Um, yes. I'm sure it does."

Oh, dear. Martin shook his head, wondering what it would take to draw Colin Peters out of the dusty realm of academia and into the modern world. A shotgun, perhaps.

"Mr. Lovejoy certainly seems to understand popular tastes," Colin ventured after a moment.

From that telling sentence, Martin deduced that poor Colin didn't. For some reason he couldn't fathom, since they were nothing at all alike, Martin liked Colin a lot. "Phin is a genius," he said simply. "He has an absolutely infallible grasp of what the public wants." Plus, he was rich, which was a great advantage when one journeyed into untried business territory.

"I'm a trifle concerned about how the Indians in this picture will be depicted," Colin murmured. His voice was so soft, Martin barely heard it.

"That's your department," Martin said cheerfully. "You get to tell us what to do." Eyeing his assistant and remembering one or two of his stuffy college professors, he amended, "Within certain boundaries, of course. After all, we have to stick to the story." He laughed with what he hoped sounded like unconcern.

"Yes." A double vertical dent appeared above Colin's nose. He looked troubled.

"Phin would never do anything that wasn't of the highest moral and ethical caliber, Colin."

"Yes. I'm sure."

Phineas Lovejoy, financial genius behind Peerless Studio and Martin's best friend from boyhood, had discovered Colin for Martin. If anything had been needed to cement their friendship forever and ever, it was this. Martin had been getting physically worn out from doing all the legwork for Peerless. Not that he didn't enjoy it. Nor did he resent the necessity for his energy being spent in so many different endeavors. Not at all. Martin believed wholeheartedly in the future of Peerless, and in the motion pictures themselves.

But he was human, and his physical resources weren't infinite. He did, in fact, get to feeling run down from time to time. After making twenty moving pictures for Peerless back-to-back, he was darned tired. Since it was his job to find actors, locations, food, lodging, horses if necessary, and, in the case of this particular picture, a tribe of Indians for Peerless's use, and since he was a perfectionist, he worked constantly. He was very happy to relinquish his research duties to an employee.

Therefore, sensing a twinge of doubt in his new assistant and believing he knew what had caused it, he hastened to eliminate it. "Think of it, Colin! This is your opportunity to educate the public about the Indians."

"Which Indians?"

Martin looked at him, feeling as blank as he undoubtedly appeared. "Why, the ones in this picture."

"I see." Colin nodded again.

Martin, perceiving a grave lack of imagination in his

companion, gave it up. Not everyone held his views on motion pictures. Martin saw the emerging industry as something close to the salvation of mankind.

What better way to prove to the residents of the world that, underneath all their surface differences, men were alike everywhere? How better to show people that we all have the same desires, aspirations, and goals for our lives? How else to show the world that everyone in it deserved to live a life free from strife, hunger, and war? How better to show people where areas of famine, drought, flood, and other pockets of need were? After all, if no one knew where want lurked, no one could help the wanters, could they?

Ever since Martin had become involved with Phineas Lovejoy in setting up and operating Peerless Studio, he'd felt himself to be on a mission. The world had been damaged enough by megalomaniacal dictators, separatist fearmongers, socialists, anarchists, and so forth. Martin's plan was to create universal understanding among the world's people. *That* would put a kink in the Kaiser's tail! Pompous, strutting, insufferable—He realized he'd become sidetracked and shook his head to clear it.

"I'm sure you'll find the leading lady of our picture a delight. Her name is Brenda Fitzpatrick."

"I see."

Colin's enthusiasm was liable to get him into trouble if he didn't try to curb it, Martin thought ironically. "She's a lovely girl. Modeled hats and gowns in New York City before she was picked up by a company doing musical comedies on Broadway. Got a great voice, although, of course, we won't be able to exploit that in a silent picture." He laughed again. Colin didn't.

Martin went on. "She's been very successful on Broadway. I'm sure when you meet her, you'll understand why. She's a true beauty." Because he wanted to stir his companion, if only a little bit, Martin winked. He tried to make it a lascivious wink but, having had little to do with lasciviousness in his life, wasn't sure he succeeded.

"Oh."

At first Martin thought he'd failed to instill even a tiny degree of intrigue about Miss Fitzpatrick in his assistant. Then he saw a dull red flush spread over Colin's neck—and he felt guilty, both for trying to disconcert Colin and for even hinting that Brenda wasn't what she should be.

Because she was. Bright, charming, not unlike one of those splendid peonies they had back east, Brenda was a real brick. There wasn't a hint of temperament about her. "But she's a fine girl. An upstanding girl. I understand she's been supporting her family for some time, because her father became ill and died when she was a young girl."

"Hmmm. Too bad, that."

"Yes. But she's so pretty that it wasn't hard for her to get modeling jobs. And then the stage came along." It sounded romantic and exciting to Martin.

"I see," said Colin.

Martin was very, very glad when the two of them exited a stand of sycamore and incense cedar trees and saw the lodge where the cast and crew were to be housed during the filming of *Indian Love Song*.

Colin feared Martin must think him a stodgy old thing and regretted it. But Colin couldn't help it. He was who he was. Most of his life had been spent inside his head and at various schools and universities. He'd achieved his bachelor's degree at Boston College before he was sixteen years old, a master's degree in philosophical history at Harvard when he was nineteen, and completed the work for his Ph.D., creating in the process a philosophical and anthropological masterpiece, according to his professors, in the history and significance of modern philosophical

thought in the study of native anthropology in the western
United States last June.

Scheduled to begin work as an assistant professor at
the new university in Los Angeles in September, he'd
been at loose ends after moving to California from Mas-
sachusetts. He'd also been pretty low on funds, although
he came from a fairly wealthy family. Colin chose not to
rely on his parents' good graces now that he was a man.
He believed men ought to be able to take care of themselves. If they couldn't, then perhaps one or two of Mr.
Darwin's more controversial theories ought to be put to
the test.

This job, therefore, was a godsend. Not only would he
be able to do what he loved—research—but he'd be able
to witness work in a new and booming industry. Colin
was fascinated by moving pictures, and he went to see
them as often as he could.

The expressive side of his nature, however, had not
been nurtured, and he wasn't very good at showing people
how he felt. And now Martin Tafft, a fine man and one
whom Colin liked a good deal, believed him to be a
stuffed shirt. Colin sighed, and wondered if he'd ever
learn how to live in the world and not in his head.

An opportunity for practice occurred not more than
two minutes later, when Martin opened the heavy door
of the wooden lodge and the two men entered the main
parlor.

A large wooden structure built late in the last century,
the Cedar Crest Lodge had been the scene of many par-
ties, the headquarters for many hunting expeditions, and
the vacation home of choice for wealthy Southern Californians who wished to rest and relax near their homes.
Not everyone cared to spend their holidays in the big city,
and the mountains in the area had been discovered to be
ideal for such a purpose.

The half-timbered building had an odd but appealing

quality about it, Colin thought, and didn't look as out of place as might be supposed. One normally didn't expect to encounter a faux Tudor edifice in the middle of a California forest. But the Cedar Crest gave the appearance of being both rustic and elegant, a combination difficult to achieve but very effective.

With appreciation, Colin entered through the heavy double timber doors of the lodge and left behind the brightness of the day. Inside, the furnishings were warm and comfortable, but they also exuded qualities of excellence and luxury. No shoddy, splintery old wooden chairs for visitors to the Cedar Crest, as one might encounter in several dude ranches in Wyoming or Montana. Such discomfort was not what wealthy Southern Californians expected during their days of rest. All of the Cedar Crest's furniture was crafted of native wood, sanded to a fare-thee-well, and polished until it gleamed.

The lodge, inside and out, was a fine example of the new Craftsman school of architecture, Colin noted to himself, although he didn't mention it to Martin because he sensed Martin wouldn't care. Long ago, Colin had learned to temper his thirst to gain and disseminate knowledge with caution. Not everyone in the world was as eager to learn about everything in it as Colin himself. Nor, it was true, did most people possess the spongelike quality of Colin's own intellect.

With a sigh of regret that it should be so, he followed Martin into the lodge. The day outside was sunny but chilly, and a fire had been built in the huge fireplace in the parlor. The pleasant aroma of wood smoke made Colin think of a trip he'd taken to Montana once. He'd never quite understood why people who trucked with long-horned cattle seemed impelled to make furniture out of the horns. Some of the ugliest hat racks and chairs he'd ever seen lived in Montana. It was almost enough to make him glad he didn't.

He was surprised to see four people kneeling on the gorgeous Bokhara rug in front of the roaring fire. He squinted, trying to discern what the people were doing.

"Snake eyes! Blast!" cried one of them, and Colin blinked. Good heavens, were they throwing dice?

"Seven!" cried another—a woman, much to Colin's shock—and then she crowed, "I win!" She gave a delighted whoop, making Colin's considerable mind go blank for a moment—but only a moment.

He couldn't see her face because her back was to him. He did notice that she had very light, golden blond hair piled on top of her head in the mode made famous by Mr. Gibson. Her hair gleamed in the firelight and reminded Colin of some old, polished Roman coins he'd seen in a museum once.

Since Colin's thirst for knowledge was all-inclusive and often unintentional—his mind absorbed trivia read in newsprint and periodicals with the same zest as it did tidbits gleaned from musty historical texts—he recognized that she wore a pinafore gown. If he'd been asked, he couldn't have said where he'd learned the name of that particular style of dress.

However he'd learned it, he also knew the gown had been sewn of velvet the color of priceless sapphires. Underneath the dress the woman wore a lacy white lawn blouse. Her clothes were very well made. Colin knew these clothes had cost a lot of money, and he deduced therefrom that the young woman was probably Miss Brenda Fitzpatrick, who was a successful actress. These days actresses earned far more than, say, college professors. Colin's turn of mind wasn't bitter, and he didn't resent the fact, but only noted it with interest. His assumption of the young woman's identity was confirmed only seconds later.

"Shoot, Brenda, you always win." A young man laughed and handed the woman something. Colin thought he detected the light of worship in the young man's eyes, and his gaze thinned. As much as Colin understood the things that made up the world, he did not understand human emotions. At all. He'd like to learn; it was only that he'd never had the time.

The woman rose from the floor with a grace Colin appreciated on an instinctive level. Her movements were fluid, and she swept the young man a deep, if comic, curtsy. "Thank you, Gil. You ought to know better than to play dice with me by this time."

Colin frowned slightly. The only jarring note in the picture the young woman presented—besides that of dicing with three men, which was so outlandish as to be almost off the scale of social normality—was that voice. The tone was delightful; bell-shaped and liquid. The accent screamed Lower East Side.

Good God, had this woman truly made a success of herself on the stage? With that appalling accent? Colin found himself fascinated by her, his intellectual thirst craving to know everything there was to know about her.

"Brenda," Martin said, laughing and gesturing the woman to come to him and Colin. "I want to introduce you to my new research assistant—and my own personal lifesaver—Mr. Colin Peters."

When she turned, Colin felt as if someone had punched him in the solar plexus. Good God, the woman was amazing! As petite as a Dresden doll, she appeared fragile in the firelight, yet substantial. That is to say, her figure was substantial. In a small way. Dash it, she had the most delicious body Colin had ever seen. And he hadn't even seen it, really.

Her mouth was as red as roses and bowed beautifully, her lips neither too full nor too thin. Her nose was an artist's dream. Her face was a perfect oval, and her chin was as delicately molded as Eve's in Michelangelo's painting on the ceiling of the Sistine Chapel.

Colin had never beheld a more beautiful woman. She looked almost unreal, she was so perfect. He tried to calm his buzzing senses with the practical knowledge that she undoubtedly owed a good deal of her magnificent shape to boning, and at least some of her coloring to paint, but he wasn't entirely successful.

"Mr. Peters," she said, and her blue eyes, which matched her gown to perfection, sparkled like sapphires. She'd managed to subdue her New York accent for the introduction. "How nice to meet you. Martin's told me so much about you. I'm Brenda Fitzpatrick." She walked like a sylph over to Colin and held out a tiny hand.

Colin stared down at that hand, marveling that it looked so innocent for one that had only lately held a pair of dice. Astounding. Clearing his throat and his mind of irrelevancies, he took her hand and shook it. "Very pleased to meet you, Miss Fitzpatrick."

"Oh, please call me Brenda. Picture sets are so casual, and we're all like a big family."

"I see. Charmed, I'm sure."

Colin, who had never behaved in any but the most dignified and reserved manner, hardly recognized the thin, shaky voice that issued from his throat. He was behaving like an imbecile, and all because Brenda Fitzpatrick was lovely. How unsettling. Since, however, it was his habit, the trained scholar inside of him noted his peculiar behavior with interest, as if he might document it later in an educational monograph.

Brenda's eyelids fluttered, giving Colin a splendid view of her eyelashes, which were thick and, unless he was much mistaken, homegrown. Her skin looked like white rose petals with a mere hint of pink—natural pink, it was, too—staining her cheeks. So much for his paint theory. In short, she was the most spectacular female Colin had ever encountered.

Then she grinned up at him, revealing teeth like pearls,

and startling him because he hadn't expected such candid humor from this source. "May I call you Colin? I know it's probably shocking to someone who hasn't been in pictures for long, but trust me, we'll all be pals before long."

Blinking, unsettled both by her beauty and the renewal of her accent, Colin stammered, "Oh. Certainly. I'm sure," and felt himself shrinking in his own eyes. He stood up straighter. He did have an advantage over many people in that he was tall and straight and, while he might be an egghead, he didn't really look like one. Except for his extremely thick eyeglasses, which took that opportunity to slide down his nose. He pushed them back irritably.

Evidently sensing some of Colin's tension, Martin broke in with his customary easiness and charm. "I can't tell you how happy I am to have Colin assisting me on this picture, Brenda. He's an expert on just about everything there is to know about American history. He's really keen on Indians."

Her blue eyes opened wider, a feat that amazed Colin, who wouldn't have believed it possible until he saw it. "Is that so? How fascinating."

He didn't believe her. Not only was her accent enough to let anyone hearing it know her for an unlettered booby, but nobody thought his work was fascinating except Colin himself. Some of his initial and unexpected ardor cooled. "Indeed." It came out more stiffly than he'd intended.

"I think it's marvelous that you know so much about the Indians," Brenda went on, apparently either not noticing or choosing to ignore Colin's awkwardness.

He didn't believe that, either. "Yes," he said. "I find my work interesting."

"He's a walking encyclopedia," Martin said, slapping him on the shoulder and making him jump. "Just the man we need for this picture."

Brenda gazed appraisingly at Colin, making his discomfort acute. He'd not encountered many self-assured women in his life; this one disconcerted him.

"I'm sure you're right, Martin." She smiled at Martin and transferred her smile to Colin. "I'd be interested to know something about the Indians if you ever have time for it, Mr. Peters."

If there was anything needed to break the spell Brenda Fitzpatrick's loveliness had spun around Colin, it was this artless comment. He detested people who spoke about "the Indians" in that magnificently casual and totally uninformed way.

Realizing this was only one more of God's little jokes—a pea-sized brain in a beautiful package—Colin shook off the remaining remnants of the magic he'd been under. "I fear there is no such thing as 'the Indians,' Miss Fitzpatrick." His voice was cool. "There are several tribes belonging to a race of people we have come to designate as American Indians, but they are no more akin to each other than a German is to a Spaniard."

"Really? I didn't know that."

Good heavens, she didn't even flinch from his tone. She must truly be a good actress because she even looked interested. What was the matter with this woman? Was she too stupid to understand he'd just tried to make her feel foolish?

Brenda darted a quick glance around the room. Her attendant swains had given up waiting for her and wandered off. Colin saw them standing in a clump at the other side of the room, lounging and smoking in an artistic grouping of chairs and sofas, gazing at Brenda and chatting with each other. It looked to him as if they were all three trying to pretend they didn't want to be the first to race to her side after she stopped toying with Martin's research assistant.

He started when Brenda laid a small hand on his arm

and stepped closer to him. He barely stopped himself from taking a startled step back.

"Listen, Mr. Peters," she said in an undertone, as if she didn't want to be overheard by anyone else. "I know you think I'm nothing but a pretty face, but I really am interested in the Indians—at least the Indians in this picture. I'd appreciate it if you could help me to understand a little bit about them."

For the third time in less than five minutes, Colin didn't believe her. "I'm sure I'll do my best to provide you with any information you require," he said in his best schoolmaster's voice.

She sighed, dropped her hand from his arm, and stepped back, still gazing up at him. She opened her mouth, closed it, then opened it again to say merely, "Thank you." She turned away from him.

Colin could have sworn she braced herself before she took off at a jaunty but extremely dainty pace toward her flock of modern courtiers.

"She's a lovely person," Martin said at his elbow.

Surprised because he'd forgotten there was anyone else nearby but Brenda, Colin turned and stared at Martin for a moment before his wits gathered themselves together. "Er, yes. She's lovely." That much was true, no matter how little of solid worth Colin had detected underneath her surface beauty.

But Martin shook his head. "No, I don't mean only that she's beautiful. A blind man could see that. But she's got a good heart, too. She's a fine person." He tapped his head. "She's smart, too."

He watched Colin as he spoke, making Colin feel vaguely like a bug pinned to a board. It was as if Martin, a scientist, was assessing him through a microscope. It was an uncomfortable feeling.

He also didn't buy the part about Brenda Fitzpatrick

being smart. Unless Martin meant smart in the ways of the world, which Colin didn't doubt for a second.

"Not everyone knows that," Martin went on. "Few people have the wit to see past her physical beauty to the beautiful woman underneath."

Now there, to Colin's mind, was a tolerably poetic way of phrasing a basic quality of human nature about which Colin himself was uninterested. Martin Tafft obviously made his living in the realms of fiction. "Really?" he said politely.

Martin sighed. "Really."

"I suppose I'll have to take your word for it." Colin felt a little small after he said it. While he didn't usually find much to interest him in the world around him, except when he was digging into its history, he always tried to be polite.

But Martin said, "Oh, I expect you'll learn for yourself one of these days." And he turned and walked away.

Colin, feeling insignificant and unimportant, decided to go up to his room on the second floor of the lodge and change for dinner. He had to walk past Brenda Fitzpatrick and her throng of worshipers to get to the stairs, and he had the fanciful notion that they were all staring at him with disfavor. Worse, he was pretty sure they were amused by him, as if he were some kind of object of fun, like the class pundit or the teacher's pet or something.

Never, in his wildest dreams, which occasionally visited him during especially deep sleeps, would he have envisioned himself as the man of Brenda Fitzpatrick's dreams.

Two

It came as no surprise to Brenda that Colin Peters considered her a pretty bit of fluff and nothing more. After all, she'd been cultivating that very image for most of her life. Exactly half of her life, actually.

At present twenty-four years old, Brenda had been either modeling or acting, first in various vaudeville milieus and later on the legitimate Broadway stage, for twelve of those years, ever since her father died. What's more, she'd done a darned good job of re-creating herself, if she did say so herself. Indeed, she'd enjoyed it, since the world seemed more willing to accept fluff than substance in its female populace. Brenda had been accepted beyond her wildest expectations.

Usually she was pleased by her success. Today she wasn't. Accustomed as she was to conquering men with little more than a smile or a discreet lowering of her eyelashes, today she wished her armaments contained more formidable weapons. For instance, a vast knowledge of American history with which she might have impressed Colin Peters, would have come in handy.

The fact was that, as odd as the notion seemed even to her, she'd taken one look at Colin, with his thick glasses slipping down his patrician nose and his air of having his head in the clouds, and known without a doubt that she'd just encountered the man of her dreams.

She frowned inside, never once allowing that frown to surface. She knew better. Frowns not only caused wrinkles, but they gave one's face a forbidding aspect that was death to models and actresses. "Bother."

No one, with the exception of a very select number of family members and friends, knew that Brenda possessed a hungry and considerable brain. Most people considered her little more than a gorgeous commodity. A decoration. Window dressing. A man's expensive accessory.

The truth of the matter was that Brenda had, by clever and industrious design, created an image for herself that allowed her to earn a considerable income, independent of most of the restrictions usually placed on women. The good Lord knew, the world neither wanted nor needed women with brains. Ergo, she'd created of herself a package of prettiness. An empty shell. Not, she sometimes thought, unlike one of those Russian eggs that jewelry fellow, Faberge, designed, the ones that were all magnificence on the outside and contained nothing but air inside. One of her admirers had given her a Faberge egg a couple of years back. It now resided in a bank vault in New York City, along with hordes of diamonds, emeralds, rubies, pearls, and other pricey gifts, given to her by licentious men who'd hoped to get into her drawers by giving her trinkets. None had succeeded.

And now, darn it all to heck—Brenda had acquired a rather colorful vocabulary during her formative years on the stage—she'd met a man whom she instinctively knew was the only man in the world for her, and he'd bought her image. Hook, line, and sinker, the rat.

Although Brenda wasn't contemptuous by nature, she had a cynical thought as she watched Colin march up the Cedar Lodge stairs. *He,* she thought, would be perfectly happy with a vapid shell of a woman. He'd probably be proud to have a porcelain doll on his arm to show off to his friends. She could probably have him on those terms with a snap of her fingers.

But that wasn't what Brenda wanted. She was sick of being an ornament. She craved something more from life, although, she acknowledged with the deep self-knowledge she'd acquired over the years, she'd live with this fiction of herself as long as it worked for her.

She also knew that, when her looks faded, she'd settle for lots of money and a big house with a huge library in which to slake her thirst for knowledge, if that was all she could get. She was not, by temperament, a solitary creature, however, and if she could find a good man with whom to share her intellectual—and physical—passions in the big house, she knew she'd be a lot happier.

That Colin was the man she wanted, and that she was the woman for him, she discerned in her innermost soul.

Now, how the devil was she supposed to make *him* know it? She muttered, "Bother," again and decided to recruit Martin in the task.

With her customary skill, she dislodged herself from her group of admirers—long ago she'd begun to consider these young hangers-on as akin to a pack of dogs sniffing at a bitch in heat—and sought out Martin Tafft. Good old Martin. He was one of the nicest men she knew, as well as one of the smartest. If he wasn't so blasted busy all the time, Brenda might have plied some of her charms on him. She wouldn't mind being married to a nice man, especially if he had a lot of money. And Martin, if what she'd heard was true, was well on his way to becoming one of America's new "movie millionaires."

She found him in the back parlor of the lounge, deep into a discussion with a man she didn't recognize. When she entered the room, the two men turned. Martin smiled in greeting. The other man's mouth fell open, and he goggled at her. She was used to it.

Pasting on her "perky" smile, she moved toward the men. "Hello, Martin." She nodded to the man, who didn't seem able to control his jaw muscles. They still sagged, revealing a set of fine choppers. Brenda was impressed.

Martin elbowed the man at his side, who closed his mouth with a click of those strong teeth. "How-do, Brenda. May I introduce you to Mr. Septimus Cadwallader, who is engineering the transport of several Indians from the reservation in Arizona Territory to work in our picture?"

She held out her hand and gave Mr. Cadwallader an up-voltage version of her usual friendly smile. This one generally left men gawking in appreciation, and Brenda always tried to please her audience. "How do you do, Mr. Cadwallader? Thank you for your help in our picture."

"Hoo dow you dew?" Mr. Cadwallader stuttered, and corrected himself. "I mean, who do you dow? I mean—"

"She knows what you mean," Martin interrupted gently. He often took pity on Brenda's victims, and she appreciated him for it.

Because she wasn't sure of Mr. Cadwallader's state but figured he was unfit to entertain a question, she asked Martin, "When do the Indians arrive?"

"Tomorrow afternoon. We'll have a run-through in the morning, just to get the cast and crew familiar with the story line. I'll introduce everyone tomorrow morning, and then introduce the Indians as soon as they get here."

"How many will be coming?" The notion of a tribe of Indians arriving by truck train tickled Brenda's ironic side, although she knew good and well that there wasn't anything amusing about what the white men had done to the Indians during the last half-century. While she didn't have the time to indulge her intellectual curiosity as much as she'd like, she read a lot. What she'd read about the Indian conflict had left her emotions in turmoil. She'd absolutely love to discuss the matter with Colin. Among other things.

"Fifteen. Young men, for the most part. There's the part of the Indian maiden, of course, but we're using a white girl for that. Heavy makeup."

"Right." Which, of course, meant that the Indian maiden in *Indian Love Song* would look like a white girl in heavy makeup. Brenda didn't even sigh. She was used to that, too, by this time. "Say, Martin," she said, "when you're through with Mr. Cadwallader"—she gave the other man yet another version of her brilliant smile and had the satisfaction of watching him swallow convulsively—"may I talk to you for a minute?"

"Sure. Be right with you. We're almost through here."

While Martin tried to get Mr. Cadwallader's attention to unstick from Brenda and refocus on the matter under discussion, Brenda wandered over to a table in a corner, comfortably set between two of the Cedar Crest's homey easy chairs.

She saw several books on the table, among them an interesting one that looked as though it was made from birch bark. Brenda knew Indians used to build canoes out of birch bark, but she'd never known books to be printed on it.

She picked up the book. It contained poems by a gentleman called Charles F. Lummis, whose name she recognized from a collection of photographs she'd seen once at an exhibition, and she commenced leafing through it. She was engrossed in one of the poems, which concerned the preservation of America's wildlife, when the door opened. When she looked up, she beheld Colin Peters in his evening garb.

Holy cow. While she'd noticed his dark good looks before, what had at first intrigued her was his brain. Now, since he didn't see her standing in the corner, she was able to observe his physical attributes in more detail.

They were considerable. Brenda, who knew better than most people how much good looks counted in the world—far too much—was impressed. While she would have cultivated his acquaintance even if he'd looked like a toad in order to satisfy her insatiable craving for knowledge, she knew good and well it would be more fun to get her education via a source as handsome as Colin Peters.

"Martin," Colin said before the door closed, "I'd like to talk to you about something." He noticed Mr. Cadwallader's presence for the first time and his step hitched. "I beg your pardon. I didn't realize you were engaged."

Brenda, watching, grinned. She'd noticed before that very intellectual people didn't pay much attention to the world around them. She might have anticipated Colin's social ineptitude had she been anticipating much of anything.

It was also true, she knew, that men in general paid little attention to anything beyond their particular fields of interest. Most men, for instance, wouldn't have cared enough about Martin's conversation with Mr. Cadwallader to hesitate interrupting them. But she also knew that men like Colin, who lived in their heads, were especially obtuse. She sighed inside, wondering why Colin, of all the men in the world, should appeal to her so blamed much.

"Oh, hello there, Colin," Martin said in his customary genial manner. "We're almost through here. Please allow me to introduce you to Mr. Cadwallader, who's going to be importing our Indians for us." He chuckled softly.

As much as she liked Martin, Brenda wasn't sure she admired his choice of words in this instance. She didn't approve of speaking about people, even red Indians, as though they were mere merchandise. Not that she herself wasn't merchandise, to be used and exploited for as long as her looks lasted. She sighed, and decided she and the

American Indians—or whatever they were, according to Colin Peters—had a lot in common.

"Oh. How do you do, Mr. Cadwallader?" Colin frowned. "Actually, Martin, it's regarding the Indians that I wanted to speak to you."

"Very well, Colin." Martin turned to Mr. Cadwallader. "Is there anything else we need to discuss, Septimus?"

Mr. Cadwallader, who kept darting glances into the corner where Brenda stood—Colin was as yet oblivious to her presence—jerked his head toward Martin. "What? I mean, I beg your pardon?"

Martin, who understood these things, having worked with Brenda before, said kindly, "Is there anything else we need to discuss before you leave?"

"Oh." Mr. Cadwallader shook his head like a setter emerging from a stream and gulped. "Er, no. I don't think so."

"Actually, I have some questions," Colin put in.

Both of the other men looked at him. Martin nodded. "All right, but I don't think any of your questions have to do with transportation, do they?"

"Transportation?" Colin frowned more deeply, giving his face a dark, fierce expression that Brenda hadn't anticipated. She found it curious. Perhaps there were untapped depths of passion inside Colin Peters. On the other hand, he might well be as dry and dull as he looked. Both possibilities suited her. She craved his brain.

"Yes," said Martin. "We're discussing the number of vehicles necessary to transport fifteen Indian men from Los Angeles to the Cedar Crest Lodge. Septimus here operates a motorized transport service. The men will arrive by train, and it will be much faster to drive them up here by motor than by horse-drawn wagon."

"Oh. I see."

Colin pushed his glasses up his nose. It was a gesture, Brenda realized, that was useful for several reasons. There was the practical reason of placing them properly so that he could see through them. But the gesture was also good for giving him something to do with his hands when, for example, he needed to think or stall for time. Brenda respected such gestures. She had quite a few in her own repertoire, although she'd wager her last dollar that Colin didn't understand the significance of his own signature gesture.

"Er, no. I don't need to talk about transportation."

"Good." Martin gave him another smile and resumed with Mr. Cadwallader. "Then I guess we'll see the Indians tomorrow afternoon. Thank you for your help, Septimus."

"Oh, sure. That's what I do." Mr. Cadwallader shot a fairly desperate glance into Brenda's corner, as if he knew the moment of parting was at hand and wanted to forestall it but didn't know how. "You're welcome. Sure. Any time."

Martin took Mr. Cadwallader tenderly by the arm and led him to the door. "There. We appreciate your care in the matter."

Brenda knew he was trying to ease Mr. Cadwallader out of the room without hurting his feelings. She considered Martin Tafft a true jewel among men. He tried always to treat people as he would like to be treated. Brenda's mother had taught her the Golden Rule in the cradle, and Brenda often thought that if the world operated by this simple principle, the world would be a darned sight nicer place to live in. Martin was one of the few people in it whom she'd found shared her belief.

Colin stood scowling as he watched the two men walk to the door, his hands stuffed into the pockets of his trousers, thereby ruining the elegant lines of his dinner suit. Brenda, who had studied such things, knew the suit must have cost him a pretty penny. She found it amusing that he cared so little about his appearance, he didn't even think about sticking his hands in his pockets. Deciding it might be interesting to watch and listen unobserved for a few more minutes, she sat in one of the armchairs, still holding the birch-bark book.

It was an odd and rather pleasant experience for Brenda to be a spectator. As a rule, she was the spectacle. She'd come to tolerate it, but she didn't enjoy it. The adulation of the theater-going public had provided her with a great income, and she honored it for her family's sake, but it played hob with her own personal needs and desires. She wondered if Colin was in as sour a mood as his expression indicated.

She didn't have long to wonder. Before Martin had eased Mr. Cadwallader out of the room and returned to his side, Colin said, "I say, Martin, have you read this drivel?" He waved what Brenda recognized as the script of *Indian Love Song* in front of Martin.

Martin blinked at the pages flapping before him. "Drivel? I'd hardly call it drivel, Colin. It's a fine story."

"It's absurd!" Colin's voice had risen.

Martin transferred his puzzled gaze from the script to Colin's face. "What do you mean? It was written by a very competent fellow, John Pinkney. Why, he's had six plays produced on Broadway."

Again waving the script, Colin said, "But his facts are all wrong."

Martin's look of befuddlement intensified. "Facts? What facts?"

Colin started flipping through the script angrily. "Why, just look at this." He folded back several pages of script, held the document in front of Martin's nose, and tapped at it with one slender, elegant forefinger. "Here. Where the woman is captured. Why, it's idiotic! No self-respecting band of Sioux warriors would ride into a town in a pack like wolves, pick a woman up from a crowded thoroughfare, and carry her off like that."

"Actually, they abduct her from a party."

Colin rolled his eyes. "That's even worse. For one thing, they'd be shot on sight, and for another, they just didn't do things like that. During the time period in which this story is supposed to be set, white people feared and hated Indians, and Indians feared and hated them back—and for good reason on both sides."

"Hmmm." Martin rubbed his lower lip as he peered at the script. Lifting his head, he shrugged slightly. "It makes for a fine story, Colin." The words were simple, the tone was gentle, and there was a good deal of puzzlement still in Martin's face.

Brenda felt sort of like giggling, although she also felt sort of like cheering Colin's indignation on behalf of a defeated people. How strange.

Colin sputtered, "But—but—"

Martin laid a hand on the other man's arm and guided him into a chair. He sat in another and leaned over so that he presented a picture of interested intimacy, as if he understood Colin's qualms—although Brenda would bet anything that he didn't—and wanted to calm them. "See here, Colin. You're the expert on Indians, but I'm sure I've read somewhere that Indians used to take white captives occasionally."

"Of course they did." Colin threw his hands in the air and exploded. "But not like *this!*" This time he whacked the script with his open palm, making Martin jump. "This is idiotic!"

The gesture didn't do much for Brenda's nerves, either, but she didn't make a noise. She found Colin's outrage fascinating.

Colin leaned over, too, so that the two men were almost nose-to-nose. "Listen, Martin, when various Indian tribes took captives, they were almost always children. Very seldom were adult women taken, and never adult men. The warriors would sooner kill the adults, and often the children. Later on, they'd take children as a matter of course, and they'd either integrate the children into their tribal life or use them as bargaining tools with the whites."

Ew. Brenda wasn't sure the American public would enjoy seeing a picture about that sort of thing.

Evidently Martin felt the same way. "Colin, nobody's going to go to a picture if it depicts blood and gore and captured kids. It's much cleaner to have the woman captured in town, off the porch of a house, without any bloodshed, and then rescued. It also provides plenty of scope for the love story."

"The *love* story?"

Colin was incredulous, although why he should be was a mystery to Brenda. He must know that most moving pictures were romances of one sort or another. She was only glad this particular one was going to end happily. Half the time the heroine died in the end, and Brenda didn't consider that much of a romance.

"Yes," Martin said mildly. "This picture is a love story. A romance, if you will."

"But—" Colin's brow furrowed, revealing two deep vertical dents above his nose. He shoved his glasses up absently.

"I'm afraid we're taking a little poetic license here, Colin."

"A *little?*"

"Only a little. For the sake of the story. Surely you understand poetic license. If it weren't for poetic license, where would Sir Walter Scott be?" Martin laughed at his comparison.

"This isn't Scott," Colin muttered, sounding stubborn. "It's more like rot."

That was a good one. Brenda approved. If a guy was going to argue, it was good to disarm his opponent with word play.

Martin chose to ignore the "rot" part. "No. It's more

like H. Rider Haggard, I suppose. It's an adventure. A romance. A high-spirited lark." He thought for a second. "Like 'Tom Sawyer,' only for adults."

Colin's lips pinched together, and he said, "For adults? I'm sure." He took in a deep breath and, letting it out on a long sigh, seemed to collect himself. "I beg your pardon, Martin. I don't mean to be a stumbling block for you. I'm here to assist you. It's only that I hate to see misconceptions perpetuated like this." He went back to tapping on the script, which was much less jarring to his listeners than whacking it.

Martin patted him on the knee, and Brenda was reminded of a father administering gentle guidance to a high-spirited son. Martin was going to be a wonderful father someday—if he ever had time enough to find himself a woman to wed.

"It's all right, Colin. I understand your protest springs from your own integrity, and I appreciate it, believe me. But in this case, we're filming a story. A fantasy. A romantic romp. The public won't actually believe it just because they see it on celluloid. People are smarter than that."

Horsefeathers. Brenda could have disabused dear Martin of *that* misconception in a minute if she chose to do so. But she didn't. She owed too much to the public's gullibility.

Colin appeared doubtful, and Brenda was glad. He might be really smart, but at least he could recognize hogwash when he heard it. Most of the smart men she'd known didn't recognize anything beyond their own desires and were perfectly happy to bend the truth to fit their wishes. While she valued the public's credulity because it provided her family with a good income, she neither trusted it nor approved of it. Most men, for example, considered her a featherheaded fool because that's what she led them to believe. Which went to prove that it was they, and not she, who were dim-witted.

"Do you really think so?" Colin eyed Martin, clearly skeptical.

Martin nodded with enthusiasm. "Certainly! Why, they know exactly what they're getting when they visit a motion-picture house these days. They're going to get a rip-roaring tale of adventure and an hour's worth of holiday from the everyday drudgery of life."

"I thought you wanted to bring the world together," Colin said, his voice traced with darkness and suspicion.

But Martin laughed again. "I do. Of course I do. And the pictures are the way to do it. Why, imagine it, Colin. The entire world will see future Peerless pictures. We can educate, enlighten, entertain, and encourage people of all nations. We can make the world come together as one. The possibilities inherent in moving pictures are infinite."

"I don't understand how perpetuating a silly myth about Indians capturing white women will promote world understanding."

Brenda didn't, either, and she was glad Colin had mentioned it.

"Oh, well, this is different. This is a story. An escape, if you will, from life's little problems. No one will take it seriously, but it will make Peerless a lot of money, and then we can use that money to film more ambitious projects."

Brenda, who had known Martin for several years, could see he was warming to his favorite topic. He was such a dear man, really, even if he remained remarkably naive, to Brenda's somewhat jaundiced eyes.

"Think of it, Colin. With the success Peerless is having, we'll soon be able to produce some truly sweeping projects. Mr. Lovejoy and I have been working on a picture idea for *The Hunchback of Notre Dame,* and plans are already underway for a production of *Cleopatra.*"

"Really?" Colin's dark eyebrows lifted, and he looked less dubious. "That's better, I suppose. At least the *Hunchback's* good literature." He eyed the script he clutched with something that looked mightily like loathing.

"Oh, yes. And we're not merely looking to great literature, either. Think of the magnificence of this vast country of ours, Colin. Don't you think people the world over would flock to see some of its glories? New York City! The Grand Canyon! The Pacific and Atlantic oceans! The sweeping plains and the bleak deserts! Think of the possibilities."

Colin thought. "Hmmm. We're already having trouble absorbing all of the immigrants flocking to the United States. We'd better not look too grand and glorious, or we'll have even more problems."

Brenda could tell that Martin didn't fully appreciate Colin's practical approach to the moviemaking process. He frowned. "That's not the point. The point is that pictures are the first universal means of communication ever invented."

After thinking about it for a moment or two, Colin nodded slowly. "I see what you mean. They're purely visual, and the human story is more or less the same the world over, I suppose. Very well, I'll grant you that point, but the point I want to make is that this script is nonsense."

Martin heaved a gigantic sigh. "Colin, when you were a boy did you ever read *The Adventures of Robin Hood?*"

"I don't think so."

"Tom Sawyer?"

Colin shook his head.

Patently confounded by such lapses in his companion's early childhood education, Martin said, *"Horatio Hornblower? Five Weeks in a Balloon? A Tale of Two Cities? David Copperfield?"*

The dents above Colin's nose deepened. "I didn't read fiction as a rule. I was too busy studying."

Martin sat back in his chair, lifted his hands in the air, and let them fall, stunned. "I can't believe you grew up without stories."

Brenda couldn't believe it, either. Heck, the only thing that had kept her going during her early years were the books her father read to her. The wonderful, fantastic stories she still loved today.

"Oh, I had plenty of stories," Colin said quickly. "But they were true. They weren't—made up."

Shaking his head, Martin muttered, "How bleak your life must have been."

Colin sat up as if he were offended. "Not at all. Merely because my parents didn't believe in filling their children's heads with applesauce didn't make my childhood bleak. It was quite interesting, actually."

"I see." Martin considered Colin in silence for a second. "Um, I don't suppose you had much use for fun when you were growing up."

"Fun?" Colin had taken to scowling again. "I'm not sure what you mean. We went to the zoological gardens to study the animals quite often. And we all enjoyed going to the Museum of Natural History when we visited my aunt in New York City. The Boston Symphony is famous for its quality, and we always had season tickets to hear the symphony."

"I see." With an enormous sigh, Martin rose from his chair. "I'll tell you what, Colin. If you can try to remember that this picture we're doing is only for fun—er, that is, that it's fiction, since you don't understand fun—and doesn't have much to do with reality, I think we'll all be better off."

Colin didn't like it. He rose, too. "Well . . ."

"I promise you that we'll endeavor to stick as much to reality as we can, but there are some elements of the story that just have to be in the picture, and that's that." An idea struck him and he smiled. "Tell you what: You help me in this picture, and I'll set you to work on some more ambitious and more educational Peerless pictures after this one's over. Will that suit you? I can almost see a sweeping saga documenting the Indians of the United States."

Still frowning, Colin murmured, "I suppose it will have to suit me, although how you're going to document every single tribe, I have no idea. The picture would last hundreds of hours."

Martin chose to ignore his assistant's lack of gusto and clapped him on the back. "Fine. That's good. Well, then, I see you're all set for dinner. I'd better go upstairs and change, too." With another cheery pat on Colin's back, he headed toward the door.

Colin watched him go, his expression dour. Brenda decided she might as well let her presence be known, although she expected Colin wouldn't approve of having been eavesdropped upon. Not that she couldn't soothe his nerves in a minute or two. She was an expert at manipulating the human male.

She stood and laid the book down upon the table, making sure she made only a very small rustling noise. As she expected, the rustle attracted Colin, who swiveled his head and directed his scowl at the corner. He was surprised to see her, so she gave him one of her more softly luminous smiles.

"I'm sorry, Mr. Peters. It's improper of me, I know, but I couldn't help but be fascinated by the information you gave to Martin. About Indian abductions, you know."

He goggled at her for only a moment. Then his sour expression altered slightly, until he looked more irritated than angry. "Were you?"

"Oh, yes." She walked up to him, exuding charm and grace, and held out her hand, which she placed delicately on his arm. He looked down at it as if it were a rattlesnake poised to strike. Brenda thought he was cute as a bug. "And if you wouldn't be terribly bored, I'd love to hear more about the subject."

"You would?" Clearly he disbelieved her.

Little did he know. While Brenda could and did read everything she could get her hands on, she preferred hearing interesting historical facts imparted verbally. Were she a wealthy man, she'd have been a scholar, and she'd have haunted the lecture halls. Since she was a woman, and beautiful, she was limited in her options.

This was one option she didn't aim to let pass. "Oh, my, yes." With a discreet flutter of her eyelashes, she added, "Would you be very bored if I were to sit with you after dinner? In one of the smaller parlors, perhaps? I'm truly eager to learn about the Indians. For the picture."

He snorted and then looked embarrassed. "I beg your pardon, Miss Fitzpatrick."

She waved his apology away and purred, "Brenda, please."

Was it her imagination, or did a faint blush stain his cheeks? Hmmm. Interesting.

"Yes. Well—well, certainly. I'll be happy to talk to you after dinner." He bowed stiffly. "Now, if you'll excuse me . . ."

Liar. He wouldn't either be happy to talk to her. But he would be eventually. She'd see to it.

"Thank you so much." If the smile she gave him in parting didn't knock him cockeyed, it sure wasn't her fault.

Three

Brenda didn't succeed in knocking Colin cockeyed. Although the information might have disappointed her for a moment had she known it, she would have been pleased to learn that she was right about one thing: It wasn't her fault.

Because, while Brenda was extraordinarily adept in her own behavioral adaptations, so was Colin at his. Always a quiet person, even as a child, he'd had ample time to study the care and feeding of human animals, with the majority of whom he had nothing whatever in common.

He'd long ago ceased believing that an attractive, vibrant woman, by some fluke of nature, might be so desperately attracted to him that she'd spend an entire evening—or even a meal—hanging on to his every word and gesture. He was not, however, unaccustomed to pretty women using him as bait as they trolled for more likely candidates to reel into their creels.

By this time, in his thirty-first year, Colin could no longer be crushed by such behavior. He understood that each species exhibited its own mating customs, and he accepted this one as part of the human mating ritual. Some human females played upon the vanity and jealousy of some human males as a means of luring them into their sticky webs.

He'd been used as a tool for exciting jealousy before. He knew that he was good-looking enough to make it not entirely impossible for a pretty woman to want to meet him. He also knew that, after the initial introduction and subsequent conversation were concluded, there wasn't a woman in the universe, save a few too ugly to find anyone else, who wasn't bored to tears by his interests and his enthusiasm for them.

Therefore, when he found himself sitting next to Brenda Fitzpatrick at dinner that night—Martin had reserved a large table for the primary staff and stars of the motion picture—he was prepared to fight his personal attraction to her tooth and nail.

It wasn't going to be easy, however. She was even more beautiful this evening than she'd been this afternoon. Her evening gown of pink silk brought out the shell pink blush of her cheeks and, since it was high-waisted and low-necked, it revealed a tantalizing expanse of creamy skin.

Colin steeled his nerves and vowed to keep his masculine instincts under control. It would be fatuous, and he knew it, to allow himself to develop a silly crush on her.

Fortunately, since he lived primarily in his brain and paid little attention to the world around him, even when that world contained an object as alluring as Brenda Fitzpatrick and it was only inches away from him, he succeeded admirably. He was unwittingly abetted in this cause by the male lead in *Indian Love Song,* Leroy Carruthers.

Carruthers hadn't achieved fame and fortune on the Broadway stage, but he had a tremendous appeal—according to Martin Tafft—on film. This was a very good thing for Carruthers in Colin's estimation since, while the actor was a handsome, upright, and noble-looking fellow, his voice sounded sort of like that of a toy poodle that had lived next door to Colin's family as he grew up.

"I love the premise of this picture, Martin," Leroy yipped at one point.

He had a habit of making *ah*s out of his *r*s, as if he were some kind of American aristocrat; a Boston Brahmin, perhaps. Colin had met the type before. At once he admitted to himself, since his academic integrity had bled into the rest of his life, that for all Colin knew, Leroy *was* an American aristocrat from Boston or somewhere else. The good Lord knew, there were lots of them running around these days. Cattle barons, land barons, railroad barons, merchandising barons, and oil barons seemed to be popping up all over the place. Maybe Leroy was a son of one of those robber barons.

"Fancy," Carruthers continued, squeaking away as if he figured everyone didn't notice his voice, "a beautiful woman"—he lifted a glass to Brenda, who smiled and lifted hers in return—"captured by a lovesick savage—"

Colin snorted. Brenda turned her head quickly and peeked at him. He pretended not to notice.

"—and then rescued by so unlikely a fellow as a college professor on holiday from Harvard." Carruthers laughed uproariously, reminding Colin of a hyena he'd seen in a menagerie. "Not, of course, that the public won't understand from the moment they see me in the role that the professor is an adventurous sort." He preened himself like a parrot, running his fingers over his pencil-thin mustache and smiling a benevolent and superior smile. Colin grimaced before he could stop himself.

He didn't realize Brenda had leaned over to whisper in his ear until he felt her warm breath on his cheek and caught the faintest hint of her perfume, a subtle and seductive floral scent. He jumped only slightly and gripped the table, hoping she hadn't noticed.

"He's really an ass, isn't he? But he's kind of a nice guy, once you get to know him." Her delicate laugh sent a ripple of hot shivers tingling up Colin's spine.

Because he figured he ought to say something, he gasped out, "Er, yes. I'm sure you're right."

When he turned his head, he found her grinning at him as if she understood his exact state of mind. Which, dash it, she probably did. She was an expert at these sorts of petty flirtations. "About which part?"

He blinked and pushed his glasses, which hadn't slipped, farther back on his nose. "I beg your pardon?"

"The ass part or the nice guy part? Which part are you sure I'm right about?"

She'd ended her sentence with an *about,* which was something Colin customarily couldn't tolerate, but her question rather amused him in spite of her grammatical construction. He smiled back at her, hoping he didn't look like a smitten blockhead. "Both, actually."

Her smile broadened, and she winked at him. "Good answer. You're a real smoothie, Colin."

He was a real *what?* Too astonished to think for a moment, Colin dipped his spoon into his consommé bowl and only then remembered the bowl was empty. Dash it, he was allowing this woman to disconcert him, and he didn't approve. He knew better than this. While he understood very little about women as people, he was wise to one or two of their wiles, and he recognized this one. She must have her eye on Martin or one of the members of the cast, and she was using him to promote jealousy in the object of her desire. Could it be Leroy Carruthers?

Colin eyed Carruthers from across the table. At present, Carruthers was simpering and gesturing and carrying on in his high, squeaky voice like a caricature out of a Dickens novel. Colin glanced again at Brenda, who was occupied in gazing demurely at her empty soup bowl and pressing a crease into her napkin.

No. Colin couldn't believe that Brenda Fitzpatrick, who must have her choice of any man in the universe, would use him, Colin, as a tool to attract Leroy Carruthers. She was probably after Martin.

Anyway, unless Colin missed his guess, Carruthers was most likely after Martin, too. As Colin wasn't one to make caustic conjectures about his fellow human beings, having been victimized in that regard himself, he recognized this one as another effect of Brenda Fitzpatrick's influence. He really needed to guard himself better.

He started contemplating his impending study of the Gabrielino Indians of Southern California's San Gabriel Valley, and managed to distract himself until the fish course arrived. When the white-sleeved waiter gently slid his plate onto the table, Colin stared at the defunct piscine creature laid in front of him, and his brain didn't immediately recognize it as his own personal dinner. "My goodness, I had no idea their culinary skills had progressed to such an extent," he murmured, thinking of the Gabrielinos.

"I beg your pardon?"

Startled out of his fishy concentration, Colin realized what he'd done and felt his neck warming. It seldom annoyed him when things like this happened, but in this case he wished he'd kept his mind focused more on dinner and less on the Gabrielinos. He turned and offered Brenda a small smile. "I'm sorry, Miss Fitzpatrick—"

"I thought we'd agreed to call each other Brenda and Colin," she said in a soft, silky voice that still held a trace of New York, although it was less noticeable this evening. Apparently, she'd studied voice and could be New Yorky or not, depending upon her whim at any given moment.

"Had we?" Colin took a deep breath, wondering if it would be stupid to fight with her over the question of names. Probably. He allowed his smile to get a tiny bit bigger. "I believe you're right. I'm sorry, Brenda, but my mind had wandered to a research project I'll be starting in the fall."

Her eyes opened wide. My goodness, they were blue. As blue as the sky on a clear day. As blue as the Pacific Ocean in the fall, when the sun shone full upon it. As blue as—good God, whatever was he thinking? "Er, yes, actually. Really. That's what I was thinking about."

"You're doing a research project on cooking?" She looked puzzled.

Colin was puzzled, too. "Cooking?"

She wrinkled her brow in confusion. It was a lovely brow. White, smooth, sort of glowy in the soft light of the lodge's magnificent dining room chandeliers. Mentally, Colin shook himself.

"I guess I misunderstood you. I thought you said something about culinary development."

He understood now. She wasn't stupid after all. Rather, her stupidity couldn't be proven by this particular conversational lapse, since it was his. "Oh." He forced a small chuckle. "I see what you mean. No. That was a slip of the tongue. My tongue. That is to say—"

She was staring at him as if he were a rare and interesting life form. Colin couldn't recall the last time he'd been this embarrassed.

"I mean," he floundered on, "I was thinking about the Gabrielino Indians, who did a lot of fishing, and, er, thinking about some of their skills in preparing fish."

"Oh." Her brow unwrinkled, but she still looked confused. Colin didn't blame her. "I see, I think."

They both turned to their plates, and Colin shoveled in a piece of fish much less politely than his mother had taught him to do. Brenda, he noticed as he chewed, was as dainty with her silverware as she seemed to be with everything else. She cut a very small bite of fish and gracefully lifted it to her beautiful lips. Dash it, he wished he hadn't thought about her lips as being beautiful. She chewed like a lady.

He noticed her hands, too. They were small and smooth

and porcelain-white. Her fingernails, although not long, were shaped and buffed and very, very pretty. She must take awfully good care of them. And that, he snarled internally at himself, was a stupid thing to think. Of *course* she took good care of her skin and hands—and every other part of her delectable body. Her looks were her livelihood, for heaven's sake.

All at once, he stopped chewing.

Her looks were her livelihood. He peered at her, hoping she wouldn't catch him staring. Fortunately, her attention had been caught by her right-hand neighbor, and she didn't notice his glance.

He'd never considered what a burden it must be to have to pamper and protect and cultivate the package one presented to society, and to know that it was your only means of income—and that, with the inevitability of the years, it would fade, and you'd be without the means to earn your living. He hoped very hard that Brenda was saving her money during these years of her success.

All he had to do to earn a living was be himself—with the occasionally forced social grace tossed in for a bonus—and he was set for life. When he got old and gray, he wouldn't be out of a job; rather, he'd probably have solidified his academic reputation, and students would be flocking in droves to take his classes.

It was something to think about. And it was a lot safer than thinking about the Gabrielinos' penchant for fish. He ate another bite of his present fish and enjoyed its savory flavor. They'd used a mighty tasty sauce on it.

"I do like fish, don't you, Colin? When it's prepared as well as this one is."

All his nerves seemed to jangle at once, and he cursed himself for being so sensitive to her voice, which wasn't all that great. All right, she had a nicely modulated tone, neither too high nor too low, and not breathy. He couldn't stand breathy female voices. But she couldn't seem to rid herself of traces of that ghastly New York accent. Whatever the quality of her voice, there was no reason for him to react to it like this. He gave himself a hard mental shake.

"Yes, it's very good."

"Do you know what kind it is?"

"Trout," Colin said immediately. While he'd never made a study of fish, he'd been on enough nature expeditions in the course of his education to be able to recognize a trout when he ate one.

"Really? We don't have trout back east. I like it a lot."

Colin cleared his throat and made a determined effort to play the role of socially adept gentleman. "Er, one time when I was in Iceland—"

"Iceland," she exclaimed. "How fascinating."

She sounded sincere. Colin decided not to dip into that pool at the moment. "Er, yes, it was rather fascinating. Anyhow, we were served a fish that tasted exactly like salmon—"

"Oh, what's salmon? I've never even heard of it."

Peering at her, Colin could determine no reason she should appear so avidly interested in salmon, but she did. Nevertheless, he answered her politely. "It's a fish native to the northwestern territories. Delicious. It swims upriver every year to spawn. Sometimes bears will wait on the banks of the river and scoop the fish right out of the water, they're so numerous." He wondered if he should have used the word *spawn* in Brenda's presence, but it was too late now.

"Oh." Her expression conveyed distress for a second. "Poor fish."

She probably didn't know what *spawn* meant. "Er, yes. Well, at any rate, this fish we ate in Iceland tasted like salmon to me. Salmon has a red flesh, and this fish didn't, but the taste was remarkably similar."

"Was it salmon?"

"No." He grinned. "It was an ocean trout. I was very much surprised to learn that."

She contemplated this information for a moment. Just as Colin was beginning to feel monumentally stupid for having told such an insignificant and ridiculous story to so beautiful and sophisticated a woman, she said, "How strange. You wouldn't expect an ocean trout to taste like a freshwater salmon, would you? I mean, it is odd. I don't blame you for remembering the experience because it's intriguing."

Actually, she was right. Surprised, Colin said, "Yes. Yes, it was intriguing."

Her face held a world of fascination. "But, do those poor fish really have to swim upstream to lay their eggs? Isn't that very difficult for them, even without the bears?"

"Yes," said Colin, surprised by the question. Apparently she did know what *spawn* meant. "It's very difficult. They even have to climb up waterfalls in some places."

Her eyebrows dipped a trifle. "Are you joking with me, Colin? If you are, I don't appreciate it, because I'm really interested."

"No!" Horrified that she would think such a thing, he hurried on. "Good heavens, no. I so seldom find anyone who's interested in my research that I never joke about it." Or about anything else, although he didn't mention that, because it seemed somehow rather pitiful at the moment. It wasn't his fault he'd been more interested in books than people, although it had made him a trifle dullish. "Believe me, while the mating ritual of the salmon might seem strange and to require astonishing vigor and persistence, it's far from being the most unusual. The mating life of species is a fascinating subject. The salmon demonstrate Mr. Darwin's theory of survival of the fittest remarkably well."

Her wide smile made him feel pretty darned foolish, and he gave himself another mental whap in the chops.

Imagine, speaking about such things with a female. Even an actress. He ought to have his head examined. Brenda herself seemed far from shocked, which didn't surprise him a bit. She was probably used to hearing more racy talk than this from any number of people.

"I'll have to look it all up in a book sometime, I guess," she said after a very long minute.

Colin grunted.

"You promise you're not joking about the salmon?"

"Absolutely not." His voice was sterner than it needed to be, but he still suffered from acute embarrassment.

"I see. Okay, I'll believe you for awhile, then—until I find out you're teasing me." She gave him one of her beautiful smiles.

"I never tease," he said solemnly.

"Really?" She ate her last bite of fish. "I love to tease and joke around."

Colin might have predicted that. "Yes, I'm sure." Thank God they'd veered away from mating rituals.

"But I've been on the stage half my life, and that's just part of it, I suppose. Theater people are loads of fun. Sometimes. When they aren't wanting to commit suicide."

Her comment, spoken in a casual and easy way, managed to divert his attention from his own mortification. His eyebrows soared, and he must have appeared either astonished or horrified because she laughed gaily.

"It's true. Theater folks are a sensitive, high-strung lot for the most part. They have lots of ups and downs, partly because the business is so uncertain, and partly because that's the way they are. They live through their emotions, I suppose because they have to. I like them a lot. Most of them."

Hmmm. Colin, who enjoyed learning about things no matter where they presented themselves, asked, "And are you like that, too, Brenda? Up and down, I mean. High and low."

She shrugged, attracting Colin's attention to her creamy shoulders and distracting him from the subject under discussion momentarily.

"Not so much," she said.

He'd forgotten his question. Fortunately, she went on without waiting for him to add a comment, so it didn't matter.

"I went on the stage because my family needed money," she said matter-of-factly. "My poor mother didn't know what to do after my father died. She used to make clothes for other people, but that didn't generate much income. I was quite a pretty girl"—she smiled in so self-deprecating a manner that her words were free from any hint of vanity—"and I had good hair, so I went to Bloomingdale's and applied for a job modeling hats. They took me on. That was a pretty good job, and steady work, but I got to talking with some of the other models, and a couple of the girls and I decided to try our luck at one of the musical comedy theaters in town. I was very fortunate to be picked up. Thank God I have a voice. Which, I might add, I've been trying to rid of its ghastly New-Yorkiness for years now." She heaved such a heartfelt sigh that Colin almost believed she was as unpretentious as she sounded.

He caught himself staring at her, blinked, and turned away. He wished they'd replace the fish course with the roast beef so he'd have something to do with himself besides fiddle with his napkin and feel uncomfortable. "I'm, ah, sure that you were more than merely fortunate. Surely you have talent. You mentioned your voice, for instance." He elected not to add that he was pleased to know she was working on the accent.

Again she shrugged. "I'm no more talented than lots of other girls. I'm prettier than some, which is another piece of luck, and I can carry a tune. I guess I have a knack for projecting personality onstage or something. Some people don't. It's an odd commodity, stage presence. There are many, many people who are more innately talented than I am, believe me, but they don't project it as well."

He guessed he'd have to believe her, since he had no means of comparison. He'd never been to a Broadway production, musical, comedy, drama, or any other sort. He didn't do those sorts of things when he was in New York City. He paid visits to the Museum of Natural History.

However, he couldn't fight a strong gut instinct that she was trying to put one over on him. He'd met perishingly few beautiful, successful women in his day, but he couldn't imagine one as beautiful and successful as Brenda Fitzpatrick being so casual about her own accomplishments. "Um, I'm sure the competition must have been tremendous," he offered, hoping to nudge her natural egotism out of wherever she was keeping it hidden.

"Oh, sure." She smiled at the waiter who set a plate before her. The waiter, a young man probably working at the lodge for the summer, couldn't maintain his stony expression in the face of her smile and turned red.

"Thank you," Colin said to the waiter, thereby surprising himself. He seldom thanked waiters because his mind was generally occupied in thinking about something other than food when he was eating.

"I'm really kind of a fraud," Brenda said after she'd tasted her roast beef. "Mmm. This is delicious."

"A fraud?" Colin stared at her. Then he recalled the beef. "Yes, it is good."

She swallowed and began carving another piece of her meat. "And I suppose it wasn't fair of me to become so successful. After all, there are hundreds of women who are dying to make it big on the stage. I just sort of showed up and got a job, they liked me, and here I am. I don't have the ambition a lot of other actresses have."

"No? How do you account for your success?"

"Luck. Luck and timing. And determination. I can't discount the fact that we desperately needed the money, and I was willing to put myself on display to get it. It's been a good thing for my family, so I don't feel too guilty. We could have had a really hard time of it if I hadn't had a face and a voice and the gumption to use them."

"Er, if you don't think the question impertinent, do you mind telling me how old you were when you set out to earn an income for your family?"

She laughed, a golden, tinkling laugh that made his head swim for a second. "I don't mind at all. I was twelve years old when I started modeling hats. Lucky for all of us, I looked older when I made myself up, so I could do the live shows in front of all those female gorgons. Mrs. Vanderbilt." Brenda wrinkled her nose, giving Colin some indication of her comic inclinations. "Mrs. Morgan. I'd almost feel sorry for her if she wasn't so darned rich. Imagine, having one's husband frolic all over the country with his mistresses in tow, while you hold down the house. If it's the Morgans' house, I suppose a woman can learn to adjust."

She laughed again, a wholehearted, gutsy laugh. "And that nose of his! Why, it just makes me laugh to think that he considers himself God's gift to womankind, when if he weren't rich, he wouldn't be able to find a woman to save himself."

But Colin's brain had got clogged back there in Brenda's twelfth year. Good God. He couldn't even imagine a twelve-year-old girl setting out independently to earn a living for her family. He began to have a niggling sort of respect for Brenda Fitzpatrick, although he knew better than to allow it to grow. For all he knew, this was merely a publicity story she'd developed over the years to make her softhearted and softheaded fans feel sorry for her.

He recalled Martin telling him something about Brenda having supported her family after her father died and wondered if he was being needlessly hard on her. But no. As a dedicated researcher, he'd learned to take everything regarding human nature and its history with a grain of salt. He decided to take Brenda's story with two grains. After all, Martin had undoubtedly heard this story from Brenda's own lips. Martin, not an academician, and a good-hearted man into the bargain, wouldn't have doubted it for a second.

Whether he believed her story or not, Colin had to admit that her life had been poles apart from his. "What about school? Did you manage to squeeze school into your work schedule?" She spoke well. Perhaps she'd studied after work. Or before work.

She shook her head, making the light glint in her hair. She had perfectly lovely hair. This evening she had it dressed simply, in a poof on top of her head. Pink pearls had been twined into the soft waves. For some reason, her hair made Colin's mouth water.

He was only hungry, he told himself, and took a bite of beef. It was awfully good.

"No. I'm afraid I wasn't able to attend school after my eleventh year."

"Oh." Colin couldn't imagine such a thing.

She peered up at him slantways and grinned. "You're scandalized, aren't you? I'm an uneducated twit."

Exactly what he was thinking, actually. He stammered, "Oh, no. Not at all." Stuffing a bite of beef into his mouth, he thought frantically. After he swallowed, he said, "You're very well-spoken, in fact."

She threw her head back and laughed that full-bodied laugh of hers, drawing the attention of several other diners, and embarrassing Colin. Martin smiled at him from the head of the table. Leroy Carruthers looked at him with scant favor from over the flowers displayed in the centerpiece. Colin took a bite of his potatoes and wished he didn't feel so warm.

"Let's just say I read a lot," Brenda said after a moment. "And I've done lots of stage work. I guess some of the grammar and stuff rubbed off."

"I see." He felt unaccountably silly. It did seem a shame, though, that this woman, who obviously had a brain cell or two to rub together, had been forced to give up her education for the sake of her family at the tender age of twelve. "Er, how many people are in your family?"

"Well, let's see. There's my mother, of course, and Billy and Tom. They're the twins. And then there's Kathy, the youngest. She's only fourteen now, but she's doing very well." Leaning closer to Colin, she said confidentially, "She had scarlet fever about six years ago and hasn't been very strong since. The fever weakened her heart, according to the doctor. But she seems to be improving all the time. She's quite a musician. Plays the piano in church when she's up to it."

Colin was no genius when it came to detecting emotions in people. Indeed, he couldn't even identify his own most of the time. But he saw an expression of anxiety pass over Brenda's face. Either she was a genuinely superior actress or this particular part of her story, and her concern on her sister's behalf, was true. "I'm sorry to hear it. I hope she will continue to get stronger."

"So do I. She's a sweetie. She deserves to live in health." She sipped some of her wine, as if she wanted to give herself a space of time in which to brighten her mood. When she spoke again, her tone was lighter. "Anyway, Billy and Tommy are both at college now. In Philadelphia."

"Are they? And you're paying for their education?"

"Sure. It's the best way to earn a living these days, I

think. To get an education, that is. Not everyone can take
to the stage like I did. And I wouldn't really want my
brothers and sister to have to go through the life, either.
It's too uncertain, and there are pitfalls galore. Anyway,
I don't think Kathy would ever be able to endure the strain
of life in entertainment."

Colin blinked at her, wondering again if she was trying
to gain his sympathy for some strange or fell purpose.
He couldn't think of one to save himself. "Er, well, your
theatrical career must pay well, though."

"Oh, sure. The pay's great. But it's not what I'd have
chosen for my life if I'd been in a position to choose."

"No?"

"No."

Hmmm. He might as well ask. Her answer might possibly shed some light on his currently befuddled state of
mind regarding her. "What would you like to have done
instead?"

She gave him a broad grin, one of the impish variety
that Colin had begun to think of as exclusively hers. "You
won't believe me."

Quite possibly. Nevertheless, he said, "Try me," and
smiled at her.

"I still don't think you're going to believe me, but I'd
have loved to be a librarian."

Good God. She was right. He didn't believe her. In
fact, her glib and astonishing answer to his question
cinched it all for Colin. She was toying with him for some
motive he couldn't fathom. But what was it?

He scanned the table, looking for personable men. Except for Martin and Carruthers, there didn't seem to be
any. The others were either old and gray or young and
callow.

Not that Brenda Fitzpatrick would be the first woman
who wanted to snare herself a rich old husband or a virile
young lover, Colin supposed, but the fellows seated at the

table were so—so—Well, they weren't suitable. The old ones were too old, and the young ones were mere boys. He turned to look at her, and the possibility that she might have a yen for a wealthy old husband or a simpering young lover irked him. Surely she wasn't so conniving.

Besides, none of the men or boys dining with them this evening would need such provocation as Brenda might be exciting by paying attention to Colin. If she crooked her little finger, they'd all come running. She didn't need Colin to achieve success with any of them.

What could it be, what could it be?

"Don't forget," she said, jarring him and returning his attention to her, "we've got a date after dinner. You're going to tell me all about the Indians."

The Indians. Honestly. She didn't really expect him to buy into that one, did she?

Nevertheless, he'd already committed himself. He smiled. "Of course. The Indians."

"Thank you. I really appreciate this."

Right. Colin refrained from uttering a sarcastic snort only with difficulty.

Four

Brenda was frustrated when she went upstairs to bed that night. She neither liked nor was accustomed to feeling this way. Oh, it was true she'd finagled Colin Peters into sitting with her after dinner and discussing Indians, but their conversation hadn't satisfied her.

For one thing, he'd been remarkably disinclined to speak with her at all. She'd detected his reluctance clearly in the rigid lines of his body, his stilted manner of speech, and in the way his lips pursed when she asked questions. It was as if he found her not merely boring and stupid, but pesky as well.

While Brenda was too sensible to be arrogant about her looks—after all, they weren't her fault—she wasn't used to men being as indifferent to her feminine charms as Colin seemed to be. She'd spent most of her life marketing her looks, for heaven's sake, and, until Colin Peters came along, she'd been very successful at it.

It had been an annoying evening. Oh, sure, she'd learned a lot about the Gabrielino Indians, but she didn't *want* to know about them. She wanted to know about the Indians who were supposed to take her character captive in *Indian Love Song*.

When she'd told Colin so, he'd looked aggrieved and superior and said there were no such Indians. She didn't believe him. She'd even argued with him about it, but he was adamant. He even got huffy.

"Never, in all of the chronicles about Indian culture that I've perused, have I read of such a thing," he said grimly. "And in all of the interviews I've conducted, I've never heard of it, either."

"But surely Indians took people captive."

"Of course they did." He was getting snappish.

"So why do you say that this particular capture is incredible?"

"Because it is."

"But *why?* "

"It's utterly nonsensical."

Which still didn't tell her why the scenario was so incredible and nonsensical. She'd been grateful when Martin had turned up, because she'd been on the point of becoming almost as testy as Colin. But Martin was a great gun, and he bought her and Colin a drink, and they'd ended up being civil to each other.

There was no doubt in the world that Colin Peters puzzled her, though. He was everything she'd ever wanted to be herself. He was, as well, everything she could imagine ever wanting in a man—and he apparently desired to have nothing whatsoever to do with her.

Was it because she was an actress? Surely not. Brenda had never met a man anywhere who wouldn't have been as happy as a cat in cream to have her on his arm. Men were so simple. So predictable. So—so—so unutterably stupid about such things.

If she were stuck with an empty-headed, brainless, ornament of a man, she'd be bored sick in a minute. But she was a woman, and women were more sensible than men. Men seemed to go out of their way to secure feebleminded female decorations unto themselves. She'd been hiding her own brain long enough to have figured out that aspect of the masculine character.

"Bother," she muttered as she slid out of her evening gown. The gown had been a success, at any rate, although she knew she'd look good draped in a sheet. She never failed to thank the good Lord for giving her looks, because she knew they were the only thing that had saved her and her family from a life of grinding poverty.

Speaking of looks . . . She glared at her reflection in the mirror, squinting hard. Was she losing her looks? Was she getting old? Wrinkled? Did she have crows'-feet? Was there something physically wrong with her, to account for Colin remaining so completely unimpressed?

No. Darn it, there wasn't a single thing wrong with her. She looked just as good as ever.

So why was it that Colin Peters, the only man she'd met in a jillion years to whom she'd even consider getting close, seemed immune to her physical allures? It was all very irritating, and she vowed that she'd try harder in the morning.

"No such Indians, my eye," she grumbled as she toweled her face dry after washing it in the sink. Thank God for money and running water, which was so much easier to wash with than bowls and pitchers. One never managed not to drip, and those chintzy oilskin squares most hotels placed on the floor were never big enough.

After slathering cream on her face to keep her complexion soft, she sank into her bed. It had been made up with silk sheets especially for her by the hotel management, because she was a star. If they only knew, she'd as soon sleep on percale because the fabric didn't slip so much.

Cradling her head in her cupped hands, she stared at the ceiling. "There's got to be some way to get him to climb down from his high horse. He probably thinks I'm nothing but a pretty face."

And why shouldn't he? She'd cultivated that very image for half of her life. Anyway, so what? Men didn't care about anything beyond a pretty face, so why should her own pretty face be a drawback in her attempt to get Colin Peters to teach her everything she wanted to know about Indians?

Shoot, this wasn't fair. Why should her success in one aspect of her life play hob with another one?

"He's not getting rid of me that easily," she vowed to the ceiling and to herself. "And I'm going to turn him into a human being, too. I can do it. Heck, after creating myself, I reckon I can create a human being out of a brick."

On that cheery note, she turned over and shut her eyes, only to sit up straight in bed a second or two later, a horrible thought having struck her.

"Good God! Maybe he's a fairy!"

Feeling deflated, she sank back onto her pillows, turned over, and decided Colin Peters could go straight to hell.

Two open flatbed trucks rattled into the lodge yard at four o'clock the following afternoon. Brenda ran outside to meet the Indians in the trucks, curious to get to know them. She'd never met an Indian before.

"Oh, there you are, Brenda." Martin smiled at her, and the two of them walked to the yard where the motorized trucks were going to be unloaded.

"Howdy, Martin," said she, getting into the spirit of a picture about the Wild West. "I hope you're putting these fellows up in the lodge and not making them sleep in tents or something."

"Brenda." Martin offered her a fake frown of injury. "You know me better than that. Peerless honors all of its actors, even the Indians."

Even the Indians. Brenda felt a slice of bitterness cut into her heart. "That's very nice of Peerless," she said, her voice betraying only a little of the acidity she felt.

"I've noticed that about Peerless. They're even nice to women, of all unworthy creatures."

Martin's brows creased, and she felt kind of mean. Never, in the few years she'd known him, had she experienced anything but respect and friendship from Martin Tafft. And she had to admit that he'd never treated her any worse than a man—or any better, for that matter, which was almost more of a test of a person's basic integrity than the other way around. She appreciated people who considered women equal to men.

They weren't, though. Women were infinitely superior to men, if only because they had to battle so hard to achieve the same rewards that were handed out to men as a matter of course. She never brought the subject up because she knew it would be ridiculed, and she'd be considered an oddball.

She didn't need a charge of eccentricity to be lodged against her at this point in her life. Maybe when she retired, she could recline in her huge house amid her immense wealth and enormous library and make snide and cynical comments about how the world worked. But at this point she needed the world and all of its imperfections, because they worked to her advantage.

Colin was already standing beside the trucks, scowling at the Indian men who were disembarking when she and Martin arrived. Because she was still annoyed with Colin, both for snubbing her last night and for perhaps being a man who preferred men to women, she walked over and stood next to him.

Brenda was surprised to see that all the men, whose dark skins, broad faces, and black hair clearly proclaimed their race, were clad in trousers and shirts and jackets, just like everybody else. She didn't know what she'd expected. Something more native, she guessed, although she knew it was silly of her to be disappointed. Had she anticipated breach clouts? Tomahawks? War drums? Feathers and paint? Silly Brenda.

Colin still looked pained. Brenda, feeling none too gently disposed toward him this afternoon, said, "What's wrong, Colin? Don't you care for this particular breed of Indian?"

He frowned down at her. "Don't be ridiculous."

Peeved, she said, "Okay." Then she gave him one of her most charming smiles and was glad when he blushed.

She was interested to note that three of the men getting out of the trucks carried baseball bats. Another one carried a baseball. When he stepped onto the dirt of the lodge's yard, he started tossing the ball into the air and catching it casually. All of the men appeared ill at ease. They eyed the white folks standing around as if they expected to be shot at. Brenda's heart went soft. She didn't blame them for being wary; as a culture these people had been through hell.

Because she couldn't tolerate the gaping social divide that seemed to widen between the two groups as they stood there and eyed each other, she made the first move.

"It's so good of you to come help us with this picture," she said suddenly, and stepped across the invisible line separating them. Having studied human nature for years and years, she had detected at once the leader of this particular grouping: the man tossing the baseball. She walked up to him and stuck out her hand.

He stared at her hand, his face completely expressionless. He did stop tossing the ball, which Brenda appreciated. She decided that her best recourse in this awkward circumstance was her outgoing nature and the truth.

"I'm sure you've never been in a situation like this before, so it's all strange. And I haven't, either, really. But I'm very glad to be working with you. Won't you shake hands?"

After another moment or two—the time seemed interminable to her—the Indian stuffed the ball into his pocket, wiped his hand on his trousers, and shook her hand. "Uh, sure."

A probably unreasonable feeling of accomplishment rushed through her. Her smile broadened. "I'm Brenda Fitzpatrick. I'll be the lady you guys capture and carry off." Because she wanted to make this man feel at ease and sensed that accusing him or members of his group of indiscriminate kidnapping wasn't the way to do it, she added hastily, "Although I know that's stupid, and you never did anything like that. It's for the pictures, you know. They like to make a drama out of everything."

The man said, "Uh—" and seemed to run out of inspiration.

She got the feeling she was confusing her audience and was irked with herself. "I'm sorry to blather on so. But it's very nice to meet you. I hope we can all get to be friends. What's your name?"

"Jerry Begay."

That didn't sound very Indian to Brenda, although she knew herself to be ignorant about such things—which was partly Colin's fault, blast him. "Mr. Begay. Well, it's very nice to meet you."

He nodded. The other fourteen red men had gathered behind Begay and were staring at Brenda with faces empty of emotion. Accustomed as she was to adjusting her behavior according to the signs she detected in her audience, Brenda found this lack of visual and emotional clues as to what these men were thinking disconcerting. Feeling more nervous than usual, she took a step back and looked at Colin.

He was glaring at her as if he considered her the biggest ass in the world, and she resented it. She was only trying to make these people feel welcome. Which, in her considered opinion, was a lot better than what anyone else connected with Peerless was doing.

Nevertheless, she gestured to Colin. "Mr. Begay, this gentleman is Mr. Colin Peters. He's studied a lot about various Indian cultures."

Begay looked at Colin, and Brenda thought she detected something in his eyes, although she couldn't recognize what it was. He nodded at Colin.

Colin, nudged out of his stiff posture by Brenda and Begay, walked over and held out his hand. "Hello, Jerry. Good to see you again."

Brenda felt her eyes widen. "Good heavens, do you mean to tell me you two already know each other?"

"Yes," said Colin, looking at her with displeasure. "It was to my great benefit that Mr. Begay allowed me to stay with his family for a month two summers in succession while I was in school. This was in Arizona Territory."

"Right," said Begay, shaking Colin's hand. He had a gruff, sandy voice that reminded Brenda of the desert from whence he came.

"How's the family?" Colin asked, as if he'd only just then remembered the social custom of inquiring about people's personal lives when one hadn't seen them for a while.

"Good."

Conversation ceased and both men stood there, Colin looking uncomfortable, Begay just looking. Once more Brenda stepped into the breach. "Well, isn't it nice to renew acquaintances?"

Neither man agreed or disagreed, and she felt like socking both of them for being impossible clods. Instead, she caught Martin's eye. "Let me introduce you to the man who's putting this whole picture together, Mr. Begay. This is Martin Tafft. Martin, meet Mr. Jerry Begay." She beamed at the two of them, hoping some of the tension surrounding this meeting would snap.

Martin shook Begay's hand. "Pleased to meet you, Mr. Begay. Glad you could come. We had trouble finding enough—er—Indians to play the number of roles we had to fill."

Begay shrugged. "I seen pictures where they just dress whites up in buckskin and pass 'em off that way."

So had Brenda. She smothered a giggle. She did, however, begin to sense that there were depths to Mr. Begay that she hadn't at first fathomed.

Martin shifted uneasily. "Ahem. We at Peerless try to be more accurate in our depictions."

Colin uttered a scornful huff. Again, Brenda felt like smacking him. She was pleased to note that Mr. Begay seemed to have some manners. He only nodded at Martin and didn't even look skeptical.

Another silence fell over the group, rather like a smothering fog, and Brenda decided to take matters into her own hands. "Well," she said brightly, clasping her hands and smiling gamely at Begay and his men, "why don't you come with me and I'll take you into the lodge." She gave Martin a quick, hard look. "These men *will* be taking rooms in the lodge, will they not?"

Martin, taken aback by her tone, jumped and said, "Of course. Of course. Here, I'll go with you."

Brenda turned to Colin and asked coldly, "Will you come with us, Colin? Or is this not one of your duties?"

He glared at her for approximately three seconds, then barked, "What does that have to do with anything? Of course I'll come with you and help." He proceeded to ignore Brenda then. Turning to Martin, he said, "I have to talk to you about this, Martin. And soon. This whole thing is getting out of hand."

Brenda wanted to ask what whole thing but didn't believe the moment was opportune. If he was going to complain about her, she'd have something to say about it, though.

Long ago she'd learned to stand up for herself, and if this possible pansy intended to ask Martin to make her butt out of his supposed business, he was going to have a fight on his hands. This was her business, too, darn it. It was her livelihood. She had every right in the world to ask questions of the man hired by Peerless Studio to assist with research. Heck, it was his *job* to help her understand Indians. Or, if not exactly his job, he should at least be expected to answer civil questions civilly.

Feeling unusually feisty, Brenda marched alongside fifteen Navajo Indians and two employees of Peerless Studio up the porch steps to the enormous and terribly elegant front doors of the Cedar Crest Lodge. She noted with interest the looks of fascination, not unmixed with disapproval, on the faces of several Cedar Crest employees when they espied the Indians, but she ignored them.

If any employee of the lodge, within her hearing, behaved rudely to any of these men, however, the lodge management would hear from her. Fortunately, she had enough wealth, status, and social clout to make a difference in the world. The knowledge made her feel better.

Life got complicated for a while at the registration desk. Only one of the Navajos, Jerry Begay, could write his name in English. Martin, Brenda, and Colin attended to the others, Colin advising her and Martin about spellings and so forth. Brenda was impressed by his knowledge, even though she still resented him for being cold to her. Eventually, the registrations were taken care of, and a couple of scared-looking bellboys were dispatched to lead the new cast members to their rooms. Brenda watched them go with a sense of satisfaction that was out of proportion to the amount of help she'd been, but she couldn't help it.

She felt sorry for those men. Indeed, she identified with them. Those Indians were in many ways akin to the women of this world. They were discriminated against for no reason, denied privileges any white man, even the basest and least intelligent, were granted as his birthright, and were generally considered of less intrinsic value than white men. It wasn't fair, and she knew it. A victim of this sort of abuse herself, she felt a good deal of affiliation with this small tribe of Navajos.

The baseball accouterments they'd carried with them from Arizona interested her. Maybe they'd got a team together among themselves. Something started tickling her brain, and she grinned to herself.

"What's up?"

She looked over to find Martin smiling at her. "Oh, I was just thinking about ball games," she said airily. "Do you suppose those men like to play ball games? They have bats and balls with them."

"Yes, they do like to play ball games."

Brenda, who had been speaking to Martin, turned when Colin answered her question. She decided not to take him to task for interrupting, since he'd told her what she wanted to know. "Really? Hmmm. I wonder if we can get up some games between the crew and the Indians. That might be fun."

Martin's brow wrinkled. "I don't know. It might breed unhealthy competition."

"Not with me managing the teams, it won't," Brenda said with self-assurance. "I won't let it."

"Honestly," Colin muttered, as if he could think of only one thing more idiotic than baseball, and that was a woman managing a team of Indian baseball players.

But Brenda was having none of that. She squinted at him. "You don't know anything about it, Colin Peters."

She resented it when he rolled his eyes.

"You're right," he said. "I know nothing about playing ball games. Or you."

The way he said it gave her to understand that he didn't want to know anything about either of them, either. Which was too darned bad because, she decided then and there, she was going to pester Colin Peters until he either came clean and admitted he was a fairy or unbent enough to be her friend. Or—although she hardly dared think about it—something more.

She only sent him a sweet smile and sailed over to speak with one of her beaux, who'd been trying to catch her eye for several minutes.

Colin watched her walk away and wondered what it was about her that seemed to bring out his least congenial side. He wasn't by nature rude, and his parents had taught him vigorously and early how to behave in public. He'd known from the time he was three years old that women were objects of respect and consideration, even those who behaved in ways that would never be tolerated in men. The three-year-old Colin hadn't questioned these teachings; he'd merely obeyed the rules of the game. It hadn't mattered to him anyway, since his mind was invariably on things other than social situations.

Yet here, in Brenda Fitzpatrick, he'd discovered an object of irritation that he couldn't seem to rise above. Was it because she was so enticing? Perhaps. He pondered that aspect of her being for a moment, and decided that, while it was annoying to have her physical presence forever jostling his senses, there was more to his aversion than that. If it was aversion. Dash it, he was only confusing himself.

"I have a feeling this is going to be a lively production."

Colin turned to look at Martin, who had spoken. "Er, yes." Jarred out of his contemplation of Brenda, he decided now was a good time to discuss some things with Martin. "I need to speak to you, Martin. About those Indians."

"Sure." Martin gave him a grin that held a modicum of wariness, as if he anticipated something unpleasant to come. "Let's go sit in the parlor."

"Very well."

Colin noted with some vexation that Brenda was

watching them as if she wanted to be part of this discussion, whatever it was. He didn't want her to be. She was only a woman and an actress, and had nothing whatever to do with the important aspects of the picture. With something that might have been interpreted, even by himself, as pique if he'd seen it in another man, Colin deliberately turned his back on her and walked along with Martin.

"I'm really glad it's Brenda who's playing in this picture," Martin told him with a pleased sigh. "She's so down to earth. No squeamish Mimi, Brenda. She'll have made friends of everyone in a day or two."

"Hmmm."

"Yes, indeedy." Martin rubbed his hands together in pleasure. "We're fortunate to have her. She's smart and funny and a real joy to work with."

With whom to work, Colin thought peevishly. Not that it mattered, and not that he generally spared a thought for other people's grammar. It must be that his senses were disordered by that wretched woman. "Hmmm," he said again.

"It's wonderful that she's the actress playing opposite those Indians, because everyone likes her, and she likes everyone."

"Indiscriminate of her," Colin murmured nastily.

Martin didn't seem to have heard him, which was probably a good thing. "I don't think I've ever met an actress who was so little spoiled by her success," Martin went on. "Probably has something to do with the circumstances. She's had to shoulder more responsibilities than most of us."

"Hmmm." Colin didn't like the turn this conversation had taken. He definitely felt no need to find admirable qualities in Brenda, who had become a painful thorn in his side.

Which made no sense. She hadn't done a single thing

to him except ask reasonable questions. Colin generally approved of intellectual curiosity. He couldn't understand why it should annoy him in Brenda. Bosh.

He was only suffering from apprehension about the misconceptions regarding Indian culture that this picture was going to depict. He abominated such shoddiness in so potentially powerful a medium. The dime novels and yellow press were bad enough. If people began flocking to see pictures that portrayed Indians as one, single, huge, savage culture, true history was doomed to be lost in a mire of inaccuracy, melodrama, fear, and speculation.

Martin, apparently perceiving that his friendly comments were being wasted on an unreceptive audience, sighed and sat in one of the Cedar Crest's large, comfortably padded Stickley chairs. "Okay, Colin. Out with it. What's eating you?"

Brenda, as bright and brash as a new penny, arrived at that moment, lifted the skirt of her ankle-length beige skirt, and sat with a flounce and a big smile. "Yes, Colin, please tell us. What's eating you?" She looked as sporty as her clothing, and she seemed to fit into the Cedar Lodge's casual elegance as if she'd been crafted specifically for it. Or it for her.

Colin felt a prickle of vexation that she, who was uneducated and a female to boot, should have such a marvelous grasp of the social aspects of life, while he, who'd been gifted with a big brain and a huge education, should be a dunce in such matters.

He frowned at her and then endeavored to ignore her. "It won't do, Martin. Those Indians, I mean. They're Navajos, for heaven's sake."

Martin blinked at him. "Yes, I believe they are. We were able to hire several of them, and Lord knows they need the work. The reservation isn't a hotbed of industry, I understand."

"Of course it isn't." Both Colin's irritation and his

sense of the injustice of it all made him snappish. "But those men aren't of the tribe called for in the script." He tapped his rolled script lightly on the arm of his chair.

Brenda caught Martin's eye and winked at him. Colin saw the gesture and resented it.

"Well," said Martin, judiciously rubbing his lower lip with a fingertip, "I suppose you're right. I mean, the script calls for Apaches—"

"Which is only one more idiocy," Colin interrupted brusquely.

Martin looked at him blankly. "Is it?"

Colin threw up his arms. "Of course it is! I thought this thing was supposed to take place in the Dakotas."

"It is."

The fact that Martin appeared totally bewildered grated on Colin's nerves like a metal file, although he knew he was being unreasonable. Why should Martin Tafft know anything about these things? He was a picture-maker, not a researcher. He was irked anyway.

"Well, then, the whole thing is crazy," he said. "If the thing takes place in the Dakotas, the Indians should be one of the Sioux tribes. Probably the Hunkpapa or Santee. The Apaches were in Texas, Arizona, and New Mexico. Anyhow, even if this picture was supposed to be set in one of those territories, the Indians who just arrived on the set are Navajos."

Martin sat still, and Colin got the impression he was trying to think of something to say. He felt a trifle ignoble, since he knew Martin to be a man of honor and integrity who wouldn't knowingly perpetuate false information—if he thought it was important. The problem as Colin saw it was that neither Martin nor anyone else except himself would probably consider this matter important.

"Um," Martin said after a couple of seconds, "I understand your concern, Colin—"

"I don't," Brenda cut in abruptly. "Who's going to

know?" She shrugged, holding her arms out and looking adorable, and Colin wanted to stamp his foot and holler.

"I don't believe you need join us in this discussion, Brenda," he said in a cold voice.

"I do." She eyed him arctically. "I don't know who you think you are, Colin Peters, but I can tell you that I have as much or more at stake in this picture than you have now or ever will have. I want to know why this Indian thing is so all-fired important."

"Because the truth is the truth, and people oughtn't try to alter it."

"Do you think Martin's trying to alter the truth?" She was beginning to sound belligerent.

"I don't know if he wants to, but he's going to do it if this picture continues with those men in it."

"That's silly, Colin. Nobody's going to know what kind of Indians those are." Martin, Colin noticed with a stab of guilt, had commenced tugging on a lock of his hair.

"I'll know," he said. "And anyone who's ever bothered to take an interest in such things will know, too."

"How will they know?"

The question, although valid, irked Colin. "For one thing, these men don't look at all like the Sioux."

"Nobody in the whole world but you will know that," she pointed out tartly.

"That doesn't make it right."

"Fiddlesticks. Anyway, they aren't supposed to be Sioux. They're supposed to be Apaches."

"But that's crazy, too!" His voice had risen, and he softened it when he added, "Besides, the language is different."

"The language? What does that have to do with anything?"

"What does it have to *do* with anything?" He'd lost his temper entirely and shouted the question at her.

She leaned forward pugnaciously. "Yes, that's what I asked."

"Well—well—well—Well, you can't have a bunch of people who are supposed to be Spaniards speaking German, can you? It works the same way with Indians."

"I'm sure it does," Brenda said, and Colin noted a certain smugness in her voice that he didn't trust. "And it matters just as much, too. Which is not at all."

He eyed her doubtfully. "What do you mean?"

Martin, who had let go of his lock of hair, smiled gently. "It's a silent picture, Colin. Nobody will ever know."

Brenda smirked.

Blast. They were right.

Five

Brenda knew she should feel some kind of triumph after Colin stalked away from her and Martin that morning, but she didn't. Something was going terribly wrong, and she couldn't figure out what it was.

For heaven's sake, she didn't want to antagonize the man. She wanted to lure him into her circle. She wanted to pick his brain and make him teach her everything he'd ever known about anything.

Obviously, she was about as far away from her goal as she was from the moon. With a shrug, she turned back to Martin. "I get the feeling he's not happy with us."

"No," Martin said with clear distress. "He's not. I don't know what to do about it, though. I admire his academic integrity, but he doesn't seem to grasp that this is only a story. It's entertainment. If it can be made educational, too, more power to it, but this one can't be. It's a story."

Brenda pondered Colin's back. It was a nice back, broad and straight, and it was attached to a pair of lean hips and long legs that looked to her as if they might sport a muscle or two. Funny. She'd never considered academics as a particularly strenuous pursuit, but it was plain that Colin had traveled into many remote and rugged areas to acquire his education. She appreciated the result. "I have a feeling our Colin hasn't had much to do with fiction in his life."

"No," Martin said sadly. "I'm afraid you're right." He heaved a huge sigh. "He's been a great help so far, but he can't seem to get his mind adjusted to the difference between the university and the motion-picture venue."

Brenda thought for a moment, then brightened. Her nature was optimistic, and very few things got her down for long. "I'll bet I can help him out."

Martin chuckled. "If anyone can do it, you can."

"You betcha." She left him with a jaunty wave and a big grin, and went off to chat with some of her admirers. She was going to set up a baseball game, by gum.

On Sunday morning, the day after the arrival of the Navajos, Colin had been trying to read in his room when a commotion in the lodge yard nudged him out of his chair. He felt crabby this morning, a result of his conversation with Martin yesterday. And Brenda, blast her. Why had she interrupted their discussion, anyway? It wasn't her place to interfere.

He knew he was being unreasonable. He was also being cowardly. Because he was so upset about how the conversation had concluded yesterday afternoon, he'd taken his evening meal in his room in order to avoid having to speak to Brenda again that day. He was afraid he'd either blow up again or apologize, and he didn't want to do either of those things.

He wanted her to go away.

So he'd taken dinner in his room. The whole time he ate, a book propped in front of him, he envisioned Brenda being lively and charming downstairs in the dining room. Surrounded by her many friends and glittering like a diamond in the lights of the chandeliers, she was unquestionably the center of attention. How she kept her good humor in the face of all the inanity encircling the making of a motion picture eluded him. The process was driving him loony.

That must be the reason for his foul mood, although Colin still wasn't satisfied it was the only one. As a rule, he didn't allow himself to become ruffled by stupidity since he'd been beleaguered by it all his life. But Brenda . . . Well, Brenda Fitzpatrick was more than stupid. She was—she was—

"She's not stupid," he muttered at his book, and realized he'd allowed his mind to wander again. With a sigh, he rose from his comfortable easy chair and wandered to the window to see what all the noise down there was coming from. Maybe more Indians had arrived. Perhaps the studio had imported some Apaches, and they were staging a real fight in the yard.

His cynicism was getting out of hand. Cynicism wasn't an attractive personality trait, and Colin tried to avoid it. A woman's voice caught his attention.

"Steee-rike!" rang out loud and clear in the pine-scented morning air.

Brenda's voice. He felt it in the marrow of his bones, even though he'd only heard it for the first time two days earlier. He drew the curtains aside and threw up the window sash. Leaning out, he perceived the source of the racket.

Some sort of ball game was in hot progress right below his window. He squinted through his glasses, frowning at the scene unfolding beneath him. Brenda glanced up and saw him, and Colin got the uncanny sensation she'd been waiting for him to appear. She shot him one of her brilliant smiles and gave him a friendly wave.

He couldn't account for the effect her smiles had on him. It was as if one of Brenda's smiles shone brighter than the sun and blotted out any other light source in existence during its brief life on earth. He couldn't see anything but her when she smiled at him that way. His entire being centered on her.

"Get a hold of yourself, man," he growled under his breath with unnecessary savagery.

"Colin!" she called out gaily. "Come down and play ball with us!"

She was as lovely as ever even though she stood in full sunlight and was receiving no help from subdued candle glow, he noted with annoyance. Not that he'd have expected anything else of her by this time. Beauty was her stock in trade, and she used her own as if it were as important as—as—honesty. Integrity. Brains. Honor. He grunted and told himself there was no need to dig for reasons to dislike her. There were plenty extant already, even if he couldn't name one offhand.

Today she was clad for sport, in a light green outfit that would have looked right at home on the golf course. Not that Colin knew any more about golf courses than he did about baseball rinks. Stadia. Whatever they were called.

Her hair gleamed in the sunshine, and the shade dappling her as sunlight filtered through the tall trees cast intriguing shadows on her face. It irked him that she was the most beautiful woman he'd ever beheld because it would be much easier to ignore her if she were ugly.

He was about to decline her invitation politely—he had about as much interest in ball games as he had in joining the circus—when Martin joined Brenda's chorus. "Yes. Come on down here, Colin. We're having fun!"

Martin, too, was dressed sportily. In a moment of snappishness, Colin wondered if all motion-picture people were as vain about their wardrobes as these two seemed to be. Sinking even farther into malice, he decided they only dressed as they did because they could afford to. They could, if they chose, do something useful with their money. But did they? No. They spent all of it on fripperies.

Martin waved again. "We're having a great time! Come and join us!"

Good Lord. Colin detested games. They were childish pastimes and unsuited to a man of his education, self-respect, and position in life. Unlike an actor, who made his—or her—living pretending and could, therefore, behave in any sort of way he felt like even if it was demeaning or stupid, Colin believed he owed a certain consideration to his accomplishments. He wasn't about to toss away his self-respect for the sake of a game. He scoffed. Since he didn't want to hurt Martin's feelings, he did so internally. Again he opened his mouth to decline the invitation to join the game, politely of course.

Again he was thwarted, this time by a deep bass voice that held an element of gruff timelessness. He pushed his glasses higher on his nose and squinted through them. Good God, was that Jerry Begay?

It was.

"Come on, Colin. You used to play ball with us when you lived with my family." He smiled up at Colin.

Colin couldn't hide his astonishment. While he knew better than to believe the common myth among America's white citizens that red men were inscrutable and unemotional—or even red, for that matter—he wasn't accustomed to seeing Begay playing baseball with a bunch of actors. He wasn't accustomed to seeing him smile, come to think of it. He knew good and well that the Navajos considered white men beneath them to as great a degree as white men considered Navajos beneath them.

"Come on!" Brenda urged again, trapping him in the beams of her sunny smile. "Baseball's a lot of fun! You can probably learn how to have fun, too, if you try real hard!"

And if that wasn't a completely snide and unwarranted

comment, Colin didn't know what was. She was trying to be funny at his expense, and he didn't like it. Unfortunately, the people around her laughed. They would. They were probably blinded by her beauty, the fools.

He glared at her for no more than a second, but it was fully long enough to understand that she had intended to needle him and would undoubtedly continue to do so, especially if he refused to join in her silly game. Blast. And he'd fallen for it. Furious with her and with himself, he snapped out, "Very well. I'll be there in a minute." Then he slammed his window shut with a little too much force, wheeled around, and began muttering.

"This is ridiculous," he growled as he yanked off his jacket. "I have no more interest in baseball than I have in flying to the sun, like Icarus." He untied his shoes, shoved them from his feet, and then stopped moving. Shoes. What other shoes had he brought with him?

Thinking back for a moment, he thought he recalled that Brenda and Martin were wearing canvas shoes. Tennis shoes, Colin had heard them called.

Colin didn't have any tennis shoes. The only shoes he possessed were serviceable and highly polished numbers suited to his position as a city-dwelling academician. Unless— Hmmm. He went to the closet, thrust aside his dressing robe, and smiled. Ah, yes, there they were. Bending over, he grabbed the grubbiest pair of shoes he'd ever seen except on the reservation.

So be it. If those silly people were going to insist upon him playing games with them, they were going to have to take his research shoes along with the rest of him. The shoes were big and clunky, but they'd seen him through more expeditions into more wilderness areas in more states, territories, and foreign lands than Brenda Fitzpatrick could ever even dream of.

He shoved his feet into them, wiggled his toes, and tied the laces, pleased with himself. Then he stood up, looked down at his shoes, and uttered a short curse. He'd forgotten to change his trousers and shirt.

Mumbling under his breath some more, he went back to the closet and grabbed his research clothes from their hangers. As he buttoned up the old plaid flannel shirt, ripped here and there during various interesting encounters with unusual flora and repaired inexpertly by his own hands around campfires in all sorts of out-of-the-way places, he grinned. He could hardly wait to see the look on Brenda Fitzpatrick's face when she beheld him now. Ha!

She thought she was so smart in her fancy sporting clothes. She expected him to show up in a suit and tie and shiny shoes, didn't she? By God, she'd learn there was more to Colin Peters than a brain.

The little fool. She had no idea that there were places in the world where fancy clothes counted for nothing. Less than nothing. What mattered in the wild were quick wits, a cunning intelligence, and rugged determination. Colin possessed all three qualities in abundance, and he was just going to show them all today, and that was that.

He knew he was being childish and couldn't seem to stop it to save himself. After he'd yanked on his faded denim trousers and retied his "explorer" shoes, he slapped a soft cap onto his head—might as well go whole hog—and left his room, trying to remember if baseball was the game in which one struck at the ball with a stick or tried to throw it through a hoop.

Brenda knew that the surge of glee she experienced when Colin capitulated to their exhortations was probably unworthy of her finer emotions. She didn't care. Let the man make a fool of himself. He needed it, the pompous ass.

She wished she believed herself. "Batter up!" she shouted, aiming a mock frown at the Indians' bullpen.

A young man, probably not more than fifteen or sixteen and looking as if he'd rather be elsewhere, got up from a bench under a spreading oak tree and walked over to home plate. Brenda thought this boy was some kind of relative of Jerry Begay, but she hadn't figured out all of the relationships yet. The only one of the Navajos who spoke at all was Jerry. She'd been trying to humor them into loosening up but hadn't succeeded so far. There was lots of time in which to do so, and she was an expert, so she didn't despair.

She smiled at the boy, whose dusky skin darkened slightly. Hmmm. Interesting. She didn't know Indians could blush. "Ready?" she asked him kindly.

He nodded, cleared his throat, took his position at the plate, and nodded to the pitcher. It looked as if he'd had lots of practice playing baseball because his pose was comfortable and easy.

The pitcher for the Peerless crew was Gilbert Drew, an actor who played a supporting role to Leroy Carruthers. Gil was supposed to be an army captain in *Indian Love Song*. He thought he was hot stuff, but Brenda liked him anyway, mainly because she recognized the frightened boy beneath Gil's swagger. She was peculiarly adept at filtering through people's surface poses and lighting on the essentials they tried to keep concealed. Which was one of the reasons her failure to penetrate Colin Peters's defenses galled her.

"Let 'er rip!" Gil called, and gave a comical windup. His aim was good in spite of his bravado, and the ball sailed right over the plate.

The boy at bat swung hard, Brenda heard a tremendous crack, and she saw the ball fly off the bat and through the branches of a gigantic fir tree growing next to the Cedar Crest's west wall. She took off her baseball cap—

given to her by a smitten New York Giants baseball player last autumn—and squinted into the tree. "My goodness, I think that's a home run."

The boy, who hadn't stuck around to listen to her judgment on the play, had already started flying around the bases. The outfield of the Peerless team raced into the trees, hoping to recover the ball. Brenda wished them luck. She'd bet that ball was history. Which reminded her of Colin, and she turned around to see if he'd shown up yet.

Her breath hitched in her chest. Great God almighty, could that man walking down the steps of the Cedar Crest's back porch and looking like a cross between a Greek god and Sir Richard Burton, actually be Colin Peters? It was all she could do not to gawk at him as men had been gawking at her for lo, these many years. She stood up and slapped her cap back onto her head.

This would never do. She grabbed for her customary insouciance with determination and managed to sling a grin in Colin's direction. "You made it!" she crowed, feigning delight. In truth, she'd as soon he'd not have come at all, if his altered appearance was going to affect her like this.

This wasn't fair. She'd had him all figured out and then he'd gone and changed the rules on her. She'd never have expected to encounter Colin looking like a romantic character out of an African safari. Or one of Mr. Roosevelt's dashing Rough Riders. Bother. This was so like him. Thank heavens he still wore his glasses. If those went, Brenda was doomed.

He pushed the glasses up his nose as she thought about them, and she felt minutely better. "Yes," he said, sounding put out about it. "I made it."

"Good."

The boy who'd hit the ball rounded third base and raced for home, and his team cheered his performance. Thanking heaven that he'd provided a distraction, Brenda turned away from Colin. "Good work! That was a super hit."

He smiled at her and nodded once. It was a small nod and an even smaller smile, but Brenda accounted it a victory. She'd loosen these guys up yet.

"Good work, Notah." Colin held out his hand to the boy.

Brenda's head swam. Good heavens, he seemed to know every Indian here personally.

"Thanks, Colin." The boy shook Colin's hand shyly and trotted back to his bench, where he was greeted with smiles and slaps on his back.

Brenda turned a narrow gaze upon Colin. "My, my, you know everybody, don't you?"

"I know some of these men," he said stiffly. "I lived with them for two summers."

"Hmmm. Yes, I remember."

"Which team should I play for?" he asked, and looked around, as if he were missing something. "Where's Martin?"

"He's out looking for the ball. As for which team, I think the Indians need you more than the Cowboys—"

"Indians and Cowboys?"

The look he gave her was so near a sneer as made no matter, and it infuriated Brenda. "Yes. The teams chose their own names, and if you object, then you just should have been here sooner, I guess."

"I see." He looked about as charming as sour milk tasted.

"Anyway, you can be on the Indians' team, because there are only fifteen of them, and there are about thirty ready to play for Peerless."

He gazed at her as if she were an annoying bug he couldn't shoo away. "Thank you for your opinion. I'll find Martin and ask him." He turned and started walking away from her.

Brenda's nature was basically calm. She possessed an even disposition, a good sense of humor, and an enormous tolerance for the foibles and failings of her fellow creatures on God's earth. When Colin dismissed her as if she were of no more worth than a spent rifle cartridge and set out to ask somebody else his question, her temper blew up like a firecracker. She took a furious leap at his back and grabbed his arm, succeeding in swinging him around to face her because he was so startled he had no time to brace himself.

"You will not ask Martin!" she hollered, sticking her face right up next to his, a feat that compelled her to stand on her tiptoes. "I'm the organizer of this match, and *I'll* tell you where to go!" She'd like to tell him where to go.

He scowled down at her; then his gaze slid sideways until his eyes were staring at her hand gripping his arm. "There's no call for violence, Miss Fitzpatrick."

"Like hell!"

Never, in all of the years she'd been working as a model, in vaudeville, and on the Broadway stage, had Brenda succumbed to the urge to use the foul language she heard every day and speak the word *hell* aloud. She thought it all the time, just as she silently swore like a sailor when annoyed, but she never, ever, allowed her knowledge of profanity to taint the air around her.

She didn't care that she'd done so now. In fact, she was only vaguely aware of having uttered the word. She was too angry.

"I'm not getting violent, damn you. I'm telling you how things are. Now, if you're going to play this game, I'll tell you which team to join because it's *my* call."

His lips thinned. His black eyebrows drew down into a fierce *V* over his nose, and those two deep creases appeared between his eyes. Brenda experienced a sudden and violent urge to kiss him silly. Good Lord, she was losing her mind.

"Very well," he said, although his lips didn't move a millimeter. He must really be furious. She told herself she was glad. "I'll go over and sit with Jerry's team."

"Good." She gave a sharp nod, turned on her heel, and flounced back to home plate.

Her own position in this game was nebulous. She'd organized the teams and kidded everyone into joining one or the other of them. Then she'd joked around some more until she'd succeeded in making them accept each other as fellow human beings instead of white men and red men. By this time, she'd succeeded so well that they were actually being friendly with each other, but she'd decided not to play today.

She enjoyed baseball but figured her talents as mediator would be more appropriate for this first game on the set of *Indian Love Song*. She hoped there would be many more games, because sports always seemed to ease the tensions that abounded during the production of a motion picture.

At the moment, she was acting as manager for both teams, as well as umpire, so she took up her position behind the plate and squinted off into the trees, slamming her fist into her mitt and wishing she were slamming it against Colin's head, and hoping the guys would find the ball soon so they could get back to playing. Her heart was thumping like an itchy dog's hind leg, her skin felt flushed and prickly with rage, and she wanted to rush back to Colin Peters, hit him several times, and then throw herself into his arms. Damn him.

"We found it!" The victorious cry came from Martin, who crashed out of the trees and into the lodge yard, the baseball held aloft as he spoke. "Got there just in time to save it from being grabbed by a bear cub."

"A bear cub? Are you serious?" Thank God for Martin

and his bear cubs. Brenda was pretty sure nothing less could have distracted her from the villainous and entirely too appealing Colin.

Behind her, Colin said, "It's unwise to get between a cub and its mother, because female bears can be ferocious in the protection of their young."

Martin laughed. "We didn't really meet a bear cub, but it makes for a good story. We actually found the ball under a pile of pine needles and being scolded by a squirrel. There's a lot to this nature stuff, isn't there?"

Brenda laughed, glad no one had commented on Colin's pedantic little lecture. She was afraid the man was going to be taken in severe dislike if he kept it up. "Indeed, there is." She brushed her hands together in a businesslike manner. "Okay, so it's now one to nothing, Indians." She glanced over to the bench. "You guys ready?"

Jerry Begay stood up, grabbed a baseball bat, tugged his hat down, and walked to the plate. He looked mighty serious about the game. She gave him a smile; he nodded and took his stance. She gave a mental shrug. Some people took sports too seriously.

Gilbert Drew squinted at the plate and the man beside it, tugged the brim of his own cap like a real baseball player, gave another comical windup, and let fly. Jerry swung and missed.

"Strike one!" Brenda called. She glanced at the bench to find Colin glowering at her. She glowered back, stuck out her tongue, and then felt foolish.

Jerry didn't flinch. He only repositioned himself and awaited the next pitch. Gil lobbed it into the dirt a foot in front of him this time. Both Jerry and Brenda had to jump back to avoid getting hit on the bounce.

Brenda threw the ball back to Gil. She had a good, strong arm and her aim was good, and she was proud of it. No fainting lily, she. No, siree. She could bat and field with the best of them. Again she glanced at Colin. Again he glared back, the rat.

The third pitch went right smack over the plate, and Jerry banged a hard line drive to center field. The center fielder, a set designer named Wilbert Penny, couldn't handle it and hurt his hand trying. Then the right and left fielders collided behind him, since neither was looking out for the other, and the Indians had another home run.

After wincing in sympathy, Brenda couldn't help but laugh. What a bunch of clods. She applauded Jerry around the bases and cheered him home. This was fun, in spite of some sourpuss men she could mention.

They called the game complete after five innings. Brenda figured it was a mercy since by that time the Indians led eight to nothing. Colin had struck out once and homered once. She didn't know whether to be pleased or irked by his relative ease with a bat and ball. She'd been kind of hoping he'd be clumsy and awkward at the plate. Well, you couldn't have everything.

She was pleasantly tired, unpleasantly sweaty, and very cheerful when she, Martin, Jerry, and Colin walked back into the lodge to wash up for lunch. "Will you join us for evening church services, Jerry?" she asked as they walked.

He gazed at her blankly, and she realized he probably wanted nothing whatever to do with the white man's church but couldn't figure out how to say so without being rude. Colin huffed irritably, a habit he had when in her company, and which she disliked intensely.

"You might find it interesting," she said in an attempt to cover her gaffe.

"No, thank you," he said in that grumbly, echoey voice of his.

"You know," she said, seizing the opportunity to extricate herself from a socially awkward situation, "it's too bad the pictures aren't able to accommodate sound. You've got a great voice."

The look he gave her was almost as blank as the one she'd received when she'd asked about church. She sighed, wishing somebody else would step in here and save her from more fumbling. She wasn't generally this inept in social situations. She wasn't generally talking to Indians, either.

"It's an interesting thing about voices," Colin said suddenly, surprising Brenda, who hadn't even considered the possibility of rescue from that source. "So many things go into the tonal quality of a person's voice."

"Do they?" She hated it that she was interested, but she was interested in everything and couldn't help it. "Like what?"

"Oh, many things. Forgetting the physical for a moment—after all, anything from a cleft palate to a bronchial condition to a sore throat can affect the sounds that issue from a mouth—I've found that people who live in atmospheres polluted by smoke and chemical waste often have husky voices."

"Ah," Brenda said. "Like people who smoke tobacco a lot. Their voices are often deep and raspy."

"Exactly. I don't know enough about it to explain the phenomenon, but I suspect smoke and other pollutants aren't healthy and most likely affect one's lungs adversely."

"I'm sure they are and do."

"Jerry, on the other hand, lives in an atmosphere almost one hundred percent pure." He nodded to Jerry, who nodded back. "And, while Navajos smoke pipes during certain of their rituals, they aren't as apt to be heavy smokers as city white people."

Jerry nodded again and made a gesture with his right hand, which Brenda, who had studied gestures as part of her job, had never seen before. It was a kind of chopping movement.

"The air in Arizona Territory is dry and hot and so clean it can make one's lungs hurt for the first few days one is breathing it," Colin continued.

The gestures used by these two men in communication intrigued Brenda. Now, if it had been Martin making the comment, he'd probably have clapped Jerry on the back. But Martin was a whole, integrated human being, complete with heart, soul, and mind. His emotions were open, his gestures generous and spontaneous. He wasn't merely an ambulatory brain, like some people. She sniffed.

Then she took herself to task for being a snob. Colin, although he'd had to be dragged reluctantly into it, had actually played a game today. What's more, he'd comported himself pretty well. She had no idea if he'd enjoyed himself, although she allowed that, while he hadn't complained, he hadn't jumped up and down or laughed a lot, either. Or at all, actually.

The old poop.

By this time they'd entered the lodge, and the small party broke up. Brenda skipped up the stairs, trying for all she was worth to maintain her perkiness in spite of her bedraggled condition. She had an image to uphold. Halfway up, she turned and waved to the gentlemen. "See you guys at lunch."

"See you then," Martin said, smiling at her with what she knew was genuine friendship. She really liked Martin.

Jerry said, "Good afternoon, Miss Fitzpatrick," and sounded like a royal duke bidding a peasant good day. His formality tickled her.

She looked at Colin. He looked back and made a sound she couldn't identify. She shook her head, turned, and headed to her room. There she bathed and changed her clothes and headed to the dining room, ravenous.

Six

Brenda had mixed feelings about religion. On the one hand, she believed in God. On the other hand, she'd grown up in New York City and had seen what she considered terrible injustices being perpetrated under the very noses of the high clergy of several different denominations, and none of them seemed to give a rap. She believed that if a guy overtly proclaimed his Christianity, he darned well ought to live as if he meant it.

She'd seen with her own eyes the magnificence of many of the churches in her native city, magnificence that must have cost millions of dollars. And, in the same church family, hundreds of parishioners starved to death or died of diseases fostered by poverty and filth. One of the richest churches in New York City owned the vilest slum properties she'd ever seen and could scarcely make herself think about.

She did think about it, though, and she gave. Although she'd never considered herself as belonging to one particular church or denomination, she gave as much money as she could to charities supporting the needy. If it weren't for astounding good luck, she might have been needy herself, and she knew it.

Therefore, when she got dressed to attend evening services at the small chapel about two hundred yards down the road from the Cedar Crest Lodge, she did so for the sake of her image and not because she felt any particular desire to participate in the service. She also wanted to see if Colin would join them.

He did. She thought she was more pleased than not, although she decided to withhold judgment until the service had concluded. She hoped the congregation would be asked to sing hymns, because she wanted to hear his voice. In truth, she wanted to know everything there was to know about him, even though she knew her desire to be foolish.

She told herself that another reason she should be glad he was going to church with her and Martin was that it would give her one more opportunity to conquer his aversion to her. Darn him anyway. He had no right to hold her in aversion.

This evening she'd taken special care with her toilette. She was going to make Colin Peters pay attention to her, whether he wanted to or not. She had dressed appropriately for church, in a lavender pinstriped tailored suit. Its long, fitted jacket complemented her figure quite well, and the narrow pleated skirt and straw hat with dyed ostrich feathers set off her fair complexion—a little sunburned now and dotted with a sprinkle of freckles—to perfection.

Brenda, who had managed to learn just about everything there was to know about how to enhance her appearance, did not despair of those freckles, although she knew fashion told women that elegance eschewed them. Any proper woman should, according to popular wisdom, try to eliminate freckles with bleach or powder or whatever else it took. She knew, however, because she'd honed her skills of observation to razor sharpness over the years, that those few freckles could serve to fascinate.

Any man she'd meet would look at her and see beauty

and refinement. When he looked more closely, he'd see freckles, and they'd set him to wondering.

Let him wonder, the pigheaded highbrow. She'd get him.

She decided she didn't need a parasol, but she put on her best kid gloves. Then she took up her Bible. She carried it with her always when she traveled, because it had been given to her by her paternal grandmother, whom she'd loved deeply, and having it reminded her of her family. She didn't read it often, but every now and then she dove into it, and even enjoyed some of it as long as she didn't get stuck in long lists of begats.

She preferred the Psalms. And the Song of Solomon. For a moment, she considered the possibility that Solomon had looked like Colin. Without the eyeglasses. She expected Solomon had been a dark-haired man with that same olive complexion and similar piercing brown eyes. Perhaps Solomon, being a king and possessing good vision, would have had a slightly more imperious cast to his expression, although Colin could be pretty darned imperious when he wanted to be. She sighed and told herself not to think about Colin. Or the Song of Solomon; she'd allowed her thoughts to dwell on lusty matters too much today already.

Imagine, wanting to attack Colin Peters and kiss him senseless. Why, if she kept this up, she wouldn't know herself anymore.

Because she'd learned long ago how to make an entrance, she waited until all the men in her entourage were gathered in the lobby at the foot of the stairs before she descended. She kept her satisfaction, which was considerable, contained when she heard conversation cease as all eyes turned to gaze upon her. She paid particular attention to Colin, who's eyes opened wide, then thinned as his lips pinched together.

Which wasn't precisely the reaction she'd been hoping

for, but at least it was a reaction. Darn him, why couldn't he be as predictable as all the other male animals in the world? Still and all, she knew her role and played it.

It had taken Brenda great care, thoughtful planning, and intricate execution to achieve the reputation she now enjoyed. In every venue she'd ever appeared, she was regarded not merely with respect and admiration for her beauty and skill as an actress, but with honest sympathy and congeniality, as well. Not for her the reputation as a prima donna who threw temperament around like confetti and who used people like cleaning rags. She appreciated her audiences too much to treat them badly, and she wanted them to like her.

Therefore, while she made every effort to play up her natural good looks, she then invariably went out of her way to act natural, as if she were the girl next door. She'd discovered some time ago that the discrepancy between her appearance and her behavior charmed people. Especially men, who were simple but vain creatures. No man would admit to having been captivated by a woman's devices. Heck, no. Men liked to believe they were the captivators.

Fat chance. Most of the men Brenda knew, with a few exceptions like Martin Tafft, were obtuse and conceited and difficult to take seriously.

Unfortunately for her, Colin Peters was not at all obtuse, seemed to possess little or no conceit, and she found herself taking him far too seriously. She wasn't easily defeated, though, and she was going to keep working on him.

She wondered if she should have lost her temper at him this morning. Too late now, but she did wonder. In fact, she'd wondered about it all through her bath and luncheon and afternoon in the parlor as she attempted to read Owen Wister's *The Virginian*. It was a great book, but Brenda couldn't keep her mind on it.

She reached the bottom of the stairs, grinned heartily, and held her hand out to Martin. "All ready?"

"We're ready." Martin didn't go so far as to wink at her, but he gave her an answering grin.

Good old Martin. He knew all about her designs and devices; they'd discussed them. What's more, he approved of them and of her, and she liked him for it. "How far away is this chapel? I think we should walk."

"You'll get your skirt dusty," Colin pointed out, sounding grumpy, as if he considered women's skirts idiotic things.

She gave him a deliberate smile. "Why, thank you for thinking of my skirt, Colin. I believe I can keep it out of the dust, though, and I'd like to walk. The air is so fresh and delicious up here."

He frowned heavily. "Very well."

Brenda wasn't sure, but she thought she detected a hint of sulkiness in his voice. She hoped it was there, because it would mean she'd affected him. Perhaps not in the way she wanted eventually to affect him, but it was a start.

"Here, Brenda, please let me carry your Bible."

It was one of her group of attendant admirers, and Brenda bestowed a gracious smile and her Bible upon him. "Thank you, Henry. It's very kind of you to offer."

Henry blushed. Brenda shot a quick peek at Colin and found him scowling and looking aggrieved, as if he didn't approve of Henry's overt puppy love. The big *putz*. It would do Colin Peters a world of good to be taken down a peg. What he needed was to fall in love. And to have his love remain unrequited. That would teach him.

Since Martin was in charge of the Peerless setup here in the mountains, and since Brenda liked and trusted him, she took his arm as the group set out to walk to church.

* * *

The Peerless crowd took up three whole pews in the small church and garnered stares from the rest of the congregation. Colin wasn't enjoying himself one little bit and couldn't understand why he'd decided to join this party. He didn't care about attending church, and he didn't like being the center of attention. In fact, he hated it. Unless he was lecturing, of course, but that was a different matter entirely.

He pushed his glasses up his nose and noted with disapproval that Brenda accepted the stares and amazed looks as if they were nothing out of the way. And, for her, they weren't.

He'd feel better if she'd preen or bask in the admiration of the masses or do something else that would indicate her vanity, dash it. But she didn't. She didn't even studiously ignore the rest of the congregation. It would have been ludicrous to have done so, but Colin didn't want to allow her even that much astuteness. In fact, she handled her celebrity brilliantly. In this instance, she offered a congenial smile to the world at large and sat down with no fuss at all.

It really wasn't fair of her to act like a normal human being, and Colin didn't like it. He also didn't believe it. All this grace and charm was only a pose; he knew it. She'd forget herself one of these days and act like the temperamental so-and-so she really was. He could hardly wait.

In the meantime, he sat next to her on the bench. In order to do so, he had to scuttle in front of Henry, the ridiculous, lovesick toady, knocking him slightly sideways and sending him bumping into another pew. Henry frowned at him, and he frowned back. Drat the silly puppy. Colin was doing him a favor, if he only knew it.

"I beg your pardon, but would you please hand Miss Fitzpatrick her Bible?" Henry's voice was as cold as Flagstaff in winter.

Colin turned to glare at him and realized he had something in his hands. It was Brenda's Bible. He took the Bible. "Yes. I'll be happy to."

Henry gave a low growl, then said, "Thank you," as if he begrudged having to say the words politeness dictated. Silly little twit.

"You're welcome." So much for Henry. Colin sat and practically flung the Bible into Brenda's lap. "Here. That fellow wanted me to give this to you." He heard "that fellow" growl again.

Brenda gave a start and turned to stare at him. "Good heavens, Colin, I'm sure Henry didn't mean to put you out. Is my grandmother's Bible *that* heavy a burden?" As Colin seethed, she leaned forward on the pew and looked at Henry with one of her glorious smiles; the ones that seemed to fade the sun, blot out the moon and stars, and obscure everything else around them. Colin shook himself internally and told himself to get a grip. "Thank you, Henry. I appreciate your kindness."

Henry, needless to say, blushed. Colin wanted to throw something. A fit, maybe.

Colin only became aware that the congregation had been buzzing like a hive of agitated bees when the organist started playing and folks shut up. When he glanced around, he saw that nearly every person in the place was still staring at Brenda, but they'd evidently stopped talking about her.

"I don't know how you can stand being the center of attention all the time," he grumbled under his breath.

"I'm used to it." She shrugged. "It's a living."

"I'm sure it feeds your ego considerably." It was snippy, and for the life of him, he couldn't figure out why he'd said it. He wasn't normally petty.

"I'm sure it would if I let it." She chuckled, a low, sweet sound that made gooseflesh rise on Colin's arms and made him think of lush tropical forests and making love on a mossy bank beside a waterfall. With birds chirping sweetly in the trees. Surrounded by flowers; flowers that emitted the same sweet fragrance he could smell now, very faintly, and which he'd come to recognize as Brenda's scent. His sex responded immediately to the happy notion of making love with Brenda. Thank God nobody could see. How embarrassing.

This, he realized immediately, is why he found Brenda Fitzpatrick so blasted bothersome. She had this terrible effect on him. He hadn't even been able to concentrate on his reading this afternoon because he kept replaying their conversations in his head. He had been totally engrossed in the study of the socioeconomic conditions prevailing in the Belgian Congo and the decline of the head-hunting and pygmy populations therein. Fascinating subjects, both of them. Until he met Brenda. She made him feel out of control. He hated the feeling with something akin to passion.

"But you don't let it go to your head?" He manufactured a pretty good sneer to go along with his doubtful tone.

She was still smiling at him and making him feel sort of like a snotty schoolboy when she answered him. "What's the point? People are only intrigued by who they think I am. I'm fortunate to be attractive, and a pretty face is nothing I attained by my own efforts. It's a gift from God. That's all."

That's all? That's *all?* This, from a woman who earned more money in a week than Colin and a dozen academicians like him could make in a year. She was shrugging off the insanity of people who worshiped her as a goddess for doing nothing but being pretty! And she was saying she wasn't at fault; that God had created her! Colin had a notion his sense of outrage about the whole thing wasn't rational, but it was there.

He said dryly, "How fortunate, then, that God waved

his magic wand over you." That was probably blasphemous, especially as he was at present sitting in a church, but he was too angry to care.

She laughed again softly. Lord, he wished she wouldn't do that. Her laughter did strange things to his senses. He pretended to become absorbed in the hymnal, which was pretty much like any other hymnal he'd ever seen.

He jumped almost out of his skin when she poked him in the ribs with her elbow. He swiveled his head and glowered at her, incensed.

She grinned. "Get over it, Colin. I can't help what I am any more than you can help what you are. I wish we could be friends."

"Friends?" The idea wouldn't have occurred to him in a million years. Friends with Brenda Fitzpatrick, star of comedy stage and celluloid? Absurd. Ridiculous. *He* was a serious scholar.

"Sure. I'd love to learn more from you about the Navajos. It must have been fascinating to have lived with them on the reservation."

Recalling the miserable conditions prevailing on the reservation, Colin shuddered involuntarily. He eyed her for a long moment, and then an amusing thought struck him. "Very well, Brenda. I'll tell you about life on the reservation." He smiled, thinking of all the stories about starvation and disease, filth, flies, and misery, he'd be able to impart. Little did she know what was in store for her.

She beamed at him, making him feel only a bit guilty. "Thank you, Colin. I really appreciate it."

He doubted she would for long. This would bring her down, though; he was sure of it. This would teach her to—to—to— To what?

As the minister started speaking, Colin couldn't remember why he was trying to teach Brenda Fitzpatrick anything at all, much less a severe lesson in the tragedies of history. He began to experience a vague and unsettling notion that his attitude about Brenda owed more to emotion than to reason. He'd never allowed his emotions to dictate to him before. This was very irksome.

He blamed Brenda.

The next morning Brenda approached Martin and Colin somewhat tentatively. She didn't want to get barked at before breakfast. They were discussing last evening's sermon, much to her surprise. She greeted the two men and then stood by, silently listening to them talk until her excitement overcame her and she had to join in.

Colin said, "It was Paul who did it. Peter wanted the church's headquarters to stay in Jerusalem. For the first fifty years or so, Christianity was only another sect of Judaism, and that would have made sense."

"Is that so?" Martin took a bite out of his apple and squinted into the distance where the cameramen were setting up to film the first sequence of *Indian Love Song.*

Colin nodded. "Sure. Haven't you ever wondered why the Christian center ended up in Rome, even though the Romans used to take sport in persecuting the Christians?" He seemed to be interested in the proceedings, too.

Brenda wished she could snag him, lead him off into the woods, and pick his brain about the history of Christianity. All of this stuff was so interesting. "I didn't know that, although it makes sense. About being a sect of Judaism, I mean, and the headquarters being in Jerusalem. After all, Jesus was a Jew."

Martin laughed, evidently finding Brenda's assessment somewhat outlandish. Colin nodded, but it seemed like an approving nod. Unless Brenda was imagining things.

"Right," he said. "Most people seem to overlook that salient point when studying their religions. There were huge arguments over whether or not Gentiles—Greeks and Romans, for instance—needed to convert to Judaism before they could call themselves Christians."

"Oh, my! My goodness, I never knew that." She wished she dared ask how in heck he knew all this stuff but knew he'd only sneer if she did.

Colin made some kind of noise that she interpreted as signifying his lack of amazement at her ignorance. She chose not to get upset.

"The earliest Christians were divided as to whether they still had to follow Jewish law, or if they could safely abandon it without being damned. The laws were extensive and governed all aspects of life, from circumcision to what kinds of foods one could eat."

Circumcision? Brenda blinked at him, wondering if he was trying to embarrass her. No. He was still studying the set construction crew casually, as if he talked about such things every day. Which he well might, for all she knew.

"It was Paul who introduced the concept of spirituality's ascendance over works, deeds, and rules, so to speak."

"What do you mean?" This was so fascinating. Brenda almost wished she could chuck making the picture and simply hang out with Colin for a couple of months. Or years. Or lifetimes.

He twitched his shoulders, as if he were slightly peeved to have to be telling her these things. "He eschewed following the Jewish laws and preached simple belief and faith in the man he'd come to consider the Messiah. He's the first one who told people they need only believe that Jesus was the risen Christ in order to be saved and given eternal life. So to speak. I imagine he considered the legend about the temple curtain tearing when Jesus died as signifying the removal of intermediaries interceding between God and man. His concept of the faith was direct, from man to God."

"My goodness." Now *this*, thought Brenda, was keen stuff. She wished she could pick his brains some more, but Martin started talking, and she decided to give it a rest for the time being. She'd get him later.

"This is going to be a great picture," Martin announced with enthusiasm.

Martin was always enthusiastic. It was one of the things Brenda liked about him. He shared her appreciation for the good things life had sent him. Unlike her, Martin was apt to get upset and depressed when things didn't go his way, but other than that they were a lot alike. Brenda figured his tendency to become distraught was because he hadn't faced enough real hardships in his life. Long ago Brenda had figured out that worry didn't change anything.

As for Colin . . . Well, she just didn't know about Colin.

She was glad he seemed less hostile this morning than he had yesterday evening. She couldn't figure him out. At the moment, he was standing in his shirtsleeves with his arms crossed over his chest. He looked grouchy. He always looked grouchy.

"You know, Martin, this is all wrong," he said at last, as if he couldn't keep silent another moment longer. "Those structures aren't the kinds built by the Hunkpapa. The Hunkpapas' tipis are totally different."

Martin heaved a sigh. "They aren't supposed to be Hunkpapas. They're supposed to be Apaches."

"But they aren't right for Apaches, either, whether you're talking Mescalero or Chiricahua or any other variety. In fact, I can't imagine any self-respecting Indian building something that nonsensical for his family to live in. Canvas! And flowers! My God."

"This is a picture, Colin," Martin reminded him.

"I still don't understand why everything has to be

wrong just because it's a picture," Colin said stubbornly. "No Indian would paint a flower on his tipi."

Brenda kind of agreed with him, although she understood Martin's point of view, too. "Nobody's going to know," she said, hoping to forestall another big brangle.

"That's not the point." Colin gave her a hot scowl, which she didn't appreciate. "Or perhaps it is. Why should the motion-picture medium spread false information when it would be just as easy to do it right? I don't understand."

"Next time," Martin said. "Next time, we'll consult you first. We don't have the time or the money to do it with this picture because everything's already ready."

Brenda could tell Martin was trying to keep his upper lip stiff. She'd bet anything he was about ready to pop Colin a good one, poor guy. Not even Martin's patience was infinite.

"Oh, fine," Colin said, crabby as all get out. "So what if it's wrong, as long as it's ready?"

"Colin, we've been over this ground before." Martin's voice sounded strained, and he reached for that tuft of hair he tugged when he was under severe stress. Brenda had begun to think of it as his worry lock.

She decided to step into the fray. What the heck; Colin already found her irritating. Might as well give him one more reason to loathe her.

"Colin, stop your grousing. You can't change it now."

He turned on her like a fury, so suddenly that she actually stepped back a pace. Peeved with herself, and with him, she braced herself, set her chin, and frowned back at him.

"Why not?" he said, his voice loud. "Why can't it be changed? For heaven's sake, thousands of people are going to see this picture—"

"More like millions," Martin murmured under his breath.

Colin swirled the other way and gaped at Martin. "Millions? *Millions!* Then for heaven's sake, you *have* to change it. Why, the whole world will be laughing at us!"

Brenda caught Martin's eye and winked at him, hoping to buck him up.

"Colin." Martin was plainly reaching for patience. "You're wrong. Nobody will know except you and maybe a few other people who've learned a little bit about various Indian markings and so forth. Nobody will even notice those tents—"

"Tipis," Colin tossed in crossly.

"Tipis. Nobody's even going to see them, because the audience is going to be too involved with the story to notice. The only time those tents—tipis, I mean—will be shown is during the post-abduction scene, when the Apache warrior carries Brenda into the village."

"Apache warrior," Colin said in a tone of unutterable contempt. "In the Dakota hills. In tents that look as if they came from a girl's camp."

"Look, Colin, I'm really glad you're here to help us keep things as accurate as possible, but some things just aren't possible."

"Why not?" Colin threw his arms out, as if piqued beyond bearing. "Why can't we at least paint some appropriate symbols on the tipis and get rid of those idiotic flowers? Flowers!"

"Don't have a spasm, Colin," Brenda said, not as acerbically as her words might imply, but in a light voice she hoped conveyed a spirit of fun. She turned to Martin. "You know, Martin, that's not really a bad idea. We can paint over those flowers. They aren't my idea of Indian artistry, either, if you want to know the truth."

Martin frowned, and something that sounded like a cross between a groan and a moan issued from his throat. He didn't let up on his hair. Brenda feared he'd snatch himself bald if he kept that up. In order to perk him up, she said brightly, "I love to paint. I'll be glad to help."

She ignored Colin's unflatteringly wrinkled nose. The miserable poop. How did *he* know whether or not she could paint?

"Well . . ." Martin let go of his hair and began rubbing the bridge of his nose with a finger. "I suppose it won't delay shooting any. We're only going to rehearse this afternoon, anyway, and if you really think you can paint over the flowers this afternoon and evening—"

"Sure we can! I'll recruit all my friends to help." Brenda was already sorting out assignments as she spoke. Henry could mix the paint, Eddie could slap white paint over those ghastly flowers, and she and Gil and a few of the others could make new symbols on the tents. Tipis. Whatever they were. Something occurred to her and her smile faded. "Er, what symbols can we use that will look like Apache stuff?"

"They shouldn't be Apache," Colin ground out through his teeth.

"Yes, yes, I know. But you're just going to have to accept the fact that we're going to be wrong in this particular instance." It annoyed her when people refused to face reality. Hell's bells, she'd been facing reality since she was twelve years old. Now she was rich. There was a lot of good to be gained from playing the cards as God dealt them to you instead of whining about not having been dealt a better hand. She'd have to try to explain that concept to Colin one of these days, if he ever climbed down from his high horse long enough to listen.

Seven

Rehearsal went fairly well, except that Colin kept interrupting the action to explain why they were doing everything wrong and to offer suggestions as to how it could be made right.

Martin almost understood Colin's feelings on the matter, but he understood even better that Colin wasn't helping to bring about the completion of the motion picture. He wasn't doing much for its quality, either. Martin knew how to make movies; Colin knew history. Martin was beginning to believe the two milieus were incompatible.

"No, no, no!" Colin cried at one point, rushing up to Martin and yanking on his arm. He looked horrified, and Martin thought at first that an accident had occurred. He ought to have known better.

The actors stopped what they were doing, which was faking an abduction. Jerry Begay, for whom this was an embarrassing proposition—Martin could clearly discern that he felt not merely silly but preposterous, pretending to kidnap Brenda—let go of her faster than a normal man could sneeze. Brenda straightened with a sigh, put her fists on her hips, and stared at Martin and Colin with a resigned expression on her face.

Martin thanked God it was Brenda, and not a dozen other actresses he'd worked with, who was playing this part. She was the only one Martin knew who'd put up with this sort of nonsense without throwing a temper tantrum.

"What is it this time, Colin?" He tried to keep the annoyance he felt from creeping into his voice, because he truly did honor Colin's knowledge. If the man could only learn to curb his insistence on applying his knowledge to every situation he encountered, this would go a lot faster.

"It's ludicrous to have Delsin fall from his horse." Delsin was a young cousin of Jerry Begay. "He's a superb horseman. And so were the Sioux."

Martin took a deep breath and counted to five. He wasn't mad enough yet to go all the way up to ten. "They aren't supposed to be Sioux. They're supposed to be Apaches."

"Oh, God." Colin stabbed a finger to the nosepiece of his glasses, then raked his fingers through his hair as if he were sliding into despair. "This is impossible."

"I'm sorry, Colin. You get to repaint the tents—"

"Tipis! They're tipis!"

Martin sighed. "You get to repaint the tipis. But I'm afraid we're just going to have to differ about what tribe these people are supposed to be from."

"It doesn't make any difference anyway. No Apache would fall off his horse, either, unless he'd been shot from its back." He glowered at the scene he'd stopped. "And they don't use saddles, either."

"No saddles. We can take care of that in a jiffy." Martin, pleased to concede this point and hoping it would mollify Colin enough to leave him alone for a while, waved to a member of the crew. "Take the saddles off the Indians' horses, Sam!"

Sam returned a small salute and went off to do Martin's bidding.

"No falling off the horse." Colin still looked unhappy.

Martin heaved a gusty sigh. "I'm sure we can shoot the scene and keep Delsin on his horse. It was supposed to be a moment of comic relief in the middle of a huge catastrophe."

Colin's eyes were squinched up tight, and his frown looked as if it had been shellacked into place. Martin got the impression that Colin had never encountered comic relief in his life until now and wished he hadn't this time, either. He probably wouldn't recognize a joke if it bit him on the butt, and he undoubtedly watched one-reel comedies with an eye to catching mistakes.

Martin could envision it. *No, no! You can't fry an egg on a sidewalk! It's not only unsanitary, but city sidewalks never really get that hot!* He shook his head to clear it of irrelevancies.

"Any Indian from a horse-riding culture falling from a horse without intense provocation is simply inaccurate. I don't see anything funny about it," Colin said, confirming Martin's suspicions.

"Delsin can keep his seat on the horse," Martin said. "If he can do it without a saddle."

"Of course he can. He's an expert horseman. All of what we now call the Plains Indians—although there were really no such tribes extant until the white man came—can ride without saddles. They're probably the finest horsemen in the world. Well, except for some Hungarians."

Martin cut Colin's lecture short by saying hastily, "I'm sure that's true." Although he was nearing the end of his patience, Martin managed to achieve a conciliatory tone.

Colin nodded and didn't continue his lecture, an example of forbearance of which Martin approved. He was afraid to ask, but he did so anyway, somewhat tentatively. "Um, anything else?" He'd rather get it all out and over with now, before Colin stopped the action again. Rehearsal would go on all day at this rate.

"There's lots more, but I suppose there's nothing to be done about any of it at this late date. I really do wish I'd been consulted about what should go into a picture containing any of the American Indian cultures before the work had gone this far."

"Me, too," Martin muttered. He squinted at the set, saw that Sam was taking care of the saddles with the help of Delsin, and noticed Brenda watching him and Colin. He sent her a wry smile, knowing she'd understand his frustration with the way things were progressing. She was a most sympathetic person, and infinitely practical.

Which gave him an idea.

Maybe he could sic Brenda on Colin. Humanize him a little bit. If anybody could do it, it was Brenda. Even if she only persuaded him not to interrupt rehearsals every five seconds, she'd be doing Martin a great favor. He waved to her, and she waved back and started walking toward them.

When Martin glanced at Colin, he noticed that his frown had intensified as he gazed at Brenda. What the heck was going on here? No man ever frowned at Brenda. She was too lovely to be frowned at, and too agreeable to be disliked.

Leave it to Colin to be contrary. Martin was tugging on his favorite hunk of hair when Brenda reached his side.

Poor Martin. Brenda could tell he was nearly at the end of his tether. And, while she admired Colin for his devotion to historical accuracy, she deplored his interference in this case. After all, it was only a picture.

"I see we did something else of which you disapprove, Colin," she said when she got close enough to be heard. "You're going to have to stop interfering, you know, or we'll never get this thing done." She spoke lightly, but she meant every word.

"Would that be so great a tragedy?"

"Mercy, Colin, you sound even grumpier than usual today. And yes, it would be a tragedy, because Peerless Studio would lose a lot of money if the picture didn't get made, and that would mean a lot of people would be out of employment, you and I wouldn't get paid, the Indians wouldn't get paid, and none of the rest of the staff would get paid.

"I'm sure Martin and Mr. Lovejoy will take greater pains to achieve historical accuracy in future Indian pictures, but this one's ready to roll, and it's impossible to alter most of the scenes now."

"I don't see why."

She eyed him for a moment, then turned to Martin. "Do you want to explain the business to him, or would you like me to do it?"

Looking as if he couldn't take any more, Martin said, "You do it. I've got to go over the next scene with Al." Al was Peerless Studio's premier set designer. Brenda figured Martin wanted to make sure Al hadn't included flowers on anything other than the tipis.

She smiled sweetly at Colin. "Where would you like me to begin, Colin? With the financial aspects of making a picture, or the duty owed to financial investors, or the hundreds of jobs the pictures are providing to workers, or what?"

He crossed his arms over his chest and frowned some more. He looked remarkably like a pouty adolescent. "You needn't explain anything to me, thank you. I understand the business end of it. It's only that I deplore all of the inaccuracies."

"I know you do. We all know you do by this time, believe me. But you're causing delays, and that's not fair to any of us, even your precious Indians."

"They aren't my *precious* Indians."

"Whatever they are, they're as irked by your interference as everyone else."

He stood still, fuming, and didn't speak. Brenda felt a little like a schoolyard bully, but he really did need to know that his behavior wasn't admired.

"Listen, Colin," she said more gently, "I know you're basically a scholar, and I understand your desire to depict Indian lore honestly on celluloid. But in this case, it's too late to alter much of the script. By the time a cast goes on location, things are pretty much set in concrete. The most you can do at this point is—well—have the saddles taken off the horses and the tipis repainted." Which gave her a brilliant idea.

"I suppose you're right. I don't like it, though, because it's all wrong." The admission sounded as if he'd had to drag it from his throat in chains.

"I know." She made herself sound more sympathetic than she felt. "But you'll at least have an opportunity to be accurate with the tipis. Why don't you stop watching the rehearsal, since it obviously upsets you—"

"I'm not upset!"

Brenda eyed him thoughtfully. "Right. But you're not enjoying it much."

"No," he conceded. "I'm not enjoying it. At all."

"Well, then, why don't you spend this rehearsal time making sample designs for us to paint on the tipis? That would be useful, and it would save Martin's poor hair."

Colin took a deep breath. "I don't mean to be an impediment to the production's progress," he said grudgingly.

"I know." Brenda kept her own voice low and free of accusation. It wouldn't do to humiliate the poor man just because he was an egghead and didn't understand the practicalities of life. "This is the first time you've worked on a motion picture, and you're not familiar with how things are done."

He nodded. "With luck, it will be the last time, as well," he said wryly.

She tilted her head and observed him. He was a stupendously handsome man, for a brain. Not that brainy men weren't generally handsome, but one didn't normally associate the one with the other. "It would be a shame to lose your expertise."

He snorted. "No one wants my expertise. Obviously."

"That's not true. Or not entirely true, anyway," she added honestly. "Martin has too much to do already. He really needs assistance. The trouble is, you aren't of much assistance to him when you interrupt his work all the time."

He didn't like it. He hated it, even. Brenda could clearly discern the rebellious lines around his mouth and eyes. He wanted to holler at her and tell her she was a nitwit and a dunce and that she didn't know what she was talking about. If he took a minute to think honestly, however, he would have to admit she was right.

After another moment or two, during which he was unquestionably stewing, Colin huffed, "You're probably right. I don't belong here."

"That's not what I said. I think the pictures need people like you." Not that there were any other people like him, at least none that she'd met. "But you've got to learn to take things a little easier. Relax some. Let some things slide. It won't kill you to enjoy life a little bit."

He huffed again.

She went on. "I know, the scholar in you rebels at allowing inaccuracies to pass by without comment, but there's only so much that can be expected of the movies. It's a brand-new industry. Martin's the hardest-working man I know, and he tries diligently to make things right. He's the best, Colin. He really is."

"I know he's a very nice person."

"He also knows what he's doing on a motion-picture set."

"I'm sure he does."

"And if you'll give him a chance—work with him instead of against him—I'm sure he'll be happy to be more accurate in his portrayal of the Indians in future pictures."

Colin turned a troubled glance upon her. She was surprised to see that he didn't look angry anymore. Actually, he appeared distressed. "You know, that's part of the problem. Right there."

"Right where?" she asked, confused.

"What you said. 'The Indians,' is what you said. And there is no 'the Indians.' That's the whole problem in a nutshell."

"Yes," she said on a huge sigh. "I recall you saying that before."

"It doesn't seem fair to me that first we steal their land and destroy their livelihood and culture, and then we portray them in an altogether false light. It's like stealing everything a man owns and then saying not merely that you didn't really do it, but that, even if you did, it doesn't matter, because he was wrong to live that way in the first place."

Put that way, it didn't seem fair to Brenda either. She nodded. "But it's another point that will have to wait to be made for another picture. Maybe we can have a parade of tribes in a picture someday or something. Right now, we're trying to make this particular picture, *Indian Love Song,* and we'll never get it finished if you don't let Martin and the rest of us do what we've been hired to do."

He turned again and gazed at the set. He looked unhappy, and Brenda was sorry about that, but honest to God, sometimes you just had to tell a man the truth. Neither of them spoke, and Brenda heard the light spring breeze rustle the pine needles above their heads. The birds chirped merrily. Or perhaps not merrily. Recalling Colin's lecture about the blue jay and the scarlet tanager, she wondered if the birds were having a huge argument in bird talk, and she just couldn't understand the words.

"You know," she said, having been struck by an interesting notion, "sometimes life's more fun when you don't know everything."

He frowned at her, leading her to believe that he wasn't ready to admit defeat yet. "I don't believe I know what you mean."

"I'm sure you don't. But it's more fun for me to think that when the birdies chirp in the trees, they're happy and not fighting with each other."

His brow wrinkled, displaying those two deep ruts above his nose that made Brenda go a little crazy inside. He gazed up into the trees towering over their heads. "Why shouldn't they be happy?" he asked, as if he were honestly curious.

She shook her head, wondering what it must be like to take every single solitary thing a body said absolutely seriously. She'd have to teach this guy a joke or two one of these days. "I don't know."

He was patently puzzled. Brenda didn't think she could explain if she tried, so she didn't. She patted him on the arm as if he were a strange little boy instead of a bullheaded, albeit brilliant, young man. "It's all right, Colin. Why don't you go back inside the lodge and work on those Indian symbols? All right? Then you can supervise us when we paint them on the tipis."

Which was something to look forward to—if one enjoyed being pecked to death by a petty martinet as one tried to follow his instructions. God, she'd be glad when this picture was over. She wanted to take Colin Peters by the scruff of his neck and shake him until his brains scrambled and he turned human. He'd be wonderful if he were only human.

"Well . . ."

"Please," she said, her tone faintly begging. "You're only succeeding in irritating everyone on the set here, and it's all to no avail. You'll be doing all of us, and yourself, too, a big favor by butting out."

She wasn't surprised to see his scowl deepen. "I don't believe that's true. And even if it is, that's hardly a lady-like way of expressing it."

Darn him anyway, the stuffed shirt! "Mercy me, I didn't know you cared about such things. You astound me." If she put any more ice into her voice, it would freeze solid before it left her mouth. She added an imperious sniff, hoping to make him feel like the toad he was.

"Oh, very well." He turned on his heel and started walking back to the lodge, his hands jammed into his pockets. He looked dejected.

Brenda didn't care. She was beginning to wonder what she'd ever seen in the man. Oh, granted, he was good-looking. And he was smart as a whip and knew everything, and she really, really, really wanted to pick his brains—but not at the price he exacted. She couldn't stand people who disapproved of everything. She generally chalked such punctilio up to the fusspots knowing nothing about the perils life could fling at a person.

If you'd never been tested by life, you couldn't expect to understand how difficult it was to uphold society's strict conventions as one struggled to survive. If he'd ever been down as far as she'd been, he'd learn to appreciate the important stuff and let the rest slide.

"Drat the man," she muttered. Even though she knew she was right and he was wrong—pigheadedly, irrationally wrong—her heart hurt. Fiddle.

"Brenda, may I speak to you for a minute?"

When she turned, she saw Martin approaching, a troubled expression on his face. Hardly surprising. Dealing with Colin Peters and his meticulous demands was enough to trouble anybody. She decided to forget about the ache in her own heart and smiled, because she sensed

Martin could use a few smiles today. "Sure thing, Martin. What is it?"

He took her arm and guided her over to a spreading oak tree. "Listen, I'm beginning to think hiring Colin was a bad idea. He's brilliant and knows everything there is to know about Indians and so forth, but he doesn't have the least idea how pictures are made. He's driving me crazy."

As Martin had begun tearing at his hair, Brenda didn't doubt him for a moment. And she was sympathetic. "I'm sorry, Martin. I know you need assistance. I guess we were all hoping that Colin would turn out to be the help you needed, but he's turning out to be a hindrance."

"You can say that again."

She didn't bother.

"Um," Martin continued, "I wonder if you'd be willing to do me a favor, Brenda."

"Sure." She lifted her eyebrows in inquiry. "What is it?"

"You might not like it," he temporized.

She shrugged. "We're friends, Martin. Friends help friends."

"Thanks." He appeared sincerely touched by her simple statement of fraternity. "But—well, I don't want to jeopardize our friendship by what I'm going to ask you to do."

Brenda was beginning to be alarmed. In order to make herself feel better, she asked jokingly, "Good Lord, Martin, you're not going to ask me to assassinate the fool, are you?"

Her question shocked Martin so much, he actually gave a start of surprise. "Good God, no!"

She laid a hand on his arm, sorry she'd shaken him. His nerves must really be on edge if he could no longer recognize a joke when he heard it. "I didn't mean it,

Martin. Just ask your favor, and I'll tell you if I'll do it or not."

"Good. I mean, thank you." Martin took a deep breath. "Listen, I know you won't want to do this, but—well—" He stopped speaking, as if he'd suddenly forgotten all the words he'd ever known. Then, in a rush, he asked his question. "Will you please take Colin in hand and try to calm him down?"

It was Brenda's turn to be startled. Her mouth opened, but Martin forestalled speech by hurrying on.

"You see, you're the only person I know who has the delicacy to take the matter in hand without crushing the poor guy. He's not a bad fellow, you know. He just needs to be—well—socialized, or something. He needs to loosen up and learn not to take everything as if it were a life-or-death problem."

Her opinion exactly. "Hmmm." She still didn't know about this. It sounded mighty tricky to her. "He doesn't like me much, you know." The knowledge made her furious. It also made the ache in her heart throb.

"Nonsense. He's just never met a beautiful woman before and doesn't know how to act around you. I've known men like him before. When they're young, all the other children tease them about being brains, and when they grow up, they've never learned how to behave around women. You can teach him."

Poor Martin. He sounded desperate. Still Brenda hesitated. This sounded like a mighty shaky endeavor. "I don't know. . . ."

On the one hand, Martin was asking her to do what she'd been wanting to do ever since she met Colin: hang out with him. She could, with Martin's blessing, ask Colin questions until the cows came home, if she did as Martin asked her. On the other hand, she didn't like rejection and rebuff any better than anybody else on earth, and she had a feeling that, if she did this favor for Martin, she was going to experience both before she wore down Colin's defenses—if she ever did.

She'd been telling herself she could wear him down for a couple of days now, but that was before she'd realized what a tough nut Colin could be. Now she wasn't sure.

Darn it, of course she could wear the man down! She was an expert, for heaven's sake.

But did she want to? It would be tough. *He* would be tough.

What did that matter? Martin needed her. Martin was her friend. Brenda tried never to let her friends down.

She heaved a pine-scented sigh. "Oh, all right. I suppose he can't hate me any more than he already does."

Martin's relief was palpable. "Bless you, Brenda." He eased up on his hair and smiled. "And he doesn't hate you, you know. He finds you as delightful as we all do; it's only that he doesn't know how to express himself. I have a feeling he mistrusts his emotions."

"If he has any to mistrust."

"I'm sure he does." Martin appeared doubtful. "Somewhere."

"Hmmm." Brenda went back to the rehearsal in a less sunny mood than was customary for her.

Colin sat in the front parlor of the Cedar Crest Lodge, gloomily staring at the pieces of paper in front of him. He'd drawn several symbols that could be painted on the tipis. He should be happy to have scored this one small victory. He wasn't happy at all.

Dash it, why was he being so unconscionably persnickety about this silly motion picture? He didn't care one way or the other, really, if Martin and his company depicted Indian life accurately. For heaven's sake, it was a piece of fiction.

The awful thought that he was trying, in the only way he knew how, to impress Brenda Fitzpatrick attacked him, and he groaned softly. Good God, could that be his problem?

He had a feeling it not only could be but was. What a lowering realization. When he was a child, he used to sneer at boys who made asses of themselves trying to impress girls. Now he was doing the same thing, and such behavior was even more asinine in a man his age than in a boy.

Was he really so little attuned to the behavioral norms prevailing in society that he was stooping to such childish tactics?

Yes, he was.

With another soft groan, Colin buried his head in his hands. And what had he accomplished by behaving thus? He'd succeeded in alienating practically everyone associated with the picture, including Martin Tafft, whom he admired greatly, and Brenda Fitzpatrick, who was the one he'd been trying to impress in the first place.

"Idiot," he growled at himself.

Colin continued to flog himself mentally for the rest of the afternoon. Along about five, as he was trying to decide which of his drawings would look best on the tipis and vilifying himself as an unmitigated nincompoop, the front door to the parlor opened. He didn't look up, since he was sunk in self-pity and knew that whoever it was wasn't interested in speaking to *him*.

"Colin?"

He jerked and spun around, nearly tipping his chair over backwards. He had to grab the table to prevent an accident. Good Lord, it was Brenda. Had she come in to scold him some more? He probably deserved it. Because he was anticipating nothing good from this source, and since he was ashamed of himself for his earlier behavior, he only nodded at her and said, "You startled me."

"I'm sorry. I didn't mean to."

Good heavens, the woman was beautiful. Colin decided it wasn't kind of God to have spent all of that beauty on one person. He ought to have spread it out some in order to spare the rest of humanity these painful episodes. "It's all right. I was—concentrating on these pictures." He waved a hand over the papers on the table and silently called himself a liar. He'd been mired in remorse and self-pity is what he'd been, and he knew it.

"Oh, how nice. May I see them?"

At least she didn't say *can* when she meant *may.* Realizing this was the fussy Colin passing another judgment on something nobody in the world but him cared about, he swore at himself and told himself to stop judging others. "Of course you may."

She wafted over to him on a cloud of femininity. Colin swallowed hard. He'd never realized how difficult it could be to maintain one's dignity in the presence of so tantalizing a creature as Brenda. Determined to redeem himself in her eyes, if possible—and he doubted it was possible, since he was stuck in a sinking pit of self-loathing—he said politely, "I'm not sure which symbols would be best for film. Perhaps Martin can help us decide." It hurt to add, "Although you're familiar with the industry. I'm sure you can say if one is better than another. Cinematically speaking, I mean."

He was an ass. That's all there was to it. There was no wrapping it up in clean linen. He was an ass, and that was that.

"Oh, I like this one." She held up a paper and indicated a stylized drawing of a hawk in flight. "It reminds me of the wide open spaces."

The Black Hills were about as wide open and spacious as a railroad boxcar, what with all the trees and boulders lying about. Colin gritted his teeth and didn't say so.

"Yes. That's a good one. I saw it first in a Chiricahua village in the Arizona Territory."

She turned those huge blue eyes upon him and he went light-headed. "My goodness, but you've done some interesting things. I'd love to hear about some of your travels."

He was, to put it mildly, skeptical. No one was ever interested in his travels. "You would?"

"Oh, yes. I've never been anywhere except cities. Mind you, I've traveled quite a bit because of the business I'm in. And I know New York City like the back of my hand. But I've never had the chance to explore the different cities I've been to, much less explored any of the western territories, although I did do a show in Denver once. But that's the closest I've ever come to a frontier. I'm sure they must be fascinating."

He allowed himself a very small smile. "I'm sure the westerners who live there would say the same about New York."

She laughed. Her laughs played hob with his senses, and he had to clamp down on his heated reaction to this one. "You're probably right."

He couldn't manufacture a laugh to save himself, but he did produce a fairly decent smile. "Oh, yes. I've known many a cowboy who'd love to see a big city like New York or San Francisco."

"San Francisco's a nice place. Very lively, and the people are friendly."

"Yes, I found the same thing."

Whoopee. He'd discovered one thing they had in common: San Francisco. Perhaps they should celebrate.

Ass. He was an ass.

Still smiling, she resumed studying the sketches he'd made, eventually pulling out five of them. "I think these would look best." She shot him a quick glance. "Mind you, I don't know anything about Indians, but if they're compatible, they'd look great in the picture."

Dash it, she was worried about him throwing another tantrum over authenticity. As if authenticity mattered a toss. "They're compatible." Because he couldn't seem to stop himself, he amended, "That is to say, they're all symbols common to various southwestern tribes, although they don't all come from the same one." Now why, he asked himself bitterly, had he felt compelled to deliver that miniature lecture? It wasn't as if anyone cared.

"Oh? Which ones are from which tribes?"

She sounded interested, and Colin didn't believe it. Rather stiffly, he said, "You needn't humor me, Brenda. I know I behaved badly, and I'm sorry. I'll apologize to Martin as soon as I see him."

"I'm not humoring you!" She eyed him for a moment. "You know, Colin, there are some people in the world besides you who are genuinely interested in these things. You're not the only one."

"Oh?" That was news to him.

"Indeed. Why do you think I asked you to explain about the Indians before?"

He had no idea, actually, unless it was to make the other men on the set jealous. He opted not to tell her so. "Um— I guess I hadn't considered why you asked."

She shook her head, as if she could scarcely conceive of so obtuse a scholar. "It's because I want to *know,* Colin. I find such things fascinating. I didn't have the opportunity to attend school after my twelfth year, and I—well, I know it sounds dramatic, but I can't help that—I thirst for knowledge. If you'd be willing to instruct me in some of these things, maybe I can reciprocate."

"Reciprocate?" This sounded scary. "How?"

She winked at him. "You'll find out."

And that, as they say, was that. His heart had commenced hammering like a Mescalero war drum, and he sensed a trap not unlike that set for soldiers riding into a box canyon with Indians perched on cliffs surrounding them, prepared to pick them off like ducks on a pond. It was no use warning himself. Colin succumbed. "Very well," he said with as much firmness as he could summon. "I'll be happy to teach you whatever you want to know."

"Likewise." Brenda stuck out her hand. "It's a deal."

And, although he couldn't even begin to imagine what she knew that he'd want to learn, Colin shook her hand.

Eight

After a delicious meal in the Cedar Crest's main dining room, during which she chatted amiably with Martin and tried to draw Colin out, Brenda went for a short walk around the building. She was steeling her nerves to tackle those stupid tipis. And Colin. The prospect held no appeal.

During dinner, Colin had been almost amiable, although he didn't speak much. Which was probably just as well, since he seldom seemed to have anything to say unless he was correcting something somebody else had said. She chuffed into the darkness. If it were anyone else supervising the tipi painting, Brenda would be looking forward to it. She enjoyed stuff like this: getting together with friends and tackling projects.

In this case, she was dreading it. Why, oh why, couldn't Colin be just a little more human? He was so handsome. And he was so exactly what Brenda had always dreamed about in a man—except that he was a stuffed shirt and an old poop, and he didn't like her. She considered this combination of characteristics monumentally unfair.

Nevertheless, after she'd walked around the lodge twice, listened with pleasure to the owls hooting in the trees and the rustle of the breeze among the leaves, she

knew she had to do it. She'd promised Martin she'd try,
and she'd never broken a promise yet.

So she trudged up the wide, beautiful oak staircase of
the Cedar Crest Lodge, went to her room, donned the huge
blue smock she wore for messy makeup jobs and other
dirty work, and headed downstairs. The Peerless crew had
confiscated the screened-in back porch of the lodge for
this evening's activities, and Martin had set up two of the
studio's portable lights. The specialized lights were used
for filming and were brighter than normal house lamps.
Tonight they'd provide perfect illumination by which to
paint the tipis.

She took in a deep, preparatory breath before she
stepped onto the porch, prepared for just about anything.
If Colin had arrived before her, he might already have
stirred the crew to anger or mutiny. Or Martin might have
prevailed and kept things calm and steady. Or the Indians
might be there, telling them all what to do. She didn't
know what to expect when she opened the door and offered a cheery salute to her Peerless friends.

"Hello, everyone. Are we all ready to fix these tipis?"
She spotted Jerry Begay, who was looking at one of the
flowered pictographs with scorn. Gil Drew, who'd started
daubing white paint over the flowers on another tipi,
looked up at her and winked.

She waved back and walked over to stand beside Jerry;
she, too, peered at the tipi. "Hi, Jerry. Those flowers are
pretty stupid, aren't they?"

"Yes." He didn't elaborate.

"Well," she said in as sprightly a manner as she could
summon, "we'll get them fixed tonight."

Jerry grunted. His expression was so generally enigmatic that Brenda never knew if he was grumpy or happy
or what. Tonight was no exception.

She heaved a large internal sigh and gave up on the
flowers, but she didn't allow her misgivings to show. Rub-

bing her hands together in a gesture of enjoyment—falsely assumed—she said, "Do you agree with the pictures Colin did to replace the flowers? There are lots more, if you don't like those."

Oh, dear, perhaps she shouldn't have said that. Colin might take her offer to Jerry as a slight upon his own selections. Piffle, this was like walking on eggshells, and she didn't like it. She cast a swift glance at Colin and noted with relief that, although he was watching her exchange with Jerry, he didn't seem huffy.

Jerry shrugged. "They're all right."

Faint praise. But she hadn't expected anything more from this particular source. "Well, then, let's get at them. Do you need help painting over the flowers, Gil?"

"I don't think so. My artistic talents aren't even being tested in this enterprise. Slapping white paint over flowers is quick work."

He gave his audience a general, all-purpose grin. It was a grin Brenda recognized as one designed to garner approval. Poor Gil. He was such an—actor. Funny she'd never noticed how desperate most actors and actresses were to be loved. Was she like that? She had no idea.

Leroy Carruthers was in a corner mixing paint. "I've got the black stuff here, stirred to a fare-thee-well and ready for the artistes." He splayed a hand over his heart. "I, too, am an artiste, but I shan't attempt to paint this evening. I," he said in as grand a manner as Brenda had ever heard, "have four thumbs on each hand and dill pickles where the thumbs should be."

They all laughed, and Brenda silently blessed the ham for making the atmosphere light. Martin and Colin had begun conversing in the corner opposite Leroy's. Brenda walked over to join them, bracing herself for unpleasantness.

Squinting hard, she couldn't detect any rancor issuing from the two men. Not even from Colin, a circumstance that faintly surprised her. She'd have expected him to have become fussy in the hour or so since dinner. He'd been almost pleasant at dinner. She judged he'd apologized to Martin as he had to her, and Martin, ever gracious, would have accepted the apology with generosity and grace and not referred to the afternoon's squabble again. She took heart. Maybe this wouldn't be as awful as she'd feared.

"Hello, Martin. Good evening, Colin. Ready to start?"

Martin smiled brightly. "Hey there, Brenda. We sure are. Gil's working on covering up the flowers, and we have the sketches right here." He brandished a sheaf of papers. "If we each take a tipi and a sketch, we'll have this problem corrected in no time at all. I'm sure the tents—I mean, tipis—"

Colin sighed. Eyeing him hastily, Brenda judged he was embarrassed about having made such a stink about tipis versus tents.

"—will be dry by tomorrow, and we'll be able to film the abduction scene early in the day."

"Good." Brenda smiled at Colin. "Are we using the same pictures you showed me this afternoon, or have you chosen others?"

"I brought the ones you chose," Colin said stiffly. "I didn't think you wanted my interference."

She felt like telling him not to be so darned touchy but restrained herself and merely nodded. "All right, then. Let's get started." She took the sketch of the hawk, then waited until she saw which tipi Colin selected to work on. She took the one next to his.

"This way, you can tell me if I go wrong," she explained when he looked disconcerted at having her nearby. What was the matter with the man?

"I'm sure you won't go wrong."

If Colin got to sounding any more wooden, they'd be able to use him as a tent pole, Brenda thought sourly. Nevertheless, as she started painting her hawk with the paint

Leroy Carruthers had mixed, she searched her mind for things to ask him. She finally decided on the subject at hand. "Um, which picture are you going to paint?"

His lips were set into a grim line, and he looked as if he wasn't enjoying himself. "I'm doing the mountain and the river." He didn't expound upon his statement.

Brenda mentally rolled her eyes. This was going to be difficult. She didn't want to fail Martin, but if she was going to have to drag every single tiny sentence out of Colin's mouth, she was going to wear herself out pretty darned quick. "Um, is that the one with the horizontal zigzag lines and the straight lines in front?"

"Yes." He set his lips again and continued painting, keeping his eyes on the canvas tenting in front of him and never once looking at Brenda.

Gad. "What tribe is that one from?"

He shrugged slightly. "Several different tribes use these same symbols. They're fairly common."

"Ah." She was interested in spite of herself. "Why do you think that is?"

Another shrug. "I suppose because the design makes sense."

She set her paintbrush down and scooted over on her knees to peer at the picture at Colin's feet. "What do you mean?"

His hand stilled and he stiffened. Brenda sighed and went back to her own tent. Tipi. Whatever the heck it was.

"Well," he said presently, as if he'd had to collect his wits before he could answer her, which was ridiculous. Brenda felt like flinging paint at him. "You see that these zigzag lines look vaguely like mountains? And the straight lines can easily be seen to depict a river. The symbols are recognizable for what they are, and I expect that's what makes them so popular with different tribes."

She decided to stay where she was, although she

wanted to see the picture again to make sure she knew what he was talking about. "That makes sense."

Silence fell between them. Brenda was vaguely aware of the others chattering nearby, but she was primarily concerned with making friends with Colin, so her concentration on that problem was intense. After racking her brain for a moment, she came up with another question. "Do many tribes have similar bird pictures? Similar to this one, I mean."

She heard Colin draw in a deep breath and release it with what she presumed was annoyance. For Martin's sake, she held her temper in check. This situation wouldn't last long, she told herself, and she could certainly stand Colin Peters's contempt and pickiness for another three or four weeks.

Three or four weeks. She almost groaned aloud.

But no. She could do this. She'd never failed yet to make friends out of enemies. Not that she'd ever had many enemies.

Colin finally answered her question, and her thoughts scattered like dandelion fluff. "Yes, most tribes depict birds of one sort or another. Different native cultures have quite elaborate symbols to depict matters of importance to them, and many consider birds important."

"They do?" Again she found herself genuinely interested. She squinted at the bird on her own tipi. It looked pretty good, if she did say so herself. "Why are birds important?"

"Various reasons."

For a minute, she thought he was going to leave it at that, and she tried to decide whether to be irked or not. Then he continued speaking, and she decided to keep her temper inside for a while longer.

"For one thing, the bird can fly and is often thereby considered as existing without the limits under which humans struggle."

Brenda thought about it as she stroked paint onto the canvas. "I see," she said at last. And she did. Failing a scientific foundation for the phenomena of life, it made sense to look to beings in nature and to ascribe wondrous properties to them. "Very interesting."

She saw Colin's head whip her way and turned to see why he was staring at her. He seemed to be studying her face intently, as if he were trying to determine if she was lying. She didn't relish his doubt.

"I found your explanation very interesting," she said with a hint of pepper in her tone. "I don't know why you're so darned eager to doubt my curiosity."

"I beg your pardon."

"No need to beg." She was beginning to feel peevish and tried to curtail her mood's slide downhill.

The evening progressed more smoothly after that, although Brenda continued to find it difficult to converse with Colin. It was as if, having decided he'd behaved badly earlier in the day, he didn't want to open his mouth now.

Colin Peters was turning out to be a very difficult man.

"Yes," Colin said to Martin, who was critically surveying the tipis set up in preparation for filming. "They look much better now."

It was the morning after the painting party, and Colin still felt edgy, embarrassed, and uncomfortable. He'd vowed to keep his opinions to himself unless they were asked for, but already he was finding his vow challenging to keep.

For one thing, he still deplored the nonsense of mixing up tribes when it would have been so easy to use the right ones. Or, if the only Indians they could find who were willing to appear in the picture were Navajos, the least they could have done is shoot the silly picture in Arizona or New Mexico.

Too expensive, probably, he thought glumly. This mountain was near enough to the Los Angeles-based Peerless Studio as to be economically feasible to use as a stage set. Rather, a moving-picture set.

For another thing, he resented the notion of any Indians at all riding into a settled town and carrying off one of its citizens for no reason. Even if the citizen abducted was as lovely as Brenda.

Granted such a notion held a certain appeal—Colin sometimes thought life must have been simpler in the old days, when knights kidnapped their brides—it still wouldn't have happened. Never. Ever. Not even during the very height of the Indian wars.

But, as he'd discovered to his distress and mortification, the script was written and nobody was going to change it for the sake of historical accuracy or his scholarly objections. He wished he'd never made them, because now he felt not merely unwelcome but stupid. It was a new experience, feeling stupid, and he didn't like it.

"All set, Martin? Hello there, Colin. Beautiful day, isn't it?"

Colin turned at the sound of Brenda's cheery voice and almost fell over backwards in shocked dismay. Good God, she looked like a ghoul!

She noticed his astonishment and laughed gaily. "Isn't the makeup ghastly? Dead white with black accents isn't very flattering, is it?"

Actually, she'd probably look beautiful in black-face. He didn't say so. Striving to achieve a smile as easy as hers, he said, "Er, yes. I mean, no." Dash it, he was blundering like a noddy. In a last-gasp effort, he blurted out, "I wasn't expecting it."

"It does look a little odd for everyday viewing, doesn't

it?" Martin chuckled. His spirits were high this morning, too. Colin figured he was glad to be getting on with things, and a stab of guilt made his innards cramp. He'd really made a pain of himself yesterday.

"White makeup looks better on celluloid than regular makeup—or no makeup," Brenda explained. The twinkle in her eyes increased markedly. "Gee, it's so seldom I get to clarify anything for you. It usually works the other way around."

She would have to say that, wouldn't she? A little awkwardly, Colin said, "Nonsense."

"Is it?"

She didn't wait for his answer but turned to Martin. Colin appreciated her restraint, since he had no idea what to say. "Are we ready to start filming?"

"Yes, indeedy." Martin rubbed his hands together and looked pleased with the day and with everything in it.

The day was fine; Colin had to grant that. The mountain air was crisp and clean. Small animals chattered in the trees and birds chirped in a frenzy of spring fever. The greens and golds of the mountainscape appealed to Colin's senses. It was one of the few times he'd noticed he had any. He'd seldom taken time to observe the world around him; today his lack of prior interest seemed a shame. Not that most of the world was as beautiful as this. It still undoubtedly held things that would be of interest to him. He'd have to pay closer attention to his surroundings in the future.

Jerry Begay, clad in some sort of buckskin garment that, Colin assumed, the costume department had judged to be of generic Indian design, walked over to them. He nodded to Colin and Martin and smiled at Brenda. Colin was nonplussed by the smile. Jerry must feel at ease with Brenda. How strange. Colin himself turned into a fumbling dolt whenever he was in her company. This was all very discouraging.

"Hello, Jerry. Ready to kidnap me?" Brenda smiled happily and shook Begay's hand.

"I reckon," said the phlegmatic Navajo. He cocked a dark eyebrow at Martin. "Shall we mount up?"

The so-called Indian tribe was supposed to ride into the town, capture Brenda while the townspeople screamed in horror, and then scurry back to their camp. The abduction was to take place on the vast front porch of the Cedar Crest Lodge, which was almost more ridiculous than if they'd snatched her from a street. Colin didn't say so, although he had to bite his tongue to keep silent.

"Right," said Martin. "Let me get over to the porch. Remember to have everybody on horseback keep to the grassy places until you get to the porch, because we don't want the horses kicking up a lot of dust and interfering with the camera's focus. When you get to the porch, it's all right to churn up some dust, because it'll make the scene look ominous."

Ominous. Good God. Colin peered at Jerry, eager to see his reaction to these instructions.

"Right." Jerry turned and walked away.

Hmmm. Colin guessed he wasn't surprised. Jerry Begay had learned to expect idiocy from white men.

"I've heard that Indians are silent and inscrutable," Brenda murmured, "but I didn't believe it until now."

Colin couldn't help himself. He said, "They are neither silent nor inscrutable. Jerry Begay is a fine man who feels out of place here among a group of white people with whom he has nothing in common. He, and most in his culture, don't show their emotions to strangers." He shut up then, sensing he'd said enough—if not more than enough.

He expected some kind of sarcastic retort from Brenda. Martin was too kind to resort to sarcasm. Colin was, therefore, taken aback when Brenda peered at him musingly and said, "Hmmm. I guess that makes sense. Sure. I'd be silent and inscrutable, too, if I were plunked down in the middle of a Navajo village."

"Er, yes," he said. "That's the point exactly." And he was astounded she'd understood it so quickly. One of these days, he'd have to remember she wasn't a feather-headed imbecile.

She nodded and walked off to take her place on the porch. Martin, who had seemed uneasy at Colin's comment, relaxed after he heard Brenda's, "All set, Martin!"

He said, "Come on, Colin. Let's go over to the porch. It's always exciting to get the first scene in the can."

Colin knew that *in the can* was a term used in the motion-picture industry to signify having captured something on celluloid. He understood why the term had come into use, since movies, after being shot, edited, spliced, and whatever else needed doing, were shipped to picture houses in flat cans. One can contained a reel. A reel consisted of a thousand feet of film, and it was only recently that moviemakers had begun creating what they considered works of art using more than one reel of film. Colin didn't know much about art, but he was withholding judgment on the issue. He had his doubts.

In justice it must be said, however, that Peerless was doing a good deal to promote the industry, and Colin, ever just, gave Peerless its due. Peerless was among the first studios to make what were termed "feature" films, longer pictures that told a full story. They still primarily produced split-reel shorts, which most often consisted of a comedy on one half of the reel and a short drama or a series of scenic views on the other, but they were making great strides in longer pictures. *Indian Love Song* was an example of the latter. Colin rather crossly thought that it wasn't going to enhance Peerless's reputation any.

But then, he was probably wrong about that. His experience with public taste wasn't vast, but he wasn't impressed with the few examples he'd seen so far. The public would probably lap up this nonsensical feature film like hot chocolate.

He was feeling crabby and depressed when he and Martin reached the trees a few feet from the Cedar Crest's front porch. Martin's chair was there awaiting him, and Colin noticed another chair placed near Martin's.

"I had them get a chair for you, Colin. You can see how we do this."

Ashamed of himself for his earlier unkind thoughts, Colin muttered, "Thanks," and sat on the chair next to Martin's. He renewed his vow to keep mum and not complain.

Almost at once, his vow was challenged. Brenda stood on the porch in a frilly gown that made her look as if she'd just stepped onto the porch from a fancy dress ball to take the air. Were Jerry and his bunch supposed to capture her in *that?* He had to chomp down hard on the inside of his cheek to keep from asking.

She called to Martin, "Are we ready? Shall I start fanning myself?"

"Just a minute." Martin scurried over to the cameraman, who'd set up his equipment in front of the porch. The two men held a brief conversation. Then Martin trotted over to the mounted Navajos, waiting in the trees a few yards from the porch. He looked pleased when he returned to the chairs. "All right, we're almost ready. Find your mark, Brenda, and we can go."

"Right-o."

Colin marveled at her good humor. Even when she got mad—as, for example, when she was scolding him for being a fusspot—she didn't hold on to her anger. Offhand, Colin couldn't recall ever having met such a sunny-natured woman. He hadn't expected her to possess such a quality, mainly because she was so lovely. Colin had always believed beautiful women were spoiled and unpleasant. It pained him to admit that Brenda Fitzpatrick seemed to be neither.

Lord, it was difficult having one's preconceived notions knocked about like this. Because he was feeling uncharitable and cross, he folded his arms over his chest, slid down in his chair, and stared balefully at the porch.

Brenda took her mark, which had been chalked on the porch floor, leaned against the railing, and commenced fanning herself. She looked for all the world like a southern belle resting after dancing her feet off at a plantation ball. She also looked darned near irresistible, and Colin wished she didn't. Dash it, this experience was difficult enough without his lusting after the leading lady.

"Good!" Martin called to Brenda. "Remember to look startled when you hear the hoofbeats."

"You bet," Brenda said.

"Isn't she wonderful?" Martin murmured.

Colin figured the question to be rhetorical, so he didn't answer. He'd have had to agree, however. She really was remarkably wonderful. As an actress, of course.

Martin stood, lifted his megaphone, and shouted into the trees. "Ready, Jerry?"

Jerry uttered a grunt, which both Colin and Martin assumed was consent. Martin called, "All right, then. Action!"

The cameraman started cranking, the camera commenced its ear-shattering clatter, sprockets chunked out onto the ground as the scene progressed, and Colin watched it all with interest. Jerry Begay, leading his pack of fellow Navajos, clad in costumes native to no Indian tribe Colin had ever studied and riding horses no self-respecting Navajo would ever ride, let out a whoop and rode into the camera's range. Colin's frown of disapproval deepened as the action unfolded.

Brenda, apparently hearing the sound of the horses— although how anyone could hear anything at all over the noise of the camera was a mystery to Colin—drew herself up and peered off as if into the distance. She lifted a hand to her forehead to shade her eyes, which was idiotic if this scene was supposed to be taking place at night, and drew herself up further. Her face assumed an expression of dismay that gradually altered into one of terror. She opened her mouth and let out a scream that sliced through the air like a knife.

Colin winced. Darn it, she was supposed to be acting; she didn't need to shriek like a banshee for real.

The horses rode up to the porch and the Indians pulled them to in a cloud of dust. Brenda began backing up, which was also stupid. Why didn't she just open the door and escape inside the building? Colin, recalling his vow, didn't ask.

"I hope that's not too much dust," Martin muttered. He called to Brenda and Jerry, "Good! Good! Keep it up. Jerry, try to look more menacing."

Colin grunted but didn't speak. He was proud of his reserve. He shook his head when Jerry plastered an expression of evil intent on his broad brown face. The Indians, Colin noticed, hadn't been forced into wearing white makeup, but they'd had their own natural reddish-brown complexions enhanced a good deal. Colin disapproved. Such magnifications of the differences among peoples could only lead to further misunderstandings and bigotry. Again, he held his tongue.

"Excellent! Wonderful!" Martin sounded as if he were overjoyed with Jerry's altered expression.

Colin rolled his eyes.

Brenda, meanwhile, had lifted an arm and was holding it in front of her in a fending-off gesture. Colin thought contemptuously that any female who acted this stupidly deserved to be kidnapped and run off with. Except, who'd want her?

Jerry crept toward her, a tomahawk in his hand. Colin

sat up straight. A tomahawk? Good God. He sank back in his chair and didn't protest, although everything inside him rebelled at the notion of a Navajo, pretending to be an Apache, operating on the home ground of the Sioux, using a tomahawk to kidnap a white female who obviously lived on a plantation in Georgia or somewhere equally southern. Lord, this was awful.

Brenda cried out some phrases that were supposed, Colin imagined, to be protests. She looked the part of a panic-stricken belle, although her words belied her act. "Good, Jerry," she said, still looking horrified. "Bend forward a little more. It'll look more creepy that way."

Jerry grunted and lifted his tomahawk. Colin could scarcely bear to watch.

"Good," Brenda said, although her appearance of terror didn't alter. "Now I'm going to scream a little bit more. Don't be alarmed."

She did as she'd warned them. Jerry didn't flinch, although Colin did. The woman had a shriek like a train whistle, and it hurt his ears. Poor Jerry, who was even closer to her than Colin, must be suffering greatly.

But Jerry didn't seem to mind. He stalked Brenda until she was flat up against the wall of the lodge. Then he let go of a volley of Navajo. Colin hoped the camera wasn't aimed at his face or the whole world would know these weren't Sioux. Or Apaches.

No. That was silly. Only scholars like Colin—or Indians from the respective tribes—would know the difference in the speech patterns of the Navajo and Sioux. Or Apaches. God, he couldn't stand much more of this.

Brenda let out another squawk when Jerry threw his tomahawk aside—another irregularity that would have gotten him low marks in any Indian tribe in the world—and plucked her right up off the porch. He flung her over his shoulder and ran across the porch, down the steps, and to his horse. The horse whickered nervously. There again,

Colin thought sourly, was a mistake. Indian ponies were trained to within an inch of their lives and would never balk at anything their masters did.

He sighed. Nobody else cared. He had to keep that in mind or he'd go crazy.

Jerry flung Brenda onto the horse and leaped up behind her as effortlessly as if he did such things every day. Now *that* was a demonstration of riding skill of which Colin approved. It was the first time in the whole picture he'd had occasion to applaud.

Other cast members, led by Leroy Carruthers, poured out of the door, pretended to be aghast by what had just happened, and started yelling and screaming. Leroy and a couple of the other men fired blanks at the escaping Indians, heedless of the possibility of hitting horses or the woman they were supposed to be protecting. Colin forced himself to keep his eyes open and watch. This was terrible.

Martin, he noticed, was enjoying himself hugely. He kept calling out encouraging words to Brenda and Jerry and the other Indians. Colin watched him with interest. He truly did love this industry. If only he loved historical accuracy as much, Colin might be happy, too. Not, of course, that anyone cared if he was happy.

He was getting maudlin. He sat up straighter and watched the band of Indians race off into the woods on their sluggish mounts. He reminded himself that nobody but him cared if the horses were sluggish.

"Good!" Martin shouted. "Great! I think we've got it on one take! Perfect!"

He rushed over to the cameraman, who gave one last crank of the camera, which spat out one last sprocket and stopped cranking. He shook out his arm as if it hurt, which it probably did. Curious, Colin heaved himself out of his chair and joined the two men in time to hear their conversation.

"What do you think, Ben? Was the dust level all right?"

"I think it'll be fine," Ben, the cameraman, said. "We'd better look it over before we put it in the can, but I think it's a good take."

Martin nodded enthusiastically. "Good. Good. Do you think we should do another take just in case?"

Ben shook his head. "Naw. Let's see this one first. I think it'll be fine."

"Great." Looking as pleased as punch, Martin lifted his megaphone and bellowed into the woods. "Great job, Jerry and the rest of you. Brenda, you were wonderful. You can come out now. As soon as we do the shot with Leroy on the porch, we'll move the camera to the Indian village and shoot that scene next."

A bunch of people leading horses and Brenda, still atop one of the beasts, ambled out of the woods. Brenda was laughing happily, evidently at something one of the Navajos had said. The whole group of them were smiling.

How did she do that? Colin wondered. How in the name of mercy did she manage to put everyone, even a tribe of Navajo Indians on foreign soil, at ease? He'd never seen anything like it in his life.

He discovered he envied Brenda Fitzpatrick her way with people and could hardly believe it of himself.

Nine

When the camera next began cranking, Brenda watched Colin rather than Leroy Carruthers after the first few minutes. She wondered if Colin would recognize himself in Carruthers's character. It was painfully obvious to her that the actor had modeled his actions on Colin's.

If Colin did recognize himself, she hoped he wouldn't be dreadfully offended. After all, although Carruthers was acting like an intellectual stuffed shirt and an impossible purist in this scene, he was eventually going to become the hero of the picture.

"Gadzooks!" Carruthers cried as he did a comedic double take. "Have those beastly savages actually made away with the love of my life? Horrors!"

Everyone watching him laughed. Everyone but Colin. Brenda saw his eyes narrow, his arms cross over his chest, and an expression of suspicion creep over his elegant features. Oh, dear, she hoped he wouldn't be too upset.

"Egad, what to do? What to do?" Carruthers continued, running across the porch and peering off into the distance like a flustered scientist watching an experiment dissipate. "Should I grab a horse and follow my darling into the mysterious blackness? Or should I, the quintessential absentminded professor, think about it for a year or two and then take some kind of action?"

More laughter. Increased dubiousness from Colin. Brenda gnawed on a knuckle and continued watching him. He must have felt her intense concentration on his person because he turned his head and sent a quick glance her way. She smiled at him and wiggled her fingers in a "hello" gesture. He didn't respond, but frowned harder and turned to watch the end of the scene.

"Good!" Martin called through his megaphone. "Great, Leroy! Perfect characterization!"

"It should be," Carruthers responded, still in character. "I patterned it after the real thing."

Oh, dear. Brenda wished he hadn't said that. Scrutinizing Colin closely, she couldn't detect whether he understood the meaning behind the actor's comment or not. He was smart enough to catch on, but she didn't know if he had the social intuition to do so. She'd met other men— most men, in fact—who wouldn't recognize themselves when acted on stage if they were given a magnifying glass, a mirror, and a hundred years of study in which to do so.

Suddenly Colin turned around and walked over to her. She was so surprised, she barely had time to produce a serene smile for his benefit. She didn't want him to know how worried she was. He'd certainly not thank her for fretting about his feelings being wounded. She said, "Leroy's a wonderful actor, isn't he?" because she couldn't think of anything else to say.

"I guess," Colin muttered.

Put out by his tepid response, Brenda said, "I think he's captured the moment very well." She didn't say anything about Carruthers's characterization, which he'd also done very well.

"Hmph. I wouldn't know, never having been in that position before."

"That's the whole point," she said dryly. "That's what acting is. Actors interpret scenes and behave as they believe a normal person would behave under the same circumstances. I mean, one doesn't have to discover a dead body to understand the horror such a discovery would evoke in a sensitive person. Or even an insensitive one," she added trenchantly, because his attitude irked her. As usual.

Martin called out, "Great! You're doing great, Leroy! Now go and tell the others the girl's been snatched!"

"I suppose so." Colin appeared unconvinced.

They both watched Carruthers without speaking for a moment. The grinding clamor of the camera filled the air, and the sound of sprockets chunking onto the earth gave a curious rhythm to the ungodly noise. The actor yanked open the lodge doors and pretended to give an alarm to the rest of the participants of the ball. Several more actors in evening costume ran out onto the porch and began milling around, some wringing their hands in consternation, some peering off into the distance.

"Perfect!" Martin shouted. "Wonderful! Look scared, ladies! Remember, everybody's best friend has just been abducted by Indians! Explain it all to them, Leroy!"

Carruthers started an animated depiction of someone telling a tale of awful importance to the other actors. He did a great job, looking to Brenda exactly as she'd expect Colin to look in the same circumstances. Only more ebullient. Brenda couldn't imagine Colin flinging his arms around in that uncontrolled manner.

Several of the female actors commenced clinging to each other in terror. One of them pretended to faint. Another pressed a hand to her bosom and let out a shriek of mock horror.

"Perfect!" Martin called, pleased with his cast.

"This is ludicrous," Colin grumbled.

"Fiddlesticks. You just have no imagination." She expected him to take instant exception to her judgment.

He didn't. He looked at her for a moment, his brow

furrowed into those two parallel lines that made Brenda weak in the knees, pushed his glasses up his nose, and frowned at the scene again. "Perhaps."

Perhaps? His qualified response astounded Brenda. "You mean you admit it?"

"I don't admit anything, dash it. I said perhaps I lack the sort of imagination that can take pleasure in nonsense of this nature."

"I see." Drat the man. He was so difficult. "Don't you ever feel the need to escape from everyday life?" she asked curiously. "I mean, don't you ever get tired of being serious and studious every minute of the day?"

He glowered at her for a second, then turned back to the scene. "No, I can't say that I do."

"Do you ever go to the moving pictures?"

"Sometimes." The admission came out sounding grudging.

"Do you enjoy them?"

"Some of them. Not the ones that depict history inaccurately."

"Don't you ever take comfort in pretending? Even if that means pretending things happened differently from the way they really did?"

"No." The word was clipped.

She heaved a large sigh. "That's too bad."

Turning completely away from the action and eyeing her suspiciously, Colin said, "Why is it too bad? Is it wrong to prefer reality to idiotic fantasy?"

"Tosh. This is fun." She squinted at him. "I really do believe you'd be happier if you learned how to have fun, Colin."

"I doubt it. Not if fun means appreciating inaccurate depictions of historical events."

"I'm not talking about that. I'm talking about taking things a trifle less seriously. Enjoying life."

"I enjoy life perfectly well, thank you."

"If what you do is enjoying life, then I'm glad I don't."

"And . . . cut! Perfect. Great! One take, just the way I like it!" Martin chortled with pleasure as he rushed up to the porch of the Cedar Crest Lodge. "Wonderful job, ladies and gentlemen. You can pack up those costumes now. We won't be needing them anymore."

The cast members congratulated one another and went back inside the lodge. Brenda watched Colin watching them. He appeared both frustrated and angry. She shook her head, wondering how to get through to him the notion that life wasn't all hard labor and study. She was startled when he turned on her almost ferociously.

"Was that man using me as his model?"

She blinked at him, astonished at his question and unsure how to answer. She didn't want to hurt his feelings— if he had any. On the other hand, it might be good for him to know that people found him fodder for fictional fussy professors. "Um, I believe he may have been."

He swallowed, and some of his ferocity fled. "Do I really act like that? Like a blind, dumb animal with no understanding of human fellowship?"

For goodness sake, he'd pegged himself to a *T.* Brenda hedged. "Well, I wouldn't say *that,* exactly. But, um, perhaps you do appear slightly blind to the conventions of societal behavior and the finer points of, um, fraternity."

"Good God." He looked stunned.

Feeling small and unkind and not liking it, Brenda said, "Mind you, I'm not saying it's true, but sometimes you do give the impression that you don't give a hang about anything or anyone but your precious academia."

"I see."

"That doesn't mean you *don't* give a hang," she hurried to explain. "Only that you give that impression. Occasionally. Every now and then."

"I see."

She gazed at him inquiringly. "Do you care about your fellow human beings, Colin? I mean, as a rule?"

He gave her a hideous scowl. She thought at once that he'd make a perfect Jack the Ripper should Peerless ever decide to fictionalize that twenty-year-old, particularly ghastly series of murders.

"Of course I care about my fellow human beings! Why do you think I despise this picture and the caricatures it's making out of Jerry and his family?"

"Oh," she said, musing for a moment. "That makes sense."

He snorted.

"Brenda!"

She glanced up and saw Martin waving at her to come back onto the set. With one last glance at Colin, she headed over to the faux Indian village. She called back, "Will you talk to me later, Colin?"

He looked surprised. "About what?"

She shrugged. "Everything."

Without waiting for a reply, she started trotting to the set.

Colin watched her uneasily. What the devil did she want to talk to him about this time? Was she going to press him for more details about Indian life? He snorted derisively, feeling as low as he'd ever felt and knowing beyond a doubt that no beautiful woman would care to gather information from him if there was another source available.

Or perhaps she was going to try to teach him some social graces, which was almost as awful a prospect as the first one. The notion that she believed he needed to be taught how to behave in company made his heart squinch painfully. Of course, her idea of proper social behavior and *real* manners probably differed considerably. *He* hadn't been caught tossing dice on the floor of a fancy hotel.

He knew all about the social graces, dash it. His mother, a fine woman and a great lady, had drilled him in polite behavior from the cradle. So had his father, who had greater social deportment than Brenda Fitzpatrick would ever possess. If she thought she was going to turn him into a grinning dimwit like that idiot Carruthers, she had another think coming.

Although, he acknowledged reluctantly, it might be pleasant to spend some time in her company. She was an enjoyable companion; the first female, in fact, to achieve such a status in his life. Even his mother, whom Colin loved dearly, was boring as all get-out when he had to talk to her for any length of time.

Strange that it should be an undereducated actress who kept his interest alive in conversation. Colin, feeling even more low and confused than he had a minute earlier, put his experience of Brenda to a rigid test. He was a male, after all, and she was the most tantalizing female he'd ever met. Could it be mere sexual attraction that kept him interested?

He thought about it, studying the overall impression Brenda created from all angles. All angles were equally delectable and attractive, to be sure. But, he decided after a long and hard examination, there was more to her than physical beauty. She was an interesting and interested colleague. He wasn't sure he liked admitting it, mainly because it would be much easier to dismiss Brenda if she were merely a sexual object.

Bother. Colin had never found life particularly difficult until he'd been hired by Peerless Studio as Martin Tafft's research assistant. In all the other venues he'd operated, his knowledge and insistence upon accuracy had been prized. Here, on the set of this mindless motion picture, it was deplored. He probably should have sought different employment this summer, but he'd been interested in how pictures were made, so he'd grabbed this one eagerly. Showed how much he knew about anything.

The notion that Brenda found him dull and boring surely didn't thrill him. He ought to have admitted that he did enjoy pretending, at least in his head. He'd always considered his fanciful side to be a weakness. Maybe it wasn't.

"Dash it, of course it is." Fancy could only get a researcher into trouble, and Colin knew it.

Was there a way to separate the researcher from the man? The idea was new to him, and he mistrusted it. His parents, both of whom were thinkers and teachers, had deplored any tendency in their children to forsake pure research for invention, considering tall tales and fairy stories as beneath their notice. Colin had considered them thus, too, since he'd been taught they were incorrect and, therefore, wrong.

Maybe there was a place for the imagination in the world of scholarship.

Good God, what was he thinking?

The camera started its thunderous cranking noise, drawing Colin's attention out of the mire of confused thoughts and into the reality of filmmaking. He watched the scene unfold with distaste.

"Look scared, Brenda!" Martin called through his megaphone. "Jerry, keep that nasty expression on your face. It's perfect!"

Perfect, his eye, Colin thought grimly. This whole enterprise was a travesty.

Brenda managed to snabble Colin that evening after dinner. She was tired after a strenuous day's work during which she'd been kidnapped, carried off into an alien environment, and made to don an Indian dress, complete with buckskin fringe and beadwork, all of which Colin considered ethnically wrong, and set to grinding corn—all for the sake of the Peerless Studio—but she wanted to help Martin in any way she could. Therefore, she aimed to fulfill her promise to try to civilize Colin.

It wasn't an easy task. "Um, I think you'd better reconsider that move, Colin," she said, holding her exasperation at bay with difficulty. What she really wanted to be doing was sleeping, but she was at present in the parlor, trying to teach the man how to play poker.

"Why?" He looked grumpy. No surprise there.

She pointed at the cards in his hand, which he was obligingly showing her—the only obliging thing he'd done since they'd met—and explained, "You have two pairs. You don't want to discard one of either set in the hope that you'll be dealt something better because there's no telling. That's the sort of optimistic play that ends up with people losing their shirts, not to mention the family farm and everything else—and I know you don't have a family farm to lose. It's a figure of speech." She sighed and told herself not to get sarcastic. "In poker, you're better off keeping what you have, if you have anything at all."

His concentration was intense. Brenda wondered if he was this contentious whenever he set about learning something new. Perhaps that's what scholars were trained to do, but it was rough on their teachers.

He pointed at her cards. "But you have a—what do you call it? A flush? Two pairs can't beat a flush, can it? Wouldn't I be better off—or not any worse off, at any rate—if I tried to pick a better hand?" He squinted at the paper she'd given him, upon which she'd written down the various combinations of winning poker hands.

"Yes, but remember that if we were playing this game for real, you wouldn't know what was in my hand. All you'd know is that you have two pairs in your own hand. Now that's a pretty good hand as it stands, and if you keep your face straight and stop scowling and continue playing, you might draw a third or even a fourth seven or five."

"This is a very frustrating game. I don't like not knowing what's going on." The scowl Brenda had noted before deepened.

She repressed a soulful sigh. "Yes, I've noticed that quality in you."

He looked up at her, squinting with suspicion from behind his thick spectacles, which he pushed up his nose. She smiled wearily and decided poker wasn't the best game to be teaching him tonight. She didn't have the energy or patience for it. Thank God the horde of young men who had been her constant attendants since she'd arrived at the Cedar Crest had been shipped off to Los Angeles after the ballroom scene. She was sure she wouldn't have the wherewithal to deal with Colin and them, too.

Martin strolled over and peered at the game in progress. Brenda wrinkled her nose at him, and he winked back. "How's the game coming, you two?" he asked jovially.

Well and good for him to be jovial, Brenda thought bitterly. Martin wasn't attempting to teach Colin Peters how to play poker. She was beginning to think that teaching Colin anything at all was a task beyond her feeble skills. How had all his other teachers accomplished the task? Somebody must have, since he knew so damned much.

Colin grunted something Brenda didn't catch.

She said, "I think I'm too sleepy for it, to tell you the truth."

Colin's head jerked up and he stared at her the way he'd seconds earlier been staring at his poker hand. "Do you want to let it go for now?" He sounded hopeful.

She grinned at him. "Would you mind? Maybe we could have a nightcap in the bar instead." She saw with interest and some vexation that Colin looked disapproving, from which she gathered that the females in Colin's family didn't frequent bars. They were probably all as stuffy and pedantic as he was.

Heavens, what a thought: a whole family of frigid academicians. She wondered how many of them there were and had a sudden vision, spawned, she was sure, by her state of exhaustion, of dozens of Peterses spreading their wintry influence on the eastern seaboard until the whole East Coast froze into a solid cake of ice.

Colin plopped his cards on the table. "I don't mind at all." As if he feared she'd change her mind, he rose and hastened to hold her chair for her in a gentlemanly manner she'd bet her last dollar he wouldn't have done if he'd been interested in the game.

She exchanged a wry glance with Martin and rose with as much grace as she could summon. "I think I'll have a Manhattan."

"A Manhattan it is," Martin said. "What about you, Colin? I'll tell the bartender what you want while you two pick up the cards."

Colin appeared disconcerted. Brenda assumed it was because he didn't drink. She asked, "Do you like sweet drinks? You might like a Manhattan."

"I don't know." His furrows were deep. Brenda had a mad urge to smooth them out for him. Lord, she must be tired! "I, ah, don't drink much."

She patted the cards into a neat stack, then took his arm. "I don't, either," she said confidentially. "But I'm tired tonight and think it will help me sleep."

"I don't need help sleeping."

He'd gone stiff at her touch, and Brenda wasn't able to stifle her sigh this time. "Lucky you." To Martin, she said, "Order him a Manhattan, too. If he doesn't like it, he doesn't have to drink it."

"Right-o." Martin sauntered off to the bar.

Watching his receding back, Brenda murmured, "I swear, he never gets tired. He expends as much energy as any of us, but he doesn't seem to feel it as the rest of us do."

"It's probably his metabolism," Colin said.

She peered up at him and noticed that he didn't look so stiff. She figured it was because she'd given him a reason to assume his professorial pose. What the heck, she might as well play along. "What's a metabolism?"

He didn't appear too shocked by her lack of knowledge. She gave him a figurative tip of her hat for it, although it most likely only signified that he was too accustomed to her state of ignorance to show how much he deplored it. He said simply, "It's the rate an individual's body uses the fuel with which it's been supplied."

"Oh." She blinked and wondered what to ask next. She had no idea.

Fortunately, Colin didn't let her befuddlement stop him; she should have expected as much. "Everybody's body is different." He glanced down at her and looked away again quickly. "As you know already." He sounded very formal, and Brenda had a notion he'd realized he'd begun talking about bodies to a female and was embarrassed.

"I see," she said, although she didn't see anything. "So Martin's energy level is higher than mine?"

"Not necessarily." He cleared his throat. "You see, it may only be that he consumes fuel at a higher level than you do. Or perhaps his body is more efficient in its fuel consumption."

"Oh." She hoped he'd drop this subject, because he was making Martin sound like an automobile, and she had an urge to giggle. Obviously, she was in no condition to try to understand the lesson he was attempting to impart. They'd reached the bar, thank God, and she saw Martin at a table in a corner.

She appreciated this bar. She appreciated the whole Cedar Crest Lodge, if it came to that. It was a tasteful and refined place. Brenda, who hadn't grown up with any refinement at all, enjoyed it when she sat in it. The lodge, and this bar, were both masterpieces of polished wooden beams and understated elegance. The whole shebang reminded her of old money. Like the Vanderbilts or the Morgans or the Astors. Or, better still, like one of those old British families who'd been spitting out dukes and earls for centuries. She sat with a sigh and leaned back against the soft cushions of her chair. "If I fall asleep, just nudge me."

Martin chuckled. "Sure thing."

Colin looked faintly shocked. How unusual. With a little grin that probably looked as dry as it felt, she murmured, "I didn't mean it, Colin. It was a joke." She took a sip of her cocktail. It was delicious, and the warmth of the alcohol spreading through her gave her hope for the night. She usually slept well, but when she was working, sometimes she suffered from insomnia.

With an effort, she sat up straighter in her soft, comfy chair and asked Colin, "How do you like your Manhattan?" After his first sip his nose had wrinkled and he looked disapproving, so she anticipated his answer.

He surprised her. Before he answered, he took a second sip, stared across the table and over her left shoulder, appeared to think for a few seconds, and finally said, "It's pretty good." He took another sip and nodded. "Yes, it's quite tasty."

Good grief. Not for the first—or even the hundredth—time, Brenda wondered what it was like to test everything with such care before rendering an opinion. Heck, she'd only had to set foot in the Cedar Crest Lodge to realize she liked it. She'd bet Colin hadn't allowed himself to form a verdict yet, and they'd been here for several days. He undoubtedly had to put the question to some sort of scholarly test. Curious, she asked, "What do you think of the lodge, Colin?"

His brow wrinkled again, he pushed his glasses up his

nose, and he looked as if he intended to mull that one over for a year or three before rendering a judgment on the subject. Brenda guessed her tiredness had made her short-tempered, because his attitude grated on her nerves like a file.

Turning to Martin, she said, "I think it's a wonderful place. I'd like to spend a couple of weeks every summer up here to rest and relax in."

Turning a weather eye upon Colin, she noted his expression and decided he didn't respect her opinion of the lodge any more than he respected anything else about her. She wanted to snap at him. Maybe slap him around some. Instead, she lifted her Manhattan and took another sip. She didn't drink very often and never gulped. One was her limit, and she intended to savor this one.

"It's a great place," Martin concurred. "I discovered it last year when I was looking for a suitable location to shoot a mining film."

"A mining film?" Brenda's interest was piqued.

"I don't believe there are any mines up here."

Brenda and Martin both turned to look at Colin. He gazed back, noted their expressions, and lifted an eyebrow. "That is, I believe there are many mines down the mountain and around San Bernardino and in the Mojave Desert, but there aren't any up here to my knowledge. The ore fields are down there."

"And you ought to know," Brenda murmured. She added to herself, *since you know everything.* She didn't say that part aloud.

"Right." Martin seemed relatively unfazed by Colin's input. "I found that out last year. I was hoping to find a place that was out of the heat of the desert, which is why I went up into the mountains in the first place. It's much prettier up here." He smiled his regular happy smile. "Unfortunately, it didn't work out. I fear we'll be shooting the picture in the desert. I get mighty tired of deserts, but it's where we film most of the cowboy pictures and so forth."

Colin nodded and looked as if he were only barely restraining himself from saying, "You should have asked me first." Asking Colin first, Brenda knew, even though she was sure Colin wouldn't understand, would have taken the fun out of Martin's enterprise. Seeking advice was all well and good, but sometimes life was more interesting when you allowed yourself to discover some things on your own.

"Are you going to make that picture next, Martin?" she asked in order to take her mind off Colin and how irritating he was. And how much she wished he wasn't.

"I'm not sure. I still haven't found a suitable site. I'm working on it, though."

She shook her head slightly. "You do too much. You never take any time for yourself."

"Oh, I love what I do. It doesn't seem like work to me."

Colin nodded his agreement, and Brenda was amused. How funny. These two men, who were as different as night was from day, had something very important in common. She didn't share this aspect of life with them. While she enjoyed her work to a degree, she'd just as soon be able to retire somewhere and read for the rest of her life.

Suddenly she saw Colin stiffen, as if a mob of people had taken to speaking ungrammatically in his hearing. Or maybe done something worse, like mistaken a Navajo for an Apache. Actually, he looked as if someone had struck him hard and knocked him cockeyed.

Good heavens, perhaps he'd had a reaction to the alcohol in his drink. Brenda had heard of some people who couldn't tolerate even a drop of alcohol.

She heard Colin mumble, "Good God."

He seemed to be staring at the door of the bar, which was at her back. She swiveled in her chair and looked to see if they'd been invaded by wild Indians. Frowning, she decided that wasn't a funny thing to say any longer, if it ever was.

A young man had entered the bar and was now glancing around with an uncertain air. He was a nice-looking lad: tall and straight, with dark wavy hair and a strong chin. He held his hat in his right hand and licked his lips nervously. He looked vaguely familiar to her.

It hit her after only a very few seconds. She sat up ramrod straight in her chair and turned her startled glance upon Colin. He still sat rigid, staring at the boy. All at once he stood, bumping the table and sending his chair skittering across the polished cedar-wood floor.

"George," he said, in a voice Brenda had not until now heard issue from his lips.

The young man at the door turned and squinted through the dim bar lighting at Colin, his uncertainty falling away. He still appeared uncomfortable when he smiled, lifted his hat in a gesture of greeting, and said, "H'lo, Colin."

"George!" Colin said, more loudly.

"Who is it?" asked Martin with interest, obviously unperturbed by the newcomer's entrance.

"It's George," Colin said. He sounded as if he'd been struck over the head with a large rock and stunned.

Brenda decided she might as well ask. "Who's George?"

Colin swallowed hard. "My brother."

No wonder they looked vaguely alike. How fascinating. She watched as the brothers met a few paces away from her table. They shook hands.

They shook hands?

Brenda knew she was way too exhausted when she experienced a sudden furious impulse to holler at the formal, stodgy brothers to forget about shaking hands and hug each other.

Ten

Something was very wrong. Colin resisted the impulse to grab his younger brother by the nape of his neck, shout obscenities, and shake the news out of him. He was none too gentle, though, when he barked, "What in thunder are you doing here?"

George's lips tightened for a second. "Visiting you, Colin. Didn't think you'd mind." There was the faintest taint of insolence in his tone.

He was also hedging, and Colin knew it. "Aren't you supposed to be in school?" Colin knew he was. What's more, George's school was in Pennsylvania. George shouldn't be within three thousand miles of California.

"Not any longer."

Colin felt his anger rise and his gaze thin. "What do you mean, 'not any longer'? I know good and well you haven't graduated yet."

A flash of temper crossed George's face. "And I'm not going to graduate." He sounded defiant, as only a thwarted adolescent can sound. "I dropped out of school."

"You *what?*" Colin hadn't meant to bellow, but he could scarcely believe his ears and bellowed anyway. Impossible! Yet if anyone in the family were to fail in life, he supposed George was the one.

George took a step sideways, as if to walk around

Colin. "You heard me." Now he sounded sullen. "Why don't you introduce me to your friends?"

Colin knew to the instant when George saw Brenda. He'd evidently been too nervous to notice anyone but Colin before. But when his eyes bugged and his mouth fell open and he started gaping, Colin knew he'd spotted Brenda. He turned, too, and had to acknowledge that Brenda Fitzpatrick, when viewed for the first time, could dazzle a man. He was in no mood to be honest with himself or he'd have owned that she still dazzled him, and he'd known her for days now.

Both Martin and Brenda rose from their chairs. Martin looked curious. Brenda smiled, which was enough to overwhelm a young lad like George. Colin took him roughly by the shoulder. "Come with me. As long as you're here, I might as well introduce you."

"As suave and chivalrous as ever, I see," George muttered sourly.

"Don't push it, George. Do Mother and Father know you're here?"

"No."

Now he was sulky. Colin wanted to shake him until he rattled and then batter him around for a while, but that would have to wait. Brenda was on her way over to them, along with Martin, although Colin was positive George hadn't yet so much as registered Martin's presence, so brilliant was Brenda's.

She was also very gracious. Colin admitted it to himself, although he'd never do so to anyone else. She gave George a warm, welcoming smile. "Hello there. Welcome to the Cedar Crest Lodge. I understand you and Colin are related."

"Th-thank you, ma'am." George swallowed. "Yes. I mean, yes, we're related. Colin and me, I mean." His face burned a fiery red.

Irked with his younger brother for being a harebrained

twit as well as a college failure, Colin said harshly, "Miss Brenda Fitzpatrick, please allow me to introduce my younger brother, George. George is—visiting from back east." Damn him.

"How do you do, George? It's so nice to meet you."

She held out one of her lovely, tiny hands to George, who dropped his hat in his eagerness to shake it. Colin cut the handshake short by introducing Martin. "Martin Tafft, my brother George."

"How-do, George. Good of you to visit us. Colin's been trying to keep us straight, but he hasn't had much luck so far." He chuckled, and Colin's insides clenched. Martin thought he was being funny, Colin supposed, but Colin didn't see any humor in the comment.

"I'm sure," George said with a hint of malice in his young voice even as he smiled and shook Martin's hand. "Colin's aim in life is to keep everyone straight."

Colin caught the sharp glint in Brenda's eyes and could have kicked his brother from here to Sunday. Anyone would think Colin was some sort of monster, the way George talked. Yet Colin had never given George any reason to think ill of him. He'd only ever tried to help him with his lessons, and there was nothing wrong with that, even though George had always been a recalcitrant recipient of Colin's assistance. A couple of instances tiptoed through Colin's mind, and his lips tightened.

George, although smarter than most human beings on earth, was probably the least ambitious member of the Peters clan. Sometimes people equated his lack of intellectual curiosity as a sign that he was unintelligent. Colin knew better. The boy was only lazy; perhaps even good-for-nothing. As this latest escapade of his proved.

"How long do you aim to visit with us, George?" Brenda asked courteously. Colin was sure she didn't care in the least, but was merely being polite. Even he, who didn't normally notice people's faces, could detect the fatigue in hers.

George shot Colin a hasty glance. "Er, I'm not sure, Miss Fitzpatrick. This visit was sort of—sort of a surprise."

"Unequivocally," Colin growled. George looked peeved.

"Well, I hope you enjoy your stay. This is a lovely place. Perhaps we can all go horseback riding together one of these days."

"I'd like that," George said quickly, flushing a deeper red as he did so.

This was ridiculous. Colin wasn't going to stand here in the middle of the Cedar Crest Lodge's bar and watch Brenda Fitzpatrick make mincemeat of his idiot brother. "I suppose you can room with me as long as you're here." He pitched his voice to a tone he hoped would curtail further conversation. Brenda needed her sleep. So did he, for that matter.

Brenda seemed a little surprised, but she didn't take him to task for his abrupt manners. Thank the good Lord for small favors, he thought caustically.

"It's very nice to meet you, George, but I'm afraid we've had a strenuous day. I think I'll go on up to my own room." She gave him a parting smile that probably finished George off, blast her. "Good night."

"G-g-good night," George stammered, confirming Colin's assumption.

Martin said, "Think I'll go on up to bed, too. It's been quite a day, but we got a lot done." He was clearly delighted about it. "Will we see you in the morning, George?"

George hadn't entirely recovered from Brenda's smile, but he did manage to stutter, "Oh, thank you, Mr. Tafft. I'd like that a lot. I'm very interested in the pictures."

Martin nodded, as if he'd already deduced as much. Everyone in the world seemed to be interested in the pictures these days, fools that they were. "Good night," Colin said to Brenda and Martin, more curtly than he'd intended.

Brenda shot him a curious glance but didn't scold him for being a pill. "Good night," she said in that beautiful, melodious, albeit slightly New Yorky voice of hers.

Colin wished that hearing her voice didn't send waves of heat through him, but it did. Every dashed time. He could just imagine what Brenda's voice was doing to his impressionable younger brother. He and George watched as Brenda and Martin left the bar, chatting in low voices. George, he noticed, was gawking after Brenda as if she were a lifeline and he a drowning sailor.

Feeling out of sorts and very touchy, Colin whirled around. "All right, George, what's going on? What's this about dropping out of college? And what do you mean by haring off across the country without even telling our parents?"

George heaved a big sigh. "For the love of God, Colin, let me at least sit down before you tear me to pieces."

He sounded dispirited, and for the first time Colin wondered if there was something more to George's defection than mere irresponsibility. He muttered, "Very well. Here." He gestured at the table Brenda and Martin had vacated. They sat, and George at once began fiddling with an empty ashtray on the table. He looked around as if with fascination.

"This is a nice place, Colin. What kind of picture is this going to be?"

"I'll tell you later. First you tell me why the deuce you're here instead of in school where you belong."

George heaved a long sigh before he spoke, and then his tone was unhappy. "I didn't belong there. I didn't fit in, didn't care for my course of study, did a lousy job at it, and hated every minute of it."

Colin felt his eyes widen as his fury rose. "So you

dropped out without telling anyone and headed west. Hoping to seek your fortune in the moving pictures, I presume." Although Colin was often abrupt and untactful, he'd never heard his voice drip venom as it was doing now. He was surprised by it, although he understood why he felt George's defection so deeply, because it was a betrayal of everything Colin himself had ever valued in life.

George waved a hand in a gesture that spoke of weariness and defeat. "For Pete's sake, Colin, you don't have to be so damned heartless."

"Since when have you started swearing, George? Is that what they taught you at college?"

"Oh, God." George propped his elbows on the table and buried his face in his hands. "If you'll listen to me, I'll tell you what they taught me, Colin. But I don't want you to be interrupting all the time. You're smarter than I am, and you use words better, and I already feel bad enough about this without you playing older, better brother and pounding me to a pulp with your superior wit."

Scalding words piled up on Colin's tongue, and he swallowed them with a good deal of difficulty. He wanted to spew them out all over George and render him sensible of the huge mistake he'd made by leaving school without their parents' knowledge or consent. He knew if he said what he wanted to, George would only withdraw from him, however, so he held his tongue.

Not that Colin cared on a personal basis. He was so angry with George, he could have beaten him about the head and shoulders with great joy. But above anything else, Colin honored their parents, who had reared their children with affection and great care, and instilled in them—or in Colin, at least—a vast respect and love for education. Colin believed he owed it to their parents to get to the bottom of George's latest regression into the realm of capriciousness and frivolity.

"Very well," he said through gritted teeth. "Tell me what happened."

George gave another airy, helpless gesture with his hand. It was a slender hand, with long, tapering fingers. Colin's own hands were much more blunt than George's. He wondered if that meant anything; if a man learned in such things could discern a person's character by the structure of his hands.

He jerked himself back to the present. George's problems were of immediate concern. Colin could look into the representative properties of hands later. "Well?" he urged, none too gently.

George sighed again. "I'm not cut out for biology and physiology, Colin. Nor for science of any kind. I know Mother and Father were hoping I'd become a naturalist, but I hate that stuff. Spiders make me crawl, mice make me sick, and the great out-of-doors only makes me feel dirty." He seemed to be searching Colin's face for any signal indicating understanding, if not approval. He didn't find any.

"Oh?" So far, Colin could drum up no sympathy. There were lots of things one could study, and the mere fact that George didn't want to be a naturalist didn't preclude a hundred other vocations. "Why didn't you tell them you wanted to study something else?"

"They seemed so keen on my becoming a naturalist. God knows why."

"Nonsense. They'd have been happy if you'd ever shown any aptitude or interest in another field." Colin sucked in a breath and curbed his biting words. "As I recollect, you never showed interest in anything but lounging around and reading novels. But the university offers many courses of study. Surely you could have found *something* there that interested you. Even in the humanities." He tried not to make the word sound like a curse.

George lifted his head and stared straight into Colin's

eyes. Colin had the strangest sensation that he was looking into his own eyes, so alike were the brothers' ocular organs. "That's just the problem, Colin. I—" He stopped speaking abruptly.

"What's the problem?" Colin knew he should probably stop frowning, if only to make George feel more comfortable talking to him, but he couldn't make himself do it. He was enraged, and there was no disguising it.

George looked very unhappy—as well he might, in Colin's opinion—when he said, "I don't want to study anything there."

It was too much. Colin spat out, "For God's sake, George, have you no common sense at all? What do you expect to do with your life if you're not trained for anything? Do you expect to be able to make a living by staring up into the blue sky and counting clouds? Or reading novels? Or do you expect our parents to support you until they die? Or me? Do you expect *me* to carry you around like a sack of oatmeal forever?"

George's head fell back and he commenced staring at the ceiling of the Cedar Crest bar. He looked both frustrated and nettled, and his attitude rubbed Colin raw.

"Well?" he demanded, furious. "What is it? Or perhaps you'd like to be a common laborer. I don't suppose a man needs a college education to work with his hands. You can mow grass or plant crops. Would you like to go into farming? Of course, you have no business sense, so you'd certainly not make a go of it, but the world always needs farmers. Or laborers. You can dig ditches. There's nothing innately dishonorable about manual labor. Is that what you want?"

"No!" Something in George seemed to snap, and he jumped up from his chair. Slamming his hands to the table and leaning on them, he looked Colin straight in the eye. "No, Colin, I don't want to dig ditches. I don't want to be a farmer. What I *do* want is to have my wishes respected for once in my life."

"Respect," Colin ground out through his teeth, "has to be earned."

"Right." As if he were a balloon and someone had just pricked him, George deflated. He stood back and jammed his hands into his trousers' pockets. "And, of course, since no one in the family ever cared enough to ask me where my interests lie, none of you knows anything about them."

"You have a voice," Colin reminded him. "You could have spoken up. I never noticed you being particularly shy about voicing your opinions before now. I'm sure our parents would have been thrilled to have been spared the cost of your first two years at college if you'd ever bothered to tell them what you really wanted to do." George probably wanted to be a juggler in a circus, thought Colin savagely. His brother always had been a frivolous sort of fellow.

"Right. You're right." George swung around, dropped his chin broodingly, and stared at the floor. "It's because I was a coward and didn't tell anyone what I wanted to do. That's why nobody ever knew."

Exasperated almost beyond bearing, Colin said in a voice gritty with suppressed fury, "Why don't you tell me now?"

George turned again, eyeing Colin with grave misgivings. Small wonder, given Colin's state of rage, although he couldn't feel guilty about it to save himself. George was a noddy and that was that. "Well? Out with it. Maybe we can salvage something from this deplorable situation yet."

"Don't sound so encouraging," George advised bitterly.

Colin only expelled a huff of breath.

"All right," George said. "I don't suppose you know this—I'm sure no one else in the family does—but I'm an artist, Colin. I'm good. If our parents ever wanted to spend money on an education for me, they'd have done better to send me to art school."

"An *artist?*" If there was anything more asinine than

being a juggler in a circus, it was being an artist. That was only Colin's opinion, but he judged it a sound one. Artists were notorious for their penchant for insanity, drugs, and alcohol, and for killing themselves and making everyone who cared about them miserable. He clenched the hand resting on the table into a fist. He wanted to sock his crazy brother in the jaw with it.

"Yes," George said simply. "I can't help it, you know. I was born this way."

"Good God." Colin shut his eyes and tried to calm himself. But—for the love of God! An *artist?* He didn't think he could stand it. He was sure their parents wouldn't have been able to stand it. It was probably a good thing that George had come to him instead of going back home with this outrageous story. When he opened his eyes, he saw George licking his lips and looking miserable. He ought to look miserable, the damned fool.

"I thought somebody in the pictures might be able to use me," George said in a small voice. "I know they use set designers and people to draw the subtitles. I'm very good at calligraphy."

A memory shimmered indistinctly in the back of Colin's mind. "Yes. I recollect something of the sort."

George used to do the titles for the amateur theatricals the Peters children presented. And he'd painted sets for school plays. Odd how no one in the family had taken any particular note of his interest in that sort of thing, or of his talent, which was considerable. Of course, that was because everyone else in the family possessed some common sense. They knew better than to consider art as a means of making a living.

Not George. Never George. Colin sighed heavily and stood up. There was no sense prolonging this conversation. Neither brother was up to it tonight.

"Come on," he said. "I'll take you upstairs. Do you have luggage?"

He could almost see the relief flood through his brother's solid body. Funny, no one looking at George would take him for a booby. He appeared so solid and stable. What a liar appearances could be.

"Yes. I left a bag with the man at the desk." He licked his lips again. "Thanks, Colin. I appreciate you putting me up for the night."

"Yes, well, you need somewhere to stay, I suppose, until we can figure out what to do with you."

"You sound as if you're having to deal with a stray cat or a mad aunt," George said cheerlessly.

"That's exactly how I feel." *Unkind, Colin. Very unkind.*

He didn't apologize.

Brenda awoke on the second day of filming *Indian Love Song* feeling tired and somehow dispirited. She wasn't sure why this should be, unless it was because she was sick of her life. She was tired of never being able to do as she pleased, of always and forever being on display. Even when she went for a casual walk in the park, people recognized her. That was because of the moving pictures. Sometimes she wished she'd stuck to vaudeville and the legitimate stage and never ventured into the pictures.

But no. She had too many people dependent upon her to have passed up the opportunity to make money in this new and exciting industry. And she was making money. Heaps and piles of it. Not only was she a respected comedic actress, but she'd also been asked to model for magazine ads and to endorse products. Now she was not merely an actress and singer, but she was also recognized as the "Maiden Dew Skin Lotion" girl. There was lots of money to be made in commercial advertisements these days.

Everything she did, though, plastered her face before the public. Sometimes she just wanted to don a pair of her brother's trousers and go riding in the woods in Vermont or upstate New York, but she couldn't.

As sure as she appeared anywhere improperly clad, she'd run into a photographer or a newspaper hound after a story. And people like that loved nothing better than to find a celebrity appearing in public looking disreputable or unkempt. Newspapers and the public thrived on scandal. Which was one of the reasons Brenda had never, ever, not even once, allowed her name to become linked with that of any man. It was also true that she'd not yet met a man with whom she wanted more than a casual friendship.

Until she met Colin Peters.

Which was why her ambivalent feelings about Colin troubled her. He could be such a pompous ass sometimes that she wanted to leap on him and scratch his face with her fingernails, just like a cat or an hysterical woman. Invariably, her violent urges were accompanied by the almost unbearable desire to kiss him and make mad, passionate love with him.

Brenda had never been to bed with a man. She was sure anyone who knew anything at all about the acting life wouldn't believe it, but it was true. She'd never found a man attractive enough to make her want to jeopardize her reputation and, as a consequence, her family's welfare. Unfortunately, Brenda, all by herself, constituted her family's welfare.

One of these days her brothers would be out of school and earning a good living. And her sister was also headed for a good career although, Brenda knew, the opportunities for women were nowhere near as good as those available for men. It wasn't fair, but nobody seemed to care about that but her. And Kathy's health was fragile. She shouldn't be obliged to work hard, because she had a weak heart.

"Lord, girl, get a hold of yourself." She scowled into her mirror, then smiled. Ah, that was better. Even if she didn't feel like smiling, she looked happy. Nobody but her would ever know.

Something tickled at the back of her mind, something she ought to remember and which was very interesting, but . . . Oh! That's right. Colin's brother. Colin hadn't been happy to see poor George; it had been obvious from the moment he'd spotted him.

Brenda's mood brightened considerably. *She* was happy George had come, whatever Colin was. In fact, she could hardly wait to talk to him and find out what he was doing here. She wondered if he'd run away from his ever-so-proper home.

Feeling better about her life and the day, she plopped a straw hat onto her golden curls and left her room. She found George in the dining room at a table with Martin and Colin and hurried to join them, smiling broadly.

"Good morning, everyone!"

They all looked up at her. Martin smiled. Colin frowned. George looked smitten. They were all reactions she'd expected. Damn Colin for being such an intolerable stuffed shirt.

"Hey there, Brenda," Martin said happily. He was almost always happy. It was because he loved his work. Brenda envied him that.

Colin, who also loved his work, was different. He managed to stop scowling long enough to say, "Good morning," but she could tell he wished her elsewhere.

George had to gulp before he could form words. "G-good morning, Miss Fitzpatrick."

She gave him a warm, inviting grin, hoping it would help him relax a little bit. When she saw his dark eyes open up as wide as saucers, she guessed she'd overdone the inviting part somewhat.

George hurriedly stammered, "Y-you look beautiful this morning." Then he blushed.

Brenda felt herself go warm and melty inside, both in

sympathy and in appreciation. The poor boy couldn't be more than eighteen or nineteen, and he was in patent distress about something. Even so, he'd managed to pay her a pretty compliment, something his older and probably smarter brother had never done, the wretch. "Thank you very much, George."

Martin had risen to hold a chair for her, and she smoothed out her skirt and sat. She did look good. She had to. Looking good was her livelihood. Today she'd chosen her lilac silk with the high, lacy collar. She looked rather like a forest sprite in this dress, which had seemed appropriate to her, considering the location of the lodge.

A waiter appeared, and she gave him her order for breakfast. The others were lingering over their coffee. Since Colin seemed disinclined to speak to her and looked more than usually gloomy, and since George was evidently tongue-tied, and since Martin was studying a list, presumably of things to do, she decided to initiate a conversation about the picture. It seemed a logical and unexceptionable topic of conversation, and one not even Colin could disapprove of, unless he was even more fussy today than he normally was.

"Is that the shooting schedule, Martin?" Her tea arrived, and she sipped it, grateful to have something to do with her hands.

Martin looked up from his list. "Yes. We've got to get the Indians' parts finished today, because they're returning to Arizona tomorrow."

She nodded and shot a quick glance at Colin. She half expected him to renew his objections to the Indians, but he didn't. He looked like a broody hen; probably worrying about his brother. She wondered what George's situation could be to bring him here, to a brother whose displeasure at his popping up was overt.

"I hope you'll enjoy watching this picture being made,

George," she said in an effort to draw him out. "It's not as much like a play as lots of people think."

"Sarah Bernhardt was in a picture that was exactly like a play," said Colin in his crabby voice. "They even had a stage and a curtain."

Brenda eyed him with disfavor. "Yes, Colin, but no one's done a picture like that since. Perhaps you haven't noticed."

He glared at her. "I noticed."

"Then perhaps you failed to notice that the motion-picture medium offers a wider range of possibilities as to scenery, movement, and drama than that proscribed by the stage."

"Yes," he said, evidently loath to admit it. "I understand that, too."

She nodded sweetly at him. "Ah. From your comment, I'd not gotten that impression."

Martin said hastily, "Here, George, would you like to come with me? Our first scene is going to be one in the Indian village. The only actors will be Indians."

George shot a glance at his brother, then rose as if he couldn't do so fast enough. "I'd like that, Mr. Tafft. Thank you." He smiled shyly at Brenda. "Enjoy your breakfast, Miss Fitzpatrick." Then he blushed, as if he wished he'd been able to think of something more cogent to say.

"Please," she said, wishing she could put the boy at his ease, "call me Brenda. I hope we can be friends."

He stuttered out something that sounded remotely like thanks and fled, hurrying after Martin as if he feared being left behind. He didn't say good-bye to his brother.

Colin muttered, "Good gad," under his breath.

Brenda's eyes thinned, and she peered at him coldly. "Some lousy kind of big brother *you* are!"

Eleven

Colin felt his eyes narrow, his lips pinch, and his color heighten, as his anger rose. Along with anger was another emotion he couldn't pinpoint, but it didn't feel good.

He hated emotions. They were so—so—uncomfortable. He much preferred the silent, unsentimental world of academia. He was comfortable there; ever so much more comfortable than when he was forced to confront the unstable whims, fancies, and moods of people like Brenda Fitzpatrick. Or his brother George.

He lifted his eyebrows in what he hoped was a sardonic expression before saying frostily, "And what, pray, do you know about the kind of brother I am?"

She sat across from him and looked about as mad as he felt. Her breakfast had not yet been served, and she stabbed at the table in front of her with a slender, beautifully manicured forefinger. "I know because I've seen the two of you together. And apart. And that poor boy is terrified of you, in case you couldn't tell for yourself."

Terrified? Again Colin's eyebrows lifted like larks soaring. "Terrified? Of me? You're out of your mind. Not to mention a meddling busybody."

"Oh, pish! I can't even imagine what the rest of your family is like if poor George came to you instead of going home when whatever it was happened."

"What do you mean?"

"Obviously something happened, and he's either very sorry or very embarrassed about it. What I don't understand is why he came to you, of all people."

"And why shouldn't he come to me? What do you mean by that?" His sense of outrage was growing by the second.

"I mean you're an evil-tempered, unsympathetic brute, is what I mean. I can't imagine coming to you for help for anything at all, but if George chose you over the other members of your family, they must all be even worse than you, which is almost impossible to imagine, and also must mean that you come from a miserable tribe of trolls and ogres!"

Her voice had risen, and when she came to the end of her unconscionable condemnation of his family, she sucked in a huge breath, as if trying to cool herself off. Colin was pretty hot himself. He'd opened his mouth to refute her charges when the waiter came with her soft-boiled egg, toast, and sliced orange, and he had to swallow a furious retort.

It took her only a second to reconform her face from an expression of wrath—although what she had to be wrathful about, Colin had no idea—to one of serenity. "Thank you so much." She smiled at the waiter, who looked like he might faint with only a little more encouragement from her.

Colin snorted, furious that this insufferable woman could have tricked so many people into believing her to be charming.

Oh, very well, dash it, she *was* charming. Sometimes. Not this morning. And seldom to him.

She whacked the top off of her egg with a knife as if she wished it were Colin's head, then glared at him. "I have no idea what George has done to earn your disapprobation, but it can't be all that bad. For heaven's sake, the boy can't be more than eighteen or nineteen."

"He just turned eighteen," Colin said, begrudging her the information, since it proved her right about his age, if not a single thing else.

"Eighteen." She took a bite of egg and a bite of toast and chewed them, swallowing before she followed up on her statement of George's age. "Eighteen years old. A child. An infant! And you're treating him as if he were the Big Bad Wolf and had just eaten all the little piggies, who were probably Navajos masquerading as Apaches in Sioux territory. I can't imagine anything else that would get you so het up."

Colin drew in air, offended almost beyond bearing. "Sarcasm does not become you, Miss Fitzpatrick. Be careful, or your many fans might come to realize you're not the saint you pretend to be."

She swiveled her eyes up and gazed at the ceiling in a God-give-me-patience expression that Colin resented like thunder. "If anyone thinks I'm a saint," she said, and there seemed to be hot coals burning her words, "it's not my fault."

He snorted again, although he had a niggling feeling she was right. Dash it. "At any rate, you know nothing whatever about my brother, my family, or me, and I'll thank you to keep your opinions to yourself."

She eyed him malevolently. He got an eerie sensation of blue lightning issuing from her gaze, sort of like fiery pitchforks from hell. Because her scrutiny made him uncomfortable, he picked up his coffee cup and drained it. The coffee in it had gone cold and tasted vile.

"I don't know a thing about you, your family, or George," Brenda said in a measured cadence that reminded Colin of a death march. "But I've met you and I've met George, and I've seen the way he looks at you, as if he expects you to take out the horsewhip and flay the hide from his back. If you had any kind of decent relationship with your brother, he wouldn't look at you like that, and you know it. Why, the poor boy looks as if he'd just confessed to breaking a bone china teacup and is expecting you to shoot him for it."

With a feeling of smugness he knew was probably unworthy of a gentleman, Colin snapped, "He did something infinitely more awful than breaking a teacup, as a matter of fact."

Her eyes opened wide. Colin had to look away from them. She was so damnably beautiful, and those eyes of hers seemed to suck him in until he was left wallowing in a sea of sensation. He despised sensation almost as much as he despised emotion. Both phenomena were futile and a waste of time, and he neither understood nor approved of them.

"Oh?" she said. "And exactly what criminal act did he commit? Murder? Mayhem? Calling a tribe by the wrong name?"

His lips tightened for a second. "No. As a matter of fact, he left school without telling our parents or anyone else."

She blinked.

"He hared away from Pennsylvania and came all the way out here to California without communicating his bolt to a single other person."

"That's it?" She sipped her tea, watching him over the rim of her cup as if she expected him to spring the real story on her any second.

"That's it?" He repeated her words incredulously. "That's *it?* What do you mean, 'That's it'? Isn't that enough?"

She didn't answer immediately, but polished off her egg. When she did speak, her voice was pitched to sound reasonable, and it made Colin's teeth grind. "Leaving school doesn't sound like such a terrible infraction to me. Maybe he didn't like college. Maybe he discovered he wasn't much of a student. I'm sure that's an awful catastrophe in your family, but it wouldn't be for the majority of human beings in the world."

If he ground his teeth together for much longer, he'd wear them down to little pearly stubs. He unclenched them with an effort. "I'm sure you place no value on education, since you don't have one—"

She sat up as if he'd slapped her. "Oh! Why, you miserable, insensitive brute! Of course I value education! That's the very reason I'm sending my brothers and sister to college, you rotten snob! But *they* want to go! If they didn't, I'd help them find some other type of work."

He didn't like being called a snob. It hit too close to the bone. Nevertheless, he continued in the coldest tone he could manufacture, "My family is and has always been cognizant of the worth of a good education. Not only is an education of inestimable value to the basic character growth of a human being and a sure road to a successful career in any endeavor, but education has been a highly prized achievement in my family for generations. No one in the whole family has less than a basic college degree."

Brenda gazed at him, her lips a thin, tight line. She didn't look overly impressed, and her attitude infuriated him. He continued, "The fact that George chose to drop out of college without a word to anyone is not something any member of the family will take lightly. It was neither right nor well considered of him, and as far as I'm concerned, he has every reason to feel abashed and ashamed of himself."

She bit into her toast savagely and followed it up with a swig of tea. Her anger was so great that she didn't even bother to appear ladylike, although she did anyway, much to Colin's disgust. He'd really like her to act like the filthy street urchin she was underneath all her fine trappings, if only just once.

"All right, Colin. I'll grant that he was wrong not to

have consulted your parents before he made his escape—"

"Escape!"

"His escape," she repeated in a menacing tone. "Because it must have felt like an escape to him or he'd never
have bucked family tradition. He was wrong not to tell
anyone. But he was undoubtedly fearful of encountering
the very condemnation you've been heaping on him since
he walked into the bar last night. I don't blame him for
it. You're awful to him. And all because he doesn't want
to continue his higher education.

"For heaven's sake, Colin, I know you think you walk
on water and that scholarship is the only thing worth a
damn in the world, but there are tons of other ways to
make a living!" She took a deep breath. "I know you
don't like me, and I know you think I'm silly and ignorant, but I'm not. And *I* never had the opportunity to get
an education! Everything I know I learned from books
or people who were kind enough to answer my questions—unlike some people I know. Does that make me a
bad person?"

He'd like to say yes but couldn't. "Of course it
doesn't," he growled angrily. "But at least you pursued
a career and made something of yourself."

She threw her hands up in the air. "What's to say
George won't make something of himself?"

He leaned forward and almost spat the words into her
face. "For God's sake, Brenda, he wants to be an artist!
An *artist,* for the love of God!" He threw his hands up,
too, as if he couldn't even conceive of something more
nonsensical than a Peters wanting to be an artist.

"An artist?" She gazed at him blankly. "What's wrong
with being an artist?"

He rolled his eyes in a gesture very similar to the one
she'd given him a few moments earlier. "It's idiotic, that's

what's wrong with it! How many people do you know who make their living via the arts?"

She shrugged, making the lilac silk of her gown ripple in the morning sunshine sifting through the lodge's curtains and making him think of the fleshly treasures the fabric hid from his eyes. Lord, she was gorgeous. He wished he'd stop noticing. A person would think that, after a while, familiarity would breed nonchalance. It hadn't with him regarding Brenda, dash it.

"Hundreds," she said quietly. "I know hundreds of people who make their livings in the arts, Colin Peters. I'm one of them, in fact. And the opportunities are endless here, in Southern California, in the motion-picture industry."

"Motion pictures," he said as if they tasted bad. "I can't believe you said that."

"And why not? You're earning a good salary working for Peerless, aren't you?"

"This job as research assistant is only a summer stopgap job until school starts in the fall and I can begin teaching at the new university in Los Angeles." He glared at her and felt like adding a *so there,* just like a little boy.

"But you *are* working in the pictures." Her gaze narrowed again, and she looked as if she were pondering something for a second or two. "Is that why he came here, do you think? Because he hoped you might be able to help him get a job in the pictures?"

"I don't have any idea!"

"Why not? Didn't you ask?"

Her question tripped him up for a second. He opted not to answer it, because he thought she'd use his *no* against him. He said instead, "He oughtn't have done it; that's all I know."

She pressed her lips together. "I'm sure it is. And I'm sure poor George wishes now that he'd braved the ire of your parents. It couldn't be any worse than your callousness."

"Callousness? Is it callousness to believe he ought to have faced up to his responsibilities like a man and not run from them like a little boy? For God's sake, you were only twelve years old when you started making your way in the world! You didn't travel halfway across the country to snivel to your big brother that you wanted to be an artist. For heaven's sake!" He was so wrapped up in indignation that it finally suffocated his words, and he couldn't go on.

She eyed him levelly for a moment. "Yes, but my circumstances and those of your brother were different. My parents were Irish immigrants and poor as church mice. When my father died, it was either work or die. I didn't have much choice in the matter."

"Nonsense. You could have sat in a corner and cried."

"I did plenty of that," she said, and a bleak expression entered her eyes.

He didn't want to acknowledge that look, which he knew resulted from deep pain in her past. "But you didn't stay there and whine! You got out and worked!"

"But isn't that what George is trying to do? He came here, to you, looking for work, didn't he?"

"It's entirely different."

"I don't think so."

"Well, you're wrong." Colin decided he'd taken enough abuse for one morning and rose abruptly. "I have to get out there and make sure Martin doesn't have the Indians singing ragtime songs or something equally heinous."

She lifted her cup so roughly that some of the tea slopped into her saucer. She didn't seem to notice, as she was glaring arrows and spears at Colin. "It won't matter if they sing anything at all, since nobody watching the picture will be able to hear them."

"That's not the point."

"Oh."

A frenzy of resentment overtook him. He put his hands on the table and leaned over until he was nearly face-to-face with Brenda. "And I don't know why you're blaming me for this fiasco. It isn't my fault George ran away from school. And it isn't my fault that I think he was wrong to do so without consulting our parents first. I'm not the villain in this piece." Deciding with some satisfaction that this was as good an exit line as he'd be likely to come up with under the circumstances, he turned on his heel and marched out of the restaurant.

His heart was pumping like a piston, his nerves were skipping like children playing hopscotch, his blood felt as close to boiling as it ever had, and he wanted to break something. Preferably George's neck. Or Brenda's.

He absolutely hated to acknowledge that he'd much rather be making mad, passionate love to Brenda than doing either of the above.

Brenda watched him stalk away from her and wondered what had possessed her to attack him like that. It wasn't her business if George and Colin were having problems with each other. And really, if she looked at the situation calmly, she agreed with Colin. George's action had been cowardly.

Of course, he was very young.

Then again, she herself had been even younger when she'd begun supporting her family. Colin was right about that, too.

But the circumstances had been so different. George had been brought up with, if not wealth, then at least comfort. Brenda's family had never been comfortable. They'd always existed on the slim, perilous edge separating survival from starvation. In an odd and hideously ironic blow of fate, her family had been better off without her father than with him.

That sounded unfair and cruel, although Brenda didn't

mean it as such. She'd had to be intensely practical almost from infancy, and old habits died hard. Financial circumstances weren't the only important aspects of life. She sighed heavily.

She, better than most people, understood that when people intoned in their superior, preacherly voices that money didn't matter, it was because they had plenty of it. And they were right. If one had money, it didn't matter a rap. If one didn't have money, it mattered almost more than anything else in life.

Darn it, why was she being so gloomy this morning? Because she'd quarreled with Colin was why, and she knew it. Blast her ready tongue.

She ate her orange in a moody silence, wishing she could replay her last scene with him. She'd hold back her sarcastic opinions if she had it to do over again. It would have been far more reasonable of her to have asked Colin civilly what had brought George to California. If she'd done so, he might even have allowed her to help him deal with his brother.

Fat chance of that now. She'd attacked, he'd parried, and they'd been at each other's throats in an instant. Whatever was it that made Colin and her rub against each other so irritatingly and so constantly? They caught fire like a match to dry kindling every time they spoke to each other. She didn't understand it. She'd never, ever had trouble getting along with people before she met him. She could get along with people she hated, for heaven's sake, and she didn't hate Colin. Far from it.

Unfortunately, real life, unlike life as portrayed in the pictures, didn't allow for second takes. She smiled grimly, recollecting Martin's always-present ambition to capture every scene in one take.

With another hearty sigh, she sipped the last of her tea and recalled her first meeting with Colin. She'd had such high hopes for a relationship between them. There seemed perishingly little chance of that now. She wouldn't blame him if he didn't even want to tell her about Indians any longer.

On that depressing thought, she left the restaurant and ambled outdoors to watch the filming, which was again taking place outside the lodge in the huge clearing that formed the lodge's yard. As she stopped in front of the lodge doors and peered around, Brenda wondered how much forest had been cut down to accommodate the human beings who chose to take holidays on this spot. Had birds and animals been displaced? Lost their homes? Died from having their sources of food eliminated?

Good God, she was getting positively morbid. Instead of thinking about dead deer and birds, she ought to be marveling at the beauty spread out before her. It took a little effort, but she dragged her mood out of the swamp of misery in which it seemed inclined to wallow and concentrated on the magnificence of her surroundings.

There was a whole bunch of beauty around here, and no mistake. She'd always loved the mountains. She used to perform in the Catskills sometimes, and in the Adirondacks, at various hotels and lodges. She'd loved the life available to her there: long walks in the woods, swims in the lakes, boating, fishing, even doing nothing but staring at the blue, blue sky and making animals out of the clouds. She smiled slightly, remembering. She'd been allowed very little of that sort of relaxation in her life, as she'd been working constantly for years.

Not that she regretted a single instant of the life she'd been forced to live. It had saved her family, it had saved her, and it was, therefore, a blessing. Brenda knew that far too many people perished when their lives were visited with the type of tragedy that had hit her family. She was fortunate. She was blessed.

Why the deuce wasn't she happy, today of all days, when the sun shone, the birds chirped, the squirrels chattered, she was making tons of money, and her family's welfare had been secured for as long as any of them lived? Bother. Human nature was so illogical and perverse sometimes. With a parting slap on the paneling of the lodge doors, she quickened her pace, descended the steps, and walked out to see what was going on with the filming of *Indian Love Song*.

The first person she saw when she walked onto the area marked off for the Peerless set was Colin. Funny how her eyes seemed drawn to him, not unlike steel shavings to a magnet, no matter how mad at each other they were.

Actually, it wasn't funny at all.

Colin and Martin were deep in a discussion. Brenda was pleased to note that neither man appeared angry or frustrated. That must signify that Colin approved of whatever was going on in the Indian village. A miracle in itself. She decided not to join them; she didn't want Martin to be hit by shrapnel from any ammunition she and Colin might shoot at each other.

Instead, she glanced around the clearing until she spotted George. He was looking small and alone, perched on a stump close to the forest. She sensed he was trying to disappear while, at the same time, absorb everything he saw. She walked over to him and smiled.

He'd been engrossed in watching the cameramen set up their machines and the set designers tweaking tipis and fire logs into proper position, and so forth. When he saw her, he jumped a little. Brenda stifled a sigh. Sometimes she wished she could be simply another person on earth, instead of a "star." On the other hand, if she were that, her family would be in much worse shape than it was. She guessed she'd take things the way they were.

"Oh! Good morning, Miss Fitzpatrick." He flushed. "I mean, Brenda."

She imagined her smile growing more tender, because

that's how she felt. With a quick fluff of her skirts, she sat on the stump next to George's. "Good morning, George. It's interesting to watch the moviemaking process, isn't it?"

"It sure is." He sounded faintly wistful.

She decided to take a chance and plunge in. What the heck? She'd never minded her own business before. Why start now? "Is that why you came to California? To see if you could get a job in pictures?"

He glanced at her, and his flush deepened. George's complexion echoed Colin's, but George wasn't as swarthy as his brother, evidently because he hadn't spent so much time outdoors. Colin must have lived under Arizona's blazing territorial sun for months and months. Small wonder he looked rather like a pirate—until one got to know him. Then one realized he was nothing like a pirate. There was nothing of the swashbuckler in him. Instead of swashing and buckling, Colin read and learned. And fussed. Brenda sighed aloud this time.

"Um, I'd sort of thought about getting work in pictures," George admitted, sounding as uneasy as he looked. "Colin thinks I'm being silly."

Brenda didn't turn to watch him because she didn't want to cause him any more embarrassment than she could tell he already felt. "Were you considering acting?"

She hoped he wasn't; most of the actors she knew were either star-blinded fools or merely mad for attention. Her case was so different, she felt guilty sometimes for having achieved her level of success.

He cleared his throat. She could tell he was terribly nervous. "Er, no. Actually, I had hoped to get in on the production side of the industry."

The production side? He sounded very mature about his ambition. It surprised her, because she'd gathered from what Colin had told her that George's trip to California had been impetuous and thoughtless. She slid a glance his way. "What do you mean?"

He flipped a hand in the air as if his meaning was as irrelevant as his ambition. Brenda's heart squeezed for him, because she knew his own ambition wasn't irrelevant at all, but only different from his family's ambition for him.

"Oh," he said in a muffled voice, "I'd gotten the notion that I might work as a set designer or something." He glanced at her, as if expecting to see contempt on her face. "I suppose that's probably pretty stupid, isn't it?"

"No," she said simply. He jumped again, as if the one word had been so unexpected as to have shocked him. Poor George. She went on, "Set designers are in great demand nowadays." She gestured at the Peerless set. "This set is much simpler than most, because of the nature of the picture. But, you know, George, Peerless is planning to shoot *Cleopatra* pretty soon, and they're going to need magnificent sets for that. And there are lots of other pictures that require complicated sets. Good set designers are hard to find. You could do a lot worse. And it wouldn't hurt to see if you could get hired by one of the studios."

"Really?" His eyes were huge. They were almost as pretty as Colin's, but they didn't move Brenda as Colin's did. She considered this a very bad sign.

"Really." She decided it would be best not to think about Colin's eyes. They watched the set preparations in silence for a few moments. Then, curious, Brenda asked, "Have you read anything about the pictures, George?"

He sat up straighter. "Oh, yes. I've read everything I could get my hands on. Not about the acting part," he hastened to assure her, as if he considered acting on a par with street sweeping. "I've read about the cameras they use and the methods of set design and construction. I—" He stopped speaking suddenly.

Brenda decided to overlook the slur against actors because she knew he hadn't meant it to be disparaging. He was probably speaking to her as he might have spoken to Colin, had Colin not slammed the door on conversation. "You what?" She smiled again, making sure it was a sweet, encouraging smile this time. She saw him gulp.

He lowered his gaze and lifted his shoulders until his head was almost lost in a hunch of unhappiness. "I, ah, am an artist. Of sorts. That is to say, I like working in art better than anything else. I like to draw and paint." He sounded as if the admission shamed him.

"That's wonderful, George. I've always envied people who could create things on paper and out of clay and marble and stuff like that. I've got ten thumbs. Can't draw a straight line with a ruler." She spoke lightly.

His head jerked up and he stared at her. "Wonderful? Ha." Now he sounded bitter. "When I told Colin about it, you'd have thought I'd confessed to having taken to theft and murder."

She laughed. "I can imagine. Colin isn't vastly interested in anything outside his very narrow field of study, is he?"

"He—"

George stopped speaking and swallowed again. Brenda sensed there was a tremendous war being waged inside him and didn't speak, hoping he'd blurt out what he'd been going to say.

"Actually," he said after a moment of struggle, "he knows just about everything about everything. His interests are vast."

"They are?"

George nodded. "Oh, yes." A faint smile touched his lips.

Brenda was intrigued. "I must say I'm surprised. I thought he'd gotten mired in Indians and never looked at anything else." Prior conversations with Colin started knocking at her brain's door, and she perceived it was she who'd become mired. Colin had imparted fascinating tidbits of information about any number of things, now that she allowed herself to recall them.

"Oh, no." George sat up straighter. "I remember when I was growing up—Colin's thirteen years older than I am, you see, and he used to take care of me quite often—why, he used to take me everywhere. It was a lot of fun."

"Really?" Her amazement must have been clear, because George blushed again.

"He's really not as bad as he acts most of the time. Honest. He's only—passionate, I guess is the right word." George heaved a large sigh. "He was great to me when I was growing up, although he tried to steer me away from art. I didn't mind. I was so glad he took an interest in me, and he's so darned smart, and he was so good to me." He seemed to run out of words with which to express his mixed feelings about his older brother.

A little of the fog began to dissipate from Brenda's mind. "Is that why you chose to come to California when you left school, George? Because you thought Colin would be more understanding than the rest of your family?" She saw his eyes widen in horror, guessed the reason, and hastened to say, "I'm sorry. I'm afraid I'm a terribly snoopy goose. I asked Colin why he was so upset about your appearance—and he told me. I'm sure he wouldn't have if he hadn't been so surprised."

"I see." George's words came stiffly, and he sounded so much like his older brother that Brenda couldn't hold in her laugh.

"I'm not at all appalled by your actions, George, so you needn't think I'm going to lecture you."

His shoulders relaxed slightly.

"Although," she temporized, because she felt she should, "I do think you ought to call your parents and tell them where you are. They'll be panic-stricken if the school makes contact with them and they don't know where you are."

He picked up a twig and threw it into the trees. "You're right, of course," he said dispiritedly. "I suppose there's a telephone in the lodge. I guess I can place a long-distance call from there."

"Sure you can. You'll have to go through the long-distance operator. Peerless always makes sure there's telephone communication available, no matter where they're filming."

"I'll try to place a call tonight." He sounded glum.

Brenda felt better about him now that she knew he'd actually studied the profession he wanted to become a part of and wasn't merely a starry-eyed kid. George had aroused her sympathy and she wanted to help him. "Why don't you let me talk to Martin about you? I have no idea what tests prospective set designers are put to before Peerless hires them, but I'm sure he can tell you."

Again, his eyes opened wide. "You mean, you think I'm not an idiot for wanting to try to make a career in the motion pictures?" He sounded perfectly astounded.

"An idiot? Good heavens, no! The industry is growing like a patch of mushrooms these days. They're going to need more and more talented people to do the work. You might as well be one of them. I'm sure it would be more fun to earn a living doing something you like than something you merely tolerate. Or something you outright hate." With a pang, she remembered her mother, who'd taken in laundry before her husband died. Thank God those days were over for good.

He blinked, as if he'd never heard another human being express his own inner thoughts out loud—and casually, at that, as if there was nothing innately wrong with his desires. She grinned, knowing full well what he was thinking. Laying a hand on his shoulder, she said, "Don't worry, George. Not everyone in the world thinks academia is the only life worth living."

She thought it might be, but that was not the point at present.

"Thank you," he said humbly. "I can't tell you how much I appreciate this."

"You just did." She left him with a wink that made his mouth drop open.

Men. They were all alike. Except Colin, damn him.

Twelve

"You *what?*" Colin's fury rose like the mercury in a thermometer on a hot day.

Brenda appeared as cool and collected as ever; as if she hadn't just proved herself to be an interfering meddler, a pest, a bother, and a detriment to humankind. "I said," she said, and there was a distinct chill in her voice, "I persuaded Martin to take your brother on as sort of an apprentice."

"I swear, I can't believe anybody—" He didn't finish the sentence, mainly because he didn't know what to say. He was angry. Irate. Furious. He wanted to thump George until he was nothing but a pasty lump. Then he wanted to hurl him off the mountain. Then he wanted to jump up and down and stamp his feet and holler and yell and rip things up and use that damned baseball bat of Jerry Begay's to smash all the windows in the lodge.

"Fiddlesticks," said Brenda, as if he weren't standing there seething like a volcano ready to erupt. "George came out here to work in the pictures, and I just got him a job. I should think you'd thank me instead of pitching one of your fits."

"I'm not pitching a fit!" Colin roared at a fitful pitch. "I'm—I'm—"

Dash it, he was jealous. Of his younger brother. Good

God. This was the most damnable thing that had ever happened to him.

"You're what?" Brenda asked, clipping the words very short.

Not in a million years would Colin admit to being jealous of George. He was humiliated internally by his reaction to Brenda's interest in George; he'd be flayed alive before he'd admit his condition to anyone else. "I'm astounded that you should take such a responsibility upon yourself." Which was a lie. Nothing Brenda did could astound him anymore. "Don't you believe you overstepped the bounds of propriety at all? Or don't you know what they are?"

He saw her face drain of color, and then two hectic red patches bloom on her cheeks. He mentally punched himself in the jaw for being a boor, much as he wanted to punch George for not being a scientist.

"No," she said frigidly. "I do not believe I stepped over the bounds of propriety. And yes, I do know what they are."

She wheeled around as if she couldn't bear to be in his company for another second longer. Colin's insides cried out to her not to go, that he couldn't stand her absence, although he wouldn't have said so aloud if he'd been granted the privilege to study in all the libraries in the universe and all the time in the universe to do it. He might be a fool, but he had his pride, for whatever good it was to him.

She must have heard his insides pleading, because she turned around again as precipitately as she'd done the first time. "Anyhow, I don't know why you're so all-fired mad at me! *You* sure didn't look as if you were going to do anything for poor George." New York had seeped into her voice with a vengeance. Colin guessed it did that when she was mad.

"Poor George," Colin mimicked. "Poor George ran

away from college like a silly half-witted schoolboy afraid of the dark without mentioning his intentions to anyone, much less our parents—who are, might I remind you, the people footing the bill for his flightiness."

"I know." Her lips tightened. "And I agree he should have consulted your parents before making the break, but—"

"But what? What justification can you come up with for that sort of behavior?" He managed a fairly decent sneer. "And you said you understood the bounds of propriety."

The angry color in her cheeks deepened. If she'd ever looked ravishable—and she did, more's the pity—she looked a hundred times more so now. Colin could scarcely keep his fists bunched at his sides. They wanted to unclench and reach for her. In fact, he had an irrational impulse to grab her in his arms, throw her up on a horse, and make off with her.

Lord, what was the matter with him? He'd never harbored fantasies about knight errantry when he was a boy. Why had he started doing it now, as an adult?

"I do not justify George's behavior," Brenda said, and Colin could tell her teeth were clenched. "I think he behaved very badly, in fact."

"But you're rewarding him by getting him a job? Is that logical? Is it appropriate? Or is it the work of a meddling busybody?"

"Damn you, Colin Peters!"

Her voice had risen, and Colin saw several people on the set turn to look at them. He said with satisfaction, "You're calling attention to yourself. I'm sure that's only natural for you, given your profession, but it isn't for me, and I'd appreciate it if you'd keep your voice down."

If looks could kill, Colin knew he'd be dead, probably skewered on a spit and roasted over a slow fire for maximum torture value.

"Very well, I'll keep my voice down, darn you. And the answer to your question is, I'm not rewarding George. I'm trying to help him. The poor boy didn't think he had any options left. It's apparent to me, if not to you, that your parents wouldn't have understood his wishes in the matter of employment. He thought you might. Obviously, he was wrong. He misjudged you, believing you might have some human feelings lurking somewhere inside that cold, fishy exterior of yours. Ha!"

She uttered the last syllable in a tone of absolute contempt. It made Colin's innards flush—and maybe his outers, too, although he couldn't see his face to tell for sure. "That's absurd." He knew it was inadequate, mainly because he believed Brenda's assessment of his parents' attitude, and his own, was accurate. He might even have felt a little ashamed of himself if he weren't so angry.

"It's not nonsense and you know it. Unfortunately, George didn't discover how mistaken he was in you until he'd traveled all the way to California. I feel sorry for him. It must be awful to have a family that doesn't care for one."

"We do, too, care!"

"Ha!"

There it was again, that one syllable that made Colin feel like a crawling worm.

"Brenda!"

Martin's voice made them both freeze. Brenda turned and forced a smile. Colin knew it was forced because he saw her struggle to produce it. There was no doubt about it: She was a consummate actress.

She waved at Martin. "I'm here! Do you need me for the scene? I have to change." She still wore the lovely lilac silk.

Colin didn't want her to take it off—unless he could help her do it.

God almighty, he was becoming a lost cause.

"No, not yet," Martin called. He was smiling up a storm and looking as cheerful as anything. Colin envied Martin his steady disposition. "I just wanted to thank you for telling me about George. He's doing a great job already!"

"Good!" She beamed in earnest this time. "I'm so glad!"

Martin and George, who waved and also looked happy, blast his irresponsible soul to perdition, turned back to the set. Colin had no idea what they were doing together, but whatever it was entailed a good deal of pointing and twiddling with various stage properties.

"There," Brenda said with a superior smirk for Colin. "I told you so. George is a talented young man, and if he doesn't want to go to college, there's plenty of work for him to do right here in California. In the pictures. And, what's more, he's smart to get in at the beginning. Pretty soon, everybody who works here will probably need a zillion college degrees, just like you have. Then we'll all be just as dull and impossible to get along with as you are. And I, for one, am glad I'll be retired by then."

She even went so far as to poke him in the chest with her forefinger. It hurt, too. If Colin had been a trace less inhibited, or perhaps if he'd read *The Adventures of Robin Hood* as a lad instead of that umpteenth chemistry book, he might have grabbed her wrist and pulled her into his arms. Instead, he could only watch as she wheeled around and marched away from him. He couldn't recall the last time he'd been this depressed.

It would serve him right if Brenda and George ran away together and got married. He slumped off to a nearby chair and sat himself down, glad nobody needed him for the moment.

* * *

Darn and blast and double heck. Brenda stalked to the lodge's porch, stamped up the stairs, marched over to a roomy wooden deck chair, and sat in a fluff of lilac silk. She couldn't remember ever being so frustrated and furious as she was after this latest row with Colin. And all because she'd been kind to his brother.

All right, so the kid had misbehaved. "I suppose you never did anything wrong, Mr. High-and-Mighty, Education-Is-the-Only-Proper-Course-in-Life, Peters," she muttered savagely. Then she decided he probably hadn't ever done anything wrong. Doing wrong had unquestionably never even occurred to him, the pickled shrimp.

Perhaps not shrimp. He was a fairly large man. Really quite large. At least six feet tall. Probably more. And very wellbuilt, actually. Darn it. It wasn't fair that he should look so good, since he was such a raging pill.

"So I don't know what the bounds of propriety are, do I?" she grumbled. "I'm an interfering busybody, am I?" She picked up a fallen pine cone and heaved it at a tall tree next to the porch. A frightened blue jay bolted out of the tree as if it had been shot from a gun.

"I'm sorry, bird." Brenda sat glowering as a blue feather drifted to earth beneath the tree. When it floated out of her range of vision, she growled, "So I rewarded him for misbehaving, did I?

"Bah!" She kicked at a post holding up the porch railing. A squirrel scolded her sharply from a tree limb. "I did no such thing! I helped the kid see what working in the pictures might be like. At least he'll know now if he wants to pursue the business or not. What's wrong with that, I'd like to know?"

She wanted to race back over to Colin and slap him silly.

No, she wanted to kick him.

No, what she wanted to do was screech at him for several hours.

She sank her head into her cupped hands and confessed to herself that what she truly felt like doing was sitting down in a quiet corner somewhere and crying. Being forever in the public's eyes had amazing disadvantages, especially when one was feeling blue. And Brenda felt exceptionally blue right now.

Where was her sunny nature when she needed it? Why should a stodgy old scholar, of all silly things, make her want to burst into tears and drum her heels on the floor?

Because she wanted him to like her is why, and he didn't. She felt very foolish when she confessed the truth to herself. Why should it matter to her if Colin Peters liked her or not?

Because she both craved the information he could impart to her and also lusted after him was why, and she knew it.

Good heavens. She'd never lusted after a man in her life. Why couldn't she have picked someone else to start with? Someone nicer and more approachable?

But no. She had to go and pick Colin Peters, who despised her.

"Bother!" There was no accounting for human nature, as she well knew. Since she didn't want to sink into a black decline, she picked herself up from her chair and decided to meander back to the set. She'd have plenty of time to change into her Indian-maiden costume later, since they still hadn't finished with the Indians-in-the-village scene.

Jerry Begay and his band were all painted up and feathered to within an inch of their lives. They were at present dancing around a roaring fire. She wondered what fault Colin would find with that scene but forced herself not to look for him. Darn him, he could just disapprove on his own.

"Hi, Brenda."

She turned to discover George had walked up and now

stood beside her. It was an effort, but she managed a smile for him. "Hi there, George. Did Martin teach you anything?"

"Oh, yes!" George practically quivered with excitement and elation. "Brenda, I don't even know how to begin to thank you for helping me like this. I never expected—I don't deserve—I don't know—"

She laid a hand on his arm to stop him before he became hopelessly tangled up in words. "Don't thank me, George. I'm sure Martin needs you or he'd have told you he didn't. He's not a man to equivocate. If he says you're going to be good at this, you will be. Trust me; Martin knows this business backwards and forwards, and it's too important to him to allow him to fib about something like that. He's a professional, in every sense of the word."

George glowed so fiercely, Brenda feared he might catch fire. He was awfully cute. Funny, that. He looked a lot like Colin, but Colin couldn't have looked cute if he'd tried. He could look dangerous. He could look supercilious. He could look angry or fussy or seductive.

Seductive? Good heavens, where had that come from?

Oh, well. Colin could look a whole lot of things, but Brenda couldn't even imagine him looking cute. Blast him.

She wanted to burst into tears and run away and hide. Instead, she smiled at George some more.

"Well, I still want to thank you," George told her, his cheeks burning like hot coals. "I—I—nobody's ever done anything like this for me before."

Of course not. Before this, George was a baby. Brenda didn't remind him of his relative youth. "Nonsense. I was glad to help." The good Lord knows, George's brother would never help him. She let go of a sniff of indignation before she could stop herself.

"Whatever you say, it was swell of you, and I won't forget it." George sounded as if he was trying to appear mature and sophisticated. He spoiled the image by dragging his toe in the dirt at his feet, thrusting his hands into his jacket pockets, and saying shyly, "And I'm sorry I didn't tell my folks I was leaving college. Colin's right about that. I should have."

"Your brother," Brenda said heatedly, "ought to be horsewhipped."

George's eyes popped open. "Beg pardon?"

She drew in a deep breath and released it slowly, irked with herself for disparaging George's brother to George. That was underhanded and dirty, and Brenda was ashamed of herself for succumbing to so base an urge. No matter what the provocation, it was beneath her to belittle Colin to George. No matter how much he deserved it, the rat.

"How did it go, George?"

Brenda almost jumped out of her skin when Colin's warm breath caressed the back of her neck and his voice sounded clear as a bell in her ear. She leaped a foot and turned to find him standing no more than an inch away from her. She gave him as good a glower as she could come up with, when she wanted to turn into his arms and beg him to forgive her for her hot tongue. Not that he didn't need forgiving for his, too, the miserable cad.

"H'lo, Colin." George looked uncomfortable. Small wonder. Brenda kept her mouth shut. "Um, it went pretty well." He took in about a bushel of air. "Actually, it went very well. Martin's a great gun."

"I'm glad."

Colin was glad? Brenda squinted at him, trying to detect any hint of scorn or disapproval or doubt. She didn't.

"That's a change of tune, coming from you, isn't it?" she asked coldly. When she saw George's raised eyebrows and confused expression, she regretted her sarcasm.

Colin peered down at her, his beautiful brown eyes reminding her of something hot and hazardous. She, the most self-assured and unflappable person she knew, couldn't hold his gaze and angled her head to stare into the trees. Why was she turning coward at this odd moment?

"Yes, it is," he said after staring her out of countenance.

Blast the man, why was he always changing on her this way? You'd think he was a chameleon instead of a stodgy old stick of a highbrow professor. She felt her body tingle at his hot glance, from her toes to the top of her head. Her nipples puckered and her mouth went dry, and she could happily have smacked his handsome face. "I'm glad of that, at all odds," she said at length, trying to sound cool and aloof.

"Me, too," said George. His voice was soft, as if he couldn't quite figure out what was going on between Colin and Brenda. Which didn't surprise Brenda in the least. She couldn't figure it out, either.

Colin turned from Brenda to George. Thank God, thank God.

"I'm sorry for the reception I gave you, George. I was surprised to see you. When you told me you'd dropped out of school without telling a soul, the first thing I did was get mad. I should have listened first and then got mad." He smiled the most charming smile Brenda had ever seen on his lips.

George's eyes grew round with incomprehension and shock, and he gulped audibly. "I—ah—I should have written or telephoned or something. I, er, don't blame you for being mad at me."

This was getting pretty sticky for Brenda, who was unused to being involved in other families' confessionals. "I think I'd better change for my next scene," she said abruptly. "I'm glad you two are talking again."

Fiddle, should she have said that? Too late to call it back now. She hurried off, glancing over her shoulder to see the two Peters brothers staring after her, George smiling, Colin with an expression on his face she'd never seen before, and which made her blood race.

Mercy and goodness, whatever did this mean?

The last scene with the Navajos went well. Brenda was pleased, although she felt slightly ridiculous the entire time the cameras cranked. She knew good and well that, while blond sausage curls were all the rage these days in the pictures, they were pretty silly if anyone involved with *Indian Love Song* wanted to be taken seriously.

Which, of course, they didn't, or they'd have had her filmed with dirty, straggly hair and smudged cheeks. Brenda knew, if the Peerless folks didn't, that it took many hours and a lot of skill to create her hairstyle. No woman could achieve the effect if she'd been captured by savages and set to work as a slave for them. She was surprised Colin hadn't already interrupted the filming with several thousand grouchy words on the subject.

But Colin didn't say a solitary thing. He only watched the scene being filmed from under a tree several yards away. He seemed different suddenly. No longer did he stand as stiff as a poker and glare with disapproval at everything. Instead, he looked as nearly casual as Brenda imagined he could look. He leaned against that tall fir tree, his arms crossed over his broad chest, one leg propped against a log, his dark hair ruffled in the spring breeze, looking more like a pirate than ever. He looked as if he might stride across the clearing and claim her as some kind of prize.

It was all new and titillating to Brenda, who didn't understand. What in mercy's name had happened to him? He seemed a totally different person. He seemed—human. Earthy. Approachable. Provocative. Arousing.

Oh, dear. Whatever had wrought this change in him, it

was probably a very bad thing for her. Almost, she wished for the old Colin back. That one was safe. This one was— dangerous.

"I don't remember if I'm supposed to hit you now or wait until you drop the bucket."

Jerry's words startled Brenda, and she realized it was the first time in her entire career that she'd allowed her mind to wander when she was supposed to be working. She glanced at him, holding her bucket close to her chest and feigning fear. Jerry was doing a great job. He looked as savage as a quiet man like him could look. "Um, I don't think it matters. You can hit me before and after, if you want to look really mean."

"Sure. Why not?" Jerry gave her a hideous scowl and swung at her, missing by the proverbial mile.

"Great!" Martin called from the sidelines. "Wonderful expressions, you two. Be sure you get close enough to make it believable, Jerry. Brenda, you were great! The way you staggered was superb!"

Superb, was it? Well, good. She dropped the bucket she'd been carrying and cowered away from Jerry, who walked up to her like a panther stalking its prey and let fly with another open-handed swing. Brenda jerked her head sideways, as if his hand had hurt her cheek when it hit, and cried out in mock pain. She pretended to stumble and fall next to her bucket.

"Jeeze, did I hurt you?" Jerry sounded horrified.

It was all Brenda could do not to laugh. Bless Jerry Begay for taking her mind away from Colin. "Good heavens, no, Jerry. I'm acting."

"Good. Jeeze, you scared me." No one would have known it, since his expression didn't alter.

Neither did Brenda's. She lifted her arm as if to ward off another blow and continued to cower pitifully. "Want to have one last baseball game this afternoon?" she asked suddenly, the thought having just occurred to her. "You

guys have to leave tomorrow, and it'd be fun to play another game." That would distract her mind from Colin,
too. The more things she could find to fill her day and
her thoughts, the better. Especially if they didn't involve
Colin. She knew he didn't like to play games.

"Sure. Sounds good to me." Jerry reached down and
clamped a hand on her arm as if he aimed to heave her
into a fire.

"Wonderful!" Martin yelled from the sidelines. "You
two are perfect!"

Brenda pretended to stagger to her feet, her face con-
torted as if she were in awful pain. "Great. As soon as
this scene's done, I'll get the teams organized." She'd play
this time, and not simply serve as manager and umpire.
That would wear her out and keep her mind occupied at
the same time. She felt better about life at once.

"That'll be fun." This time Jerry pretended to shove
her hard, and she pretended to stumble and sprawl on the
ground once more.

"Perfect! Wonderful! You two are doing a superb job!
The public is going to love this one!"

Martin's enthusiasm tickled Brenda. She pretended to
flounder in the dust for a moment or two, picked up her
fallen bucket, gazed up at Jerry in terror, and crept to her
feet as if the spirit had been beaten out of her.

Poor Jerry. It really wasn't fair that he and his people
should be portrayed as such barbarous fiends when they
were only people, like everybody else in the world. But
this was what the public craved, she supposed, and this
was how she earned her keep, so she'd do it. And Jerry'd
do it. And the misconceptions about Indians would grow
and become entrenched in the public's mind as moviemakers continued to crank out these silly pictures.

She was depressing herself again. What was wrong
with her today? She caught sight of Colin, leaning against

that tree and gazing at her like a satyr about to pounce on a nubile virgin, and she sighed.

Oh, yes. She remembered now. *That's* what was wrong with her.

Colin noticed that Brenda had sent Jerry over to ask him if he wanted to join in the baseball game and grinned to himself. She hadn't come to ask him herself.

It was working. His act was working. Maybe acting wasn't such a nonsensical pastime after all.

Not that it was entirely an act. The truth had struck him shortly after she'd stormed away from him earlier in the day, and he'd been nearly knocked cockeyed by it. He shouldn't have been. After all, he, above most men, should have recognized what was happening.

He and Brenda were performing a mating ritual! He'd initially believed it was only she who was doing the dance, but he'd been wrong. They both were. That was why they struck sparks off each other every time they talked. Only the mating game in human beings was more complicated than it was for other species. Colin wasn't a naturalist, as his parents had wanted George to be, but he knew a little bit about almost everything, and he'd studied biology.

For instance, if he and Brenda were dogs, he and she would have started out by sniffing each other, and would have mated by this time. If they were birds, he'd have strutted and preened and fluffed his fine feathers in front of her, she'd have pretended indifference, and they'd have mated by this time. If they were cats, he'd have been howling under her window and had boots thrown at him by the other lodge visitors—and they'd still have mated by this time.

But they were human beings, and human beings weren't so simple, dash it. Human beings seldom really knew what they were doing as they performed this particular rite, preferring to think of mating as something other than a natural act, and one that required thought. Which was probably a good thing, or folks would be copulating all over the place—and with perfect strangers half the time. That was no way for the world to run.

However, he lusted for Brenda. She might lust for him or she might not, but he had a notion that she did. Otherwise, why should he upset her so? It sounded like biology at work to him, and he'd made up his mind to give in to it. Why should he be the only male animal not to achieve satisfaction of a sexual nature when the call was so loud? Dash it, he was a normal, virile male.

And Brenda was an actress.

Actresses were loose women, weren't they? Not that Brenda seemed particularly loose, but she probably was. They all were. Weren't they?

For some reason, the thought of Brenda being a loose woman who would mate with any old male who came into view and sniffed around her didn't sit well with him. He figured he was only being silly. Any time Colin got jealous of his brother George, he knew it was time to act. So he was acting.

"What team is Brenda going to play on, or is she going to be manager and umpire again?" He tossed the baseball in the air and caught it, reminding himself of Jerry Begay when he'd first stepped out of the truck several days before. His decision to seduce or be seduced by Brenda had given him an odd sort of confidence, and he discovered himself behaving like any other beer-guzzling, baseball-mad American man. He'd even noticed himself swaggering a few minutes ago. How odd.

"She said she was going to play today," Jerry told him casually.

How could any man be casual around Brenda? It didn't seem possible. "I see. Where's she getting the people to play on the teams? Lots of the extras have already been shipped out."

Jerry, a phlegmatic individual, shrugged. "I dunno. I expect she's using the crew."

"I expect so." Colin saw his brother walking toward him, called out, "George!" and threw the ball at him. It wasn't a very good throw, and he was disappointed. Perhaps this typical American male pose required practice. George caught the ball anyway.

"Are you going to play, Colin?" George looked happy. Colin didn't wonder at that. George was now working in pictures, thanks to Brenda.

"Yes, I'll be playing."

"Good. I don't remember you ever playing baseball when we were kids. You were always hanging out in museums and libraries and stuff like that."

He had to say that, didn't he? Colin didn't frown; he didn't want anyone seeing how much George's comment irked him. Far better to assume superiority. "I suppose I was. How else was I supposed to get my doctorate?"

George sighed. "That's right. You're a doctor now, aren't you? Gee, Colin, I think that's swell. I'd never be able to do that. I'm not smart enough."

Although pleased, Colin wouldn't admit it. "Nonsense. You merely have other interests."

Looking astonished, George blurted out, "Well, yeah, I always thought so. But I never thought you'd admit it."

Dash it, was his little brother determined to make him look a fool? Colin frowned at George. "Don't be silly."

George shrugged.

"All right, everybody, let's form our teams!"

Brenda stood under a sycamore tree, wearing that silly New York Giants baseball cap and looking more beautiful than any woman had a right to look. George trotted over to her, and Colin saw her point to a large pine tree on the other side of the clearing, where Martin and several of the Peerless crew members had already gathered.

So, Colin thought, she's going to play with the Indians. "Where do you want me, Brenda?" He knew where he wanted himself to be, and he gave her a slow, seductive smile to let her know it, too.

She blushed, and Colin was pleased with himself. He'd never acted the dashing rake before. The pose was rather enjoyable. It would be even more enjoyable if it bore fruit. So to speak. He frowned and decided he'd have to use some kind of protection if his plan worked.

"Why don't you play with the Peerless folks, Colin?"

"I'd rather play with the Indians." He'd rather play with her, actually.

She frowned. He got the distinct impression she was trying to put distance between the two of them, and he was reminded of the mating dance of a certain genus of duck. The female duck always played hard to get, even going so far as to nip her prospective mate on the tail—but she always succumbed in the end.

When he'd agreed to work for Peerless this summer, he never figured the job would prove to be so educational.

"Very well," she said, her tone slightly peevish. "Come on."

He grinned to himself as he sauntered over to stand at her side.

Thirteen

"Slide!" Martin bellowed, forgetting for the moment that he was rooting for the wrong team. But Brenda absolutely delighted him, and he wanted her to score. She'd socked a whopper into the trees and then raced like a rabbit around the bases. Now, with her blond hair streaming and her skirt hiked up nearly to her waist, showing an undoubtedly shocking display of pantaloons and petticoats, she was headed for home base.

The cameraman who played left field had found the ball in the woods and, for once, lobbed it in a straight line to the center fielder, Gilbert Drew. Leroy Carruthers, today's pitcher, who probably ought to be distressed that he'd pitched a home-run ball, was shouting and laughing and generally making a spectacle of himself—and nobody cared. They were all having too much fun.

The Navajos, whom Martin had never seen animated at all, had jumped up from their benches, hurried to home base, and were now shouting, rooting for Brenda. Even Colin Peters, much to Martin's amazement, was hollering and cheering. He stood at home plate, too, clapping his hands, encouraging Brenda in to score.

Unless she sped up or slid, though, she'd probably not beat the ball. There was always the chance that George Peters, who was the Peerless Cowboys' catcher, would drop the ball, but he didn't look awfully clumsy to Martin. In fact, the boy had thus far shown himself to be a talented, even a gifted, artist, and Martin was pleased as punch that he'd decided to try for work in the pictures. Peerless could use him, especially with the magnificent epics the studio had planned for future productions.

Even though he wasn't sure he really wanted Brenda to slide, since he didn't want her to scrape her delicate skin, Martin cupped his hands around his mouth and again roared, *"Slide!"*

Brenda, who had grinned at him when she rounded third base—Martin was at present not the director of a picture, but the Cowboys' third baseman—slid. With a glance over her shoulder to see who had the ball, she spotted the Cowboys' second baseman, Herbert Bloom—otherwise Peerless's second cameraman—catch the ball and rush forward to throw it to George.

She shrieked, "Watch out below!" and let herself fly, hands first, arms stretched out in front of her, at home base.

Martin stood motionless, his heart in his throat, as he watched Brenda, blond hair, petticoats, pantaloons, and all, churn up about an acre of dust. He heard the ball slap against George's mitt, and he heard somebody let out an "Ooof," as if whoever it was had been hit in the stomach.

Then there was silence.

And suddenly, over the stillness in the air and the cloud of dust hovering above home plate, the umpire, one of the waiters from the Cedar Crest who'd been roped into service, shrieked in a voice too shrill to hide his elation, "She's safe!"

Both teams erupted into cheers of delight.

"Yee-haw!" hollered Gil, who had played in several cowboy pictures recently

"Hooray!" yelled George.

The Navajos let out with a variety of whoops that might have been frightening if heard under other circumstances.

And then, as abruptly as the noise had started, it ceased. Martin, blinking with surprise, looked around to see what had happened. Then he did, and his mind went blank as his mouth dropped open.

George, stunned, dropped the ball and gaped.

The Cedar Crest's helpful waiter blushed scarlet and turned his back, so as to hide his face.

Gil, standing behind the second baseman and staring, whispered, "Holy smoke."

Leroy Carruthers's eyes nearly popped out of his head.

Jerry Begay took one look at the spectacle, grinned, and turned to rejoin his tribesmen.

Colin Peters and Brenda Fitzpatrick were locked in an embrace that was truly awesome to behold. Martin wished he could capture it on celluloid and show actors how a *real* kiss looked.

Which meant, of course, that it was too awesome for public consumption. Martin trotted to home plate and put on an act. He wasn't an actor as a rule, but he knew how the job was done. He lightly slapped Brenda on the shoulder. "Great job, Brenda! Even though you're on the other team, I'm impressed!"

Colin and Brenda jumped away from each other as if somebody had run an electric current through them. Brenda touched her lips with a very dirty hand and said, "Oh, my!" Colin appeared too rattled to say even that much.

"Good job, everybody!" Martin said hurriedly, not wanting another perilous gap to descend in the conversation. He turned and beamed at the baseball players. "I'll stand drinks for everybody!" He pointed at the lodge with a bat he'd picked up from the ground. "Onward to the bar!"

A consummate professional, Brenda recovered her wits

almost immediately—much sooner than Colin, who still looked as if he'd been conked over the head with a large skillet. "Thanks, Martin!" She looked around eagerly, as if she had nothing at all on her mind but the baseball game. "So, what's the final score?"

"Five to four, Indians," Jerry Begay said. Although he'd always heard Indians were an inscrutable lot, Martin could swear there was a twinkle in Jerry's dark eyes.

"We won!" Brenda's fist shot in the air like a union organizer at an enlistment rally. "Whoo-hoo! We won!" And she threw her arms around Jerry Begay.

Jerry jerked once and looked as if he hadn't expected—or craved—such attention from Brenda, but he managed a fairly creditable hug in return. Then she turned to George and hugged him. George blushed, but even so he didn't look as embarrassed as Jerry. When she released George, she hugged Martin, who hugged her back gladly. She was a great lady, Brenda Fitzpatrick, and a good friend.

She quit then, and Martin could tell from the expressions on various faces that some of the men were glad and some disappointed. He grinned inside. Brenda was a real champ, and she knew how to work an audience.

"I have to go to my room and wash up before I go to any bar," she said with a laugh. "I'm filthy after that slide."

"But you won the game with it," Martin pointed out.

She gave him one of her characteristic winks. "When my director tells me to do something, I do it. You said slide. I slid."

They all laughed—except Colin. Martin saw him watching Brenda as if he wanted to eat her up. His eyes were as hungry as those of a starving wolf. It was another expression Martin wished he could capture on film, so he could use it to show other actors how that special yearning look was achieved. He sighed and clapped Colin on the back. "Come on in, Colin. I'm buying."

With a noticeable shudder, Colin seemed to pull himself together. He only looked a little loopy when he turned to Martin and licked his lips. "What? Oh. A drink. Yes. Sure. Thank you. I'll—I'll be there in a minute." And he took off at a lope for the lodge doors, through which Brenda had just passed.

Martin gazed after him, put his hands on his hips, and sighed. He had absolutely no idea what was going on between those two, but he wished them both the best.

How could she have done such a thing? Brenda, forsaking aplomb for the first time in her twelve-year career, bolted to the lodge, through the massive double doors, across the lobby, and up the stairs, as if pursued by demons. Hell's bells, she didn't even know how that torrid embrace had happened.

The events leading up to it were clear in her mind. She'd decided to slide in no more than a split second, when she'd realized there was no other way to score. Throwing caution to the wind, she'd heaved herself at home base. After that, it was difficult to recall what happened. She vaguely recalled a pair of strong arms reaching through the cloud of dust to grab her hands. She'd held on happily, eager to get out of the dirt. Brenda wasn't enamored of dirt.

And then, all of a sudden, she'd found herself in Colin's arms. Were they the same strong arms that had reached for her? She guessed so. They were certainly the arms that had encircled her once she'd regained her feet.

They'd felt marvelous holding her, too. She sighed deeply when she pushed her hotel-room door open. And that kiss . . .

If Brenda never kissed a man again in this lifetime,

she'd always know she'd been kissed by an expert at least once. The kiss has been—well—perfect. Astonishing. Moving. Exciting. Electrifying, even. She'd never expected a kiss to be so all-consuming. So stunning. None of the men she'd kissed on screen or on stage had stirred her so.

"They were only actors," she reminded herself. "Colin is a man." And what a man. Oh, how she wished she could learn how to reach him.

He'd assuredly reached *her*.

It was probably a mere momentary aberration. Brenda wouldn't allow herself to place too much importance on that kiss. It had been a spur-of-the-moment impulse on Colin's part, at whim, a—

Oh, Lord. It had been magnificent.

Brenda pressed her fingers to her lips, savoring the remains of the sensation. Then she caught sight of herself in the mirror and thought fled. She uttered a tiny scream.

"Good God, I've never seen me look like that!"

She looked like a waif. An orphan tossed upon the shore by a storm-tossed sea. A war refugee. A bum, actually. The glimmering blond sausage curls were no more. Her hair hung in tangled hanks, dull from the dust and dirt of the baseball game. Her gown, a serviceable pink number she'd donned for the sake of the game, was beyond redemption. The ground-in filth would never come out of it. Even if it did, the skirt and bodice both sported big ragged rips. Her underwear showed. Good heavens.

The rest of her was a wreck, too, streaked with sweat and grime. She reminded herself of some of the poor children who lived in the gutters of the Lower East Side in New York City. She was so sorry a specimen that she actually giggled as she took in the full tattered glory of her present self. Wouldn't her fans faint if they could see her now? She'd be great in one of those tear-jerking pictures the public loved so well.

Enough of this. She had to get down to the bar.

First she washed her face and hands. She'd have to take a quick bath before she joined the rest of the crew. Although she was sure no one else would bother to bathe, she valued her image too much to let it teeter now. She'd already lost her composure once today. She'd see to i that such a lapse never occurred again.

After she'd shed her dress, she brushed her hair. Wha a wretched tangle. Most of the dust and pine needles and other junk came out with the tangles, and it didn't look too horrid after a hundred or so strokes of her brush Frowning at the brush, she decided it could stand a good soak after performing yeoman's service.

Because she didn't want to take time to wash her hair she twisted it into a soft knot and pinned it at the top o her head. She'd had so much practice making herself at tractive that even this simple style worked. Brenda ap preciated her basic good looks a lot sometimes, mainly because she didn't have to spend much time enhancing them.

When a knock came at her door, she didn't bother to put on a dressing gown, thinking it was Martin or a bell boy with a message. She only held on to the doorjamb and peered around it into the hall. Her breath left her in a rush when she saw Colin standing there.

He looked as if he, too, had washed, although he hadn' been as dirty as she to begin with. She was the only one who'd slid through the pine needles and earth to score Her mouth went dry and her hands went cold, and she couldn't think of a single word to say to him. She wanted to fling the door wide, hurl herself into his arms, and beg him to have his way with her—which wouldn't do, and she knew it.

Colin had regained some of his composure, Brenda noticed. Out there on the playing field, when Martin had separated the two of them, he'd seemed fairly stunned

Brenda had been completely stunned, for that matter, but she was accustomed to being on display, so she'd been able to gather her wits together and pretend composure more quickly than he.

By this time, however, he'd regained the predatory expression she'd noticed earlier in the day. Oh, dear.

"I came to walk you down to the bar, Brenda." His voice was soft and deep.

Was it sultry, too, or was that her imagination? Oh, Lord, however was she going to hold on to her purity with Colin acting like this? She cleared her throat. "Um, thanks, Colin. I'm not dressed yet."

A very faint, very seductive smile visited his lips. "I don't mind."

His words and his manner jolted her. What did he think she was, anyway? Some kind of floozy? A doxie? A scarlet woman? She was no mere plaything, and the sooner he realized that, the better for them both. With a frown, she said tartly, "Well, I do."

His expression didn't alter. Brenda swallowed. Oh, dear. Maybe the opinion of her she deduced from his attitude was the correct one after all. She sure didn't feel like turning him away with harsh words stinging his ears. Rather, she felt like pulling him into her room and ravishing him.

This was really terrible.

"It's going to take me a little while," she said. "I'm going to take a quick bath."

"I'll be happy to wait."

Good heavens, what should she do now? This decision wasn't nearly as easy to make as whether or not she should slide. After what seemed like a century, she said, "Wait a minute. I have to get a dressing gown on."

That damned eyebrow of his lifted, and she could hear his unspoken opinion that he'd prefer it if she didn't bother with the dressing gown. She bothered anyway, her emotions in turmoil.

She was no frothy bit of goods to be toyed with; to be used and discarded like a two-cent omnibus ticket. She was no member of the chorus who was open to bids. Brenda knew many young women who'd gone into the chorus expressly to be seen and employed by rich men seeking mistresses.

That life wasn't for her. Blast it, she was a moral woman. Not only that, but she had a loving family who would be appalled if she let herself be bought by the highest bidder. The mere thought made her blood run cold. The theater had been wonderful to her, but it was a perilous place. There were pitfalls galore, especially for pretty women. So far, she'd managed to avoid them.

So far, too, she hadn't been tested. Colin was a test, darn him. She said crisply, "Wait just a minute," and shut the door in his face.

Although she half expected him to push the door open and come in before she'd made herself decent, he didn't. She didn't know whether she was disappointed or relieved. Overall, she guessed she'd prefer that he remain a gentleman. Which he did.

After she'd pulled on her blue Chinese silk wrapper and tied it around her, she went back to the door. She was barefoot, which was improper, but there were limits, for heaven's sake.

Opening the door wide, she said, "Come on in. I won't take long."

"Take as much time as you need."

His voice was casual, but his eyes were intense. They were intense at the most relaxed of times, but now, here, in her room, with her practically naked in front of him, their intensity seemed to have an entirely different meaning than was usual for them. Brenda decided she'd best not try to figure out what that meaning was.

"Have a seat," she said, gesturing at the room. She had a very expensive suite, with a small parlor, a bedroom, and a bathroom. "There are lots of magazines and books and stuff. They'll keep you amused while I bathe."

He turned that hot, hot gaze upon her, and Brenda Fitzpatrick, who was about as worldly as a person could be, felt herself blush. Darn. This was awful.

"Thanks," he said. "I'll wait in here if you want me to."

She felt her eyes pop open as his insinuation struck her. Had he expected her to invite him into the bathroom while she bathed? The unmitigated cad. She wished the idea didn't appeal to her so much.

"Yes," she said coolly. "Please wait in here."

He sat with a sigh on the big brocaded sofa stretched in front of the fireplace.

Brenda retreated into the bathroom. She even locked the door. Inside herself she felt a tumble of emotions. She was accustomed to men lusting after her, and she'd learned innumerable ways of dissuading them without earning their enmity.

She'd thought Colin was different. She didn't want him to turn out to be just another sex-crazed man hoping for a brief fling with her. She didn't know why the notion made her want to burst into tears, but it did.

"Golly, girl, you have it bad," she muttered angrily as she dipped her toe into the warm bathwater. She'd dumped in a lot of her favorite orange-blossom scent because she felt so sweaty and dirty.

It was insane of her to want Colin Peters to fall madly in love with her. Why should he? Most men, when confronted by a woman they believed could be easily conquered, thrust notions of love, marriage, and decorum out of their minds and concentrated on sexual conquest alone. The shameless beasts. Brenda soaped her soft-bristled bath brush savagely with her specially made orange-blossom-scented soap and scrubbed her back.

By the time she'd finished washing the crud from her body and scrubbing the dirt from under her fingernails, she was feeling both depressed and furious. She wanted to scratch Colin Peters's eyes out with her newly cleaned nails. She also wanted to cry.

In short, she was a mess.

Something occurred to her, and she sat bolt upright in the tub, all thought of tears vanishing in a flash. She'd forgotten to bring her clothes into the bathroom with her!

She groaned. Now she'd have to parade in front of Colin, who'd been eyeing her like a wolf after a sheep all day long, in only her dressing gown and nothing else. What would he think of her now? She had a pretty darned good idea.

Slapping the water with her bath brush and sending up a wave that dribbled over the side of the tub, Brenda swore softly. "To heck with him. If he tries anything, he'll find out what kind of woman I am."

She only hoped she wasn't wrong about herself.

It was all Colin could do to keep from breaking down the bathroom door and charging inside where he would— What? Rape her?

"Don't be an ass," he advised himself gloomily.

But he was beginning to doubt his animal-mating-ritual scenario. It didn't look to him as if she'd be all that eager to tumble into bed with him any time soon.

He didn't understand her reluctance to follow the call of nature. This was the way the ritual went, wasn't it? The male signaled his intentions and the female, after protesting for a little while, fell into his snare. Procreational activities ensued, and everyone's needs were satisfied. Colin acknowledged that the human species was somewhat more complicated than most mammals, but surely not *that* much.

Brenda, however, was proving difficult. She wasn't playing by the rules. Colin disapproved of her resistance. She probably didn't even *know* the rules.

But that shouldn't matter, dash it. These mating customs were as old as life on earth itself. They were performed by instinct. She shouldn't be able to help herself.

Moodily, he considered himself and Brenda in as unemotional a manner as he was capable. Perhaps there was something about the natural aspects of the ritual he'd failed to grasp.

The female of the species always attempted to select the most worthy object, if there was a choice. There was no obstacle there, surely. He was handsome enough, wasn't he? He was no insipidly preening Leroy Carruthers, perhaps, but he was good-looking. Even manly, which is more than could be said for Carruthers. If what Colin suspected was true, Carruthers was some kind of oddity in the natural world: a member of the species who preferred his own gender.

Colin had no quibbles with nature, however it played itself out. His concern centered around whether or not Brenda should select some other male over himself. He couldn't see why she should, given the number and general caliber of the present group of candidates. It's true that he might be a little on the intellectual side, but that shouldn't be a barrier, since she claimed to seek knowledge.

Maybe he didn't look as if he had enough money to tempt her. He was really quite well-off. All right, he was no Getty or Rockefeller—or Morgan, who had singlehandedly bailed the country out of bankruptcy a few years back.

Still, he could provide her with—with what? She was as rich as God Almighty Himself. What a pity. If she'd been on the needy side, he might have had better luck, but she wasn't needy. And he couldn't buy the diamonds and rubies and other ostentatious rocks he'd heard actresses craved. Slumping on the sofa, he thought about her possible need for money for a minute. Maybe she gave all of her money to her family and didn't keep much for herself. Maybe she'd really like a fellow who could shower her with diamonds and emeralds and so forth.

On the other hand, she didn't wear much jewelry. He'd seen her once in a necklace of pearls that he'd assumed to be genuine. That was the only jewelry he'd seen her wear. Probably some old married goat of a millionaire had given her the pearls. His stomach twisted painfully.

Unless that was his heart.

"Dash it, man, don't be an ass," he advised himself again.

He thought hard for a long time as Brenda, he presumed, was soaking in her bath. He wished he could watch her soak. Maybe help her. His rigid sex gave a tremendous throb, and he groaned.

Dash it, his plan would work. It *had* to work, unless he wanted to die from unfulfilled sexual desire. He only had to give it time. After all, it often took the male duck days to claim his mate. Humans males ought to be able to ply their wiles and wait for at least that long. Humans were the superior species, after all.

The fantasy of a naked Brenda in his bed made Colin's sex throb again alarmingly, and he wasn't sure about that waiting-for-her-to-fall scenario. Waiting was very difficult when the provocation was so great. Brenda was a most alluring female human being. Actually, she was *the* most alluring female human being he'd yet come across.

She was also bright and charming and interested in things and a darned good sport. He recollected her slide into home base with a grin. The girl had grit, all right.

Yet he couldn't allow her good qualities to fog his intentions. If he began thinking of her as an individual personality instead of an object of his sexual mating preference, his designs upon her person might become muddied. If he allowed himself to, for instance, fall in love with her—whatever that idiotic phrase meant—he'd be doomed.

The bathroom door opened, and he sat upright on the sofa. His eyes went round and his mouth fell open. Good God, she was standing there in nothing at all but her gorgeous flesh, pink now from the warm bath, her hair knotted on top of her head, her bare feet sporting ten perfect pink little toes.

Very well, she wore that blue silk wrapper, but it only accentuated the flush of her skin and the incredible blue of her eyes. He knew she was naked under the wrapper, and he knew without knowing how that her body would be spectacular. He gaped at her, speechless.

Brenda didn't notice Colin's state of arousal or his stupefaction. She was too mortified by her idiotic lapse in common sense. Why hadn't she thought to bring clothes into the bathroom with her? It was humiliating to have to parade around in front of him practically naked as she rushed to the closet to fetch clothes to wear down to the bar. She hoped he didn't take her relative nudity in the wrong way.

Whatever could the right way be?

Lord, she had to control herself or she'd be ruined. He provoked the most unnerving yearnings inside her. Every time she'd so much as looked at Colin these past several hours, visions of white picket fences and hordes of charming children swarmed into her head. Not to mention those other, darker visions, of herself and Colin tangled in the sheets of her hotel room, clinging to each other in passionate and embarrassingly intimate embraces.

Mercy. She hoped he'd chalk up the high color in her

cheeks to her recent bath and not embarrassment brought about by her own salacious thoughts.

"I'll be just another little minute, Colin," she tittered, her voice gone high because her throat was tight.

He didn't answer her. Oh, dear, was that because he was shocked by her outrageous boldness? He'd unquestionably heard all the lurid tales concerning actresses being fallen creatures and so forth. Would he believe her to be one of those poor women who threw themselves into the arms of any willing man who was rich enough to buy her favors?

Brenda knew full well that most of the women who allowed themselves to be supported by wealthy men were only suffering from the memory of poverty or its current influence in their lives, and that most of them were only determined never to experience want and deprivation again. The means open to women for achieving security were minuscule, and if a woman chose to sell herself to a rich man in order to lift herself from the gutter, so be it. Brenda was too wise to cast stones. She was only fortunate that she hadn't had to make a decision of that nature. Chance had played an enormous part in her life, and she knew it.

Before she'd left the bathroom, she'd determined exactly what she planned to wear. She didn't want to have to putter around in front of Colin in her dressing gown; that sort of delay might give him doubts about her virtue. She had enough doubts of her own without adding his to the mix.

Therefore, she aimed herself directly at the closet and turned to a powder-blue, scoop-necked pinafore dress and a frilly white lawn blouse, suitable for casual afternoon wear. She'd grab fresh pantaloons and a suitable set of undergarments from the bureau drawer on her way back to the bathroom. She'd plotted her course with intricate care so as to spend as little time as possible alone with Colin in the parlor of her suite.

She'd just taken the blouse and pinafore from their padded hangers when she felt his arms go around her. She uttered a small shriek that withered into a moan of pleasure when she felt his warm breath on her neck.

Fourteen

Colin's hands were big and broad and hard. They closed across her midsection and drew her back against his chest, which was also big and broad and hard. The hardest thing she could discern on his body, however, was his masculine member, which was at present pressing against her hips like an iron rod.

Brenda's brain screamed, *No!*

Her heart whispered, *Yes. Oh, yes.*

It was as she'd always feared. She was no better than she should be, and this was the telling moment. Everything in her cried out for her to turn into Colin's arms and succumb to the lure of his magnificent manliness.

The tattered vestige of sanity still alive in her head told her to slap the cad's face and run.

Lord, what a dilemma.

"You're beautiful, Brenda. You're the most beautiful woman in the world."

Fortunately for her, she'd learned long ago that beauty meant next to nothing in the overall scheme of things except when it came to making a living, and that was only because men were too stupid to value women as they ought. Her sanity made a tentative step toward mending its rips.

She said, "What are you doing, Colin?" She'd aimed

for a stern, icy quality in her tone, but that had been asking too much of her willpower. Her voice merely shook, which wasn't nearly as effective.

"I'm kissing you," Colin answered unnecessarily.

There was nothing whatever wrong with Brenda's nervous system. She could discern without being told that he was kissing her. Which meant her question had been silly. Through the mush in her brain, she tried to compose a sentence that would more nearly get her meaning across.

He took that moment to move his hands only slightly, but the movement was enough so that his thumbs barely pressed the bottoms of her breasts. Brenda feared her bones were melting. Her knees most definitely had lost their steel and were beginning to buckle. With an enormous effort, she stiffened them.

This was terrible. It was awful. It was despicable of Colin to do this to her. It was—it was—

Oh, God, it was wonderful.

No, no, no! She couldn't begin to think that way or she'd be lost for sure. "Colin," she said—she was astonished that her voice held such firmness. "This isn't right."

"Yes, it is."

His voice was a mere rumble, more nearly felt than heard, as it brushed across the skin of her neck. She felt gooseflesh rise all over her body. It took all the power she could command not to let her head drop back and give him better access to the tender flesh of her throat. She wanted to guide him to that little hollow between her ears and her neck that was so sensitive.

Stop it! In that direction lay ruin, and Brenda knew it, even if her emotions and nerve endings had decided to ignore the bitter truth for the nonce.

"Please let me go, Colin," she said softly. She hadn't

intended the command to be soft. She'd wanted it to come out loud and steely.

"I don't want to."

Oh, great. So what was she supposed to do now?

She knew what she wanted to do, and it was scandalous. Recalling all the injustices perpetrated against women in this land of the free and home of the brave, Brenda straightened as much as she was able, with her limbs turned to jelly and her bones to water.

But she knew what was what. This sort of underhanded seduction wasn't fair. It was as old a practice as it was an unfair one. Beastly, lust-crazed men had been perpetrating such methods on love-starved women for as long as the world had been turning. Both genders might appreciate and enjoy the act of love, but women appreciated it as an expression of that love. Men used love to get what they wanted, and that had very little to do with commitment and permanence. Brenda resented it almost as much as she longed to succumb.

"Stop doing that, Colin."

"Don't you like it?"

Fiddlesticks! If that wasn't an unethical question, she didn't know what was. "Liking it has nothing to do with it."

"It has everything to do with it. I need you, Brenda. I need you more than anything else on earth."

Right. Sure, he did. Even in her fuddled state, Brenda knew that was untrue.

Well, perhaps it was true right this minute, but it wouldn't be true as soon as he'd had what he wanted. She'd seen too much misery engendered by just such belief in men's soft lies to fall for that old line. Many's the time she'd comforted a woman who'd been led astray by sugary words murmured by a scoundrel.

"Nonsense." Blast, her voice was quivering again.

His hands covered her breasts, and she nearly lost control completely. She couldn't afford to do that. As surely as she gave herself to Colin—and she dearly wanted to—he'd just as surely begin looking upon her as a wanton hussy, sort of like a piece of candy to be tasted and discarded. If she succumbed to him now, she'd be proving what he assumed about her was true: that she was just like any other actress in the world and was, therefore, no better than a prostitute. She'd never be able to hold her head up again.

Not only that, but she'd be betraying her family. Her mother had told her over and over again that she'd rather starve in a ditch than to learn Brenda had sold herself to some man for her family's sake.

Thinking of her family strengthened her. Although Colin's fingertips were at present setting fire to her body, through the agency of her breasts, which he was caressing, she slapped her own hands over his, grabbed his fingers, and yanked them away from her.

She felt bereft. She also felt justified, and she wasn't about to lose the momentum she'd gained thanks to her mother's wisdom. "Stop that this instant!" she snapped—and she even sounded moderately irate, if a little shaky.

"But—but—"

"No buts!" She jerked away from him. A cold breeze hit her back where his warm body had been, and she shivered. "If you can't behave yourself, Colin Peters, I'm going to have to ask you to leave my room." She considered pointing at the door, but that might have made her dressing gown gape, and she was having a hard enough time rejecting him as it was.

He looked as if she'd hit him with a baseball bat instead of merely refused his advances. His befuddlement rankled, and allowed her to gather her wits together more quickly than she might otherwise have done. She'd have slammed her hand on her hips except for the dressing-gown problem.

"But—" He looked utterly helpless.

Brenda didn't buy it for a second. He was about as helpless as a wasp. Wasps looked pretty enough—sometimes—but they packed a wallop that could fell a sensitive person. While Brenda didn't claim to be the most sensitive female on earth—she'd had to learn how to parry the slings and arrows of outrageous fortune when she was quite young—she retained enough sensitivity to be offended by his evident bewilderment.

So the knave had believed she'd fall for that old you're-the-most-beautiful-woman-in-the-world routine, had he? He'd thought she'd be flattered by his scandalous attentions, had he? He'd believed her to be so lost to virtue that she'd climb into bed with him as soon as he gave the signal, had he?

Well, she'd show him. Now that she was no longer encircled by those maddeningly deceptive arms—deceptive because, while they felt as though they belonged on an athlete, they were on the body of a total scholar—she was beginning to gather herself together. She marched up to him, stopping far enough away so that if he made a swoop, she'd be out of his reach. She didn't trust herself *that* far.

"Get out of this room, Colin. I had believed you to be a gentleman, but I can see now how deceived in you I was."

"Deceived? Deceived?" He both sounded and looked as if he'd never heard the word before.

"Deceived," she said firmly. "I shall go downstairs and join the others as soon as—in a moment." She'd been going to say as soon as she was dressed but didn't want to point out her relative nudity in case he'd forgotten about it. She made the mistake of letting her gaze drop to his trousers and gasped.

He hadn't forgotten. Good God, he was huge. She knew stage actors who liked to parade around in their drawers in order to show off their assets, but she'd never seen anything like this before.

Swallowing, she allowed as to how she might be the slightest bit naive about this man-woman thing, even though she'd been an actress for half her life. She'd heard tales enough, but she'd never actually seen a hard male member before.

What was worse was that she had a compelling and completely illogical, not to mention wicked, desire to see one now. On Colin.

Merciful heavens, this was just awful. She stamped her foot to get her own attention. "I'll be back in a moment. If you can behave yourself, you may remain in my room and escort me downstairs."

She saw him swallow. "I'll behave. I mean—I mean, I'll stay here and wait for you."

"Very well." She grabbed her clothes, rushed to the bureau and snatched out some underwear—she didn't even look to see what she'd chosen—and hurried back to the bathroom. As soon as the door closed behind her, she locked it with a hand that shook as if with palsy, threw her clothes on a dressing table covered with bottles of scent, bowls of dusting powder, and her tooth powder, sank onto the pretty wicker chair with the flowered seat cushion, pressed a hand to her pounding heart, and tried to catch her breath. It took a long time.

Colin was still trying to figure out what had gone wrong with his carefully constructed plan of action when Brenda emerged from the bathroom again, this time covered from head to toe with clothing. Dash it.

She looked as if she'd been born fully clothed, as if she didn't even possess breasts, but only those two slight protuberances on the bodice of her gown. Colin knew better. Not only did she possess breasts, but they weren't slight. They were large and succulent and he wanted to feel them again. And again and again and again. And the rest of her, too.

This was awful.

She stood as straight and stiff as his sex had been only moments earlier, but she appeared much less happy. In fact, she scowled at him in a manner that might have been described as frightful if it had been on the face of any other woman when she said, "I'm ready."

So was he, although he meant something different by the words than she. He sighed. "Allow me, please." He opened the door and stood aside. She sailed out of her room on a cloud of indignation and dignity. Colin saw several damp curls caressing the nape of her neck that must have escaped her brush and hairpins. They made his heart lurch. Not to mention his sex. Grinding his teeth and telling himself to calm down, he followed her.

But the Peerless crowd in the bar was cheerful, Brenda visibly relaxed as soon as she saw them, and Colin decided he might as well join in the fun. Unfortunately, there wasn't anything else more pleasurable to do at the moment.

He'd been sitting with Leroy Carruthers and a member of the Peerless crew when he heard his brother's voice. "H'lo, Colin."

Colin glanced up and saw George smiling at him shyly. Feeling guilty that he should inspire guilt in his own brother, he gestured at an empty chair at his table. "Have a seat, George."

"Thanks." George nodded at Carruthers and the other man and sat. He looked as if he'd as soon the two non-Peters fellows would take themselves off.

Colin wasn't sure he wanted them to go; he feared George wanted to bring up unpleasant subjects and preferred to study the Brenda problem for a while. Since he was accustomed to thinking his own thoughts while in the company of others, he hadn't been having any trouble considering Brenda until George showed up. He sighed and paid attention to his brother, who seemed to be winding up to speak some more.

"I, um, asked the long-distance operator to place a call to Mother and Father, Colin," George said after taking a swig of his drink.

Colin frowned at the mug in George's hand which, he presumed, contained beer. He didn't think George should be drinking an alcoholic beverage at his tender age, although he opted not to mention it. No sense in humiliating his brother again. He'd already made George feel bad enough—and he was sorry for it, too.

George apparently caught Colin's severe glance, because he colored slightly and lifted the mug. "Root beer," he said, embarrassed about it. "I'm not old enough to drink."

Dash it, Colin wished he'd stop making mistakes with people. He hadn't meant to appear so disapproving of his brother. He really wanted to help George, but he kept embarrassing him instead. That was no help. And he was failing completely in his campaign to lure Brenda into a sexual liaison, as well.

This was ridiculous. The laws of nature dictated sexual behavior in various species. Surely he couldn't have strayed so far from the path set out by nature that his instincts no longer worked properly. Could he? It seemed unlikely, although something had definitely gone wrong with his plan of attack.

George said, "Well?" and Colin realized his brother had asked him a question.

It was his turn to flush. "I'm sorry, George. I was thinking over a—a problem—and didn't hear what you asked."

George didn't seem much surprised by Colin's lack of attention. He looked resigned, actually. Colin was ashamed of himself. "I just asked if you wanted to talk to them when the call goes through," George said, fiddling with his glass. "Our parents, I mean."

"Oh. Well—sure. Why not? I don't have any news to report or anything, but I'll talk to them."

"I'm sure they don't care if you have news. They'll be pleased to hear from you. I know they miss you."

"They do?" This was news to Colin, who never communicated with his parents unless he had something of an uplifting or educational quality to report. He didn't communicate with anyone at all merely to blather on about nothing, and he never placed calls over the telephone. He'd been operating under the assumption that, while he enjoyed hearing from his parents, they didn't much care to hear anything but newsworthy incidents from him.

Perhaps he'd been wrong about them, too. Perhaps parents enjoyed hearing from their children simply because they loved them.

Bother. Life could be very complicated sometimes. All of his carefully constructed theories seemed to be going up in smoke before his eyes.

He shot a glance at Brenda, who was playing some sort of lively card game that entailed a lot of slapping of hands on the table and laughing, and he frowned. Up in smoke, hell. His theory about her had been blown sky high. Shaking his head, he decided she was worth constructing another strategy for, although what it might be he had no idea.

"Of course they miss you." George sounded incredulous. "They talk about you all the time. They're awfully proud of you, Colin."

Wrenching his gaze from Brenda, Colin blinked at his brother. "They are?"

George laughed. "Oh, I get it. You're pulling my leg."

Colin had glanced at his brother's long legs before he

realized George had used a figure of speech. "Er, no, George. I'm not pulling your legs."

"Leg," George corrected. "Just one of them." He shook his head, as if in amazement. "I swear, Colin, you really do have your head in the clouds, don't you? I'm surprised you ever come down to commune with us lesser beings here on earth."

"I beg your pardon?" Now it was Colin who was incredulous.

As if he hadn't heard his brother, George went on musingly. "I must admit I was surprised when you agreed to play ball with us today, but you're pretty good at it. Now, if you'd only learn to talk to the rest of us in a language we can understand, you might even turn human one of these days."

Colin didn't know whether to be offended or not, but he had his suspicions. He said crisply, "I am human, for heaven's sake."

"You don't act like it," George muttered. "At least not very often."

"Some people never have any trouble understanding me."

"Brenda." George nodded wisely, which looked kind of silly for a boy his age, even though he was right. "That's only because she's as smart as you are."

What? Again Colin glanced at Brenda. His lips compressed as he studied her. She? Smart? As in intelligent? He turned his head and frowned at his brother some more. "What do you mean by that?"

"What do I mean? Well—" George appeared confused. "I meant what I said. She's smart. Intelligent. Brainy." His eyes narrowed, and he squinted at his brother. "In fact, she might even be a little smarter than you, because she's got the whole world fooled into believing that she's not smart at all."

He nodded at Brenda's table. "I mean, look at her.

She's over there, laughing and joking and playing slapjack as if she didn't have a brain in her head. But she must be smart, because she's been at the top of her profession almost since the day she started, and Martin told me she plans to retire soon. Retire!" George shook his head in wonder. "Can you imagine it? She can't be much older than I am, and she's going to retire, and I haven't even begun to work yet!"

It was on the tip of Colin's tongue to say something snide about his brother's choosing to drop out of college, and how that might retard his ambition for retirement, but he didn't do it and was pleased with himself. It occurred to him that perhaps this sort of restraint was what George meant when he referred to "turning human." He sighed heavily. Here was something else to ponder in his idle moments.

A bellboy came into the bar, looking around as if he were searching for someone. George saw him and jumped up from the table. "That must be my call." He hurried over to the boy, who confirmed his assumption, and George went out to the telephone room.

Slowly, Colin rose and followed him. This would be a test of his brother's suppositions about human behavior as opposed to his own beliefs, which had been based on serious and prolonged study. If his parents were happy to hear from him—and Colin would probably be able to discern fake happiness from the real thing, even if he wasn't the most perceptive man in the world—then he'd have to give George a point for astuteness.

He still didn't understand it. It would be much easier on him if his assumptions about instincts governing behavior carried over into the human species from the rest of the animal kingdom. Life got so confusing when you couldn't rely on instincts. Or education. What good was all of his book-learning if it couldn't even get him into bed with the woman he wanted?

Of course, he'd had no reason even to consider instinct versus learned behavior until he'd met Brenda. She was certainly a predicament in his life. Not unlike a complicated problem in algebra, with several unknowns to solve. Bother. He wished they were both dogs; it would make everything so much simpler.

On that dismal note, he entered the telephone room, where George had already launched into an explanation to their parents about how he'd ended up in California when they'd believed him to be in Pennsylvania.

Although she hid it beautifully, and only because she'd learned her craft well, Brenda's attention was focused almost entirely on Colin after they entered the bar. She wanted to punish him for taking liberties with her person, so she chose to sit with some of the Peerless crew at a table apart from the one Colin chose, but she never lost track of him.

The bastard didn't seem to be suffering unduly. She had to make a conscious effort not to grind her teeth. Or heave her root-beer mug at his handsome head. How dare he sit there and talk to his brother while she sat here playing a jolly game of cards with other men? He ought to be eaten up with jealousy, darn him!

She wondered what he and George were discussing. Colin appeared bemused. George was obviously amused. She was glad it wasn't the other way around, or she'd have feared Colin might be relating his experience in her room, and that would be mortifying.

Darn, but she wished Colin cared for her. She knew he wanted to go to bed with her, but she wanted ever so much more than that. She'd made a vow to herself and to her mother that she wouldn't succumb to a man before he offered her marriage. Colin would be the perfect man for her if only he wasn't so—well—imperfect. Actually, the only thing wrong with him was his lack of a marriage proposal. And human understanding.

Bother. What else was there? Without human understanding, Colin might as well be a mannequin. An empty shell. Granted, his was an appealing shell; still, unless there was a sensitive soul living inside it, it was no good to her.

Well, it might be of *some* good to her—if she were a different sort of woman.

Irked with herself, Brenda slapped the table before a card had been discarded. Chagrined, she shot a grin around the table. "Sorry, guys. Guess my hand slipped."

"That's all right, Brenda," Gil Drew said. He smiled at her, a little goo-goo-eyed.

Dear Gil. He was so sweet. Much sweeter than some men she could mention. Darn and blast Colin Peters for being such a—such a—such a— She couldn't think of anything bad enough. What she wanted was for Colin to possess Gil's easygoing, softhearted disposition while, at the same time, retain his intellectual capacity and interests.

Nothing was ever perfect, darn it all. Brenda knew she was being selfish to want even more than she already had, but she'd truly like to be able to fall in love with a man who would fall in love back. *And* provide the intellectual stimulation she'd craved all her life.

It was her terrible misfortune to have met Colin Peters and fallen for his brain and his body before she knew what a dreadful person he was. She had a degrading impulse to bury her head in her arms and burst into tears.

To counter it, she slammed her hand down on the next jack to appear on the table. Gil had the same impulse a split second later, and his hand nearly smashed hers flat when it landed on top of it.

Brenda cried, "Ow!" before she could catch herself, then felt guilty because Gil looked dismayed.

He leaped to his feet and rushed to her side. "Brenda! I'm so sorry! Are you all right? Did I hurt you? Oh, my God, I'm sorry!"

She couldn't help herself. Gil's concern was so absolutely what she craved from Colin that she hugged Gil. "I'm fine, Gil. Thank you. You didn't hurt me."

It was a lie. Her hand stung like fire. But it felt so good to be hugging a man, even if Gil didn't half measure up to Colin, that she continued to hug him even after she knew she shouldn't any longer. She was glad she'd given in to her affectionate impulse when she saw Colin walk back into the bar, catch sight of her in Gil's arms, wheel about instantly, and leave the bar.

Good. She hoped he was as jealous as all get-out.

Unfortunately, Gil seemed to have misinterpreted her embrace. His was getting a little heated. She gently disengaged herself from his arms. He'd started breathing heavily and was sort of red-faced. When she glanced at the others at the table, they were looking as if they wanted to be elsewhere. Oh, dear. She hoped she hadn't given Gil a mistaken idea of her own feelings in order to irritate Colin.

Lord, but life could get complicated sometimes. It had been much easier before she'd met Colin. Darn him.

In an effort to make light of the situation and, with luck, diffuse any misinterpretations Gil might have placed on her actions, Brenda said, "I'm sorry, Gil. I didn't mean to squish you."

He licked his lips. "You didn't squish me." His voice squeaked.

Interesting. When Colin was aroused, his voice went low and gravelly. She preferred the gravel to the squeak. Naturally. With great annoyance, she decided she needed to have her head examined.

All right. They'd covered that. She'd apologized. If Gil still didn't understand, she was sorry, but there wasn't much she could do about it here and now. Brenda decided to get back to the game. "Whose turn is it now?"

Ben, Peerless's first cameraman, cleared his throat. "Um, I think you slapped the jack first, Brenda."

"Right." She sat in a flutter of percale. "Let's get at it." She started turning over cards. Slowly, Gil returned to his seat. She'd have bet almost anything that he didn't want to, but would have preferred to hug some more. Too bad. She'd had enough of men groping her for one day.

Perhaps not *quite* enough.

"Dang!" she said aloud, so irritated with her heightened senses that she could happily have ripped them to bits with her bare hands.

"What's the matter?" Gil asked, looking worried.

She smiled at him and lied, barefaced, "Not a thing, sweetie." Damn Colin Peters to perdition. He could go straight to heck and take his darned hands and that other thing of his with him.

Again, she wanted to cry.

As for Colin, his internal temperature went from boiling to freezing and back again at least sixteen times after he left the bar and before he thrust the lodge's double doors open so hard they slammed the walls on either side. He stormed across the porch and down the steps, without the least idea where he aimed to go.

It didn't matter. One direction was as good as any other in his current state of misery.

She was hugging that measly little pipsqueak of an actor! She was hugging him *hard!*

Had she hugged Colin, who'd been playing the mating game by all the rules? No! She'd chosen that little, arrogant puppy of an *actor!* An *actor,* for the love of heaven!

Brenda Fitzpatrick, who had fed him that big line about being interested in intellectual pursuits, who'd claimed to be interested in learning all about "the Indians"—whatever "the Indians" were—had rejected Colin and taken up with that puny carbuncle of an actor. An actor. Good God. Colin could hardly stand it.

Fifteen

It took Brenda a long time to shake Gil Drew off her tail after the slapjack game ended. She even sank to using subterfuge in order to dodge his attentions.

Smiling sweetly, she fluttered her eyelashes. "Thank you so much, Gil, but I really don't feel like going to dinner quite yet. I'm very tired and think I'll lie down for awhile."

Obviously disappointed, Gil said, "Can I call for you later? I don't mind waiting."

Brenda didn't like to lie, but she knew that lies were necessary, both professionally and personally, sometimes. She considered this one of those times. "Thanks, sweetie. I'm going to eat in my room tonight. This picture's almost done, and I have to read some more scripts to see what I want to do next."

Gil reminded her of a chastised puppy when his head drooped, he stuffed his hands into his pockets, and he looked at her with his big, brown, plaintive eyes. His eyes weren't nearly as lovely as Colin's, darn and blast it. Brenda felt an illogical urge to shriek at the top of her lungs and yank on her hair, as Martin sometimes did when the stress of picturemaking got to him.

Gil saw her to the door of her room. Brenda knew he

wanted to kiss her, but she made a point of shaking hands with him. She felt like a rat—and it was all Colin's fault.

Innately honest, she knew that wasn't the truth. She'd used Gil because she'd been upset by Colin, and that wasn't fair to poor Gil. At the moment, however, she couldn't drum up the energy to think about how to take care of the Gil situation. Her concentration was focused exclusively on Colin. Who didn't deserve it, the lout.

She had to be alone to contemplate. If she couldn't get away by herself, she feared she'd go nuts. Therefore, as soon as Gil had shuffled off down the hall, looking discouraged and making Brenda feel guilty, she put on a dark cloak and some sturdy walking shoes, tiptoed down the hall in the opposite direction from the lobby, scuttled down the service stairs, and exited the Cedar Crest Lodge by the back door. With the hood of her cloak pulled up over her head to hide her distinctive blond hair, she hoped she looked relatively anonymous. She didn't think anyone saw her as she made her escape. As soon as she'd made her way past the first few trees, she hung her cloak on a branch because she was too warm with it on.

A late spring afternoon in the mountains was enough to brighten anyone's spirits. Brenda, who was normally happy and calm, perked up after a very few minutes of walking among the tall pines and firs, the cedars and sycamores. She loved the scent of the forest and the small animals that scurried here and there, busy about their business.

How much less complicated was, say, a chipmunk's life from her own. Chipmunks didn't worry about finding mates for themselves. They didn't care if their mates loved them or were smart or could teach them all about Indians. They didn't care about anything but operated on instinct. Relying on instinct made much more sense to her in her present chaotic mental state than the stupid way human beings went about things.

On the other hand, she really didn't know for a fact about the chipmunk way of life. For all she knew, chipmunks went through tortures of unrequited love, just as humans did.

She decided this train of thought might well lead to depression, so she discarded it. There were so many beauties up here in the mountains. Brenda enjoyed Southern California; she'd been toying with the idea of buying a home here and sending for her mother. No matter what happened, Brenda was determined to care for her mother.

A scarlet tanager shot out of a tree near her, and she smiled at it. While she missed the bluebirds of her home state of New York, she loved the birds up here. Especially those noisy, squawky blue jays. They had balls, those birds, and Brenda admired them for it. She had balls, too.

With a frown, she decided having balls was probably not a very feminine trait. Perhaps she should try to be less one of the boys and more of a soft, simpering lady.

But then she'd have men falling all over her. She had enough trouble with that sort of nonsense already.

No. She'd chosen the wisest course to follow. Her very success should have taught her as much by this time.

Except that her success had fallen short with Colin.

"Bother!" She heaved a pinecone at a tree and kept walking. The day had been perfectly gorgeous, and she didn't pay much attention to the fading sunlight as the afternoon crept on toward evening. The trees surrounding her cut out a lot of the sun's brightness anyway. It wasn't until she realized she was having trouble seeing the trail that, with a start, she decided she'd better turn around and head back to the lodge.

When Brenda didn't come downstairs to have dinner with the rest of the Peerless folks in the dining room, Colin silently cursed to himself. Trust Brenda to thwart his desires in this selfish way. All he wanted to do was gaze at her, for heaven's sake. He hadn't planned on touching her again.

Well . . . eventually, he wanted to touch her. But not tonight. Tonight he only wanted to look at her, as one might look at a spectacular painting or something. Colin had never had much truck with art, but he'd heard people say that gazing at great works of art lifted the spirit and elevated the mind. He'd feel uplifted and elevated if he could peer at Brenda for a while. But no. She was even going to deprive him of this much pleasure.

He was feeling very grumpy when Gil Drew showed up. Then he felt even grumpier. Gil had a cheery greeting for everyone. Colin eyed him dourly, wondering if he'd received more than a mere embrace from Brenda. If she preferred that callow blockhead to him, Colin would just— he would just— He didn't know what he'd do. Nothing, probably, but he'd feel really, really bad.

Unfortunately, he couldn't waltz over to Gil and ask him if he'd bedded the beautiful Brenda. Such things weren't done in polite society. Not, he thought nastily, that a motion-picture crew could be accounted as polite society. He eyed Gil with disfavor as the actor joined Martin and both men walked over to Colin. It was all Colin could do to force himself to smile at them. He wanted to punch Gil Drew in his shiny pink baby's face.

"Howdy, Colin," Gil said.

Colin wondered if the actor were being deliberately offensive, then told himself not to be ridiculous. Rather formally, he said, "Good evening."

"Gil said Brenda's having dinner in her room," Martin told him. "Why don't you join us at our table, Colin?"

He didn't want to. He wanted to storm upstairs, batter down Brenda's door, and ask her why she was hiding in her room. Was she ashamed of having made love to the silly Gil Drew all afternoon after she'd rejected Colin?

Good God, he was losing his mind.

"Thanks, Martin. Don't mind if I do." He heard the strain in his voice as he smiled and lied.

Neither Martin nor Gil seemed to notice. George joined them, and the four men headed to a table next to a window, where they would have had a wonderful view of the forest if it had been daytime. As it was, the lodge's electric outdoor lighting illuminated a few of the closest trees.

The woods appeared mysterious and enchanting, and whatever that annoying thing was in Colin's chest—the one that had been acting up ever since he'd met Brenda— gave a painful twinge. He just wanted to be with her, dash it, and he might as well quit lying to himself about it.

There had to be some way to get her. He only had to think about it harder.

"Don't you think so, Colin?"

He realized Martin had spoken to him and started, dropping a Brussels sprout he'd just speared with his fork. "Don't I think what?" he asked, deciding in an instant that it would be useless to pretend he'd been paying attention.

Martin chuckled. "Mind in the clouds again, eh? Or in the books, rather, I imagine."

Colin frowned, misliking this image everyone seemed to have of him as some kind of inhuman learning machine. He guessed he hadn't done much to disoblige folks of the notion, but he didn't like it. "I guess," he muttered.

"I asked if you don't think the picture's going well."

Colin respeared his Brussels sprout, put it into his mouth, and chewed thoughtfully. After he swallowed, he said honestly, "I don't really know. You know more about making movies than I do. I suppose it's going pretty well, considering the subject matter and the way it's being treated. At least the tipis don't have flowers on them anymore."

Everyone laughed. Colin hadn't intended his comment to be humorous, and he didn't understand their laughter. There was a whole lot about social behavior he didn't understand. He'd never much cared before. He did now, for all the good it did him. With another frown, he ate two more Brussels sprouts.

"I think it's going very well. I'll be sorry to see Jerry and the rest of our Navajo friends leave tomorrow, but they've done a great job."

Nodding, Colin said, "Yes, they have." That is to say, he guessed they had. He didn't know. Dash it, he didn't seem to know anything anymore except stuff he'd gleaned from books, and books didn't offer him any guidance in matters of the heart. He meant flesh, not heart. Whatever he meant, it was painfully obvious he'd been dead wrong about mating rituals.

After dinner, he trudged up the stairs and started down the plush, carpeted hallway to his room. As he passed Brenda's suite, he paused. He stared at the door, frowning.

Should he knock? What would he say if she answered the door and asked him what he wanted? He couldn't very well say he wanted to make love to her.

He should probably just skip it. She'd surely not appreciate his showing up uninvited, especially if she was trying to get some rest or study a script or something.

Bother. What to do, what to do . . .

With a disheartened shrug, Colin walked on down the hallway without knocking on her door. Before he'd reached his own door, he heard someone else knocking at a door behind him. Instantly, he had visions of Gil Drew being received by Brenda *en dishabille,* and being invited inside to partake of her favors.

Scowling, he turned and glared down the hall. A bellboy stood before Brenda's door, a message on a silver tray held in one hand, a gloved fist preparing to knock at her door again. The door remained closed.

After knocking a second time, the bellboy leaned down and put his mouth near the keyhole. "Miss Fitzpatrick? Miss Fitzpatrick, there's a cable for you. It's from New York City, ma'am." He sounded impressed.

Colin's scowl faded, but he was faintly troubled. It wasn't like Brenda to ignore a knock at her door. She was too nice for that—or too conscious of her image.

He felt a little mean when the latter thought tiptoed through his head, mainly because he knew it to be merely catty. Brenda had a genuinely gracious manner about her, and even though he was mad at her right now, he shouldn't fail to acknowledge it. God knew where she'd learned it, too, since she couldn't have had much in the way of training in such matters at home, having been earning her family's keep practically forever.

The bellboy knocked one more time, looking more disappointed as the minutes passed and no Brenda came to the door. At last, and with a big, sorry sigh, he leaned over and slipped the cablegram through the crack at the bottom of the door. When he walked away, his shoulders were slightly slumped. Colin could plainly see the boy's disappointment not to have met the magnificent Brenda Fitzpatrick in person and to have spoken to her and handed her the cable. Unfortunately, Colin knew exactly how he felt.

"Blast it, I'll bet she's only hiding."

In truth, he didn't believe it, but he used it as an excuse to march back down the hall and rap sharply on her door. No answer. He rapped again. Still no answer.

What the devil had happened to her? Where was she? Was she in there, injured? The notion appealed not at all, although it was more welcome than Colin's next idea, which was that she'd been so upset by him—or something else— that she'd tried to end it all. He wracked his brain, trying to recollect any signs in her indicating she was so delicately balanced that she'd take an overdose of laudanum or slash her wrists.

As hard as he tried, he couldn't conjure an image of Brenda as a suicide. Especially not merely because some unknown scholar like Colin had kissed her.

He shoved his dollop of disappointment away as unworthy.

Which still did nothing to account for Brenda's not answering her door. Such behavior was unlike her. Dash it, was she being deliberately elusive?

Why would she be elusive? Unless it was to worry him, Colin couldn't account for it. And really, if he were to be honest with himself, he couldn't account for it that way, either. He wasn't important enough in her life for her to want to worry him. Blast it.

After he quit trying to include himself into a scenario that might account for Brenda's failure to answer her door, Colin finally came to the conclusion that she'd gone out. But where?

It was none of his business where she'd gone or what she was doing. Colin knew it, and he turned and started down the hall toward his own room at a steady clip.

His feet slowed. He stopped walking.

Dash it, this was no good at all. He couldn't get the nagging image of Brenda in some kind of trouble to leave him alone. With a bitter sigh, he knew he'd get no rest this night until he made an effort to discover her whereabouts.

Of course, if he discovered she was holed up in Gil Drew's hotel room, he might just have to shoot himself, but that was a risk he'd have to take. Better to know than to continue to suffer this dreadful apprehension. Or perhaps it wasn't better to know. He guessed he'd find out.

So, assuming as nonchalant an air as he could summon under the circumstances, when his heart was beating out a rhythm of disquietude and foreboding, he went searching for Brenda.

She wasn't in the lobby. She wasn't in the dining room. She wasn't in the bar. She wasn't in the card room.

He did discover Gil Drew in the card room and felt minimally better, but not much.

She wasn't in the billiard room. She wasn't in the reading room. She wasn't in the kitchen—although the entire Cedar Crest kitchen crew turned and gaped at him when he'd looked.

She wasn't in either parlor.

"What's up, Colin? You look worried."

Colin wasn't pleased when George glanced up from a deep armchair in the front parlor, where he'd been reading a book. Because he didn't care to have the whole world know his business, Colin answered his brother casually. "Couldn't concentrate on my book so I thought I'd take a walk."

"Want any company?"

The last thing Colin wanted at the moment was company. Unless the company consisted of Brenda. He forced himself to smile "No, thanks. I'm—considering a philosophical problem."

George nodded, as if he were accustomed to his older brother considering philosophical problems. "Have fun."

Was George being sarcastic? Probably. Colin couldn't drum up any indignation at the moment. Perhaps later. He continued his search.

She wasn't in any of the hallways. She wasn't on the porch. She wasn't anywhere on the grounds.

"Dash it, where is she?"

The evening air had turned chilly. Colin crossed his arms over his chest, glad for his sack jacket, even if it didn't provide much warmth. Frowning into trees he could barely discern by the light of the lodge's outdoor lamps, he wondered if Brenda had, for some witless reason, wandered off into the woods.

It would be just like her, the little fool.

But no. That was unfair. George was right about her, and even Colin couldn't deny it and continue to consider himself a reasonable man. She wasn't a fool. She was quite clever, in fact. Maybe—although he wasn't willing to admit it yet—she was even intelligent.

Whatever her brain power or lack thereof, she was still gone. With a soft curse, Colin returned to the lodge, borrowed a blanket and one of those newfangled electrical torches from the concierge, and went outside again. He felt like a fool himself when he deliberately walked into the night-dark woods.

A sense of panic started to inch itself up Brenda's spine. With clenched teeth, she crammed it down and stuffed the hole from which it had emerged with brass and grit and a smidgen of fortitude. If she hadn't been defeated by all the other odds against her in this stupid life, she sure wasn't going to allow being lost in the woods to dismay her.

An owl hooted from a nearby tree. To Brenda, it sounded as if the bird were jeering at her. "Liar," it called to her in Owl, and she sensed it knew she was already dismayed.

Were the Owls an Indian tribe? she wondered inconsequentially. Where was Colin Peters when you needed him?

"Get a hold on your nerves, girl. You're just a bit disoriented. There's no need to lose your mind yet."

Talking to herself didn't help. In fact, the sound of her voice seemed eerie in the darkness of the forest. It also seemed to startle the animal life surrounding her. From rattling her with its chatter and hoots, it suddenly terrified her with its silence. Darn it. She wished she'd kept her big mouth shut.

But she was either walking around in circles or she'd headed in the wrong direction entirely. She hadn't seen anything that looked familiar for a very long time, and now that the sun had set, she could hardly see anything at all. She was pretty sure she wouldn't be able to recognize her own mother if she appeared in front of her.

Or a bear.

The thought of a bear materializing out of the gloom made the blood thunder in her brain and fear scream in her head.

Until she thought about the possibility of a mountain lion, and then she froze in her tracks. Good God, a mountain lion might jump at her from the limb of a tree, mightn't it?

She glanced up and saw nothing. She glanced around at ground level and saw nothing.

In fact, she couldn't see anything at all.

Sweet Lord, she was lost. She was lost in the forest at night, and nobody but God knew where she was. God and the devil.

Darn it. Why had she chosen now, of all inconvenient times, to think about the devil?

Maybe she was being punished for having carnal thoughts about Colin Peters.

Nonsense. God had created human beings. He'd installed a sexual nature along with everything else in the mix with which He'd gifted the human body. Surely He wouldn't have done that if He hadn't expected that sexual nature to kick in from time to time. How else could the human species survive?

She felt no carnal urges at the moment. All her sensations were occupied in being frightened. Darn it, why hadn't she noticed the sun getting low on the horizon?

Easy enough to answer: She couldn't see the horizon from here, in the middle of a bunch of trees.

A city girl, she was unused to trees, although she'd read a lot and therefore knew a tree when she saw one. And she'd visited the mountains before, for various jobs. She was sure she'd read once or twice about what one should do if one found oneself lost in the woods. Now, what was it? Was one supposed to stand still and wait for rescue or keep walking? She couldn't remember.

All right, so she didn't know what to do. Obviously, her sense of direction, which was pretty good when she was in familiar surroundings, had deserted her. She didn't know which way north, south, east, or west was. Even if she'd brought a compass with her, she wouldn't have known in which direction to walk, since she didn't know where she was. She'd not even be able to see the compass by this time. She'd seldom felt this stupid.

Which was nothing to the purpose. It wouldn't do her any good to berate herself at the moment. That could wait.

Although she didn't like to think about needing one, she considered whether or not she had anything with her that might constitute a weapon.

No. She didn't. She wasn't even wearing a hat with a pin in it. She wasn't wearing a hat at all.

Bother. Perhaps she should arm herself with a stick. She wished she'd thought about a stick before it got too dark to see. Did she have any matches? She seldom carried any, but she searched through all the pockets in her clothes in hope. Her hope came to naught.

The night air was getting chilly, too. But had she thought to bring along a wrap? Even a shawl? No, she hadn't. She'd hung her cloak on a tree branch and merrily trotted off to get herself lost in the woods without giving it another thought.

In fact, she couldn't recall ever feeling so helpless, and

she didn't like it at all. Where was the moon? Where were the stars? If only she had a little light, she might be able to find a stick, if not her way back to the lodge.

She decided she'd be better off standing still and waiting for—for what? For some large, hungry animal to maul her? To freeze to death?

Nonsense. One couldn't freeze to death in the springtime, could one? She recalled reading somewhere about hypothermia and wished she hadn't.

So she shouldn't stand still. She should walk. If she walked, even if she walked around in circles, she'd keep warmer than if she stood still.

Actually, her feet hurt, and she'd as soon not stand at all, but sit. But if she sat, she'd surely get chilled all the way through, and that was no good. She might also be a better target for the large, hungry animal stalking her. Wouldn't she? Or would an animal be more likely to be attracted by movement?

Feeling completely melancholy and overwhelmed, and wishing she'd read more about large beasts of the forest, Brenda nearly succumbed to tears before her staunch nature reasserted itself and told her not to be a simpering ninny. No matter where she was at the moment, she was both alive and close to the Cedar Crest Lodge. No large, hungry animal would roam this close to a human habitation, would it?

Not unless it sensed an easy meal.

"Darn it," she muttered, becoming more and more annoyed with herself. She'd never been a sissy before.

She'd never been lost in the woods before.

"Stop it!"

She heard a rustling in the woods and froze. Oh, Lord, had she roused some sleeping beast with her voice? Why hadn't she just shut up and kept walking? Or standing? Or sitting?

Darn, she wished she knew what to do.

The rustling noise didn't stop. It seemed to be getting closer. Oh, sweet heaven, what was it? Throwing caution to the wind, Brenda felt around for a tree and tried to find a branch she could break off. Perhaps she could ward the beast off with a bushy branch.

Darn it, this one was a pine tree. There weren't any bushy branches on pine trees—and even if there were, they were too far over her head for her to reach any of them.

Maybe she should climb a tree. Another tree. One with branches. Frantically, she hurried past the pine tree, holding her arms out in front of her in an effort to feel her way since she couldn't see.

Ow! There was a tree. Some kind of tree. She'd just crashed into it. It was the kind with bushy branches. Not quite heartened, she felt around the tree, trying to find a branch she could break off. She found a branch, but it was pretty thick. It wouldn't break when she yanked on it, and it wouldn't break when she tried to twist it. All she got for that particular effort was a painfully scratched palm. Growing angry with the fates as well as herself, Brenda threw herself at the branch, hoping her weight would break it off.

It almost did, but not quite. This wasn't fair. It was too unkind of the fates to stick her out here in the wilderness all by herself and not even allow her to break a branch with which to defend herself against wild beasts.

Furious, she heaved herself at the branch again. It broke with a hideous cracking sound, and she and the branch fell to the ground. It was a painful, prickly experience, and it didn't improve Brenda's mood. She didn't pause to consider all her scrapes and bumps, however, but jumped to her feet, clutching the branch by its sappy broken end. She'd never get that stuff out of her clothes— not to mention her broken flesh. Bother.

The noise didn't stop. Weren't wild animals supposed

to be afraid of loud noises? That branch breaking and her falling on top of it had made a terrible racket. Why was the beast still heading her way?

A horrible thought struck her—or, rather, another horrible thought. What if the creature headed her way was some sort of maniac who lived in the mountains and preyed on lost people and so forth? She'd read about men who, crazed by war or general everyday nonsense, took to the woods and lived in the wild. It would be just her luck to meet one now.

The noise kept coming. It was getting closer. Desperately, Brenda cried out, "Stop! Whoever you are, stop right there! I'm armed!" With a bushy tree branch. Oh, Lord. Oh, Lord.

It had a light with it, whatever it was. She wasn't comforted, although she supposed a light did exclude hungry animals. It didn't leave out maniacal mountain men.

She cried, "Stay where you are, or I'll shoot!" With her bushy tree branch. God, if she survived this night, she'd give a thousand dollars to charity. She swore it.

"Brenda?"

It knew her name! Oh, God! This was worse than she'd feared.

"Brenda, is that you? Where the devil have you been? I've been worried sick."

She squinted into the darkness, thinking the voice sounded vaguely familiar. And, while it sounded irked, it didn't sound as if it meant to roast her on a spit over an open fire or do her other harm. Too terrified to hope, she didn't answer, afraid it might be some sort of trick.

But that was stupid. How could it be a trick? Nobody knew she was out here. She still didn't speak.

The voice came again. "Where are you? For the love of God, say something, so I'll know where you are! You were an idiot to stay out after dark, dash it. It's not safe."

Colin! It was Colin! Brenda almost lost control and

burst into tears, she was so overjoyed to know it was he who'd come to rescue her.

Then it registered on her consciousness that he'd called her an idiot. Her terror turned to rage in an instant. "Is that you, Colin?" Before anything, Brenda was an actress. She pitched her question at a mellifluous tone.

"Yes." He, on the other hand, sounded irritated.

The fiend. The miserable, coldblooded, horrid, awful, woman-seducing fiend. Brenda said sweetly, "Yes, Colin. It's I, Brenda." That should give him pause; she'd used *I* instead of *me*. She wondered if he'd notice it and catalog her proper use of pronouns in the machine that passed for his brain.

"Why in the name of heaven are you out here in the woods after dark?" he asked in a loud voice. "Did you intend to spend the night out here?"

He was getting closer. A faint streak of light issued from the gloom. It wasn't much, but it was enough for Brenda to discern a tall fir tree standing only a yard or so away from her. She ducked behind it. Darn him for calling her an idiot. Darn him for coming after her himself instead of sending somebody nice to look for her. George wouldn't call her an idiot. Jerry Begay wouldn't call her an idiot. Gil Drew wouldn't call her an idiot.

It infuriated her to know she wouldn't have cared if they had. Only Colin had the power to hurt her feelings.

She raised her branch above her head, no longer heedful of the sap dripping down her arms and onto her frock.

He emerged, looking angry, holding his blasted torch up and shining it in a circle around him. "Where the deuce are you?"

She didn't answer. He started walking again. When he was close enough to her tree for her to reach, Brenda brought the branch down on his head.

Sixteen

Colin didn't know what hit him. Whatever it was didn't hit him hard, but it was plenty hard enough to tumble him to the ground. On his way down, he reached up to hold on his glasses, hit himself on the head with the torch, dropped the blanket, and sent the torch flying.

He sprawled in a pile of pine needles for a moment, confused, before he heard Brenda's voice. Only it didn't sound like her voice. It sounded like something that had come out of a crazed fishwife.

"How dare you call me an idiot!" the voice shrieked. "You devil!"

"Brenda?" Colin pushed the branch away from his face and felt his head to make sure it was all in one piece.

"How dare you? You wicked, wicked man!"

He didn't understand this at all. He thought he'd come outside in the pitch dark to rescue her, and here she was vilifying him to the heavens. Not to mention the creatures of the forest, the trees, the moon and stars, and everything in between.

In a voice he hoped conveyed concern, and determined not to lose his temper since she had obviously become deranged, he asked, "Are you hurt?"

"Am I hurt? Am I *hurt!*" she hollered. "Of course I'm hurt, you lunatic! Wouldn't *you* be hurt if somebody called you an idiot? And all because you'd gotten lost in the woods?"

He had no answer, primarily because he couldn't comprehend the question. He hadn't called her an idiot, had he? Well, maybe he had. He'd been thinking of her in unkind terms ever since he'd realized she wasn't anywhere in or near the lodge. He tested an explanation on her. "I, ah, was worried about you when I discovered you were missing."

"Missing?" she shrieked. *"Missing!* I wasn't missing! I was here all the time. I'd gone outside to *think,* you miserable toad!"

Miserable toad? Him? Tentatively, he drew his knees up, preparatory to standing. The torch's beam had gone out when it hit the earth, but there was a shaft of moonlight filtering through the tree branches. It landed right, smack on Brenda, its silvery light giving her a ghostly, shimmering appearance that was half frightening and half enchanting. It would have been a good deal more enchanting if she hadn't continued to yell at him.

She didn't wait for him to respond to her calling him a toad, which was just as well. "I was so scared! It was so dark, and I couldn't see a thing, and then you came waltzing along, calling me an idiot! You beast!"

Carefully, Colin pushed himself to a sitting position. Squinting around the small clearing, he spotted the torch. Thank God his eyeglasses hadn't come off. He hoped the torch wasn't broken beyond redemption, because it would be much easier to get back to the lodge if they could see the way.

"Well?" she stormed. "Well? Don't you have *anything* to say, you—you—you louse?"

Louse? Colin began to feel the faintest degree of resentment. Here he'd come all the way out here, into the woods where God alone knew what dangers lurked, in order to find her, and she was screaming at him and calling him names. It didn't seem sportsmanlike. "Um, I thought you'd be glad somebody came after you, actually."

"Glad? Why, you miserable goat! First you try to rape me and now you pretend to be some kind of chivalrous knight! I hate you, Colin Peters. I *hate* you!"

"Rape you?" Colin could scarcely believe his ears. "I did no such thing." Offended, he climbed to his feet, picking up the torch on his way, and began to brush himself off. He stuck the torch into his pocket for the nonce, to get it out of his way.

"You did so," Brenda declared emphatically. "You barged into my room and tried to take advantage of me, and don't you dare deny it!"

Although he would never, ever take a woman by force, Colin had to acknowledge that he had intended something of a carnal nature when he'd gone up to Brenda's room that afternoon. Nonetheless, her opinion of his intentions riled him.

Then again, perhaps her experience in the woods had unsettled her more than he'd at first suspected. Colin wasn't adept at reading human emotions and he wasn't accustomed to considering other people's feelings, mainly because he recognized so few of his own. Now, however, he squinted at Brenda and recognized a certain frenzy about her that was most atypical of the calm, steady, sunny-natured Brenda he'd come to know and—and—and—well, *know* would do at present.

Trying to pitch his voice to a soothing timbre, he said, "You're hysterical." He didn't mean it as an insult. He only stated what, to him, was obvious.

"I am not hysterical!" she bellowed.

"I believe you are, actually, Brenda." This time, he meant his tone and words to imply that he understood and wasn't going to hold her wild accusations and name-callings against her once she calmed down. To make sure she took his meaning, he smiled slightly and said, "It's all right. You'll feel better in a minute."

To his astonishment, she seemed to stiffen. He hoped she wasn't going to fall into some kind of seizure, although he'd been trained in first aid, so he probably could cope. It might even be easier to handle a seizure than this hysteria, come to think of it.

"You brute." Her voice had gone deadly calm. "You fiend. You devil. You scoundrel. You monster."

Now, Colin wasn't a sentimental sort. He'd lived in his head most of his life and wasn't accustomed to fits of fiery temperament and so forth. And, while he chalked up this wild talk of Brenda's to some kind of paroxysm brought about by fear, he didn't like it.

"Don't be silly," he said calmly. Withdrawing the torch from his coat pocket, he began studying it in an effort to make its light work again. He heard Brenda breathing in short, gasping respirations, and assumed her riotous mood hadn't abated, although she no longer screamed at him, which was an improvement. Hoping to calm her further, he said matter-of-factly, "I brought a blanket, in case you were cold." He glanced up from the torch and added dryly, "I see you didn't bother to bring a wrap with you."

When she spoke again, Colin didn't even recognize the sound as a voice. It sounded more like some kind of predatory animal poised to strike. The pitch was low, the tone menacing. "I didn't bother to wear a wrap."

It was a statement, a repetition of his, and he didn't believe she expected a response. Anyhow, he was busy with the torch, although his concern with the torch was mainly a ruse to make Brenda settle down.

"I'd been walking in the woods because of you, Colin Peters," she went on in that same lethal tone. "Because you had abused my friendship."

This was too much. Colin couldn't let it pass unremarked upon. "Now, really, there's no need—"

She went on, tromping over his explanation as if he hadn't spoken. "I'd gone walking in order to think, because I was upset and confused. Because of *you*."

To Colin, it sounded like an accusation. He didn't think she could sound much more reproachful if she'd charged him with murder. He opened his mouth to refute her allegations when again she overrode him.

"I walked for what seemed like hours. I didn't notice when it began to get dark because I was too busy thinking about things. I was too distressed about what kind of person you must believe me to be if you thought I'd approve of what you'd done."

"Dash it, Brenda, I didn't do—"

She held up a hand. He shut up. "Yes, you did," she said firmly. "And I was hurt. Very hurt. And I didn't notice when it began to get dark. And then, when I realized the sun must be setting, I tried to find my way back to the lodge. I couldn't."

"One should always mark one's trail," Colin pointed out, hoping in that way to show her that he was on her side.

It didn't work. He ought to have expected it. Her voice rose on her next words. "Don't you *dare* patronize me, you awful man! What did you expect me to do? Leave a trail of crumbs?"

Although he suspected the question to be rhetorical, he said in what he hoped was a reasonable tone, "No. The birds and squirrels would have eaten them. What the Indians do is—"

"I don't give a hang what the Indians do!"

Colin winced because she'd gone back to screeching. He deduced she was in no mood to be rational, so he decided to hold his tongue. He could teach her forest craft later, if she wanted to learn. She probably didn't. He fiddled with the torch some more.

"It got dark," she went on, lowering her voice again,

thank God. "And I didn't know where I was. There was no moon and there were no stars. I couldn't see a blessed thing."

Although he knew better, Colin nodded, understanding what had happened. "It was too early in the evening. You probably should have rested until the moon rose. It's full tonight, so—"

"Be quiet!" She stamped her foot, and he shut up, sighing as he did so. "I was scared, Colin. I was scared to death. I don't know what kinds of animals live in these woods—"

He opened his mouth to let her know, but shut it again when she screeched, "Don't you *dare!*" He sighed again.

"I was frightened," she went on. "And then I heard you coming. But I didn't know it was you. How could I?"

He didn't answer the question, prudence telling him she didn't want to know that, either.

"I didn't have any weapons. I didn't have any light. I didn't have *anything.* So I broke a branch and when you walked next to my tree, I hit you." She sniffed. "Frankly, I'm surprised I didn't faint dead away from terror."

Looking up from the torch, Colin peered at her, wondering if she were deliberately lying to him or if she'd forgotten their brief conversation prior to her trying to brain him. Also, Brenda hadn't before now appeared to be the fainting type. Perhaps she was exaggerating to make her point. "You answered me when I spoke to you," he pointed out. "That was before you hit me."

"Oh, hush up!" Folding her arms over her breasts, she turned around. She stood there, rigid, for a moment, then whirled back. "I was frightened! Terrified! Scared to death! And all you can say is, 'You answered me'! Ooooh! I wish I'd knocked you out with that branch!"

He could tell she meant it, and he couldn't fathom her reasoning. He suspected it wasn't reasoning at all, but rather another example of her state of hysteria. Surmising that she was unable to appreciate rational conversation, he said gently, "I'm sorry you were frightened, Brenda. I understand. I was worried about you, so I came out here to try to find you. I didn't mean to scare you."

To Colin's horror, her bottom lip began to tremble. Good God, she wasn't going to cry, was she? Colin had always hated it when women cried in front of him. He considered such tactics lowdown and dirty. His sisters used to cry when they couldn't get their way in any other, more logical, manner.

Brenda's voice shook when she said, "And then you trounce in here and call me an idiot. An *idiot!*" She dashed away tears. Colin felt awful. "You mean, mean, mean, mean man."

She burst into tears, and Colin stood there feeling helpless and contemptible and miserable—feeling like, in fact, exactly what she'd called him. He held out a hand uncertainly. "Here, Brenda, don't do that."

"D-d-don't do what?"

"Don't carry on so," he pleaded. "I understand that you're still hysterical, but please—"

"I am not hysterical!"

He saw her eyes brimming in the moonlight. They looked like dark pools of misery to him, although he'd never harbored fanciful thoughts before. He felt rotten.

Her mouth trembled. Emotion surged within Colin's breast. "Here," he pleaded. "Don't cry. Please."

"I hate you, Colin Peters," she stated flatly. "I hate you more than liver. More than anchovies. More than anything."

And then she launched herself at him. He staggered backwards and would have fallen flat on his back again except that he bumped up against a fir tree. His arms went around her, and he held her as she sobbed against his jacket.

For a long time—it might have been seconds or minutes; Colin didn't know—they stayed locked in each other's arms. Then Colin's brain started functioning again.

Good God, Brenda had thrown herself into his arms. *His* arms. Not Gil Drew's arms. His. Colin's. His right hand began moving of its own accord, first stroking her back, then finding the soft skin of her neck. He whispered, "You're cold, Brenda."

It was a statement of fact, and he cursed himself for not being more eloquent. But he'd never needed eloquence before. She nodded and continued to weep pathetically.

He said, "Let me get the blanket. You can wrap it around yourself."

This time she shook her head, although she still seemed wretched. He didn't understand her reluctance to take advantage of the blanket, although he wasn't going to argue with her. She was in his arms, for the love of God. Any man would be a fool to release her if she didn't want him to.

He continued to stroke her, gently running his right hand down her arm, trying to determine if she might be suffering from shock. It seemed unlikely, given that the weather recently, while a little chilly at night, was quite springlike. Her body felt like heaven pressed against him. He wouldn't mind staying like this for the rest of his life, actually, although he knew he'd tire of being vertical sooner or later.

For the first time in his life, he regretted being of such a literal turn of mind. If he had an ounce of whimsy within him, he wouldn't have considered such a thing as his feet wearing out. As long as Brenda was in his arms, he should feel wonderful.

Yet, it was true that his feet had begun to hurt. Also, he feared Brenda might have suffered more than he'd initially believed. He couldn't account for her state of panic unless something dreadful had happened to her. Perhaps she'd thought she'd seen a bear or something. He didn't believe she really had, but she might have been mistaken, which would be every bit as frightening as if the bear had been real.

He whispered softly, "Here, Brenda. Let's get the blanket. We can sit down and you can warm up." He'd be more than happy to hold her in his arms all night long, for that matter, although he didn't say so, recalling her accusations of lousehood a few minutes earlier.

She nodded, sniffling and looking unhappy. Colin picked up the blanket from where it had fallen when she'd bashed him and shook it out vigorously. Then, after thinking the matter over for no more than five seconds, he spread the blanket under a large sycamore tree. He removed his jacket and, very gently, slipped it around her. Then he took Brenda's hand and led her over to sit down upon the blanket. He sat next to her and drew up the blanket so that it covered them both.

In a voice so tender it alarmed him, he asked, "Are you comfortable?"

Again she nodded. Then she shook her head. Colin heaved a silent, internal sigh. Obviously, she was still in a state, although she no longer screeched, thank heavens. "What can I do to make you comfortable? We don't want you to catch cold."

Which was a tolerably stupid thing to say. Cold weather never hurt anyone. It was germs and bacteria that made people sick. He didn't explain, knowing she didn't care.

"N-nothing," she mumbled in what, to Colin, sounded like a last-gasp sort of voice.

"Are you sure?"

"Y-yes."

With another, bigger sigh, Colin realized he was beginning to react to her closeness. There was something about Brenda that struck him on his raw side; he hadn't even known he'd possessed one until he met her. When he'd first seen her, she'd seemed almost too perfect to be real; he'd had an easier time of it when he was still able to look upon her as an animated doll.

Then she'd begun to ask him questions about his work. Under more normal circumstances, such interest from an attractive woman would have pleased his vanity. Since he was in the unnatural setting of a motion-picture location, and Brenda was an actress and all, he'd mistrusted her motives. Not that he had, to this day, any idea in the world why he should have done so. What could her motives have been, other than a quest for knowledge? But there you go. Human beings were an odd lot; Colin knew it from long years of study. And he was as human as anyone else—if slightly more intelligent.

Unfortunately, along with his mistrust of her motives had come an understanding that, far from being some kind of perfect automaton, Brenda was entirely human. This fresh awareness had been accompanied by an insatiable lust, which was rearing its ugly head again now, as he sat under a tree in a forest with his arms around a recently hysterical Brenda.

He expelled a huge breath and wished he could be a scholar and not a man all the time instead of merely from time to time. It didn't seem right that both parts of him should be so inextricably entwined with one another in situations like this.

But this was a human condition, he supposed, and there was no gainsaying it. Because he was embarrassed by his condition—not that Brenda could see it since, except for that one shaft of moonlight penetrating the leaves overhead the atmosphere was black, he decided it might hurry things along some if he were to apologize for his behavior earlier in the day.

He supposed he owed her that, although he was slightly miffed by what he assumed would be her reaction to his present state of arousal. After all, wasn't that why she was so successful? Because men found her sexually attractive?

Actually, that probably didn't account for *all* of her popularity. He understood that Brenda was fairly worshiped by young ladies across the country. He heaved another sigh, decided he'd never fully comprehend anything he didn't read in a book, and dove in head first.

"I'm very sorry for upsetting you earlier today, Brenda."

Weak, Colin. Weak. If you expect her to let up on you, be more specific. He'd learned long ago that, in scholarship, one must spell out exactly what one meant.

She said nothing but merely sniffled, which confirmed his own assessment of his tepid apology.

So, however much he hated to do it and even begrudged the necessity since he considered Brenda almost as much at fault as he was—although he couldn't have said why—he tried again. "That is to say, I'm sorry I—ah—was forward with you. Earlier. In your hotel room."

As much as he appreciated academic honesty, he'd be dashed if he'd apologize for trying to take advantage of her—whatever that meant—because he hadn't. He'd never have done anything against her will. He'd most certainly not tried to rape her, as she'd accused him of doing.

"Are you?"

Her voice was small and weaker than he'd ever heard it, and it made his heart lurch. He also wasn't sure what to say. On the one hand, he wasn't sorry at all, because he really, really wanted to go to bed with her. On the other hand, he was sorry his bold ploy hadn't worked.

Ergo, he decided, he was sorry and could answer truthfully with the words she wanted to hear. "Yes. I'm very sorry."

She sniffled again.

"It won't happen again." Ugh. This particular truth didn't sit well with him. He had a feeling that, if he ever were to taste the full measure of Brenda's charms, his infatuation would have been satisfied and, therefore, would be over.

"Th-thank you."

She didn't sound happy about it. Given his state of acute sexual excitement, as well as the difficulty he'd had in coming up with an apology that came near the truth while avoiding its full implications, he considered her thanks lukewarm at best. He said huffily, "You're welcome."

They sat cuddled up together in the blanket for what seemed an eon to Colin, although it probably wasn't more than a minute. When Brenda spoke again, she sounded uncharacteristically diffident. "I'm sorry I yelled at you." She gave another sniffle. "I was very scared."

"I understand. The feminine temperament is notoriously unstable."

He felt her stiffen and knew he'd said the wrong thing. Dash it, she was idiotically sensitive about some things.

"And in what scholarly tome is that sentiment written?"

Her voice was stronger now, and aggressive in defense of her gender. Colin was about to retort with references when his erudite candor smacked him upside the head.

In reality, while he'd heard the psychological aspects of the male and female personality discussed and debated by others, he hadn't read much about the matter on his own. He preferred to form his own conclusions on the basis of solid facts. One couldn't do that when studying people, because people were so—unsolid. Colin therefore had always preferred history and the natural sciences to the study of human psychology.

Peeved because he couldn't cite references without pretending to knowledge he didn't possess, he said, "I understand Dr. Freud has done all sorts of studies on the topic and has concluded that women are of a generally histrionic disposition. Most of them. Many of them." He gritted his teeth and modified his statement yet again. "Some of them."

Brenda raised a hand. Colin thought she'd done so to wipe away more tears, and his heart gave a hard spasm, although he didn't do anything, not wishing to have his face slapped or anything of a like nature.

"Dr. Freud," she said in a tight voice that sounded as if it were being squeezed through clenched teeth, "is an ass. He blames all human problems on sex."

Colin blinked into the pitch-black night, unsettled by such frank speaking. "I, ah, believe he's studied extensively on the matter."

"Fiddlesticks," Brenda said firmly. "He only thinks he has. If he'd *really* done his homework, he'd understand that most of the world's problems aren't brought about by sexual frustration or misplaced sexual fantasies or sexual hysteria, but by poverty, ignorance, and malnutrition. He's a damned snob."

Good God, she was right.

He'd never admit it. With a condescending chuckle, he said, "You've studied this subject extensively, I'm sure."

He was dismayed when she pulled away from him as if he'd suddenly begun to stink. "Yes, I have, damn you! You think you're the only person in the universe who reads? Blast you, Colin Peters, I'm tired of you belittling me! I may not have a college education, but I'll bet I've read more books about more subjects than most of the other people you've met in your stuffy, confined, narrow-minded life!"

"Oh, now, really—"

"Oh-now-really, my foot!"

She scrambled to her feet, yanking at the blanket and rolling Colin, who hadn't expected such a violent move, onto the pine-needle-and-sycamore-cone ground cover under the tree. He blinked into the blackness for a second before he realized what had happened; then he, too, stood up. He fumbled for the torch in his pocket and turned the switch, hoping it would work. It didn't.

Because he was irked, both by her and by the torch, he said, "Poverty, ignorance, and malnutrition don't explain this latest outburst on your part."

"No, they do not! *You* explain this one, you condescending cretin!"

"Name-calling won't make very many people change their minds about females being unstable," he pointed out smugly.

"Oh! You drive me crazy!"

And with that, she once again hurled herself at him. This time, however, she pounded on his chest with her fists. It didn't hurt, but Colin didn't like it much. He jammed the torch back into his pocket and reached for her wrists. He didn't have much trouble subduing her.

It occurred to him that this was the last thing he'd wanted to happen. What he'd hoped for was a truce. Maybe even more than that. A friendly kiss would have been nice. A lustful one would have been nicer.

Feeling defeated and discouraged, he said, "I'm sorry, Brenda. I didn't mean to—" He was going to say *provoke you* but decided those words would be more like waving a red flag in front of a maddened bull than offering a white flag to a foe. After thinking for a second, he said, "I didn't mean to say that."

He had, but she didn't need to know it. He still held on to her wrists, not very tightly because he didn't want to bruise her tender flesh, but tightly enough to prevent her from bruising his tender flesh.

"Y-yes, you did."

Oh, Lord, she was crying again. Colin felt awful. "Here, Brenda, please don't cry. I'm sorry I hurt your feelings."

"You're a brute."

At least that's what Colin thought she said. Her words were so thick, it was difficult to tell. He wanted to deny it but knew he'd be better off not doing so. He opted for another, "I'm sorry, Brenda. Please don't cry."

"I h-hate you."

"I'm sorry." And that was the truth.

Her fury subsided so gradually, Colin wasn't even aware of it until he realized she was resting her hands on his chest, next to her head, which was pressed there. He blinked down at her blond curls, wishing he could see them better in the moonlight. Very gently, he released her wrists and put his arms around her.

Was it his fevered brain making him believe she seemed to be snuggling more closely against him? He wasn't sure, but he made a tentative gesture toward reconciliation by resting his cheek against her soft hair. She smelled like a flower. He closed his eyes and allowed his senses to luxuriate in her essence.

When he felt her hand move to his back, as if she were attempting to learn its geography, he sucked in a breath and held it. His sex, which was already hard, gave an enormous throb. Dash it, did she know what she was doing to his libido? If she did, her protests earlier in the day were totally disingenuous.

"I want you to like me, Colin," she whispered into the darkness. "But you seem to hate me."

"I don't hate you." It was true, although Colin hadn't thought about it until now.

"You do, too."

Dash it, she wasn't going to start another argument now, was she? Colin didn't think he could take it. He gritted his teeth, and answered anyway. "No, I don't."

She sniffed. "You seem to."

"I don't mean to. I—ah—don't think I know how to get along in nonacademic surroundings sometimes." He'd never admitted that aloud before. This infatuation with

Brenda was forcing him into all sorts of confessions he'd just as soon not make.

He felt her nod. "I understand."

"You do?" He wasn't sure he believed her.

He felt her nod again. "Yes. I've had to study human behavior for a long time, and I pegged you for a man who'd never had to worry about society's acceptance or rejection of him the first time I ever saw you."

Which had nothing to do with anything at all that Colin could see. For a couple of seconds. Then her meaning penetrated the sponge that was his brain, and he understood her. She was right. He'd been born into a solidly middle-class family with solid middle-class standards. He'd never had to scramble for a meal or go without one. He wasn't the product of an impoverished immigrant family as was Brenda.

Brenda, on the other hand, had been forced from her twelfth year to study middle-class mores and behavior, much in the way he'd studied Indian cultures and natural sciences. In effect, she was as much a scholar as he. And, since she was rich and he wasn't, she might even be more successful in her field of study than he'd been.

It was an interesting insight, and one he guessed he'd have to study at length later. This moment didn't seem appropriate to delve further into it.

Even if he'd wanted to, Brenda took that moment to kiss him, and all thoughts of any nature at all flew right out of his head. She kissed him!

He kissed her back with all the fervor he didn't until now know he possessed. He was terribly disappointed when she pulled away from him after several blissful minutes, during which they both investigated each other's bodies searchingly, and by hand.

Seventeen

"Oh, Colin."

After their exquisite kiss and several minutes of exploration, they'd sunk back onto the blanket—which Colin had taken care to spread out again—and Brenda was feeling dreamy. Since she'd never had much of a childhood, she'd never been able to appreciate young love under the stars. Or anywhere else, for that matter. She felt as if she were making up for lost time tonight, although she still wasn't ready to give herself to Colin or any other man before he'd made a firm commitment. Which meant marriage.

"I really was terribly frightened when I was lost."

"I'm sure of it," he said, in a voice that sounded strangely taut.

She didn't fully fathom why this should be, although she figured it had something to do with the marvelous kiss they'd recently shared. She continued in her own rapturous tone, "Isn't it a beautiful night, though?" She'd like to kiss him some more but knew that would be forward. She couldn't very well chide him for trying to take advantage of her and then try to take advantage of him.

Well, she could, but not if she expected him ever to believe another word she said.

"Yes. Yes, it is."

She realized he'd licked his lips nervously. Still, she didn't understand. Sighing with pleasure, she stretched out and wiggled until she was pressed directly against him. She thought he groaned softly but wasn't sure.

"You were right about it being too early for the moon and stars when I was so afraid." She felt quite open-minded and magnanimous about saying so at this point, since she'd been furious at him when he'd pointed it out to her earlier. "But aren't they lovely now?"

"Yes."

He was certainly a tight-lipped fellow when he wasn't lecturing. Brenda didn't really mind. She could civilize him. She'd tackled more difficult tasks in her life. "I'm sorry I yelled at you."

"That's all right."

"I don't want to fight with you."

"I'm glad."

He might have been glad, but he didn't sound it. Undaunted, Brenda went on. "But, you see, I'm not what you believed me to be."

"No?"

Was that a whimper? Brenda stared hard at what she could see of his face but couldn't tell.

"No. I get the feeling you think I'm a loose woman." She felt him take a deep breath and sensed that he'd opened his mouth, so she gently pressed her palm against his lips. He gave a small moan, which she also didn't understand. "I'm a passionate woman, Colin, but I've never been loose."

"Oh." The brief syllable sounded as if someone had tried to strangle it on its way out of his mouth.

"And, while I find you awfully attractive . . ." She drifted into silence, afraid of what she was going to say. Colin uttered another smothered moan. "Well, I do find you attractive, but I'm not willing to sacrifice my virtue on the altar of passion, no matter how much the notion appeals."

She wasn't sure what he said then, because she couldn't make out the words. It sounded vaguely like a cross between a plea and a protest. She decided to forge onward. Maybe if she confessed her own attraction to him, he'd be more apt to treat her with respect instead of as an object of his own sexual fantasy. She spared a moment to be sorry actresses had such abysmal reputations as a group.

"It's not that I don't have the normal urges common to both men and women," she hastened to assure him. "But I'm not going to jeopardize my reputation, my career, or my morals for a mere fling."

This time she was sure she heard him groan, as if he were in pain. She pulled away from him, worried all of a sudden. "Oh, Colin! Are you uncomfortable? Are you cold? Are you hurt?"

"No." His voice sounded strange. "I'm fine."

She squinted at where she assumed his face was. She could barely see it, but it looked to her as if his eyes were squeezed shut and his mouth had scrunched up. He really did seem to be in some kind of pain. "Are you sure?"

He nodded.

Because she thought he might be fibbing in order to spare his own male vanity, she reached up and caressed his cheek with her hand. He sighed into her palm, and she smoothed her fingers across his lips. There was something wrong; she knew it.

"Tell me what's the matter, Colin," she urged gently. "I can sense you aren't feeling well."

"I'm all right."

If he got any more clipped in his speech, he'd be barking like a dog. Brenda frowned into the night. "No, you're not. Tell me what's the matter. Please. I want to help you."

He sucked in a huge breath and let it out all at once.

"If you really wanted to help me, you'd go to bed with me."

She jerked away from him and stared hard through the blackness and into his face. She suppressed her first urge, which was to sock him in the jaw, when she saw how truly miserable he looked. Because she didn't want any misunderstandings to exist between them, she said severely, "And I'd like to oblige you, Colin, but I shan't do so. Not unless you offer me more than a single night of passion in order to slake your lust. I'm not that sort of woman."

"I know that. Now."

She believed him. She also believed he was unhappy about it. She sniffed. Too bad for him, the rat. If he loved her, he'd ask her to marry him. But no. All he wanted was to go to bed with her. It was all very upsetting. Standing, she shook out her skirt. "I think we ought to go back to the lodge."

"I don't think I can walk."

She squinted down at him. He still looked as if he were suffering from something dire. Her heart had taken to aching, and she wasn't sure she believed him. "Why not?"

"Sit next to me again and I'll show you."

She put her fists on her hips and continued to stare at him for a moment before she complied, being careful not to do anything that might be remotely construed as seductive. "What do you mean?"

He took her hand and laid it carefully on his thigh. She jumped up again, as if she'd touched burning coals. "My God! Is that what I think it is?"

He nodded miserably.

"Oh." She didn't know whether to be pleased or appalled. "I—ah—didn't know."

He groaned.

For no good reason she could comprehend, she felt guilty. "I'm sorry, Colin."

"Right."

"I didn't mean to let you think I—I'd—I mean—"

"Never mind. I know what you mean." He took a ragged breath. "Not your fault."

"I should say it's not." That didn't sound very nice. But Brenda didn't know how to be nice under these circumstances. The whole situation was new and bizarre and out of her realm. While it was true men had tried to seduce her before, she'd always been able to put them off with a joke. And if a joke didn't work, she'd shame them into letting her alone. She felt neither like joking with nor shaming Colin. The truth of the matter was that she wanted him as a partner in a sexual liaison almost—but obviously not quite—as much as he wanted her.

"This is very distressing," she said, beginning to gnaw on her knuckles. "Are you sure you can't walk? We can't stay here all night." Although it sounded like a sort of romantic thing to do—except that, if anyone learned about it, nobody would ever believe they hadn't done what Colin wanted to do.

"Give me a minute," he pleaded. "I'll be all right in a minute."

Hmmm. Is that how these things worked? Brenda had never been this close to capitulation before, so she had no experience—and none of the women who'd talked to her about this sort of situation had ever refused to consummate the act. Fiddlesticks. "Very well. I'll—ah—walk around the clearing for a second or two."

"Don't get lost again."

That wasn't kind of him. She decided not to say so. "I won't."

She thought he nodded but didn't lean close enough to be able to tell for sure. She didn't dare; she feared he might take her leaning as some kind of seductive ploy on her part, and she didn't want to tease the poor fellow any more tonight. She hadn't intended to tease him in the first place.

Which irked her. It wasn't her fault men found her attractive. It wasn't her fault men's libidos—not to mention their egos—were such that they assumed any woman to be fair game. It was probably men's uncontrolled sexual natures that had forced women into being creatures whom men believed were designed solely for their pleasure. This was why men liked to believe women incapable of serious thought: because if men acknowledged women's equality of intellect, they would no longer be able to think of them as objects. Brutes. They were all brutes.

She was becoming downright irritated by the time Colin at last struggled to his feet. "Better now?" she asked sarcastically and then could have bitten her tongue. She didn't want to start another fight.

"Yes. I think so." She heard him take a deep breath. "Thank you for being understanding."

That was nice of him, especially when she'd lately been on the verge of kicking him with her heavy walking shoe. "You're welcome." Deciding that wasn't enough, she went on to say, "Thank you for coming to find me." No one else had thought to do so. Then again, she hadn't called attention to the fact that she was going out for a walk; probably nobody else knew she was missing to begin with.

"You're welcome."

This conversation was leading nowhere in a hurry. With a sigh, Brenda said, "Shall we go back?"

"Yes."

But not, it soon became evident to her, immediately. Colin pulled that torch thing out of his pocket and monkeyed with it for several minutes. Brenda, who was anxious to return to the lodge because tomorrow would be another full day of filming, restrained her impatience with something of an effort. When he finally got the blasted thing to send out a thin stream of light, she expelled a breath of relief.

Needless to say, her show of impatience vexed him. He glared at her. "It will be much easier to find our way back if we have some light." His voice was snippy.

"I'm sure of it." Hers was hard.

A mood of deep depression had descended upon Brenda by the time they straggled back to the Cedar Crest Lodge. It was past midnight, and they had to awaken the night watchman to unlock the front doors for them. The fact that he did so with a broad smirk on his face did nothing to ease Brenda's state of gloom.

"This is for you."

Brenda felt ghastly the morning after her night in the woods with Colin. As ever, though, she put on a happy face, even though she was nearly asleep on her feet, her head ached, her eyes burned, and she wanted to sleep more than she wanted food, money, or sex with Colin.

When Jerry Begay's voice penetrated the fog in her brain, however, she perked up a trifle. She saw he was holding out the baseball he'd brought with his band to the Peerless lot. It was, evidently, a gift for her to remember them by.

Brenda was delighted. "Oh! Thank you, Mr. Begay. How nice."

"That's very nice of you, Jerry."

She wasn't overjoyed when she heard Colin's confirmation of her words. In point of fact, she felt like turning and hollering to him that she could speak for herself. She held in her temper and her hot words and merely smiled at Jerry.

"You're a good sport," Jerry said simply. "You play baseball like a man."

In her present state of exhaustion, Brenda's emotions were perilously close to the surface. That she'd managed to earn Jerry's respect and make a friend of him touched her so deeply, she nearly cried. Having learned to be strong over the years—and knowing from Colin how little most Indians showed their emotions except in the bosoms of their families—she didn't humiliate herself thus, but smiled and said, "May I give you something, too, Jerry? I'd like to."

He smiled. "Yes. Thank you."

She'd had no idea that Jerry would give her a gift, but she recalled reading that Indians—which tribes of Indians, she had no idea—valued tributes, so she'd prepared one for him already. She'd have asked Colin about it before offering it to Jerry but feared he'd only sneer at her. She wasn't up to being sneered at this morning.

Therefore, she'd decided to give Jerry a small music box she liked a lot. It played "Polly Wolly Doodle," which she didn't expect any self-respecting Navajo would understand, but she didn't either, and the tune was lively, so she guessed it would do. Then, although it had felt like vanity at the time, she'd also decided to give Jerry a photograph of herself. Signing the photograph, "With fondest wishes to Jerry Begay, in memory of working in the pictures together. Brenda Fitzpatrick," she hoped it, along with the music box, would be appropriate gifts and might convey a modicum of her appreciation of the band's professionalism during the filming of their scenes.

Now, as the Navajo band began climbing into the motorized trucks hired to return them to Los Angeles, where they'd take a train back to Arizona Territory, she realized she'd left her gifts inside the lodge. Frustrated with her carelessness, which had probably been a result of her state of exhaustion and unhappiness, she said,"Oh, dear, I'll be back in just a little minute. I left the things on a table in the parlor."

Jerry nodded. She didn't even look to see if Colin was still there when she turned to retrieve the gifts. To heck with Colin.

It didn't take her more than three minutes to accomplish her trip. When she got back to the truck, she stopped short when she saw Jerry and Colin chatting. Unless she was out of her mind, Colin was blushing! Now why should that be? Then Jerry saw her, she noted the twinkle in his eye, and she knew exactly why.

Darn it to the earth and skies, Jerry Begay had deduced that Colin and she were attracted to each other. Perhaps he even knew they'd stayed out late in the woods together last night. Indians were supposed to know things like that, weren't they? Obviously he'd said something to Colin about it, too. How embarrassing.

Suppressing her impulse to turn tail and run back into the lodge, Brenda donned her most blasé, nonchalant, friendly pose. "I hope you will accept these small gifts, Mr. Begay. I sincerely appreciate your help in making this picture."

Jerry nodded. He seemed especially pleased with the music box, which he turned over and over in his big rough hands. Brenda showed him how to wind it up. "See? It plays music every time you open the lid as long as you keep it wound up. But don't wind it too tightly, or the spring will break."

The Navajo nodded again. He peered at the photograph unsmilingly, and Brenda hoped she hadn't violated some sort of cultural taboo by giving it to him. He said, "Thank you," and she guessed she hadn't.

With one last handshake for Colin, Jerry climbed into the truck. Brenda heard the driver cranking away at the motor and the motor catch. The driver hurried up into the cab of the vehicle, and the truck started down the mountainside, followed by the second truck, both vehicles taking the villains of *Indian Love Song* with them. She shook her head, thinking it really wasn't fair to cast those good men as villains. There was nothing to be done about it now.

She stood there in the dust churned up by the truck wheels, waving, until the trucks were out of sight. There were lots of farewells trailing after the band of Navajos, since Martin and the rest of the *Indian Love Song* cast and crew had come outside to see the Indians off.

There was nothing the least bit villainous about those fellows. They'd been polite and quiet and gentlemanly in a way that had seemed utterly natural. Colin had told her that they were behaving as they always behaved.

In other words, they'd never been anything but themselves, yet they'd made friends of the entire crew—although they were wildly competitive on the baseball field.

It was an interesting phenomenon. Brenda, who had never, since her twelfth year, felt able to be herself, had also made friends of all with whom she worked. In her case, the result had been a lot more difficult to achieve.

Of course, Indians, no matter of what tribe, were a conquered race. She supposed white men, who enjoyed feeling superior to everyone else on earth, now considered it politic to be gracious to them. She, on the other hand, was merely a free-born white woman and, therefore, remained an object that must be subjugated to the white man's will.

Boy, was she being melodramatic this morning. To counteract her mood, she turned to Martin once the trucks were out of sight, again ignoring Colin. "What's up for today, Martin? Are we doing the reconciliation scene?"

"That's it," Martin confirmed. He rubbed his hands with pleasure. "The picture's almost in the can."

And then they'd all go home, and she'd never see Colin Peters again. Her eyes filled with tears so suddenly, she didn't have time to stop them. She wiped them away immediately. Good heavens, she was a total wreck.

She hadn't wiped her eyes quickly enough to deceive Martin, who looked at her sharply. "Is anything the matter, Brenda? Are you not feeling well?"

"Oh, no. I'm fine. Just got some dust in my eye, that's all." She laughed. "Whew! Those trucks sure do kick it up, don't they?"

"Yes," Martin said, still watching her with keen interest. "They sure do."

Thank heaven for Martin Tafft. He didn't say another word, but smiled at her and strolled over to the set. She knew he knew something was wrong with her, but Martin never pried, bless him.

Colin walked away without a word. Brenda's heart felt as if it had been ripped out of her chest and trampled in the dust.

The filming was almost over. Martin had told Colin that the whole picture would be wrapped up in another day or two. That meant he was going to have to work fast if he expected to get Brenda to succumb to his charms.

Colin frowned. What charms? Obviously, he didn't have a single charm to call his own if she had so little difficulty resisting him. Dash it, his failure to lure Brenda into his bed had been the most dismal failure of his entire life up to now. This morning, for instance, she wasn't even willing to talk to him. She hadn't even offered him a "Good morning."

He hadn't offered her one, either, he reminded himself.

But that wasn't odd. After all, he was known for his failure to pay attention to anything but books. And even if he was beginning to notice the world around him a bit more than he used to do, he was still just another fellow working for Peerless. *She* was the big name here. *She* was the star of the event. He was a nothing. A zero. A big, fat, empty, blank spot on the face of the earth.

That was no way to think. He had to buck up. While Colin had never been conceited about anything at all, much less his masculine prowess, he'd never felt like nothing before, either. His life had been spent as he'd wanted to spend it: in pursuit of knowledge. He was living exactly as he wanted to live.

Except that he'd failed to conquer the one women he'd ever really wanted. It was a lowering reflection. He sat on a stump in the shade, his eyes directed at the activity on the set, while his mind whirred in confusion.

Dash it, she hadn't reacted at all the way a female was supposed to react to the male's mating ritual. She'd even told him she wanted more than a brief fling before she'd agree to a sexual union.

The awful thought occurred to Colin that perhaps this *was* the way female humans were supposed to react to the male's courtship rituals. Perhaps, the human species being what it was, the female had instincts that weren't so well developed in most males. Perhaps they instinctively sensed that, in order to raise their young properly—and young sprouts often resulted from mating—they had to manipulate males into a commitment lasting longer than one night. Gad, what a dismal thought.

Or was it? Colin was squinting at the set construction, not really watching it, when a man cried out, startling him out of his muddled thoughts and making him pay attention.

"Look out! I can't keep my grip on it! Hold on, Carl!"

The man who'd yelled had been balanced on the top rung of a tall ladder propped against a taller tree. He'd been holding one end of a huge wooden platformlike contraption. Colin couldn't tell what it was from where he sat, so he stood up, shaded his eyes, and watched, his heart pounding with suspense.

A gasp came from the others watching the scene when the man lost his grip on the wooden thing. It fell from his hands, jolting him and making him lose his balance. He was barely able to cling to the ladder and to the limb of the tree against which the ladder was balanced. The ladder swayed perilously. Colin stared, appalled, still stunned and unable to react more cogently. Then his glance darted to the ground beneath the wooden thing.

Good God. His brother George stood directly underneath that gigantic slab of wood, staring up at the man on the ladder. Another man, poised on the edge of an outbuilding's roof, clutched the other end of the slab in both hands, but only barely.

"I can't hold on to it, either!" the man on the roof cried out in dismay. "Look out below! It's going to crash!"

"George!" Colin roared. "Run!"

To Colin's horror, George turned to look at him instead of taking his advice. Colin waved his arms frantically in an effort to get his brother to run from underneath that heavy board. For what seemed like hours, George looked from Colin to the man struggling with the board, before he recognized his own danger, turned, and started sprinting to safety.

It was too late. Colin's face screwed up into a grimace of consternation and his hands flew to his head, even as he took off running toward George.

The giant board hurtled through the air. As Colin watched, he could have sworn the blasted thing had a mind of its own. It was probably his own fright for George making him think the board aimed at his brother, even going so far as to turn end over end, thereby zeroing in more directly on George.

The board struck with a sickening thunk. George dropped like a stone to the hard earth. It seemed to Colin that the world stopped spinning on its axis for a second.

The sound of the board hitting George and then the earth smote his ears, and then there was a moment of absolute silence. Then all hell broke loose.

"George!" a woman screamed. Colin's brain registered Brenda's voice.

"George!" Colin bellowed, terrified on his brother's behalf.

"Good God!" From out of nowhere, Martin raced onto the set.

Others streamed over to George from all sides. The man on the ladder made his shaky way down. The man on the roof, his mouth having fallen open into a horrified *O*, stared at the chaos beneath him in patent distress.

Colin got to his brother first. George lay facedown on the ground, the infamous board weighing him down. With a strength he hadn't known he possessed, Colin upended the gigantic slab of wood and heaved it away from his brother's motionless body. Falling to his knees in the dirt, he reached for George.

"Be careful. Better not move him yet."

It was Brenda. Colin turned to yell at her to shut up before he realized she was only being sensible. He passed a hand over his face and fought panic. "Right. Better check for broken bones first."

"And concussion."

Brenda knelt in the dirt, too, her concentration completely on George, not giving a thought to the beautiful blue silk day dress she wore. She bent close to George's face. "George?" she said gently. "George? Can you hear me?"

No answer. Colin's heart went cold.

She glanced up, worry plain on her face. "Martin, please get the lodge's doctor out here quickly."

"Right." Martin didn't bother to check George's condition for himself, but wheeled around and sprinted like a deer to the lodge. Fortunately, the Cedar Crest had a doctor on staff. Most luxury resorts did these days.

"George?" This time it was Colin trying to determine his brother's state of consciousness. "Can you hear me?"

No answer.

He looked across George's inert form to find Brenda staring back at him. He shook his head. Her lips pressed together tightly. He feared for a moment that she might cry, but she was made of sterner stuff than that. He ought to have known her better by this time.

She licked her lips. "I've had a little experience with this sort of thing. Let me check him over."

Colin wanted to protest, but he couldn't pry his tongue from the roof of his mouth, where it seemed to be stuck. So he watched instead as Brenda first of all checked George's breathing by holding a leaf before his nostrils.

The leaf fluttered, and she looked up and gave Colin a brief, strained smile. "He's still alive." As tenderly as if she were dealing with a hurt child—which, to all intents and purposes, she was, dash it—she checked his pulse. Her smile looked more natural when she reported the results. "His pulse is strong and steady."

Colin's breath left him in a whoosh, and he feared for a second that he might pass out. It was probably only his masculine pride that saved him. He'd be dashed if he'd faint in front of Brenda and a motion-picture crew.

After she'd determined George's status as a still-viable human being, she very tenderly palpated his limbs, being particularly careful with his back. "You never know about these things," she muttered. "I couldn't see clearly, but it looked as if the board hit him on the shoulder. I think it missed his head."

"Thank God," Colin whispered, the words yanked from him by a force outside himself.

"Yes," Brenda said, sounding somewhat wry, "unless it clipped his back. The spine is a vulnerable thing. And if that dratted board caught him in the back and damaged his spine, it might be bad."

"D-don't—don't—" But Colin didn't know what he wanted to say. In truth, he supposed he wanted to tell Brenda not even to hint at such an awful possibility, but the words wouldn't come. She didn't glance up at him, but continued to test George's limbs one by one.

Suddenly, she turned to the crowd standing by. "Get me a bucket of water, somebody. Hurry."

Several men ran off to do her bidding. Colin wasn't sure, but he suspected that at this moment, she was being more sensible about George's catastrophe than he. He was so aghast, he couldn't even think, much less act. He blinked as she began to tear at her waist. It took him a second or two to realize she was taking off the sash tied there.

She held it up. "This is cotton. It will hold water, and perhaps he'll regain consciousness with cool water on his head. If he can talk, he'll be able to help us help him."

Three buckets full of water appeared as if by magic at Brenda's side. She offered the carriers one brief, brilliant smile and said, "Thank you," as she dunked her sash into the closest bucket. She squeezed the excess water out, folded the sash into a pad, and leaned over George again.

As she very gently pressed the cool cloth to the back of George's neck, then his cheek, and then his forehead, Colin heard the sound of running feet. Turning, he saw Martin racing back to the set, accompanied by a portly man in a dark suit who carried a black bag.

"Thank God," he breathed. "I think it's the doctor."

Brenda straightened, still holding the cloth to George's head. She, too, whispered, "Thank God."

It was only then that Colin realized how scared she'd been. And still was. He stared at her, stunned. Had her cool-and-collected attitude been only an act? Had she carried on so splendidly in spite of her fear? Had she been as frightened as he underneath?

When she withdrew her hand so that the doctor could have access to George, Colin saw that her hand trembled. She stood and actually swayed a little on her feet, and he understood that her poise and self-assurance *had* been an act, and an extraordinary one. She was a by-God heroine.

His admiration for her soared like an eagle. Instantly, he stepped up to her and held her arm so she wouldn't fall. She shot him a quick glance and whispered, "Thanks. I—ah—don't feel so good all at once."

He leaned close to her. "Thank you, Brenda. You were wonderful."

She seemed to sway into him for no more than a second, but his other arm went around her and squeezed her close. He didn't care what anybody thought. She might well have saved his brother's life, and he wanted her to know how much he valued her assistance.

Assistance? Dash it, she'd done everything herself. She was no assistant. She was a heroine.

Her voice came to him, small and breathy. "Um, I'm afraid I might be a little sick, Colin. Please let me go into those trees for a minute."

He'd be dashed if he'd let her go now. She might have saved his brother's life. He led her off into the trees himself.

"Please," she said, her voice a little stronger. "I hate being sick in front of people."

"I'm not people." The statement made no sense, and he knew it even as the words left his mouth. But, whatever it meant, it was the truth. Colin didn't want to be "people" to Brenda. He wasn't ready to admit what he did want to be to her, but he knew darned well it wasn't simply "people."

"Here," he went on. "Lean over and put your hands on your knees. That might help. Put your head down."

He might have been useless in helping her with his brother, but he knew what to do when one felt sick whilst on the trail. He was pleased when she did as he'd advised—and without even arguing with him first.

Colin could still see the set through the trees, and even as he lightly helped Brenda to keep her balance, he watched the doctor. His heart nearly leaped out of his chest when he saw Martin and the doctor help George to his feet. His body must have jerked along with his heart, because Brenda spoke.

"I'm sorry I'm taking so long. My stomach isn't cooperating this morning."

She sounded apologetic. Colin couldn't believe it. He turned and stared down at her. "No, no," he assured her. "I'm not being impatient. It's only that George seems to be all right. He's standing up."

"What?" She jerked upright. "Where?"

"There." Colin pointed at the scene.

Slowly, slowly, Martin and the doctor were walking George toward the lodge. Colin pushed his glasses up his nose and peered through them, wishing his eyesight were better. "Does it look to you as though his arm's hanging at an odd angle?"

She clutched at his arm with a viselike grip, peering hard herself. "I think so. It looks as if the doctor's got it in some kind of slinglike thing. That's probably only to hold it in place until he can get him inside."

Suddenly recalling why they'd come into the trees, Colin turned toward Brenda, who lost her footing and fell against him. "Are you feeling better?" He didn't want to rush her, but he had a compelling need to see to his brother's welfare.

"Yes. Yes, I'm fine now. Thanks. I guess seeing George walk helped my tummy."

"Good. Can you walk? I've got to see George."

"Yes. I think so."

She took a step, and her knees seemed to give out. She looked up at him plaintively. "Listen, Colin, I'm still a little shaky. You go on to help with George. I'll follow you when I can."

He wouldn't allow such a thing. She'd saved the entire day, for the love of God. With a short, "Nonsense," Colin lifted Brenda right off the ground. She responded with a tiny squeal.

Then she sighed, her bones seemed to melt, and she relaxed into his arms. She was light as the proverbial feather as Colin ran with her into the lodge.

Eighteen

The doctor and Martin had led George into the small parlor, where he now lay on a chaise longue. The doctor said that was the best place, because the chaise had no sides and he could work on the boy from all angles.

Martin had placed a sentry at the door, the big cameraman, Ben. Ben eyed them doubtfully. "Something wrong with Brenda?" he asked. "The doc's busy with George right now."

"I'm fine," Brenda said, although her voice sounded weak. She felt weak, for that matter. This had been a truly dreadful morning. Although it did feel rather nice to be in Colin's arms. She wished he weren't such a worm. It was very discouraging to know how deeply she cared for him. She'd always assumed she had better taste than to fall for a worm.

"Are you sure?"

It took her a second to realize it was Colin who had spoken, and that he'd been asking about her fitness to stand on her own. With a big sigh, she said, "Yes. Thank you." In truth, she wanted to stay right where she was. Which would be a disaster. It was too easy, while in his arms, to pretend that he cared for her.

But he didn't. All he wanted was a brief sexual liaison with her.

It was all too disheartening to think about at the moment. Colin set her gently on her feet and didn't release her until he was sure she wasn't still wobbly. That was nice of him. She guessed he wasn't a total worm.

Colin opened the door as quietly as he could and entered before her. Brenda glared at his back until she realized he was too worried about his brother to remember proper courtesy. So she followed him into the room.

George's back was to them, but Brenda was encouraged to see him sitting on the chaise in his underwear. Colin hurried over and stood behind the doctor, who was bending over George.

"How is he?" Colin asked breathlessly.

"I only broke an arm, Colin. I'm not deaf," George said, in a tone that sounded remarkably good-humored, all things considered.

Brenda honored him for trying to joke under the circumstances. She hurried over, too, no longer feeling lightheaded and with her balance finally restored. George's face was as pallid as a winter moon, and the grimace on his face, which she imagined was supposed to be a smile, looked only pained. He was really trying hard to be brave through his ordeal. He didn't notice her, but was squinting up at Colin, who was also pale.

It seemed to Brenda that Colin appeared nervous and didn't know what to do with his hands. She wouldn't have been surprised to learn that he wanted to hug his brother, but he couldn't very well do so with the doctor hovering over George's shoulder and arm. Gently, he felt for damage. Every time he did, George winced. Brenda noticed him gripping the chaise with his undamaged hand, and his knuckles were dead white with the pressure he had to expend not to cry out or jerk away from the source of pain.

Clasping her hands to her bosom, she cried, "Oh, George! I'm so sorry you had to have that awful thing fall on you, but I'm *so* glad you weren't hurt worse." A tear leaked out of her right eye, and she dashed it away, irked with herself for succumbing to emotion when George needed everyone's strength.

"Brenda!"

She squinted at him, wondering why he didn't sound happier to see her. They were friends, weren't they? She noticed his pallor suffuse with a deep crimson, and she understood. He was embarrassed to be seen in his undies. Only with effort did she refrain from rolling her eyes. As if she hadn't seen men in their underwear millions of times.

"Don't be shy, George. I'm an actress, remember? I've seen everything." She winked at him to keep the atmosphere light.

It was an exaggeration, but George seemed to relax, which made it worthwhile. The doctor shot her a frown over his shoulder but didn't complain about her presence. Which was a darned good thing, because she wasn't about to be ousted from this room by some old-maid doctor.

"Martin said you're the one who helped me the most when I was knocked out, Brenda. Thanks. Thanks a lot."

How sweet of him. "It was nothing, George. Anyone would have done the same."

"Maybe, but nobody else did." George managed a fairly substantial grin that faded into a moan as the doctor pressed a particularly tender spot.

"I'm afraid I'm going to have to hurt you, young man," the doctor said in a voice that tended toward a false heartiness.

Brenda supposed doctors had to be that way or their patients would object. Personally, she preferred plain speaking. "Is there anything I can do to help, Doctor?"

The doctor's eyes squinched up as he peered at her. He

looked doubtful. "I don't believe this is a job for a lady, ma'am."

If there was anything guaranteed to infuriate Brenda, it was even the slightest indication that some *man* considered her beneath him because of her gender. "I've helped during bone-settings before, sir. I'm stronger than I look."

"I'm sure that's true," the doctor said in a tone that clearly conveyed his doubt. He sounded, in fact, as if he were only humoring her. He glanced at Colin. "You're this young man's brother, aren't you, sir? Perhaps you'll be willing to assist in this next phase of our work here."

She didn't want to do it, but Brenda stepped aside. This wasn't the time to argue with the obnoxious medical man. It helped her emotional state some when Colin glanced at her, almost spoke, then pressed his lips together as if he, too, believed the doctor was wrong in his assessment of her prowess as a medical assistant.

"Maybe I can do something to help?"

They all turned to gaze at Martin, who appeared fairly shaky and definitely pale. He shrugged uncomfortably. "I, er, guess I can hold him down. Or something." As if he couldn't help himself, he added, "Although I've never been very good with these types of things."

Brenda put a hand on Martin's arm. "I'll do it, Martin. Don't worry."

"Really, ma'am, I—"

Colin cut the doctor off before he could finish his objection. "She'll do fine." Glancing at Martin, he said, "Why don't you get poor George something to drink, Martin? Maybe brandy or something to help the pain."

"I'll give him a dose of morphia after I set the bone," the doctor said, sounding a bit grumpy. "But I suppose a sip of brandy won't hurt. It's not the wonder drug everyone seems to believe it to be, you know. Not nowadays, when we have anesthesia other than alcohol to assist us."

"Get some brandy anyway, Martin," Colin said in a chilly tone. "I'll drink it if George doesn't want it."

George chuckled weakly.

Martin's spine straightened, and he grinned at George. "Right-o. I'm much better at fetching drinks than at setting bones, believe me." With a quick salute, he was off to the bar, looking much relieved.

The doctor grunted. He eyed Brenda with distaste when she stepped up to help him. She smiled serenely back at him. "And what would you like me to do, Doctor?"

What he wanted her to do was go away and she knew it, but she wouldn't give him the satisfaction.

"Very well," he said after a second or two, during which he was obviously stewing. "If you will hold his left shoulder down. He will probably jerk when I pull the bone back in place." He frowned at George. "Please lie flat on your back, young man. Here, I'll help you."

"Oh, geeze," George whispered. He'd gone pale again. Brenda understood completely.

The doctor assisted George to lie on his back, and George only offered up a couple of groans. Sweat beaded on his forehead, and he looked more scared than hurt.

"You may hold down his legs, if you will please," the doctor said to Colin. "Be sure he doesn't move too much. Neither of us will want to have to do this again."

"God, no," muttered George. The perspiration had started to drip from his face.

Brenda gave him a kiss on the cheek. "Buck up, George. You'll be fine in a little while. I wish I could do something to deaden the pain."

"Shoot me?"

Brenda smiled at him. She loved a big spirit, and George had one.

The doctor, she noticed, didn't even crack a grin.

"We'll take care of his pain afterwards." The words were clipped and cold.

Brenda, feeling a trifle cold herself, snapped, "Yes, but that doesn't help poor George at the moment, does it?"

"I know you aren't versed in medical science, Miss Fitzpatrick, but for your information, we need Mr. Peters's cooperation in the setting of this bone. If we knock him out with opium before we set it, we might not do it properly."

Not only didn't Brenda believe him for a second, but she also wanted to kick him in the hind end and tell him she knew animal doctors with nicer bedside manners than he possessed. What possible harm could it do to ease poor George's pain before the doctor set the bone? She held her tongue for George's sake, but she detested the doctor.

"Let's just get this over with."

That, from Colin, who was nearly as pale as George and was perspiring, too. Brenda felt sorry for both Peters brothers and wished she could do more to help than just hold a shoulder. "It'll be all right, George," she whispered softly. "We'll give you some painkiller as soon as this is over, and then you can sleep."

She noticed the doctor, who had been digging around in his black bag, glaring at her, and deduced he didn't approve of lay people speaking to his patients about medical procedures, even those as humane as promising relief from pain. She glared back at him and pressed gently on George's left shoulder.

The doctor snapped his bag shut with more force than seemed necessary. "Very well. Mr. Peters, please hold your brother's legs tightly. We don't want him moving."

Brenda wanted to ask if it wouldn't be better to drug the poor patient if he really wanted him to be still but didn't. She'd only aggravate the fool further, and that wouldn't do George any good.

"Here's the brandy!"

They all glanced up to see Martin standing in the door, holding up a brandy bottle in one hand and a glass in the other.

"God, I could really use a drink," muttered Colin.

Brenda couldn't help it; she laughed. So did George, thus astonishing everyone in the room. The doctor, exasperated, snapped, "Give the patient a small drink, if you must, Mr. Tafft."

Plainly cowed by the doctor's crisp manner, Martin glanced from Brenda to Colin to George and shrugged. Following the doctor's instructions, he uncorked the bottle and poured out a finger of brandy.

Brenda knew that one was supposed to savor brandy; to swirl it and sniff it and make a big production of drinking it. She'd never understood the mystique surrounding the drink and was glad when Martin eschewed such traditions in favor of speed. George, whom she'd never seen take a drink of alcohol before, sniffed the glass and wrinkled his nose.

"I think I'd prefer opium."

The doctor snorted again. Brenda grinned. Colin said, "Drink it, George. It might help."

"If I don't choke to death." He drank it, though, and then coughed, which hurt his arm and made him groan.

Brenda could hardly wait to get this over with and get the poor boy sedated.

"Are we quite ready?" the doctor asked snappishly.

George, whose eyes were watering, and who didn't seem able to talk, nodded.

Colin said, "Yes. Please. Let's get this ordeal done."

Brenda didn't speak, figuring silence on her part wouldn't hurt and might keep the doctor from being any more aggravated than he already was.

"All right. Hold tight."

Brenda pressed down hard on George's left shoulder.

She saw Colin gulp hard and do the same with George's legs. Martin shut his eyes and turned his head so he couldn't see the operation progress. The doctor positioned one hand on George's right shoulder and the other on his wrist. Then he pulled. George cried out and his body jerked, but neither Brenda nor Colin let go.

It seemed like forever that the doctor pulled that poor arm, but it could have been only seconds. There was a terrible grinding noise, George whimpered pathetically, and that was it. Almost as soon as he'd begun, the doctor grabbed the splint he'd set by and began bandaging. "Keep holding him," he said crisply.

Brenda and Colin, exchanging a glance of anguish, did as bidden. George had his eyes shut so tightly, Brenda couldn't even see his eyelashes. Tears squeezed out from under his closed eyelids and sweat poured from his body. He seemed so young and so vulnerable, and he was in such dreadful pain, that she wished she could hug him to her bosom and comfort him as his mother might have done in these circumstances, had she been here.

Which would never do. George was, to all effects, an adult man, and she was a woman, and nobody in the whole world would understand. Indeed, George's brother would probably accuse her of trying to seduce the boy.

After an eon or three, which could only have been a few minutes, the doctor tied a white sling bandage around George's neck to hold the splint in place and said, "There you are, young man. You two can release the patient now."

Brenda complied, giving George a little pat on the shoulder as she did so. So did Colin; then he sat with a thump on a chair beside the chaise and buried his face in his hands. Brenda feared he might faint.

"Are you all right, Colin?" she asked, thinking she probably shouldn't have. Men were so sensitive about these things.

But Colin nodded and didn't snap at her, so she

guessed he didn't mind too much. Martin, she noticed, was as white as a sheet and was tossing back a small brandy. She grinned. Bless Martin's heart. He wasn't shy about showing emotion. Not like some men she could name. She wanted to hug him, too, but didn't dare.

Instead, she asked quietly, "Would you like a little brandy to steady your nerves?"

"No. Thank you." Colin's voice sounded very strained and scratchy. Which Brenda understood. She felt as if she'd been dragged through a thousand miles of barbed wire fencing and then thrown into an alligator pit. And she couldn't swim.

As for poor George, she could see that his teeth were clamped tightly together. She feared he might break his jaw if he kept that up. With his left hand, he had the edge of the chaise in a death grip. He'd drawn his knees up, and she got the feeling he'd have curled himself up in a fetal position and rolled back and forth except that his right arm was in such mortal agony. She glanced at the doctor and risked asking, "Can we give him some laudanum or something else to deaden the pain now, Doctor?"

The doctor had been puttering about, putting stuff back into his black bag. Brenda disapproved. While tidiness was all well and good in its place, she considered George's plight of more importance at the moment. He looked up, frowning, which didn't surprise her. She frowned back to let him know what she thought of doctors who cared more for their darned black bags than they did for their patients.

"Yes, yes," he said impatiently. "I'll give him a dose of morphia now and leave a prescription with instructions. He shouldn't take too much, as I'm sure you know. We don't want him to get addicted to the stuff."

"I don't think you have to worry about that," Brenda said in a voice as dry as dust. "He only needs it for pain."

"For heaven's sake," Colin said, suddenly looking up from his cupped hands. "My brother is no drug addict! He needs some relief from that pain, and he needs it now. Will you snap it up a little? Please?"

Brenda gave Colin a big smile. He noticed it, blinked at her, and looked confused, as if he didn't understand why she was smiling at him. But she heartily approved his eagerness to end his brother's suffering. He so seldom exhibited the characteristics of a normal human being; the fact that he was doing so now on behalf of his brother gave Brenda hope. For what, she didn't know, but his attitude encouraged her anyway.

"Very well. Here, young man, can you lift your head?" The doctor had a teaspoon poised in the air over George's head. George couldn't see it, since he had his eyes shut.

Again suppressing an urge to sock the doctor in the chops for being a coldblooded, coldhearted, not to mention blind and deaf, son of a female dog, Brenda said, "I'll help."

Ignoring the doctor's black look, she knelt beside George and put her arms around him carefully, so as not to jar his recently bandaged arm. "Here, George, let me help you lift your head a little bit so the medicine won't drip down your chin."

George opened his eyes, which were swimming in tears of pain, and gave her a stiff nod. "Thanks, Brenda." His voice was a small, hoarse croak. "You're a real pal."

"Nuts. You're a brave guy. I'd want to be knocked clean out before anyone set any of my bones. Now drink this stuff. It'll probably taste nasty, but medicine always does."

He gave a feeble chuckle, peered up at the doctor, saw his sour expression, and frowned back. Brenda got the impression he'd like to offer the doctor a few home truths but didn't have the energy. He drank his medicine with a grimace and a cough, but he got it down.

Brenda gently helped him to lie back on the chaise, making sure he didn't do anything to jog his arm. "There. Now you just sleep, George. I'll get you a blanket."

"Thanks, Brenda."

She could scarcely hear his voice and said, "Nuts," again. She wanted to cry for the boy. He seemed so young and so hurt.

"I'll get a blanket for him. You stay here and watch him."

Surprised by Colin's sudden entry into their conversation, she glanced up and saw him watching her with an odd expression on his face. She didn't argue, but nodded and said, "Thanks."

"Really, he doesn't need anyone to watch him. He'll be fine. It's only a broken arm. It's not as if he broke his neck."

Furious at the doctor, Brenda said through clenched teeth, "He got bashed by a huge piece of lumber. It's not just his arm, for the love of God. The poor boy's a mess. And you're a stinking, lousy doctor."

"Really, young woman, I don't understand the manners prevalent in today's females."

"And I don't understand why you ever decided to become a doctor. You've got about as much compassion as a hungry crocodile."

The doctor grabbed his black bag and straightened up. Pointedly ignoring Brenda, he spoke to George. "I'll look in on you later in the day, young man." Since George was in too much agony to say anything, he turned to Martin and continued in his most cold and doctorly tone. "In the meantime, I'll get a laudanum mixture prepared for him. He can take two teaspoons every four hours, depending on his level of pain."

"Good." Brenda was generally more polite than this, but she'd begun to hate this ill-natured doctor. She didn't even care that he was trying to disregard her presence.

"The laudanum is only for the first two or three days," the doctor went on, continuing to ignore Brenda and her mood—unquestionably because he didn't give a hang what she thought of him, since she was a mere woman, and an actress at that, and shouldn't be allowed to hold opinions in the first place, much less express them. "I'll leave some salicylic powders, too. They are excellent for fever and for pain, although the laudanum is much stronger. The powders are less addictive and can be taken almost at will."

Martin, who had sunk onto the sofa after downing his shot of brandy, nodded. "I know a couple of people who take them for headaches."

"I wish I had a headache instead of this."

Brenda forced a fairly natural-sounding chuckle and patted George on the shoulder. "You're doing fine, George. You're a bully patient." She looked up at the doctor and made a face. "Even if you don't exactly have a bully doctor."

The doctor's lips pursed; then he snorted one last time, and marched out of the room. Brenda stuck her tongue out at his back. "What an icky man. I'm surprised the lodge doesn't hire a better-tempered doctor. After all, people pay a lot of money to stay here."

"I'll talk to the management about him," Martin said. He still appeared shaken. "He really was a brute."

Brenda appreciated his promise, which she knew he'd carry out, since Martin's word was gold. "Thanks, Martin. That's good of you."

He stood, hanging on to the arm of the sofa until he was sure his legs would hold him. "It's only fair. If I'd hurt myself, I'd hate to have that troll working me over."

George was beginning to look slightly healthier. He even grinned a little. "At least he set the arm."

"I still don't think he had to do it while you were awake and feeling it. I think he just likes to see people suffer."

George moaned softly. "If he does, I guess I made him happy. It was awful."

She patted his shoulder again. "But you'll be all right soon, George. I'm sure of it."

"Me, too," said Martin. Now that he was on his feet, he was looking healthier, too, and was eager to leave the sickroom. "I'll, er, go talk to the management now. The sooner, the better, and all that."

Brenda nodded. She understood. Martin wasn't exactly cut out for life in the medical field. He was better at making pretend stuff come to life on celluloid. "I'll wait for Colin."

"Good. Good." Martin fled.

"Poor Martin." Brenda smiled fondly as the door closed behind Martin's hastily retreating form.

"Yeah. He's a good guy. He gave me a job, you know."

"I'm awfully happy to hear it. Will you be working in set design?"

"Yeah. I've started sketches for an Egyptian epic."

"Wonderful. It must be either *Cleopatra* or *Egyptian Idyll.* I know Martin is looking forward to doing both of those, because he used to live in Egypt." Brenda was encouraged to note that George's words were becoming faintly slurry. "Are you in a little less pain now, George?"

He nodded. "I think so. Can't really tell."

"Good. I hope you'll be able to sleep for a long time."

The door opened once more. When Brenda glanced up, she beheld Colin coming in. It looked to her as if he were holding at least two blankets, four pillows, a dressing robe, and some slippers. She could hardly see his face for all the stuff piled up in his arms.

"Here," he said. "I wasn't sure what was needed, but I didn't want to forget anything."

She rose and hurried to help him. "I don't think you forgot a thing, Colin. Thank you."

George managed to slew his head around so he, too, could see his brother. "Yeah. Thanks, Colin."

Colin's eyebrows rose. "The laudanum's working, I deduce."

With a grin, George nodded.

"Good. Here, let's get you covered up."

"I'll lift your head, George," Brenda said. "And Colin can place a pillow under your neck. That might make you feel more comfortable."

Without answering, George nevertheless got his appreciation across; Brenda read it in his warm brown eyes— about as brown, but much warmer, than those of his brother. Acting the good nurse, she tucked him in as if he were a baby. Which was fine. She figured people in pain who'd undergone procedures perpetrated by evil witch doctors who didn't believe in anesthetics deserved to be pampered.

By the time she was through fussing, George was fast asleep. She stood back, put her hands on her hips, and gazed down on him with a good deal of affection. "There. He's all set for a little while, at least."

"Thank you very much, Brenda. You're a wonderful nurse."

Shocked, she jerked her head up so fast to stare at Colin, she nearly broke her neck. She couldn't believe he'd said that—and in such a sincere voice. "You're welcome. I only did what anyone would have done."

He shook his head. "No, you didn't. I honestly believe you could have set that arm as well as that dashed sawbones, and with less pain to George."

She licked her lips. She couldn't believe Colin was actually complimenting her and meaning it. Fearing it was some kind of joke or another ploy to get her into bed, she said hesitantly, "I didn't care for the doctor myself."

He smiled at her. "No, I could tell you didn't."

They stood there, staring at each other over the blanketed, pillowed, and exhausted form of the sleeping George, until Brenda couldn't stand it any more. The longer they stared, the more she wanted to leap over George's chaise and beg Colin to make love to her. The notion of them parting and never seeing each other again—and of never experiencing the kind of passion Colin had offered, even if it didn't include love and commitment—made her heart shrivel up.

She made a decision then. She feared she'd regret it one day, but at the moment, it seemed only rational.

Nineteen

As Colin gazed at Brenda, he suddenly found it difficult to imagine her as a bit of fluff. He'd been trying to do that, he realized now. He'd been attempting with all of his resources to think of her as just another woman, more lovely than most, to be sure, but that was all.

He'd pretended to ignore all of the evidence singling her out as a unique person, one with intelligence, integrity, spunk, honor, and huge capabilities. There was no way, in the face of her service to his brother, that he could keep the pretense alive any longer.

Brenda was about as far from being ordinary as a woodpecker was from an eagle. She was special. She was wonderful.

He was in love with her.

And, what's more, he feared this new understanding had killed off any possibility of their ever getting together. He supposed they could still be friends. That thought made his heart scrunch up into a little aching lump and his head pound.

She broke the silence, which had become thick with unspoken emotions. "Um, I think I'll stay in here with George for a while. I'm sure he won't need me, but you never know. Something might go wrong, and I don't trust that doctor to come back any time soon." She frowned, and it was a second before Colin realized her frown wasn't meant for him. "He ought to have secured a nurse to watch him, at least for a day or two."

"A nurse?"

"Yes." She cast him a quick, enigmatic gaze. "If you didn't have the money for it, I'd have been happy to pay for her."

"I don't need your money, Brenda." He knew his hot reaction to her offer was unreasonable. There was, after all, no law, of nature or of God, that dictated men should have more money than women. He, being a typical American male—although he'd have denied it unconditionally until this morning if anyone had accused him of such a thing—was offended by her offer anyway.

She heaved a big sigh. "I'm sorry. I forgot how touchy you men are about that sort of thing."

You men. Colin swallowed hard, unhappy to know that Brenda had categorized him in such a fashion. If he'd behaved decently to her from the first, she probably wouldn't have. Too late now. And there was no time left to re-establish himself in her eyes. He'd completely failed in this, perhaps the most important mission in his life. And the fact that he hadn't recognized it as a worthwhile mission until now was no excuse. He should have seen it. The fact that he hadn't only proved what George and everyone else in his family had been saying about him for years: He paid more attention to his studies than he did the people surrounding him. He cared more about historical folks than living human beings.

Dash it, he hadn't even recognized this particular characteristic of his, which he fully acknowledged and had done for years, as a flaw until this minute. But it was one. A gigantic, mind-boggling, misery-making flaw in his character. He used to laugh about it, thinking it was amusing that other people were so involved with their fellow humans. He'd considered himself immune to such frippery.

Until now.

After a second interval of silence, Brenda let out a chuff of air and said, "I'm going to sit over here and see if I can find a magazine or something to read." She headed for the sofa.

Colin watched her back for a moment, then steeled himself for rebuff and asked, "May I sit with you? I'd like to stay here with George, too." And Brenda. He wanted to stay with Brenda. For as long as she'd let him. He didn't dare say so.

She glanced back at him from over her shoulder, her eyebrows lifted above those spectacular blue eyes, lending her exquisite features an expression of surprise. "Sure. I'm glad. For a while there, I'd wondered if you even cared what happened to your brother."

Immediately Colin bridled. He opened his mouth to refute such a monstrous doubt on her part but never got it said. Brenda intervened.

"I'm sorry, Colin. I shouldn't have said that." She sounded as if she was nearly too tired to stand up any longer. When she sat on the sofa with a soft "Whew," he perceived that she was weary. Very weary.

Her interruption had given him a chance to think about his objection. Recalling his first meeting with George at the Cedar Crest, he understood how she might have come by such an opinion of him, and he was ashamed of himself.

Walking slowly over to the sofa, he said, "No. You're right. Of course you thought I didn't care. I gave you no reason to think otherwise."

He sat next to her, but not too close, fearing she'd tell him to get lost if he took any more liberties with her. His heart gave another hard spasm. He could scarcely stand to think about how badly he'd mucked up his approach to Brenda.

Mating rituals. Good God, he must have been out of his mind.

She sighed again and stifled a yawn. "I know better now."

"You do?"

Rubbing her eyes, she nodded. The gesture was uncharacteristic of her, and indicated to Colin how worn out she was. They'd been up awfully late last night, and she'd been terrified, which in itself was enough to drain a person's energy.

He'd been a beast in that instance, too. Glumly, he admitted to himself that he had a lot to make up for with regard to Brenda. In a gesture meant to mollify, he said humbly, "I haven't been very nice to you, Brenda, and I'm awfully sorry. I didn't realize what a stiff-necked bastard I'd become in the past few years."

He heard a rustle in her corner of the sofa and peeked at her sort of sideways, fearful of looking at her fully in case she intended to mock him or sneer or something. She'd reared back slightly and was staring at him with eyes as big and as blue as robins' eggs. He felt the back of his neck heat up and pushed forward relentlessly.

"And I was an ass and a fool to believe you'd go to bed with me. As if I'm any great shakes. A woman like you could have her pick of all the men in the world. I can't believe how arrogant and idiotic I was. You must despise me by this time, if you didn't already."

"Good heavens." Her voice was small and breathy. Colin figured she was just winding up to let him have it with both barrels.

But she said nothing more. Again he peered at her from out of the corner of his eye, wondering why she wasn't using this opportunity to rake him over the coals. Lord knew he deserved it. He pushed his glasses up his nose and braced himself.

Not a peep from Brenda. He finally dared turn his head and look at her. He was alarmed when he saw her, for she had her hands clutched in her lap and her head bowed. He couldn't tell if she was merely gazing at her clasped hands, trying not to laugh at him, thinking of choice insults to fling at him, or praying. He didn't know, either, which he'd prefer she be doing.

Several minutes passed in silence. Colin got itchier and itchier as the seconds dragged by, his body tense, his brain screaming, waiting for a barrage of wordy weapons to hit him. At last he couldn't stand the strain another instant longer. "Er, Brenda? Are you all right?"

She nodded and didn't speak.

Good Lord, whatever was the matter with her? He tried again. "Brenda? I'm sorry I've been so awful to you. I don't know what possessed me to be such an ass."

She lifted her head and glanced at him. At least she didn't look as if she aimed to pick up the stone ashtray from the table beside her and bash him over the head with it. Colin thanked his stars for small favors.

"An ass?" Her voice was still soft—as soft as eiderdown and as lovely as a sunset. Her voice was as beautiful as the rest of her, faint traces of New York be damned. "No, Colin, you were never an ass." Her head lowered again. "I had hoped, when we first met, that you might have been willing to instruct me in some of the historical aspects of Indian culture. I guess you had better things to do."

Once again his heart gave a large, painful spasm. "No," he said hoarsely. "I had nothing better to do. The truth was that I didn't believe you meant it. I guess I didn't think anyone as beautiful as you could possibly be interested in academics."

Her low chuckle was so ironic, it felt to Colin as if

he'd been sprinkled with alum. "That's been a problem for me ever since I was a little girl."

She spoke matter-of-factly, but Colin could guess at the pain behind the simple statement. He couldn't imagine himself, for instance, Colin Peters, being judged solely on the basis of his appearance. That society judged women thus struck him as immensely unfair, although he'd never much thought about it before. He gulped again, painfully. "I'm sorry. I hate knowing I was as unfair to you as all the rest."

She shook her head. "Oh, no. I'm used to it."

Which only made Colin, who'd always prided himself on being different from his fellow men, feel worse.

She went on. "I have to admit that it hurt, though, even though I'm not blaming you. I have such a powerful thirst for knowledge, you see. I never had the opportunity to attend school past the primary grades, and now I can't ever seem to make people believe I mean it when I ask questions about the things that interest me."

"If I'm an example, I'm sure that's true. I didn't think you meant it. I was an ass."

She glanced at him and gave him a very small smile. "Well—maybe."

His heart turned over. God, she was wonderful. Why hadn't he recognized it before it was too late? Was he one of those blind men who were fated to stumble through life not recognizing treasures until they slipped through their fingers? What an abysmal thought.

He had a sudden, painful vision of himself as a gray-haired old man, living with a gray-haired old woman just like him, stuck in a colorless union with no life to it—no humor, no glee, no fun, no interests other than what they read in books. He'd known couples like that, mainly retired professors and scientists and other academicians. They'd grown used to each other but had never experienced passion together.

God, how depressing. He turned toward her suddenly. "Listen, Brenda—"

"Listen, Colin—"

They'd spoken at the same time, and both stopped instantly as soon as they realized it. Colin gestured with his right hand. "I'm sorry. Go ahead."

She gestured with her left. "No, no. You go first."

"No, really, I didn't mean to interrupt."

"It was I who interrupted."

"No. Please."

She sucked in a deep breath. "Very well." Then she shut her mouth, and it stayed shut for so long that Colin feared she'd forgotten what she'd intended to say.

When he saw that her cheeks had started burning, his eyes almost popped from his head. Obviously, she hadn't forgotten. But what was it?

She spoke again, so suddenly it startled him. "Oh, Colin, this is so embarrassing. But—but— Oh, darn it, I'm so bad at this!"

He'd almost become accustomed to the use of epithets, which she didn't really do very often, but it still jarred on his already ragged nerves. He didn't speak, sensing they'd both be better off that way.

She burst out, "I'd love to go to bed with you!"

His mouth fell open.

Her head turned and she faced him fully, lifting her chin. Her cheeks were now a brilliant pink, which only enhanced her beauty, and her blue eyes sparkled like precious gems. "I know it's shocking, but it's what you wanted to hear, isn't it?" There was a distinct flavor of defiance in her tone.

Confusion held him speechless. On the one hand, yes, that was exactly what he wanted to hear. On the other hand it wasn't. Not at all. Since this understanding was totally new to him, he couldn't think of anything to say to her to save his life.

Suddenly she surged from the sofa with a swish of skirt and petticoat. "Oh, I'm making a botch of this!"

"No," he said feebly. "Wait."

She wheeled around and stood looking down at him, her arms straight at her sides, her fists clenched. "Yes, I am. Now you think I'm a wanton hussy, don't you?"

"No, I—"

"*Don't* you?" Her voice had risen. Darting a glance at the lump that was George, she lowered it. "You must. No woman who wasn't of loose morals would offer herself in this humiliating way."

Finally Colin managed to gather his muscles, if not his wits, together, and he rose from the sofa, too. He towered over her. She was so small and delicate and lovely. He hated himself for offering her such a scummy proposition as he'd done earlier. He couldn't quite take in the fact that she now seemed to be accepting it.

"Brenda, I didn't mean—"

"Oh, I'm making such a hash of this!" Again she swirled around. With her back to him, she lifted her hands and buried her face in them.

Colin felt terrible. "Brenda, I—"

She shook her head. "No, Colin, please don't try to make me feel better. I understand. You don't want me any longer."

He gaped at her blond curls, a little messy now after the vicissitudes of the morning, unable to speak. She thought he didn't want her any longer? Was she out of her mind? Was he out of *his* mind?

"This is the most mortifying moment of my life." The words were muffled, as if she was choking back tears. "Please forgive me. If you can, try to forget I even spoke of it."

Forget? How in the name of glory could he ever forget this? Colin gave himself a mental thump in the jaw to get his brain unstuck; it had frozen solid in shock. "No,

Brenda, please. You misunderstood me. I was—I was—I was just so startled."

She huffed. Colin couldn't tell if there were tears in the noise or not, but he feared there might be. Lord, how could he bungle everything so badly, every single time he tried? "Please. You're wrong."

"About what?"

"About me. About you. About everything." He threw up his hands, frustrated beyond bearing at his inability to articulate plainly. He'd never had this problem before in his entire life. Even when he was a boy, he prided himself on his clear thinking and declamatory proficiency. Then again, what would a boy know about a situation like this?

A watery chuckle issued from Brenda's throat. Her hands still covered her face. "That's no surprise to me."

"Oh, Lord, Brenda, don't you understand? I want you more than ever. I want you so badly, I can hardly stand it."

Her arms dropped and she turned and peered at him oddly. "You do?"

"God, yes."

She gazed at him blankly. "Oh."

"But—but it shouldn't be like this."

She glanced around the parlor. "Um, I didn't think we should do anything in here, Colin."

He ought to be writing this down. While he was generally good at speaking, his true strength lay in the written word. How nonsensical he must sound to her. He'd sound even more nonsensical if he asked her to wait while he wrote out what he meant, since he couldn't seem to say it coherently. "No, no, I didn't mean that. What I meant was that you shouldn't be giving yourself to me like this."

"But—but you just said you still want me." She looked so forlorn, it was all Colin could do to keep from grabbing her and making love to her right there and now.

"Aaaarrrgh." He rammed his fingers through his hair. "No, I didn't mean that."

"No? You mean you really don't want me?"

"No! I mean yes! Oh, dash it, Brenda, I want you terribly. But not like this."

Her lovely face assumed a quizzical expression. Small wonder. "I don't think I understand, Colin." Small wonder about that, either.

"Of course you don't. I'm not making any sense."

"Well," she temporized, "you're certainly not making yourself clear."

"I know." He jammed his glasses against the bridge of his nose and then thrust his fingers through his hair once more. What was the matter with him?

She cocked her head to one side. "Would you like to think about what you want to say for a while, Colin? We're going to be here for a few extra days, I imagine, since this accident will have delayed filming at least one day, and probably more. I don't know about the set or if that big wooden thing was broken when it fell. Or even what they wanted to use it for."

"I don't need to think," Colin told her bitterly. "I need to be flogged."

A tender smile touched her lips. "I've thought so for a long time now."

"You must hate me."

She shook her head. "I wish I did, but I don't."

"I don't know why."

"I don't, either."

The door opened behind them, making them both jump. Colin uttered a soft, "Damn." Just when he'd been on the verge of sorting out his thoughts and declaring himself. Not that she'd even consider marrying him, but that was the only way he'd feel right about this—this offer of hers.

Unless she'd decided she merely wanted to have an

affair with him. The possibility stunned him. Although he saw Martin and a white-clad nurse enter the room, the significance of their entrance didn't register on his brain. He vaguely heard people saying words around him, but he didn't understand any of them. His body and heart both received the signal when Brenda spoke, though. His senses would be able to pick her voice out of a chorus of thousands.

"Isn't that right, Colin?"

He heard and understood that. It was Brenda who'd spoken. He hadn't a clue as to what she referred, however. He said, "Um . . ."

Evidently, Brenda noticed his condition and understood. She gave him a sweet smile and spoke to the nurse. "Colin and I were just saying that we wished the doctor had ordered a nurse to watch out for George, if only for a day or two."

"I believe it was Mr. Tafft who requested my services." The nurse spoke with a lilting Irish accent. She had cinnamon-colored eyes, white-streaked red hair, apple-red cheeks, a cheery demeanor, and was as big as a barn. "Dr. Wilson is a terrible old curmudgeon, dearie. He's not got a compassionate bone in his porky little body."

"I noticed that," Brenda said, laughing as she did so.

"So did I," affirmed Martin. "That's why I requested the services of Nurse Cleary here. I asked that she stay for two days." He glanced worriedly at George. "If that's not long enough, we can extend the time."

"You're a peach, Martin."

Colin watched as Brenda hugged Martin. His hands bunched into fists, and he couldn't account for his sudden, mad compulsion to sock Martin in the jaw. There was no doubt about it: He had it bad. Martin was as good an egg as ever lived, and Colin could swear that he and Brenda were no more than friends to each other. But, good God, he was jealous of the man.

"I've got to go back out to the set now," Martin said. He glanced at Colin uncertainly, as if wondering why Colin hadn't yet spoken.

The look on Martin's face jolted Colin into action. As if a goblin had goosed him from behind, he jerked forward and held out his hand. "Thanks so much for hiring a nurse for George, Martin. I've been worried about him."

Martin seemed to relax now that Colin was speaking to him. "Good. Well, I hated knowing it was a Peerless prop that bashed the boy."

"My, my," murmured Brenda. "You're such an alliterative bloke today."

Chuckling, Martin turned to leave the room. "I'll see you two later. Let's dine together this evening. We can discuss the picture's altered schedule."

"Sounds good to me," said Brenda, her manner having undergone a magnificent change. Only a moment or so ago, she'd been near tears. Now she sounded as cheery and good-natured as ever. Colin wondered if she really had her emotions under such superb control, or if she were only a brilliant actress.

Which made his doubts begin to gnaw at his intentions again. Dash it!

But, honestly, could one believe a woman with such an easy facility for manipulating her sensibilities? Did she ever mean what she said? How could one tell?

What in the name of God was he thinking now? *He* was the one who couldn't be trusted with his emotions—mainly because he pretended not to have any. Brenda was a joy. A wonder. A breathtaking female specimen. The fact that she could function in emergencies and not reveal her innermost secrets in front of the whole world was an attribute that should be applauded, not deplored.

"Dinner," he said vaguely to Martin. "Sure. Sounds good."

Martin left with a parting wave, eyeing Colin one last

time, as though he were trying to ascertain his state of mental well-being.

Nurse Cleary set her embroidered bag on a table and went to inspect her patient, in which pursuit she pulled George's blanket down, revealing him still fast asleep. Big purple bruises were more easily evident on exposed body parts than they had been before they'd had a chance to ripen.

Colin glanced over from where he stood, noted as many of his brother's injuries as could be seen from this distance, and shut his eyes. It hurt him to see George like this.

The nurse tutted. "What happened to the poor lad?"

Thank the fates, Brenda explained. Nurse Cleary nodded and looked concerned and chuckled when appropriate. "Aye, I see how it was. The poor lad got himself knocked senseless and his arm busted. We'll see that he rests and mends himself. We won't let him do naught that might undo the doctor's work, believe me." She used the plural *we,* although Colin had no doubt as to who would be doing any restraining that might be necessary.

He believed her, too, even though she wasn't speaking to him. The militant light in her eye made him feel a little sorry for George. Although it must be admitted that George had demonstrated a particularly willful nature of late and might need some curbing during his recovery. Nurse Cleary would probably do him a world of good.

Still struggling to keep his nerves in check, he walked over to her, held out his hand, and hoped his assumption of ease passed the sharp-eyed nurse's inspection. "Thank you very much, Miss Cleary. I'm sure George will profit by your diligence."

She eyed him askance. "Aye? My, but you're a silver-tongued talker, aren't you?"

If the woman only knew. Unable to think of a suitable response on the spur of the moment, Colin remained mute and only smiled at her, thereby refuting her claim that he possessed a glib tongue. She looked as if she'd be able to check any of George's more unruly impulses without much trouble. If he gave her too much sass, she could sit on him. Poor George would never be able to dislodge her. Not only was she as big as a barn, but she looked solid, as if the majority of her bulk was made of muscle.

"Oh, aye," Nurse Cleary said, after enduring several seconds of Colin's silence, "I'll make him rest, you may depend upon it. And I'm sure he'll be right as rain in a couple of days."

"Fine." Searching his brain frantically for something else to say, Colin came up empty, so he said, "Fine" again, and smiled some more.

Brenda took mercy on them. "If you don't need us in here any longer, Nurse Cleary, perhaps we should leave you to your patient."

"Splendid," said the nurse. "I understand from Mr. Tafft that the two of you have spent a nerve-wracking morning. Get along with you, then, and if you'll take my advice, you'll both go to bed and rest up for a while. No sense making yourselves sick over this young scamp."

"Right." Colin nodded at the nurse and gazed blankly at Brenda.

Fortunately, she was endowed with social graces sufficient for the both of them. "What a good idea. I don't know how you do it, Nurse Cleary. Even being minimally involved in George's injury has given me such a turn, I believe I do need a rest."

The nurse smiled with enormous benevolence upon Brenda, to whom, evidently, she had taken quite a shine. Everyone did; charm was one of Brenda's major claims to fame, which meant she'd never want Colin in her life permanently.

Colin told himself to cease with that line of thinking instantly.

The nurse went on, "Of course it gave you a turn, lovey. But it's different when it's one of your own, don't you know. It's one thing to care for a stranger. It's quite another when you see a friend or loved one in danger and hurt."

"Yes, it is." Colin shivered in the warm room.

The nurse gave him a squint-eyed once-over. "Oh, aye. You're the lad's brother, aren't you?"

He nodded and had to suppress a very embarrassing and childish urge to cry. To counteract it, he squared his shoulders and said, "Well." Then he couldn't think of a single thing to say after the one word. Dash it, he was useless.

Again Brenda saved him. "Let's leave George and his nurse alone now, Colin. I'm sure Nurse Cleary will be happy to let us in again later, to check on his progress."

"Surely, surely." Nurse Cleary folded her hands over her huge aproned stomach and offered them a bountiful smile, like a saint blessing a couple of sinners. "The lad mostly needs to sleep now. He'll be under the influence of laudanum, too, so your chances of finding him awake will be better eight or nine hours from now."

Eight or nine hours. That would leave Brenda and him free to do—anything. He swallowed again, hard.

"Of course," said Brenda.

Colin could only nod, his vocabulary having fled long since and apparently determined to maintain its absence. He managed to recollect some of the manners his mother had taught him scarcely in time to rush across the room and open the door for Brenda. When he shot one last glance back at George's nurse, he discerned her shaking her head and watching him sadly, clearly believing George's brother to be in perhaps greater need of nursing care than George himself.

Maybe he was. He certainly was nothing like his usually self-assured self when he found himself in the hallway alone with Brenda. He gazed down at her, wondering what to say now.

She peered up at him, her expression more sober than made Colin feel comfortable. "Well?" she said after several tense moments.

Well? Well? What did she mean, *well?* Well what? Well why? Well where? Well, hell. God, he was losing his mind. No. He'd already lost his mind.

She lowered her gaze and commenced gently rubbing her arms. "I guess I'll go upstairs and rest. I think I do need a nap. Or something."

He still didn't have a clue what he should say.

Brenda waited a scant few seconds longer, then heaved a king-sized sigh and turned away from him.

Panic welled in his chest. She was leaving him! He reached out and grabbed hold of her skirt, which was the only thing he could reach. "Wait!"

She turned and stared at him as if he were a maniac—which he might well be, given the overall state of his emotions at the moment. "I beg your pardon?" She gazed from his face to his hand, which still held a chunk of her skirt in a death grip.

He released the fabric in a hurry. "I'm sorry. But, please, Brenda, don't go. Please. I—I—I—" He what? Blessed if he knew.

Fortunately, as ever, Brenda grasped the situation instantly. In a voice as sweetly flowing as honey, she said, "Why don't you come upstairs with me, Colin?"

He stared at her for only a moment before he grasped the import of her invitation. He gulped audibly, nodded, and started up the stairs right behind her. She led him to the door of her room, turned to give him one last quizzical gaze, and then, with the air of someone who'd just made a monumental decision that she feared she might regret—and soon—she opened the door and entered before him.

Twenty

This isn't right, Brenda Fitzpatrick, Brenda's conscience scolded her.

Her woman's intuition shot back, *What do you know, you old hag? I may never have another opportunity to experience Colin's love.*

It isn't love, and you know it, you naughty, passion-blinded goose. It's lust.

Lust and love aren't mutually exclusive, you know.

You're quibbling.

Brenda told them both to shut up and leave her alone. She was already as nervous as a cat on a hot stove. She had to lick her lips before she could get them apart far enough to speak. Her throat was dry as a mummy's wrappings. "Would you like a drink of something first, Colin?" First? Good God, the man would think her the sleaziest of sleazy creatures in nature if she kept this up.

"Um, sure. What do you have?"

She wished she could have a shot of rye, actually, but she only had the mildest of sherry wines in her hotel room. Brenda didn't drink much, and she only kept the wine on hand for the few times meetings had to be conducted in her room. "Ah, I have a little bit of sherry."

"Thank you. I'd like some wine."

Was he as nervous as she? He sounded like it. Taking

some courage from this evidence of his vulnerability, Brenda went to the dresser where the sherry and a couple of glasses stood. Her hand trembled as she poured some out for Colin. Then, deciding she needed something, even if she didn't drink, she poured one out for herself. After handing Colin his glass, which he drained instantly, she sipped at her own and shuddered. It would take her a long time to figure out why people liked to drink. The stuff was icky.

"Thank you." Colin stood there, looking uncomfortable and rather helpless, holding his empty wineglass.

"Would you like some more?"

"No, thank you."

"No? Well, then."

This was crazy. Brenda, who'd sworn to herself at least a decade earlier that she couldn't afford to be romantical about life and, therefore, wouldn't be, decided now that this particular decision had been a wise one. She wished she hadn't forgotten it with Colin.

However, she had invited Colin into her room for a purpose. Ergo, they'd best get at it before someone decided to interrupt them. First taking a deep breath and silently calling on God to give her strength—although what God had to do with this situation, she had no idea—she reached for the buttons on her bodice.

Colin blinked and looked frightened.

Oh, this was too ridiculous. Why should *he* be scared? *She* was the one who was the uninitiated virgin here.

It occurred to her suddenly that perhaps Colin didn't know that. Or perhaps he didn't believe it, the cad. Perhaps he believed her to be a woman of loose morals after all. Maybe he'd fallen for the pervasive opinion of actresses and had tarred her with the same brush, no matter how well he'd come to know her.

But she couldn't allow herself to get distracted. She wanted to experience this more than she'd ever wanted anything, barring security for herself and her family. Telling herself to get a grip on her nerves, she said softly, "Would you like to help me?" Then she felt as if someone had set a torch to her, she was so embarrassed.

Fortunately—or unfortunately; she guessed she'd have to decide that later—Colin started slightly and stepped forward. "Yes. Thank you."

She let her arms fall to her sides. So gently she could scarcely feel, Colin put his hands to her bosom. Her eyes closed of their own accord. This was it. This was the beginning of her fall.

No, no, no. That was the wrong way to think about it. This was the beginning of a whole new world. Yes. That was much better.

"Your—" The word ended in a croak, and Colin cleared his throat. Brenda opened her eyes again and looked up at him. "Your dress got all smudged when you were helping George."

She nodded, then forced herself to speak. "Yes. It's nothing. It doesn't matter."

"You were wonderful today, Brenda."

"Thank you."

"Lord, I'm nervous."

"So am I."

At least they seemed to be on an equal footing, although Brenda assumed Colin had at least some prior experience in lovemaking. If they were both as unskilled as she, they might be in for a bumpy ride.

She'd expected him to continue unbuttoning the front of her frock, but all at once he slipped his hands from her buttons and around her torso until he held her tightly in his arms. Ah. This was much more comfortable. Perhaps they would go through a few preliminaries before they tackled the main course. Brenda wished she'd thought of this instead of acting like a hussy.

"I've dreamed about this," Colin whispered.

"So have I."

The kiss they shared was so tender, Brenda might have wept, except she feared she'd terrify Colin out of his intentions. As she felt his sex engorge and enlarge, though, she deemed such a thing unlikely. Gaining a modicum of courage and boldness from knowing he desired her, Brenda rubbed herself gently against him. He let out a hiss of pleasure.

Ah. This was better. If one of them stopped being scared, they'd probably have a greater chance of success. Whatever success in these circumstances turned out to be.

"You're so beautiful." He nuzzled her throat, and she sighed delicately with the pleasure of the sensation.

She almost wished he hadn't said that. She'd prefer that he desire her for herself alone and not merely for her beauty, which had been a gift from nature. She was sick of men only caring about her beauty.

Silly Brenda. Her beauty was what had taken her this far in life. She'd be a fool to discount it now. She was getting what she'd wanted ever since she'd set eyes on Colin. And if it was on account of her beauty, and if this was all she ever got from him, if he refused to give her the benefit of his love or even of his knowledge and learning, at least she'd always know she'd had this much.

He'd started feathering light kisses over her cheeks and forehead, and his hands had begun roaming delicately over her back and down to her hips. She had far too many clothes on for her to gain full value of his caresses.

She lifted her lips to his and kissed him gently, wondering if he could feel the love in her heart. His own lips were soft and full and warm and brushed hers with exquisite tenderness. They were the most wonderful lips Brenda had ever seen. His tongue pressed against her mouth softly, and she parted her lips.

Oh, my, that felt good. His tongue was velvety and

gentle as it probed hers. She'd never done this before, although she'd heard about it plenty of times. Theatrical folks weren't noted for their discretion. Snippets of giggled conversations tiptoed through her mind as she melted into the sensations Colin was drawing out in her.

Her body tingled all over. She felt as if the blood had started dancing in her veins. Her nipples puckered and began to ache. She felt a quiver in her lower belly and a pressure between her thighs. When Colin's hand pressed against her hips, she responded instantly, fairly grinding herself against his groin.

Lord, she wanted whatever it was Colin had. She needed it. Desperately.

"Brenda," he gasped, and said no more.

She understood, having been fairly deprived of speech herself. Knowing she was passing some sort of boundary and she'd never be able to return, she deliberately fumbled with the buttons on Colin's jacket.

"Wait," he croaked.

To her dismay, he let go of her and backed away a step. She was about to protest when she realized he was merely shedding outer garb. His jacket flew across the room and landed with a soft plop. As if in a trance, she watched his collar studs hit the floor. Seconds later his stiff celluloid collar joined them. Then he started on his shirt buttons.

With a start, she realized he was getting ahead of her, so she began unbuttoning, too. Her nerves jangled and her fingers fumbled over their job, but at last the bodice of her frock opened. She glanced at Colin's eyes. They'd been watching her hungrily. When she pushed her dress down and it puddled at her feet, she saw him swallow.

His own shirt dropped from his fingers as if they'd lost all muscular control. He ripped his undershirt off quickly, as if he wanted to get the thing over his head before it had a chance to hide her from his vision a single second longer than it had to.

Brenda felt her mouth drop open. His chest was a work of art. She, who had seen chests galore in her day, due to the fact that most actors harbored a strange combination of egomania and insecurity in their complicated bosoms and liked to parade their wares for admiring audiences, was gratified. Colin was perfect in her eyes. Not bulky, his musculature was well-defined and beautiful. His chest was just hairy enough. Not enough to make him look like an ape, but interesting. Very interesting. "Oh, Colin."

He appeared worried for an instant, until he understood her comment had been one of approval and not censure. "I've, ah, done quite a bit of physical labor during my scholastic career. Anthropology and archeology aren't indoor pursuits."

"No." She gulped. "I mean, yes, I can see that." She paused for another second or two, taking in the glory of Colin's torso. He was tanned, too, as if he'd done a lot of outdoor work without his shirt on. She wished she could have been there to watch him. Better yet, she'd have liked to help. "I'm glad."

His slow grin seemed to heat the air between them. It took a minute for her to overcome her nervousness enough to grin back, but she did it. "Well," she said after a pause, "I like your chest. I hope you like mine."

She heard him suck in a quick breath as she reached for her corset hooks. The garment dropped onto the gown mounded at her feet. Very slowly, she reached for the straps of her fine lawn chemise. It was her favorite, a delicate, feminine garment, and Brenda was grateful she'd chosen to wear it today. She loved its broderie anglaise and satin ribbon trim and always felt especially and mysteriously womanly when she wore it. It was an odd thing, but it gave her courage, probably because it was both ladylike and tantalizing.

At least she hoped it was. From the look on Colin's face, it was plenty tantalizing. Slowly and carefully, she slipped the straps down her shoulders. Colin's breathing became heavier. Encouraging, that. When the chemise snagged briefly on her breasts, Brenda saw him swallow again. And then the chemise, too, fell to her feet to rest there along with her corset and frock, and she stood before the love of her life in nothing but her pantaloons.

"My God," Colin breathed.

Brenda took that as encouragement. Feeling both shy and bold, she asked in a voice breathy with fear and excitement, "Well? Do you approve?"

"Approve? Approve? My God, Brenda, you're—you're like a goddess. One of the vestal virgins or something."

Vestal virgins? What in the name of heaven were they? For a moment, she wondered if contemplating virgins might put a damper on this pleasant interlude. But no. A glance at the front of Colin's trousers reassured her. "Is that a good thing?"

He nodded slowly before he cleared his throat and whispered, "Oh, yes. It's a very good thing."

"I'm glad."

As if a mesmerist had snapped his fingers and brought Colin out of the spell he'd been under, he shook himself quickly and tackled his trouser buttons. Brenda watched, fascinated. She'd never seen this before. As much as actors liked to make exhibitions of themselves, no man had yet had the courage to display himself in front of her naked from the waist down. She'd had glimpses of what might await her, but she'd never seen it in the flesh—so to speak—before today.

Colin pushed his underwear down along with his trousers, and Brenda gaped at the result. He popped, heavily and fully aroused, from the fabric. His—thing—was very big. Gigantic, actually.

Brenda's eagerness suffered a slight setback. Was this right? Was it even possible? Was this the way it was supposed to work? It didn't look like it to her, although it must be. It was her turn to gulp.

"Don't be afraid, Brenda," Colin pleaded, as if it might kill him if she got scared and backed out now. "I'll be gentle."

She glanced at his face and discerned the worry there. Poor Colin. "Don't worry, Colin, I won't back out now." That would not only be unsportsmanlike—and Brenda prided herself on being a good sport—but it would be a terrible letdown. No playwright worth his salt would allow such a thing to happen in fiction. Brenda wasn't going to disappoint in fact.

After staring for fully long enough to worry that Colin might become embarrassed, Brenda dragged her gaze away from his masculine member and allowed it to travel down his legs.

Mercy sakes. Imagine an academician having legs like that. Long, lean, heavily muscled, and spattered with black hair, they looked as if they ought to belong on a cowboy. Better yet, a gladiator. Or a pirate. Somebody who did lots of athletic stuff, anyway. The phrase *columns of Hercules* drifted through Brenda's brain as she admired them. Then she took herself in hand and decided to move things along.

With trembling fingers, she untied the drawstring to her drawers and let them drop to the floor.

They stood there for several seconds, looking into each other's eyes. Then, as one, they moved into each other's arms. "God, Brenda, I've dreamed of this ever since I met you."

"I have, too." It was difficult to speak for the sensations rioting in her body. Colin's hands had started stroking her bare skin and igniting fires all over her. Heat danced wherever he touched her, and the pressure to achieve release increased along with the heat.

Suddenly, he stooped a little and picked her up from the floor. She threw her arms around his neck and held on, thrilled that he'd done such an impulsive thing. When he lowered her to the bed, she kept holding on, and they were soon entangled with each other on the soft, pillowy mattress.

"You're so wonderful, Brenda," Colin murmured onto her stomach, where his lips had roamed.

Brenda lay back and luxuriated in pleasure. "When we met, I thought you hated me."

His low chuckle sent waves of prickles through her. "No. I never hated you."

"I'm happy to hear it."

She couldn't stand just lying there any longer. As Colin's hands stroked a map of sensation from her stomach to her breasts, she allowed her fingers to tunnel through his thick, dark hair. He had beautiful hair, although she knew men didn't like to think of anything about themselves as beautiful. Men were so vain. Still, she loved his hair. Through slitted eyes, she watched his hands discover her body, inch by inch.

His skin was dark from having been exposed to the sun for so many years. Hers, as was the fashion, remained as white as milk. The contrast excited her, especially when his hands worked their way up to her breasts. Brenda was happy, as she'd never been before, that she had substantial breasts, because she'd always heard men liked women who had a certain amount of flesh on them. She wasn't huge, by any means, but her breasts were a nice handful for Colin.

He took full advantage of them, too, kneading them gently for a moment before he lowered his mouth to each in turn. Brenda gasped and closed her eyes. The sensation was almost too exquisite to bear. When he took her right nipple between his teeth and gently nipped it, she thought she might die. His tongue made magic on her skin. She began to utter little cries and moans without being entirely aware of what she was doing.

Colin, too, seemed to be absorbed in what he was doing. When she started exploring his body, he groaned. His body felt warm and hard under her eager hands, and she delighted in the contrast between it and her own. She'd sometimes wished she could examine the differences between the male and female structure, but she never believed she would have the opportunity to do so in such a splendid way. The relative hairiness of his legs and chest as opposed to hers fascinated her. She ran her hands over his chest until the overwhelming compulsion to taste him came to her. So she did. He groaned again.

And then there was his sex, pulsing and hot against her. She'd never imagined ever doing such a thing, and it shocked her for an instant, but she reached out and touched it. As soon as she did so and Colin uttered a low, breathy growl, her inhibitions fled.

"It feels so silky." She hadn't expected that.

Colin only groaned again, from which Brenda deduced that he didn't dislike her examination. Therefore, she continued, feeling the smooth, burning shaft with eager fingers.

"That feels so good," came from Colin's throat, sounding husky and strained.

"Yes," Brenda agreed. "It does."

And then there were his balls. Brenda had heard men refer to their balls, but she hadn't understood what they'd meant until this minute. How very unusual they felt in her palm. Slightly hairy, loose in their sac. Interesting. Very interesting.

"God, I can't wait any longer."

Surprised, Brenda snatched her hand away, afraid she'd

done something wrong. But no. From the way Colin acted now, she knew she hadn't. He pressed her back on the mattress and kissed her hard and long. The kiss was delicious, but what he did with his fingers was even better.

When she felt his hand cover the curls between her thighs, she bucked in shock and anticipation. Her shock faded when she understood that, as she'd explored his masculinity, he wanted to explore her womanhood. It was only fair.

Merciful heavens. It also felt sensational. She cried out softly when his fingers started probing her secret places. She was very wet down there. She hoped that wasn't a bad thing.

"You're so wet," he murmured. Since he sounded pleased about it, Brenda took heart.

She also decided two could play at this game, so she reached for his rigid sex once more. He threw his head back, shut his eyes, and looked as if he were in some kind of exquisite pain for a second.

In an instant, he recovered. "I can't wait much longer, Brenda. Are you ready? I'll try not to hurt you." He kissed her again, urgently.

"I'm ready, Colin," she whispered when he drew back to look at her, a plea in his eyes. Indeed, she was beginning to fear that if something didn't happen pretty soon, she was going to die. Her body was screaming for release by this time, in such a state of fevered excitement that it didn't know what to do with itself.

Fortunately for Brenda and her body, Colin knew exactly what to do. He said, "Don't be shocked, Brenda. I'm going to do something first."

She'd had her eyes squeezed shut, savoring the miracles Colin was performing on her body. When she felt his warm, wet tongue take over from where his fingers had been probing seconds earlier, her eyes flew open, and she pushed herself up on her elbows. Good heavens, he was licking her!

"Colin! Whatever are you doing?"

He glanced up at her, and she distinctly recognized the glint in his eyes. "This is the result of some research I did. In France."

He went back to work. Her shock lasted only long enough for her to react to what he was doing. With a low moan, she sank back and enjoyed herself. Thank heavens for France. It didn't take long. Colin had driven her to such a pitch of excitement that a very few strokes of his tongue sent her spiraling over the edge and into a climax of magnificent proportions. Her whole body convulsed, and she gasped and cried out in pleasure and astonishment.

Before she'd fully comprehended the glory of this new experience, Colin had guided his shaft to where her femininity still quivered. With one plunge, he'd buried himself in her. Brenda gasped again, this time with surprise. And a little pain. She had to admit to it. But it wasn't bad.

It wasn't really bad at all.

In fact, now that she thought about it, it was really quite thrilling. There was something astonishingly exciting about knowing that she and Colin were joined in the most intimate way possible.

"Are you all right?" The words sounded tense.

Colin had pressed his face into the pillow next to her head, and Brenda sensed he was holding himself back with a huge effort. She lifted her hands to his shoulders and started caressing him tenderly. She kissed his hair. "I'm fine, Colin. Fine." Never better, in fact.

She could sense rather than feel his sigh of relief. "Good. I'm glad of that. I didn't want to hurt you."

He lifted his head and looked into her eyes for a moment before he gave her one of those little half grins of his. She thought her heart might burst with love, although she knew things like that didn't really happen.

For only a moment, time seemed suspended. Then Colin bent to kiss her again, and he started moving in her.

"Oh, my!"

He stopped moving instantly. "What?" he gasped. "Are you hurt?"

No, she wasn't hurt. It was only that she hadn't expected anything to feel quite like this. It was—it was—it was really quite exciting. "No," she said, absorbed once more in the novelty and variety of these sensations. "Keep going. Please."

So he did. After a few seconds, Brenda got into the rhythm of it. Oh, my, it felt good. She'd had no idea. After only a few seconds more, her thoughts scattered like chaff in the wind and her body took over, reaching for the release it had only moments earlier achieved.

And then it happened. Like a crescendo in music, the sensations rose and rose until everything exploded into a shattering culmination. Brenda bucked and cried out, and ripples of release danced through her body.

With a roar, Colin, too, achieved release.

For what seemed like forever, time stood still. The only sound in the universe was the duet of gasping respirations as Brenda and Colin tried to catch their breath. The only beings in the universe were Brenda and Colin, and they were one.

Gradually, the world started slowly spinning again. Birds commenced chirping in the trees outside the window. The hotel room came into focus, and Brenda's spirit returned to her body.

When she opened her eyes at last, she discovered herself staring straight into Colin's dark, beautiful eyes. They didn't look cold any longer. In fact, his entire face, which often appeared aloof and withdrawn, held a new softness and wonder. Brenda imagined her own expression echoed his.

He moved first, lifting his hand and brushing the hair away from her face. It had come loose from its pins. Brenda supposed it was a mess, although she couldn't drum up much concern. A whole new world had just exploded into being in her life, and she didn't give a hang about her appearance.

Colin's smile was as intimate as any smile she'd ever received from a man. "Are you all right, Brenda?"

Because emotion threatened to overwhelm her, Brenda only nodded. She didn't want to cry and scare the poor man to death.

"I'm glad." He kissed her with exquisite tenderness. "I—I've never—I mean—it was . . ."

His words trailed off. Brenda understood. With an effort, she managed to whisper, "Me, neither. Yes, it was."

Somehow, in the last several minutes, they'd managed to create a unit perfectly tuned to operate as one. At least, that's what it felt like to Brenda when they sighed together and closed their eyes. Again as a unit, they moved. Colin slid to Brenda's side, wrapped her in his arms, and drew her up to his chest. She snuggled there in a kind of blissful relaxation. She felt rather as if they were floating together on a cloud somewhere above the tawdry earth.

With a sigh of absolute contentment, she smiled. So did Colin.

She didn't know how long they lay there, drifting and dreaming, before they went to sleep.

Colin came back to consciousness slowly. He couldn't recall the last time he'd felt this contented, this relaxed. Languid. Free. Glorious, actually.

And it was all because of Brenda. The perfect woman. He couldn't understand now, after they'd made love together, why she'd allowed him such intimacy. She was far too good for him. He'd never in a million years deserve so superior a person.

She was everything he'd ever dreamed of in a woman. That is to say, she was everything he ever would have dreamed of, if he'd been in the habit of dreaming. It seemed a pity to him now that he hadn't ever allowed himself the privilege of daydreams. They'd have enlivened and enriched his life. He'd been a fool to eschew such fancies as irrelevant and unimportant. At the moment, he couldn't think of a more useful task to set his mind to than spinning fantasies about Brenda.

Reality sent a sharp stake through his heart with a sudden, painful thrust, launching him back into real life with a jolt. Colin frowned, and his heart started aching painfully.

Brenda still lay curled at his side, and he still had an arm around her. He glanced down at her soft blond curls and felt like crying.

Before they'd made love, he'd told himself that once the act was done, he'd be free.

Which only went to prove something he'd known for days now: He was an ass.

Now that he'd made love with her, it was painfully clear to him that he could never have enough of Brenda. Bright, beautiful Brenda. The most perfect woman in the world.

Unfortunately, it was also painfully clear to him that there was no way in hell he could have her.

The truth was so unbearable, Colin closed his eyes against it and tried to pretend it wasn't so. Unpracticed in pretense, he failed utterly.

Twenty-one

When Brenda slowly returned to the waking world, at first she didn't remember why she felt so good. Then it all came back to her, and she smiled. Turning over, she reached out her hand for Colin. She wanted to feel his naked chest one more time before they had to wash up and go downstairs to resume their lives among the cast and crew of *Indian Love Song*.

Her hand flopped onto the sheet instead of onto Colin's hairy chest, and she opened her eyes, blinking into the soft afternoon sunbeams floating through her window.

Where the heck was Colin? Groggily, she pushed herself up, only then realizing that several previously unused muscles were annoyed at having been put to use at last. Let 'em protest, she thought happily. They'd get used to it.

She saw Colin sitting beside the window, his chin in his hands, his elbows on the sill. He seemed to be studying the bird life out there. Brenda wondered if he were cataloging the different kinds of birdy chirps. Perhaps he was studying the flight patterns of scarlet tanagers as opposed to those of blue jays, before and/or after they'd robbed other birds' nests.

"Colin?" Her voice came out low and husky.

He turned and smiled at her. This smile carried a lot of warmth and friendliness, or so it seemed to her.

She smiled back, hoping to convey more than mere friendliness with her own smile—although there was sure nothing wrong with friendship. Heck, Brenda valued friendship more than most things in life.

But she craved something else from Colin.

The more fool she. She knew she'd never get it. Colin was far too good for her, and they both knew it. He was a certified brain. She was a certified beauty. She'd known for a long time that, while the twain might meet from time to time, there was no future in it.

She opted not to dwell on the bleakness of her situation at the moment, for fear her heart would break.

"Awake at last?" His voice was deep and silky. Brenda loved his voice.

"Yes." Feeling expansive, she held a hand out, hoping he'd come to her.

After a second or two, he did—reluctantly, unless it was her imagination. She doubted that it was. She no longer believed that he disliked her, but she knew good and well he'd had what he'd wanted. The rest, for her, was all downhill from here. Her heart gave a sharp twang at the knowledge. She'd learned to be practical long since, however, and she wasn't going to spoil a perfect afternoon by whining at this point. She'd known what she was getting into when she went to bed with him.

He sat next to her, bent down, and kissed her. It was sort of a neighborly kiss, nothing like the kisses they'd shared earlier. She sighed and told herself to get used to it.

"Are you all right, Brenda? I mean, are you—well, are you hurt or sore or anything?"

How sweet. Even if he didn't love her, he at least cared a little bit. "I'm fine, Colin. Never better." She produced a cocky grin.

His eyes twinkled in response, and Brenda took heart. All right, so she'd never have him permanently; she was sure they could at least be friends. She'd take what she could get.

"Good. I was afraid I'd hurt you."

She shook her head. "No. I'm fine." More or less. At least her physical self was feeling okay. More than okay. Ginger peachy, actually. Because she felt she needed a hug more than anything else in the world at the moment, she hugged him. He hugged her back, hard, and she felt a little better. His hands even wandered a bit, giving her to understand that he hadn't yet lost interest in her entirely. Which was nice.

"I'd better get out of bed. I suppose we should put in an appearance at dinner tonight, or people might begin to talk." As far as she was concerned, they were welcome to talk. As long as they didn't talk outside of the motion-picture set. She trusted her friends at Peerless.

"I'm afraid the dress you wore when you helped George is wrinkled now, as well as dirty."

"That's all right. I have lots of clothes." Her wardrobe was big enough to clothe all the orphans in New York City, in fact. That was one of the primary reasons Brenda gave money to her favorite charity in amounts equal to what she spent on her elaborate togs. She needed fancy clothes in order to support her profession, but supporting the orphans was more important to her—and to the world.

"Here, let me help you."

"Thanks, Colin."

He must realize she was sore, in spite of what she'd told him. But of course, he'd know that. He was well versed in the scientific facts of life. He was probably thinking of Brenda now as he might think about a scientific experiment in mating among different species of animal life.

Because she felt a trifle embarrassed about being naked

in front of Colin now that the heat of passion had passed, she pulled a sheet up to cover her breasts. He sighed, and she glanced up at him quickly. He'd been surveying her unclad body. Fair enough. If she hadn't wanted him to look at it, she shouldn't have displayed it so freely. It was her own fault if he believed her to be a hussy.

What a depressing notion. To counteract it, she gave him another one of her patented good-guy grins. "Would you be a real pal and get my dressing gown out of the closet, Colin? It's blue silk. You can't miss it. It has a dragon on it."

"I know what it looks like."

"Oh, that's right." He'd seen her in it before. That first time he'd tried to get into her drawers.

Brenda mentally smacked herself. If she wanted to salvage anything of value from this experience, over and above the admittedly smashing physical stuff, she was going to have to drag her mind out of the gutter. It was imperative to cease thinking of herself as abandoned and of Colin as a predator. It wasn't true. What they'd shared was special.

Wasn't it?

Countless memories of other women—women not as fortunate in the brains and beauty department as Brenda—swarmed into her head. She couldn't even recall the number of times she'd comforted some poor, foolish female who'd believed a man's blandishments and allowed herself to be used.

Sweet Lord above, she wasn't just another one of those poor, stupid women, was she?

"Here. This is very pretty, Brenda. It almost matches your eyes, although your eyes are much lovelier." Colin held the robe for her.

How sweet he was being. Brenda appreciated it, since her mind seemed determined to make something disgraceful out of the love they'd just shared. If it was love and not a mere sexual fling.

Stop it this minute!

Her sharp commandment did little to quiet the tumult raging in her head. "Thanks, Colin." She maintained her smile until she'd shut the bathroom door behind her and turned on the tap to fill the tub.

She'd probably only felt sorry for him. Why else would so precious a woman allow him to go to bed with her?

Colin heard the water filling the tub in the bathroom and wandered back to the window to stare outside some more. This present plaguey mood was new to him. He was unaccustomed to entertaining insecurities and doubts. Still rarer for him were the dreamy moments that occasionally overtook his anxiety.

She was so wonderful. Perfect. She was magnificent. The most delightful, gracious, brilliant, kindhearted, lady-like, exciting, and seductive woman in the world. And she'd allowed him—*him*—an eggheaded scholar, to make love to her. Colin relived the past hour or two in his mind so many times, it began to take on the quality of something mystical, almost holy.

Maybe, if he was very lucky, she'd allow him to remain her friend. Perhaps she'd let him call on her from time to time, if only to go to dinner together, or talk. Maybe she'd still let him come over and tutor her in all the things she wanted to learn. She truly did have an insatiable curiosity about the things she'd never had an opportunity to study, as well as a capable, curious mind. He knew better than to maintain the fiction that she'd let him touch her again.

The very thought of marriage was out of the question. It was laughable. Nonsensical. Idiotic. Colin was a fool even to combine the name *Brenda* and the word *marriage* in the same sentence.

He'd sunk into a total funk by the time Brenda had bathed, dressed, and rejoined him. She looked, of course, perfect. She looked as if no man had ever touched her.

They walked down to the Cedar Crest Lodge's dining room together, each absorbed in thoughts of his and her own.

Something had changed. Martin couldn't put his finger on exactly what it was, but it was something. He could tell. He'd been dealing with actors, emotions, and story lines for too long not to detect a difference in the relationship between Brenda and Colin.

He'd also been dealing with human beings for too long to believe the change was entirely for the good. If life were a simple affair, like it was in the pictures, Brenda and Colin would finally decide they were made for each other, get married, and live happily ever after.

But could real life sail so smoothly? Heavens, no. People always had to complicate everything. Martin, watching closely as Brenda and Colin entered the dining room, sighed. He had a suspicion that they'd become—ah—closer, this afternoon. He had another suspicion that neither of them was willing to accept his attraction to the other as a gift from God. If they had the sense God gave a goose, they'd be happy.

They weren't happy, either one of them. The silly fools.

Considering his interference in this instance as in the light of an act of mercy, Martin rose from his table and gestured for the couple to join him.

"I'm all by my lonesome tonight," he said, smiling up a storm in order to counteract the almost palpable aura of gloom hovering over the couple. "I'd sure appreciate some company."

Brenda, bless her, managed to manufacture a friendly smile. What a trouper the woman was. Martin esteemed her as a real treasure. He hoped Colin would admit the same to himself pretty soon, or he might lose her. Colin smiled, too, but he wasn't as good an actor as Brenda, and his smile came across as brittle and forced.

"Thanks, Martin," Brenda said in her best light, bantering tone. "I'm famished."

"I'm hungry, too."

Martin eyed Colin sharply. The poor guy looked so unhappy, Martin was surprised he'd even said that much. Probably Brenda's influence, he decided. He took a bet with himself that Colin would push his food around on his plate and not eat a bite. He had more faith in Brenda. She was never a big eater, but she wouldn't give her unhappiness away by pining and going into a dramatic decline. She was tougher than that.

"I've already ordered. Chicken à la king. They make a pretty good one here."

"Sounds okay to me," Brenda said brightly. "I think I'll have the same. Colin?"

The look she gave him ought to have convinced the fool that she loved him almost beyond bearing, Martin thought with cynical amusement. But Colin, analytical as he was, would probably interpret it as something else. Martin had always suspected that scholars, if given the opportunity, could analyze the life out of pretty much anything. This was the first time he'd witnessed the process as it happened.

"Sure," Colin said, sounding vague and not altogether present, as if he was mulling over something else. "Thanks. I mean, sure, I'll have it." He blinked uncertainly. "Er, what was it again?"

Brenda patted his hand. "Chicken à la king. They make a pretty good one here. Martin said so."

"Oh. Oh, sure. That'll be fine."

Martin saw that Colin turned his hand over and squeezed Brenda's briefly. It looked to him as if the poor guy would have liked to hold her hand all through dinner and didn't dare. It also looked to him as though Brenda would have loved it if he had.

Whoo, boy, these two needed help. Unfortunately, they were both adults, and Martin didn't have a clue how to help them.

Colin and Brenda visited George after dinner. He was awake but groggy.

"How's the arm feeling? Did that beastly doctor come to see you like he promised?" Brenda grinned at the boy, and spared a moment to be glad, although she also felt guilty about it, that he'd broken the arm, since it gave her something to think about besides Colin. All the thinking in the world wouldn't do anything to alter her situation with Colin, darn it.

George grinned up at her. Her heart gave a squishy little lurch in appreciation of George's game attempt at good humor. He was a fine kid, even if he wasn't behaving in a fashion endorsed by the Peters clan.

"The doctor says I'm going to be okay," George said. "And it doesn't hurt too much. It's better when I'm drugged."

Brenda laughed. "I'm sure that's true. It'll probably hurt like heck for a while, but it'll get better. Did the doctor say if you'll regain full use of it?"

George nodded. "Yes. I'm relieved, too. I was really worried at first, because—" He shot Colin an apprehensive glance. "Well, because, you know, I—well, I'll need both my arms and hands to function properly if I aim to make a go of set designing for the pictures. And I'm right-handed, so that arm's the more important of the two."

A swell of compassion filled Brenda when she saw George's neck redden and two splotches of color visit his snowy cheeks. The poor guy. He wanted so much to make a success of his life and to prove to his family that academia wasn't the only road one could take in order to achieve it. She wished him well and aimed to help him as much as she could. He'd have to do most of it on his own, of course. No amount of moral support could make up for a lack of effort, determination, or talent. She sensed he possessed all three qualities.

"You're looking a little better." Colin's voice held no conviction.

Brenda grinned at him and then at George. "I think you look like last week's laundry left to sit, wet, in a tub until it turned all mildewy. I guess it's the bruises set against your pallor."

Colin looked shocked.

George laughed. "I'm sure you're more right than Colin is." He glanced at Colin. "Although I appreciate the encouragement. This is no fun."

Finally Colin understood he was being teased. He grinned, too. "She's right. You look like hell."

"Thanks, Colin." George laughed again and then winced. "It hurts when I laugh."

"Do you need more medication?" Suddenly Brenda remembered the nurse. "Where's Miss Cleary? I thought she was supposed to be watching you."

"She is," George assured her. "Like a hawk. She only went out to get some supper for the both of us. I understand I'm only to be allowed soup." He gave a grimace of distaste.

Brenda winked at him. "Maybe I can sneak you a steak one of these days."

"Shoot, I hope I'm not going to be laid up like this for days. Maybe another day or so will be enough. I wouldn't have to be in bed now, except that I got a little battered when that thing hit me. If it was just the arm, I'd be up and about right now."

"You're better off resting. It's always best to rest after receiving an injury. Animals know it by instinct. Sometimes humans need to be tied down." Colin looked stern.

George grinned up at his brother. "You can save the rope. My instincts are working just fine, thanks."

"Oh, George!" Brenda felt like crying, although she'd never do such a weak thing in front of the invalid. Besides, she had a feeling her tears would be more for herself than for George, and she despised them. "I'm so sorry this happened."

"Yeah, me, too."

Colin put a hand on his brother's shoulder. "I'll be back later, George. If you need something, let me know. Can I get you anything now?"

George shook his head, winced again, and said, "No, thanks, Colin. I think all I need now is some chow, and that's being provided, such as it is."

The door opened as he spoke, and Nurse Cleary entered the room bearing a tray. Colin rushed over to help her with it. Brenda was pleased to note this evidence of social aptitude in the man she loved. He wasn't hopeless by any means.

Not that she'd be the one to civilize him. In a few days, they were going to part forever. Or, if not forever, then for the most part. The idyll would be over; that was all she knew for certain.

"Thank you, Mr. Peters." Nurse Cleary flapped a napkin and tucked it into George's pajama top. "Help me sit this rascal up so he can eat his thin gruel and water."

"Ew." George made a terrible face. "Gruel? You said—"

The nurse laughed. "Only joking, Georgie, my lad. You'll get some dry bread to go with your gruel."

She and Colin assisted George to sit. Watching, Brenda

saw the sweat break out on George's forehead, and she cringed inside, wishing she could take his pain away. But he'd be better soon. Everything healed in time. Even hearts, she imagined, although it seemed unlikely right now.

As soon as George saw what lay on the tray Nurse Cleary settled across his lap, he cheered up considerably. "Say, this beats the tar out of thin gruel and water."

The nurse grinned and gave him a wink. "Sure, and it's real food you need, my boy. I don't care what the doctor says, a growing lad needs real food."

"I'll say."

Brenda and Colin laughed along with the nurse as George dove with relish into his roast beef. Brenda blessed Nurse Cleary for providing relief to her dour mood, if only momentarily.

The distraction didn't last, of course. After George ate, the nurse shooed them out of his room, and she and Colin were left with each other, the memory of a magical afternoon, and a future she couldn't even guess at. Pragmatic as ever, she decided to get as much from Colin as she could as long as they remained at the Cedar Crest Lodge.

Feeling shy but determined, she asked, "Would you like to come up to my room for a while, Colin?"

He gaped at her as if he couldn't imagine such a thing. Brenda experienced a sharp stab of irritation. "Don't worry," she said dryly, "I won't ask you to do anything you don't want to do."

"What?" He gulped. "I mean— No. I mean, yes, I'd love to go to your room. And—and—well, you don't have to do anything you don't want to do, either."

Swell. Just what she wanted to hear. She felt glum when she and Colin entered her room a few minutes later. He taught her another lesson in lovemaking that night, though, so Brenda decided she ought to count her blessings and not long for things that couldn't be.

"Cut! And . . . It's a wrap!" Martin cried through his megaphone, joy ringing in the words. "Great job, everybody. This picture is going to be a winner."

Dismay flooded Colin so suddenly that he winced, although he immediately chided himself for being foolish. He'd known there were only a few more days of filming left to be done after George's accident. He slanted a glance at his brother, who was out of bed and sitting on a stump, looking bruised but unbowed, his arm in a sling. George looked happy, too.

Might as well be, Colin thought bitterly. George would undoubtedly work with Brenda countless more times as he built a career in the pictures. This was it for Colin, and his heart hurt at the thought.

He sought out Brenda among the crowd of Peerless employees who swarmed onto the set as soon as Martin's announcement hit the air. The cameras stopped churning, sprockets stopped clunking out onto the ground, the cameramen grinned and shook out their arms, which were tired from cranking, and a general cheer went up.

Brenda appeared to be happy, too. How depressing.

Nevertheless, Colin knew better than to make a spectacle of himself by sulking in a corner. Gathering his courage in both hands and shoving his misery aside, he joined the throng, trying with all his might to look as if he was happy, too.

So what if his pose was a lie? So what if the picture was a ridiculous piece of fantastic fluff? So what if it reinforced white America's misunderstandings about Indians? So what if the story couldn't have happened the way it was depicted in *Indian Love Song* in a million years?

So what if he never saw Brenda again?

Colin's heart gave a sudden, sharp spasm. He told himself to stop brooding. If he never saw her again, the world would continue its orbit around the sun, the moon would continue its orbit around the earth, the sun would continue to shine, people would continue to misinterpret history, not to mention science, and nothing would change. Except him. He'd never be the same again.

"Colin!"

Brenda's voice cut through his gloom, and he looked up. She was smiling at him. It fascinated Colin that every time she did that, his insides lit up as if a lamp had been lighted in his soul. He didn't understand it. Such a phenomenon didn't fit into any scientific dogma he'd ever read.

To hell with science, he thought savagely, and then he couldn't believe he'd done such a heretical thing. Whatever would his parents think? Or his professors? Those dried-out, dried-up, gray-haired sacks of trivia and nonsense.

Good Lord, he was failing fast.

His mind went blank when Brenda rushed up and threw her arms around him.

"Oh, Colin! We made it! In spite of George's accident and the wrong Indians and flowers on the tipis and everything else, we made it! We can all go home again!"

His arms had wrapped around her naturally, as they'd become accustomed to doing in the past several days, since she and he had first made love.

The notion of never making love to her again almost forced a cry of anguish out of him. He suppressed it with an effort. He didn't let her go, but he did whisper, "Will that make you happy?"

"Oh, yes. I miss my family so much."

"Ah."

She seemed to sense something of a troublesome nature in his attitude, because she drew slightly back—without

releasing him, thank God—and peered up into his eyes.
Her own glorious blue eyes, even set as they were this
moment against a background of dead white makeup, were
large and luminous and remained the most beautiful eyes
Colin had ever seen.

What a marvelous specimen of the female human being Brenda was. She was, without a doubt, the most perfect example of the species ever to have graced the earth.

When her hand touched his cheek, he pressed into it,
aching for closeness. "You don't sound very happy about
it, Colin." Her voice feathered across his senses as soft
as a dandelion puff.

He took a big breath and decided he didn't care if he
made a total fool of himself. What was pride in the face
of so great a loss as this? "I'm going to miss you,
Brenda."

"You will?"

Colin didn't understand why she sounded surprised. It
must be obvious to her by this time that he worshiped the
very ground she trod upon, not to mention every other
thing about her. "Yes. Very much. Terribly." He almost
said he feared their parting would kill him, but such a
dramatic utterance went so exactly against everything of
truth and science he'd learned to value in life that he
couldn't do it.

She didn't speak immediately. When she did, Colin's
heart lurched again. "I'm going to miss you, too."

"You will?" He didn't believe her.

Again she waited for several seconds before she spoke.
Her words were very soft, and they sounded tentative, as
if she doubted he'd be happy to hear them. "Oh, yes. I—I
love you, Colin."

He blinked at her, sure he'd misunderstood. For a second, his mind raced like a guinea pig on a wheel, spinning, spinning, spinning, trying to decipher what she'd

said, sure she couldn't have said what he thought he'd heard. At last he said, "I, ah, beg your pardon?"

She made a *tsk* sound, as if she didn't want to have to repeat herself. She did it anyway. "I said, I love you."

Evidently he still looked doubtful—or perhaps dumbfounded—because she hurried on, "You don't have to love me back. I'm not trying to put any pressure on you. I'm not that type of person, no matter what you think. But I do want you to know that I love you. Very much."

He realized that tears had pooled in her eyes, and the understanding of what it had cost her to admit her love smote him. Hard. He still couldn't comprehend the magnitude of her confession; it sounded impossible to him. "You love me? Me?" If he'd had a hand free, he'd have pointed at his chest, but his hands were occupied in holding on to Brenda.

The faintest hint of exasperation visited her face. "Yes, darn it. You don't have to look and sound so incredulous. I know you don't want to hear me say it, but it's the truth, and that's that."

"No," he said. "I mean, no, I don't not want to hear you say it." Dash it, he'd never been so ungrammatical in his life. He tried again. "I mean, you can't possibly love me."

The hint grew into a certainty. She snapped, "Why not? Is there some sort of scientific principle that says an actress can't love a professor?"

"What?" He didn't understand her question. "No. I mean, yes. I mean, what does science have to do with anything?"

She rolled her eyes. "Nothing. But why can't I love you? Is such a thing so impossible?"

"Yes." Colin started feeling a wee bit more cheerful. "I mean, no. It's not—well, it *seems* impossible, but I don't suppose there's any hard-and-fast biological or physiological canon against such a thing occurring.

Stranger behaviors have been manifested in animal life before this, I'm sure. Like, say, cats nursing rabbit babies and so forth."

"Good God." She leaned back and stared at him as if he were a rare and peculiar subspecies of the genus *Homo sapiens. Homo idioticus,* perhaps.

"But—but—but—" Colin stopped stammering, drew in a breath, swallowed, and fumbled forward. "I mean, you can't love me. I'm just a stupid scholar."

She tilted her head to one side and studied his face, clearly puzzled.

"What I mean to say," he slogged on, "is that I can't believe that you, of all people, could possibly love me, of all people."

"Why not?"

Why not? Why *not?* Good question. "But—but—I'm so—so—stuffy."

She nodded. Not encouraging, that.

"And I treated you so badly."

Another nod.

"And—and—" Suddenly, the dam holding back his emotions burst, and he cried out, "And I love you more than life itself!" He didn't even qualify his sensational statement with scientific theories about how such a state of being was impossible to achieve.

"You do?"

"God, yes. And I knew you'd never marry me, so I didn't even think to ask you."

"Really? How odd."

"But—but— Dash it, Brenda, if you love me, and I love you, why *can't* we get married?"

"I can't think of a single reason."

"You can't?" Colin stared at her, bewildered.

She shook her head.

He swallowed. "Would you mind living in Los Angeles? That's where my job is."

"Not at all. I've been wanting to retire for a long time now."

"And you won't mind being married to a stuffy old professor?"

"Gosh, no. As long as you promise to practice your lectures on me."

"Honestly?"

"Honestly. And you won't mind if I buy a big house for us with a huge library and a billion books?"

"Heavens, no. I'm not one of those men who resent the success of women."

"Glad to hear it." There was a distinct twinkle in her eyes now.

Colin, still scarcely able to believe this was happening, swallowed once more, cleared his throat, and took one last chance. "So—so, will you marry me?"

"You bet I will."

Colin barely heard the whoops and cheers that went up from the Peerless folks when he and Brenda kissed each other.

George acted as his brother's best man at the wedding. Martin presented the happy couple with a complete set of Shakespeare as a wedding gift.

Brenda and Colin, who moved Brenda's mother to Los Angeles, built a fabulous estate on Sunset Boulevard. Colin was soon one of the most popular professors on the new university campus. Brenda was as happy as a cat in a cream pot with her big library and her books.

They were both delighted that their three sons and two daughters possessed both beauty and brains.

If you liked BEAUTY AND THE BRAIN, be sure to look for THE MINER'S DAUGHTER, the next in Alice Duncan's The Dream Maker series, available wherever books are sold in September 2001.

Marigold Pottersby is hanging on to her father's failing San Bernardino copper mine by the skin of her teeth when she discovers Martin Tafft plans to use it in his new film. Realizing a hefty rental fee may be the answer to her prayers, Mari agrees to let the filming begin—but she balks at the offer of a role. That is, until gorgeous Tony Ewing, the son of one of Lovejoy's heaviest investors, shows up to investigate the progress of the latest picture.

BOOK YOUR PLACE ON OUR WEBSITE AND MAKE THE READING CONNECTION!

We've created a customized website just for our very special readers, where you can get the inside scoop on everything that's going on with Zebra, Pinnacle and Kensington books.

When you come online, you'll have the exciting opportunity to:

- View covers of upcoming books
- Read sample chapters
- Learn about our future publishing schedule (listed by publication month *and author*)
- Find out when your favorite authors will be visiting a city near you
- Search for and order backlist books from our online catalog
- Check out author bios and background information
- Send e-mail to your favorite authors
- Meet the Kensington staff online
- Join us in weekly chats with authors, readers and other guests
- Get writing guidelines
- AND MUCH MORE!

Visit our website at
http://www.zebrabooks.com